SUMMER PEOPLE

SUMMER PEOPLE

SALLY BLAKELY

MIRA

MIRA™

ISBN-13: 978-1-335-01425-2

Summer People

For questions and comments about the quality of this book, please contact us at CustomerService@Harlequin.com.

TM is a trademark of Harlequin Enterprises ULC.

MIRA
22 Adelaide St. West, 41st Floor
Toronto, Ontario M5H 4E3, Canada
MIRABooks.com

HarperCollins Publishers
Macken House, 39/40 Mayor Street Upper,
Dublin 1, D01 C9W8, Ireland
www.HarperCollins.com

Printed in U.S.A.
26 27 28 29 30 LBC 5 4 3 2 1

For Georgia
From the sixth floor to the rest of our lives,
and whatever comes after that too.

then

I spend the entire year waiting for summer. Not the whole of it, but its return. The moments just before it actually begins on a calendar, when you're already calling it summer, when people are already on patios and at markets and kids are out of school. I wait for the edge between the pleasantly warm days of late spring and the heat of July, when there is nothing but a seemingly endless stretch of days ahead of you.

I used to be waiting for a trip: a group of people, an A-frame cottage with creaky floors and the rush of salt air through open windows. But even with that all gone, I still find myself waiting for that moment. Some shift in the air that starts in April and lasts through the solstice in June that signifies something turning over, starting fresh. Not fully realized yet, but getting there, waking up.

I wasn't always this way. I used to be someone who vowed that I'd never live for weekends, vacations, summers. But the habit rooted in me ten years ago. Checking off days on a calendar, marking moments by how much closer they were to summer coming back.

And it all started at a party I wasn't even supposed to go to.

one

Spring
Ten Years Ago

It was unusual for me to go to a party without anyone else in tow, and by "anyone else" I mean the five of us—me, Laurel, Gabe, Davi, and Zoey. But it was the last Friday of spring break and Laurel was out with a girl from one of her marketing classes after she'd decided to ghost the guy she'd been seeing from her econ class last week, Gabe and Zoey weren't back from their trip to Barbados with her parents until Sunday, and Davi had one of those infuriating spring colds, made all the worse by the fact that we only had so many weekends like this left between us and graduation.

But there was a call from a classmate, and springtime California air as we walked the few blocks to the house where she knew about a party. Music and drinks in the fridge and no real concept of a before or a during or an after for any of us, and then a cheer going up at the front door for someone arriving. Golden-brown hair and flashing eyes and a case of beer hoisted in the air. A second beer in the kitchen while I laughed along with everyone else, and a screen door closing behind me as I stepped onto the quiet back deck to cut through the alley and head home.

"Got to be a record," said a voice from behind me. I turned. The guy everyone had been so happy to see earlier leaned against the railing, a water bottle in hand. He was wearing a navy-blue sweater, the sleeves pushed up to above his elbows, the white of a T-shirt just peeking out underneath the neck of it.

"What?" I asked.

He glanced at a watch on his wrist. I didn't know anyone who wore an actual watch at that point, and this one looked well loved, a leather band that had been worn by someone before him. "Ten thirty," he said. "Sorry the party disappointed you."

"This is your party?" I asked, pointing back at the screen door, a rectangle of yellow in the dark, voices and a song that Laurel turned up every time it came on the radio spilling out of it.

"Nah," he said, shaking his head. A lock of hair fell across his forehead, and he pushed it back. I didn't know it was a restless habit then, that his hair wasn't pushed back by design, but by anxious necessity. "I'm just friends with the guys who live here."

"You keep them in beer," I said, settling against the wall opposite him. The light from the kitchen fell across his face just in time for me to see a smile tug one side of his mouth up. "Everyone was certainly happy to see you earlier."

"I think if you show up to any party with a case of beer on one shoulder people will be happy to see you."

"Was it on one shoulder?" I asked, pretending to think. "From what I recall, it was over your head."

"You *were* paying attention," he said, that smile stretching.

"You're the Lloyd Dobler of beer."

"Wasn't Lloyd the key master in *Say Anything*?" he asked,

crossing his arms over his chest. "You know, holds on to everyone's keys, makes sure they're sober before they drive?"

I nodded at his water. "If that's all you're drinking, you could be key master if you wanted."

He glanced at the bottle, something flitting across his face before he looked back at me. "I try to follow the water-between-drinks rule," he said. "Not big on being drunk."

"Fair."

He shifted then, like something had occurred to him, and held out his hand. "I'm Everett," he said. "Bridges."

"First and last name," I said without taking his hand.

"Something wrong with that?"

"No." I shook my head. "Everett Bridges. Sounds like you're going to be an actor or a writer or something. Am I close?"

He exhaled a small wry laugh. "Something like that."

"Sutton," I said, finally taking his hand. We didn't exactly shake them, just kind of held them there, suspended. I realized I was waiting for him to ask me my last name, probably so I could say something like *now that's more information than I wanted to give you tonight*, but he didn't. He just looked at me until the warmth of his palm started to crawl up my arm and I quickly said, "Hale," and dropped his hand.

"Sutton Hale," he said, leaning back again. I could feel my cheeks heat and was grateful for the dark. "Now *that* sounds like you're going to be someone people know."

I opened my mouth to respond, but the door flew open at that same moment, a guy in a polo spilling out and peering drunkenly around the deck until his eyes landed on me.

"Have you seen Everett?" he asked.

"I'm here, Shane," Everett said, pushing back the door where Shane had cornered him in with it. "What's up?"

"We need ice," Shane said. "And beer."

"I brought you more beer an hour ago," Everett said.

"And everyone has really enjoyed it," Shane said. "Are you drinking? Can you go? I'm about to kick John's ass at *Mario Kart* in the basement and I—"

"I'll go," Everett cut in.

"Great," Shane said, digging into his pocket. "Shit, I don't have any cash on me."

"I'll get it," Everett said.

Apparently, that was all the convincing it took for Shane. "Guys!" he shouted as he spun back toward the kitchen, the door slamming behind him. "He'll get it!" A chorus of cheers went up.

"Sutton," Everett said, reaching into his jeans pocket to pull out a set of car keys. "It's been great. I hope you enjoy the rest of your evening, wherever it takes you."

"You too," I said as he started down the back steps. And that might have been it, might have made our lives far less complicated if some cosmic force hadn't landed a fist against my stomach, punching my next word out of me. "Wait."

Everett turned with his foot on the bottom step, gaze slanting up to mine. I felt it again: heat in my cheeks, stretching down my neck and across my chest this time. "Want some company?"

The way Everett's mouth turned down at the corners, like he was trying to suppress a smile, like he *knew* I might ask, almost made me take it back. Instead, I raised an eyebrow, waiting.

He jerked his head to the side, beckoning me toward him. "Come on, then, Sutton Hale."

I followed him around the side of the house and toward what I assumed was his car: a nondescript sedan, the same as most students drove in Southern California, either handed down from older siblings or purchased as a high school graduation present by their parents. But he started across the street just as I was about to reach for the handle toward a classic sixties Bronco, the top removed and its paint the perfect shade of muted sage green.

"This is your car?" I asked as he walked around to the passenger side, unlocking it and holding it open for me.

"This is my car," he confirmed as he closed the door behind me, patting a hand on it for good measure. I took in the interior, clearly new, lovingly refurbished as he walked around the front and climbed into the driver's seat. He glanced sideways at me as I ran a finger over the brown leather of the seats. "What?"

"I can't tell if I love or hate this," I said as the engine rumbled to life.

Everett laughed as he put the car in Drive and pulled out of the spot. "Dance Hall Days" came out of the speakers when his phone connected to the stereo, loud, and he reached over to turn it down before asking, "Why's that?"

"I'm no car aficionado, but don't refurbished models like this usually go for, like . . . a shit ton of money?"

"They do tend to," he said. "But my mom's husband is into fixing up cars, so I mostly paid in labor for this one."

"Really?" I asked. Everett nodded as he turned out of the neighborhood and onto the main road, the wind whipping through my hair as we picked up speed. California was already warming up this time of year, but it was still chilly at night, and I wrapped my hands around my bare arms, suppressing a shiver. Everett noticed, and at a stoplight he reached into the back bench seat and produced a well-loved Devon College crewneck.

"Here," he said. "It's a little early to have the top off," he explained as I tugged the dark blue sweatshirt on over my head, catching a whiff of something warmly familiar, crisp pine and cinnamon, and something almost salty underneath it. "But I drove down the coast this week to surf."

"Wow." I refastened my seat belt. "So you're, like, a real Californian."

"Los Angeles born and bred, I'm afraid. Where are you from?"

"Bay Area," I said. I gave him a wry look. "Different kind of Californian."

Everett nodded as he shifted gears, which I, for some reason, found unbearably hot. We talked back and forth as we drove the rest of the way to the gas station, basic things like majors (me: culinary arts, Everett: film school), why we'd picked them, how we'd ended up at Devon in the first place. I'd ended up here because of the scholarships they offered, but it hadn't seemed meant to be until I met my friends, the people who weren't here tonight. It was as if all the other schools had been out of reach simply to pull me here, with them. But I didn't tell Everett that part of things just yet.

At the gas station, we grabbed two cases of PBR out of the cooler before starting down the candy aisle, where he paused in front of a display. "Want anything?" he asked me.

"No thanks," I said until a bag caught my eye. "Gummy worms."

He grabbed them and the sour version before rounding the corner into the chip aisle. I followed just in time for him to toss a bag of pretzels my way, followed quickly by potato chips that I only just caught.

"Quite the refined palate you've got there," I joked as he mulled over the Pringles options. He smirked at me. "Sour cream and onion." He raised an eyebrow at me. "Just in one future chef's opinion."

"See," he said as he grabbed the canister and tucked it under his arm. "Sutton Hale is a name people are going to know."

We tore into everything on the drive back to the house, tossing things back and forth, holding open bags out to each other, and it struck me that I hadn't felt immediately comfortable like this with anyone in a while. That I reserved things like this for my best friends. That I had, I realized as Everett turned onto the street where we could hear the music from the party echoing, felt so comfortable around him that I'd gotten into a car with a virtual stranger.

I examined him while he parked: good jaw, tendons working in his forearms as he twisted the keys out of the ignition, a five-o'clock shadow on his chin. From what I could tell, he looked like he used his body, and not necessarily in a seven-days-a-week-at-the-gym way, but just in a leaned-out, casually strong way. A surfing, fixing-up-cars-but-would-still-eat-junk-food-in-the-car-with-you way.

He smiled over at me then, and I didn't blush this time. I smiled back, and I think the rest of the night might have been decided right there. When he told me I was about to learn how to be the most popular person in the room and handed me one of the cases of beer and bags of ice. When everyone cheered as we walked inside and I watched people clap Everett on the back and they pulled me into their huddle too. I felt some of the warm glow that emanated from him, even then. Golden boy. Effortless. Not a care in the world. Or so I thought.

It was easy from there. A PBR toast, and staying close even when we weren't: looks across the room and returning to each other as soon as we could, like tonight's outcome was already a foregone conclusion. Everett's hand found my waist as the crowd got larger and we stumbled together, and I wrapped my fingers around his wrist to keep him there. Someone turned on something people started dancing to and I gave him a questioning look, like an invitation, and he shook his head, but it only took one tug for him to start moving with me. Before long, my hands were in his hair and his were on my hips and I felt a little drunk even if I knew I wasn't. His lips were against my ear, talking to me, and I was paying so much attention to the perfect height difference between us, him just a few inches taller than me, so he didn't have to stoop, so I didn't have to crane my neck when his hand cupped my face and he kissed me for the first time.

We laughed on the drive to his place, and the breeze didn't feel so cold anymore. Everything was warm and exciting, and the house Everett was living in wasn't far. Davi had made his sickbed on our couch back home and it would be best to avoid him, I'd told him, which was really just a way to *not* tell him that I never brought anyone home. That I always went to their place. But Everett didn't seem to mind, and his roommates were gone that weekend anyway, and his place was nice, as far as college boys' places went. There were surfboards leaned against the house out back and his kitchen was clean. He had movie artwork on the walls of his room, framed like he cared about them. An illustrated still from *E.T.* and hand-sketched concepts for the DeLorean and an old magazine ad for *Jaws* and even, I noticed with some strange twinge of satisfaction like this had all been planned, a small print of the *Say Anything* poster, Lloyd standing with his boom box above his head.

There was a desk stacked with books and notebooks and what looked like bound screenplays in one corner and his bed was made, until it wasn't, until I was pressed back against his pillows and our clothes were on the ground. It was good; great even, better than I thought something like this could be. And maybe it was whatever this ease was between us, some give-

and-take that was a little rare, but not impossible. Not with the right, handsome guy and the right back porch and the right car. It was something I'd done before, and so I didn't think that us doing this would ever matter beyond that night.

In the morning I smelled pine and cinnamon, pressed my face into the pillow before my brain caught up with my body and my eyes flicked open.

I rolled my head to look over my shoulder at Everett. He was asleep, so still and quiet that, for a minute, I craned a little closer to him to make sure he was, in fact, breathing. When I could rest assured that he was, I sat up as slowly as I could, trying not to wake him.

I never slept over. I reminded myself of that while I picked up my jeans off the floor and tugged them on, as I reached a hand under the bed to look for my bra.

"Sutton Hale," I heard, and smacked my head against his bed frame as I straightened, clutching my shirt to my chest. I looked over the bed at Everett, who was leaned up on his elbows, smirking at me. "Are you sneaking out?"

"I'm not—" I said, unsure of how to proceed. "I'm just—"

He rolled over, fishing around on the floor on his side of his bed until he sat up, holding my bra. He held it out toward me and I took it from him. "Thanks." I turned away and put it on as hurriedly as I could, slipping my shirt on over my head before I turned back to him. "Look," I started. I realized he'd been staring at his door, not sneaking some peek at me at all, and he rolled his head to look at me then, hands clasped behind it. "I don't spend the night."

"Okay," he said, simply. There was something about him, like everything was a bit of a joke, like nothing was that serious. A bored house cat. A dog stretching in the sun. Life was good and simple and laid out before him.

"So, I just don't want you to think this means something."

"Something," he repeated, with that hint of a smile behind the words.

"I'm just not, like, looking to start anything—" I said, then rerouted when he frowned. "I mean, you seem great, but we're about to graduate, and—" I cleared my throat, crossed my arms. "I don't sleep over."

"So you've said." He smiled for real at me then, in a way that would have had me crawling back into bed with him if I wasn't so determined to make my point. If I *did* hook up with someone twice, it was usually because there was a lull in coursework, or we were on summer break. *Boredom*, Laurel had once pointed out, as she tended to do. Grand proclamations about you that she made after months of study, no room for argument. *You only keep hooking up with people when you're bored.*

"Sutton," Everett said, sitting up when I opened my mouth to make yet another point. "Don't worry. I don't sleep over either."

"Oh," I said. "Well, excellent."

"For the record, you seem great too," he said. "I'd be down to hang out again in a social setting, for sure, but I'm not looking for anything either."

I considered this. Letting him in. What that would look like. "I just think it's a little complicated," I said. He cocked an eyebrow. "We graduate in two months. What—are we going to hang out a couple times, maybe do this again if we go to another party—" he snorted at this "—and then never see each other again?" Everett shrugged, like this didn't sound so bad. "I'm sure you have people in your life you'd like to spend time with before you go your separate ways. I know I do. Maybe we just shouldn't . . ." I stopped, letting the unspoken words hang there because I didn't exactly mean *waste our time* but there wasn't really a better way to put it, and by the look on Everett's face, I'd say he agreed.

"Fair enough," he said. He swung his legs over the side of the bed—he'd put on sweatpants at some point in the night, thank god, and tugged a hand through his hair. "Can I at least give you a ride home? Buy you a coffee?"

I nodded, relieved. "Sounds good."

Davi was still sleeping when I got home, and the door to Laurel's room was closed, which meant she either wasn't here, or was still asleep herself. Either way, I didn't tell any of them, and I could never really put my finger on why. Every time it almost came up, it just didn't seem important.

And it didn't matter. Not through the rest of my classes and graduation and a car ride to Malibu with Laurel and Davi, most of our things already packed into boxes and shipped off to various parts of the US. I thought that one night was the last of Everett Bridges. There was no reason at all it shouldn't have been.

two

This Summer

I need you. It's a worrying text to get from your best friend, especially when it's delivered fully out of the blue, no context provided, after she's been dodging your messages for the last several months. My communication with Laurel has been spotty for several years now, if I'm honest. But we always find our way back to each other.

I need you. Like a bat signal sent up, one that had me booking the next flight to Los Angeles to see her, and the reason I am now, six months later, driving her down the Pacific Coast Highway in the direction of a beachside resort I haven't seen in five years. We might have changed since then, but as we pull into the porte cochere outside the main building, it's clear Malibu Springs, terrible as its name may be, has not.

"I'll be right back," I tell Laurel, who is barking breakneck French into her phone. She nods and waves a perfectly manicured hand at me as I step out of the driver's side of her car.

Ralph, a front-desk staple here and someone with whom my relationship has been a bit of a mixed bag, looks up as I walk in, career hospitality on his newly lined face. "Welcome," he coos as I approach the mahogany front desk. "Checking in?"

"To the Wild Horse Villa," I say. I slide my ID across the counter before pulling up our reservation confirmation on my phone.

Ralph makes an approving face, which is strange because Ralph has only once before looked at me without disdain twisting his expression. "Have you stayed with us before?" he asks.

"I have," I say, giving him a tight smile. "But we've usually been in the Wildflower cottages."

"Ah." His tone is pinched. Something like recognition passes across his face, eyes narrowing in my direction, but his face brightens at something on his computer screen. "We have Ms. Im's card on file. You're all set," he says.

"Ralph?" Laurel asks when I hop back into her car.

"Ralph," I confirm.

"Still hates us?"

I nod as I guide the car toward the tight corner that will take us away from the main hotel and back down toward the bluff where Wild Horse Villa sits. "Still hates us."

Laurel rolls her window down and leans her head out, drawing in a breath as she shuts her eyes. "At least some things never change." I glance over at her, the narrow set of her shoulders, and wonder if she's actually looking thinner in the months since she shared the news of her divorce or if it's just all the time we haven't spent together in the last five years that's painting her image differently for me.

"When is everyone else arriving again?" I ask, like I don't already know. Like we haven't gone over the plans I made for this week a hundred times.

Laurel looks back at me, raising an eyebrow. "Gabe and Davi are on the same flight this afternoon. *He* is driving down tonight."

"Great," I say nonchalantly as I round the bend toward the

villa, its white stucco walls stark against the bright blue sky. "Looking forward to it."

Laurel snorts. "Sure you are."

I ignore her because it doesn't matter how I'm feeling about seeing *him* again. We're all here for her this week, to help as she navigates what she's calling the start of her "new life."

Laurel Im, best friend, former *Rock Band* champion, absolutely hopeless cook, is also the textbook definition of a social media star, and creator of one of the largest culture and lifestyle empires around. It started back in college: posting her outfits, recaps of her daily life, her recommendations for everything from mascara to green juices, but it wasn't until after graduation that she started to blow up. Since then, Laurel has launched a line of athleisure wear, started a podcast, signed deals with brands like Hoka and Bombay Sapphire and Knix, hosted trips where she leads tarot card readings and hikes through the Italian countryside. She is an influencer to the highest degree, maintains a lifestyle most people could only dream of, and has the best hair of anyone I know.

Her appeal only grew when she married Stephen four years ago, the boyfriend the internet was obsessed with. He was perfect for her: model-handsome and just as busy as she was, her biggest supporter and the picture of a doting husband.

That is, until Laurel told me she needed me, that she needed all of us, because she and Stephen were getting divorced. Out of nowhere, with zero warning. We agreed to gather at the resort we used to visit each year the week the divorce would be finalized to be there for her. To support her through it.

We haven't been back here in five years. Not since our last stay at Poppy Cottage, where a secret I hadn't kept alone nearly destroyed the group of friends I'd been calling family for a decade.

Nearly. Laurel's invitation, I hope, is a new beginning for all of us. To return to what we used to have: a group so tight-knit it rivaled movies, a reality so good it almost seemed made up. The kind of closeness I had searched for all my life. What has felt off track for the last five years will be righted again this week. I'm sure of it.

The Wild Horse Villa is a far cry from Poppy Cottage, but the last time we stayed there, the romance of its tiny space and desperately needed repairs was starting to wear off, so it makes sense that we move to a bigger space. That, and part of Laurel's invitation was her paying for a week in the sprawling Spanish Revival home we're dropping our bags in the foyer of now.

Not that any of us took her up on it. As soon as she sent the invite, the rest of us started our own group chat where we figured out how we'd surreptitiously pay her back so Laurel wouldn't have to spend a penny on her own divorce week, save for the party she's throwing herself on Friday and the rest of us have been left completely in the dark about.

"Here I let you make me think staying in that A-frame was so romantic," Laurel says as she sets her suitcase at the foot of the terra-cotta-tiled stairs, leaning her head back to look at the vaulted, beamed ceilings, the light filtering in through the skylights there.

"Yeah, yeah," I say, wrapping my arms around her shoulders. "You loved sharing that tiny room with me every summer."

"I will miss you always kicking me in your sleep," she says. She tucks her hands around my wrists and sighs. "I'll miss how uncomplicated things were there."

I try not to tense, to acknowledge what's obviously missing from that statement. *Until the last summer.* But it's Laurel who's brushing off the moment, breaking away from me.

"I bet I know one thing you'll love about this new house," she says, throwing her arms wide to show off the sprawling kitchen sitting opposite the living room just off the entryway. I follow her over there. "No more telling us all to get out while you cook."

"Yes, because you were so often *in* the kitchen at the cottage." I spread my hands on top of the mammoth marble island, nod at the pasta arm over the six-burner gas stove. "I want one of those in my own home someday."

"I'll get you one," Laurel says, her brief moment of melancholy from earlier erased. She spins into the living room, collapsing in a heap onto a plush white armchair there. "I'll buy you a thousand weird wall faucets!"

After thoroughly admiring the first floor, we haul our things upstairs and choose our rooms—Laurel's at the back of the house, overlooking the beach, and mine at the front, small but with a balcony off to one side. We curl up out there on the outdoor settees and peek over the wrought-iron railing every time we hear tires coming down the road until it is, finally, Gabe and Davi pulling into the driveway behind Laurel's car.

"Ahoy!" Laurel shouts down to them, the upper half of her body leaned over the railing.

"Hi!" Gabe calls, beaming up at us in khaki shorts and a T-shirt sporting the name of the college where he runs the admissions department back in Denver. "How's the view?"

"Excellent now!" I call down to him as Davi expels himself from the car behind Gabe, his curly black hair less coiffed than usual.

"Did anyone pack any Dramamine?" he says, voice bouncing off the stucco walls. "I think I left mine in the bathroom at Burbank."

"Davi!" Gabe booms, throwing a rough arm around his

shoulders and almost lifting him off the ground in the process. Where Gabe is towering and brawny, Davi is stocky. And, currently, a little green. "Forget your Dramamine! Look where we are!"

"I see where we are," I hear Davi mumble as he squints at his phone, probably responding to a work email even in his current, nauseous state. "I still don't travel well."

"You and potato salad," Laurel says. "Just get in here!"

"I have Dramamine, Davi," I call down to him as Gabe bounds toward the house, leaving Davi swaying on his feet in the driveway.

We all settle in around the island in the kitchen. I scrub a hand over Gabe's shorter haircut when he hugs me. Davi takes the pills I gave him and keeps his sunglasses pulled down over his eyes.

"Gabe, we're thinking you can have the room down here," Laurel is telling them. "Davi, there's a room upstairs with blackout curtains that has your name on it."

"Great," Gabe says. "But who cares about room assignments? Let's start catching up."

"We have to wait until everyone's here," Laurel says. "I hate repeating things. Everyone should be here by seven."

Gabe's gaze flicks briefly toward me, but I ignore it.

"So what are we supposed to do until then?" Davi asks. "Sit in silence?"

"Well, Dramamine always knocks you out," I say to him. "So at least we know what you'll be doing."

"I told Mia I'd call when we got in," Gabe says, almost apologetically. Mia is Gabe's wife, and currently on her own trip with their three-year-old twins and her sister. We all knew that part of even getting Gabe here this week meant giving him time and space to check in with them multiple times a day.

"I do have some emails I should respond to," Laurel adds a little guiltily.

The kitchen goes silent for a minute, the immediate excitement of being reunited fading from our bodies and making room for reality. That we haven't all been together—not like this, at least—for years. There have been day trips, birthday parties that only some of us could make it to. But the last time we were all in the same place at the same time was at Laurel's wedding, and on top of that not being an entire week away together, I think the day she married Stephen is the last thing any of us want to bring up right now.

"Hey, come on," I say. I need this week to be perfect. Not only for Laurel, but for all of us, so everyone in this room will see how important it is that this group remain intact. "We'll each take an hour to take care of whatever we need to, and then we'll reconvene here for drinks, okay?"

"So we'll sit in silence, drinking?" Davi asks.

It hits me how strange this is, all of us together again not knowing what to do. The transition into this trip used to be exciting, but now it feels like our first night at sleepaway camp, all of us a little unsure. I sink onto one hip, sighing. "We'll play a game or something."

"I didn't mean to make it awkward," Laurel, who has never once looked as timid as she does right now, says. Her expression pricks at something in my chest, the same thing I've been feeling since she sent her *I need you* text in the first place. Something she's not telling me in all her nonchalance about the divorce. "We can catch up now," she offers.

"No," I jump in. "You're right. Repeating things sucks."

The words are accompanied by a flash of irritation that I know, logically, is unfounded. But emotionally, I am a cracking Hoover Dam, holding back five years' worth of anger at the person who's still missing from this situation. The person who makes keeping this group intact so complicated, because it can't just be the people in this room, much as I might wish it. For this group to be intact, we still need him. The one who my rational brain reminds me isn't actually making it impossible for us to talk right now, but whom my animal brain rails against for not being able to get here earlier. The *him* of earlier. The him I don't want to see.

Everett.

three

First Summer

Gabe and Zoey broke up just before college graduation, and everything was ruined. Perhaps more accurately, Zoey cheated on Gabe just before college graduation, and not *everything* was ruined, but *we* were. The five of us—Zoey, Gabe, Davi, Laurel, and me—could never be the same again.

We'd been planning the trip to Malibu for months, a way to bridge the gap between our three years spent living together in the little brick house on the corner across from campus and our departure to different places; new jobs, the next steps in our lives that would take us away from each other.

But Zoey was officially uninvited after Laurel and I walked into our house to find her naked with a guy that was very much *not* Gabe on the couch that *I* bought for us with the scant savings from my bakery job. We had to watch in horror as the olive-green fabric undulated beneath them, both entirely unaware of our presence until Laurel—out of sheer panic, I think—hurled her untouched coffee at them, effectively ending both the act they were currently engaged in and the short life of the couch. Not that I wanted anything some stranger's bare ass had been so thoroughly ground into.

Gabe was bringing someone new on the trip to fill the space

Zoey left behind in our group. An old friend none of us had met, going on the trip that was supposed to be our last hurrah together. And of course he could, because Gabe was heartbroken, but I was still nervous about it. About someone new.

Davi, Laurel, and I drove up to the resort we'd booked back in February when the idea was first born, Gabe a few hours behind, catching a ride with his friend.

"Coastal cottages, my ass," Davi said after we'd checked in at the main building (Spanish Revival, red blooms dripping down every surface, a man who didn't look too happy to see us) and made our way along a winding, narrow road to the row of tiny pastel-colored cottages tucked along the beach.

Laurel's drooping Herschel duffel landed on the ground with a loud thwack as it dropped from her shoulder. She and Davi squinted at the structure in front of us, which was drooping about as much as Laurel's bag, the roof missing more than a few shingles and the faded blue siding several years in need of a good power wash.

"It's cute," I told them, waving a hand at the little flower boxes beneath the windows, out of which some hearty Southern Californian succulents grew. The effect was a little unnerving, like you might lean out a window hoping to pluck some rosemary from an herb box and instead wind up with a stab wound to your thumb, but to me, it spelled effort. Someone had tried to pretty this place up, even if it wasn't in obvious ways.

"Cute," Laurel repeated, her pert nose wrinkling. Five feet of pure energy, Laurel is still someone my Uncle Hank routinely describes as "spunky," a buzzing whirlwind of ideas who swept me up our freshman year of college and hasn't let go since. She is one of a very small handful of people I have let into my life and let stay, Davi and Gabe included. As such, I would do anything for her, including trying to convince her that the cottage, the front door of which was a little offset on its hinges, was the coastal getaway of her recently graduated dreams.

"Come on," I said, slinging an arm around both of their shoulders. "Let's pick our rooms before Gabe gets here."

"Gabe and *whoever*," Davi said. "Why does he get to bring someone again?"

"Because Gabe just had his heart shattered," I reminded him as I jiggled the doorknob until it gave. "And this guy is his friend."

"*We're* his friends," Davi said. "This trip is supposed to be *our* thing."

"Stop being so whiny," Laurel told him as we stepped into the cottage. "You'll probably love him. Besides, we need a fifth."

"Not the best way to put that," Davi muttered as I flipped on the lights and spread my arms in a *ta-da!* motion, though I'd never actually been to the cottage and had no real idea what, exactly, I was presenting.

It was better than the outside, at least. Small, not much more than one big open space, a bedroom downstairs and a loft with bunk beds and one twin, and a closet of a bathroom tucked into one corner, but it was cozy. There was a small vinyl-topped banquette table next to a Pullman kitchen that would serve our purposes that week, and out back—Laurel gasping and clapping her hands together as she shot toward it—a deck bigger than the whole of the house.

"Look at this," she breathed as she yanked the doors open, letting in a cool burst of sea breeze. I dropped my bag on the orange twill couch and followed her outside. She was standing at the top of the set of steps that led down to the beach, the bottom one buried in the sand. She glanced over her shoulder at me and Davi as we joined her. "This will make Gabe feel better."

We looked out at the white-capped waves crashing in, at beachgoers wandering or finding places to settle in to enjoy the late-afternoon warmth, until Davi broke the silence with what we were all thinking. "I'm so pissed at Zoey."

I sighed, exchanging a look with Laurel before resignedly agreeing. "Me too." A hot, angry point needled at me, a reminder of everything this trip was supposed to be up until a mere forty-eight hours ago. We'd still have a good week, but it—and college graduation—would now be forever tinged by what happened.

The worst part, aside from Gabe's complete heartbreak, was the fact that Zoey had been the fifth person in our tight-knit group of friends. Gabe and Zoey officially declared their love for each other at the end of freshman year, and only then after a lot of discussion and agonizing over the fate of our friend group should things ever go south between them. None of us had seen any reason to worry: They were perfect together. Until, it turned out, they weren't.

Gabe had told us in his trademark sweetheart way that he didn't want this to tear us apart, that we should all still be friends with Zoey if we wanted, but we'd all felt betrayed by what she'd done to him, too. By what it meant for all of us.

Even so, it was strange not having her there. *It's a little lopsided without her, isn't it?* Gabe had asked me just the previous night, our last in the house. I'd nodded, but in reality, I didn't know if I totally agreed.

Yes, it felt off. But somehow, what she'd done hadn't surprised me. I was livid, to be sure, but I understood, on a fundamental level, that most people would disappoint you. It was just a matter of time until Zoey did something to screw up what had been her perfect track record. It didn't mean I wouldn't have happily thrown her to the sharks for Gabe. But it did mean she'd just lived up to what I already knew was her inevitable potential.

"Maybe the friend Gabe is bringing is hot," Laurel said.

"Laurel, no," I said. "What did we *just* learn? None of us should be dating our *friends*."

"But what if he's *dreamy*?" Laurel asked. I scoffed.

"I don't care if he's Ryan Gosling. This trip is not about romance."

"What if he's Idris Elba?" Laurel asked. I ignored her in favor of grabbing Davi's hand and dragging him toward the sand. "Oscar Isaac?" she called after us. I broke into a jog with Davi, headed straight to the water. "Sutton!" she shouted. "What if he's *literally* Aragorn shoving the doors open in *The Two Towers*? You wouldn't even *consider* him then?"

"Aragorn is taken!" I called over my shoulder, just as she sprinted after us and we splashed into the water, the sun sparkling off of it everywhere.

I was slicing a baguette in the kitchen when Gabe and his mystery friend arrived that evening. Davi walked outside to help with bags, something patently unlike him, but the only thing stronger than Davi's desire to not help was his curiosity.

"Where are you going?" I called after Laurel when she hopped up, nearly upending her second glass of boxed Moscato.

"Recon!" she shout-whispered in my direction before scurrying out the door.

I laughed, shaking my head before lifting the lid off a pot on the stove, stirring the simmering pasta sauce inside. Laurel was back quickly, running into the kitchen and practically colliding with me.

"So," she said in a hushed tone. A car door slammed outside, voices floating in through the screen door. "Do you want to know?"

I shrugged a shoulder as she grabbed a slice of bread off my cutting board and broke off a bite. "Whatever."

"*Whatever*," Laurel said. "Sutton, he could be our new fifth."

"I echo what Davi said earlier about referring to us like that," I said, pointing my spoon at her.

"He's *hot*," Laurel hissed as feet sounded on the front step. I just rolled my eyes, but she pulled me deeper into the kitchen, continuing. "But, like, not in an intimidating way? He's, like . . . a little rumpled. But expensively rumpled. Like, put him in a navy-blue coastal knit sweater and a pair of round glasses and he'd be your favorite hot nineties dad, if your favorite nineties dad could also whisk you off to Spain for the weekend and keep you in bed the whole time."

I thought for a minute, trying to conjure up this image. "What?" I finally asked, just as the front door swung open.

"Laurel, you know that your *whisper* carries like a fucking foghorn," Davi said as we fell into a line, Laurel holding her wineglass in front of her face to hide her abashed grin. Gabe walked in behind Davi. His face was as familiar to me as Laurel's, all kind eyes and short brown hair, and as he hugged me to him it felt like our week there was clicking together.

Except. There was still the person walking in behind him, head ducked as he dropped the luggage Davi wasn't actually helping to carry by the front door. For a minute all I could see was the top of his head, but then he was straightening, and it was like all sound in the room died.

I don't know if I'd use Laurel's exact words to describe him, but not because she was wrong—because I'd already seen him in a well-loved navy-blue sweater at a party two months ago.

I already knew what that tousled, golden-brown hair felt like under my fingers, soft and thick and inviting. I already knew what it was to have those eyes homing in on me, the sharpest shade of gray-blue I'd ever seen, speckled toward the middle like the nexus of a storm cloud. I already knew the sound of his breath in my ear.

"Hi," he said, a grin just curling one corner of his mouth as he looked at me. I could tell he was thinking the same thing I was, gaze locked on mine even as the others stared at him like he was the newest attraction at a museum.

"Hi," Laurel and I echoed, judges before him. He was game, though, and stepped forward, holding a hand toward me to shake, the cheeky grin on his face growing.

"I'm Everett Bridges."

four

This Summer

Davi ends up falling into one of what, in college, we called his daily comas on the couch, his phone clasped to his chest even in that dead-to-the-world, snoring sleep that made him miss class on more than one occasion. Something about it makes this week feel a little more normal, until Laurel's emails turn into a hushed phone call with her manager, one she shoos me out of her room for. I return to my room where I answer my Uncle Hank's text asking if we've arrived safely, unpack my things into the dresser and closet, stare at the ceiling for a while. Usually, by this time, Laurel and I would be drinking wine on the back deck, laughing about something. Or at least talking. By six thirty, I send Gabe out to pick up the pizza order I placed, leaving me with a newly revived Davi at the counter and a pit of dread in my stomach at Everett's impending arrival.

"I see Laurel did the shopping," Davi says as I search through the pantry where Laurel shoved the two paper bags of groceries she'd carried in this afternoon. I grabbed fixings for a salad at the store earlier while Laurel stuffed Cheez-It crackers and popcorn, protein bars and Fritos into the cart. Back home, she's a devout subscriber to every meal delivery service on the planet—at least those that aren't currently sponsoring her. Her fridge is stocked with things like ready-made kelp salads and smoothie cups she only has to add coconut water to, but when left to her own devices, she is exclusively a grazer of packaged goods.

I toss him a bag of honey-mustard pretzels. "She got you your favorite."

"I knew I loved her for a reason," Davi says, ripping the bag open.

I rake my dark blond hair into a ponytail before grabbing plates out of the cupboard and setting them on the counter, collect a handful of forks out of the drawer and arrange them in a perfect fan, line up five water glasses and five wineglasses next to that. When I turn around Davi is watching me, eyebrow raised.

"What."

Davi holds up the hand he just used to pull a pretzel out of the bag, the fingers covered in the yellowy powder that coats his favorite snack splayed. "Nothing," he says. "You just seem a little on edge, that's all."

"Well, I'm not," I say. I can tell by Davi's expression that the strained edge in my voice is fully evident. "I'm fine."

"Yeah," Davi says. "I know that I'm always at my peak when I'm about to see an ex."

"Everett Bridges is *not* my ex," I snap quickly.

Davi grins, crunching on a pretzel. "If Laurel hears you using his last name this week you're going to be in *troooouble*."

I draw in a steadying breath, rest my palms on the counter behind me for support before I say anything else. When I do, Davi still looks amused. "I'm fine. I feel fine about spending this week with . . . him."

"You're going to have to land on *Everett* at some point, sweetie," Davi says. "Or we're all in for another disaster."

I hear Laurel's footsteps start to descend the stairs at that moment, her timing impeccable. I can't be sure if Davi is referring only to what happened five years ago, or to one of the several incidents that have occurred since, but either way it doesn't surprise me that he's the one bringing up the obvious tension in the room. Davi tends to be the bluntest among us. But even so, it rattles me, this reminder that, probably, I'm not the only one who has what happened at the forefront of my mind.

"Everything okay?" I ask Laurel when she appears and stops next to Davi with a slight crease between her eyebrows.

"Fine," she says almost absentmindedly, eyes scanning the kitchen. "Do we have wine?"

"Gabe's grabbing some," I say. Laurel nods, clearly distracted. "Did you and your manager get everything figured out?"

"Oh, sure," she says. She sits down next to Davi and digs her hand into the bag he offers her. "Just finalizing the details for the post announcing the divorce on Friday."

Davi and I exchange a quick glance before we look back at her.

I'd anticipated Laurel's mood might be less than her usual bubbliness this week, had thought it would be a trip spent taking long walks on the beach, talking, drinking too much, maybe burning a picture or two of Stephen. But instead, she'd asked me to organize it as if we were re-creating every one of our old traditions in this place.

It seems she intends this week to be a celebration, which would be fine, great, even, except for the fact that none of us has any idea what happened between her and Stephen. So while there's been plenty of the usual Laurel—bubbly, bright, happy—there have also been pockets of this in the last several months. Some air of distractedness around her, a glimpse of a sadness she staunchly denies feeling at all.

"Do you have to announce the divorce?" Davi asks as Laurel

takes the bag of pretzels from him. "I mean, isn't not announcing kind of the cool new announcement?"

"I think that's for baby announcements," Laurel says, tone gone light. That's the thing about these moments: They slip away quickly, and usually after someone else asks a follow-up question, makes it clear they've noticed the shift in her mood.

There's a beep at the door, the mechanical whir of the dead bolt unlocking. For a half second, I hope it might just be Gabe. Fifty-fifty odds aren't the worst I've ever had. But if this were a horse race I'd lose, because it isn't the shoulders of a former high school football star and a stack of pizza boxes coming through the door. It is instead a head of thick, golden-brown hair pushed back by a pair of sunglasses, cold-weather gray eyes underneath, a long-sleeved black T-shirt with the sleeves pushed up, the last suitcase to arrive set by the table in the entryway. It's a Bronco-driving, surfing, amusingly charming, infuriating film director. It is, despite Davi's warnings, *him.*

"Everett!" Laurel crows, hopping off her stool to greet him.

"Hey," Everett says, setting his sunglasses and keys on the table before he wraps an arm around her shoulders, envy shooting through me. Not that Laurel is hugging *him*, but that *he* is hugging *Laurel*, that their own friendship that has nothing to do with me or the rest of us is on full display. I *know* that they see each other more often than the rest of us, simply because they both live in Los Angeles and frequently overlap when they're traveling, because they're *friends.* We all are, I remind myself.

"How are you doing?" Everett asks when they release each other. The fact that Everett gets to ask this at all grates on me. After probably the twentieth time I asked her, Laurel told me in a fit of uncharacteristic exasperation that she'd delete my number if I didn't stop asking her *how she was doing.*

"I'm okay," Laurel says. "Glad we're all here."

"Me too," Everett says, eyes drifting over her shoulder to mine. "Hi."

"Hi," I say, tucking my hands into the back pockets of my jeans and shifting between my feet. I don't wave. We don't hug. Just, *hi, hi*, before it goes silent between us.

"Okay, we're all adults," Laurel says. She waves us together. "Hug and make up."

It takes a beat for either of us to step forward, but when we do, it's to practically collide in the middle, all elbows and shoulders and nothing fitting like it used to. I pat his back once, in what I think is a friendly move, but skepticism is painted all over Laurel's face when we pull apart. She is unconvinced.

"Are you good?" Everett asks, head ducked a little toward me. This, at least, is familiar. And he is too, I suppose, of course he is, but I don't want him to be. I don't want to feel *anything* at the steel gray of his eyes, the pine and salt and cinnamon scent that's now impossible to escape given his proximity. But I do feel something. Irritation. A bristle up my spine, heat coiling in my stomach, a reminder that, try as I have for five whole years, I haven't let that last summer go.

"I'm good," I say—or snap, I can't tell. There's a sound like waves crashing in the distance rushing around in my ears, a painful tick in my throat. "Are you good?"

"Great," he says, voice matching mine. A little annoyed, but trying to hide it.

"Fine," I say.

"Fine," he repeats, and *this* is why you don't hook up with, date, or become otherwise romantically intwined with your friends. Because you'll end up standing across from each other repeating things like *fine* at thirty-two years old.

Luckily, the front door opens at that moment and Gabe

comes walking back in, pizza boxes in hand, another box from the wine shop next to it balanced precariously on top. Everett and I step markedly away from each other.

"Just in the nick of time," Laurel says on a barely stifled sigh. I step forward to help with the boxes, but Everett does at the same time, and we're knocking into each other again.

"I've got it," I say as I grab the pizza out of Gabe's hands a little roughly. The box on top starts to shift and Everett, being disappointingly closest to me, grabs it before it falls, bottles clinking together inside. I pivot on my heel and march back toward the kitchen.

"Looks like things are going well here," I hear Gabe say in a low voice to Laurel at the same moment I realize Everett is following me, wine box in hand.

He sets it on the island, clearly trying to communicate something with me through the intense, pointed expression he's wearing. I ignore him and slide the pizza into the oven and set it to its lowest temperature, turning back toward the fridge, but there's a chest in my way.

"Excuse me," I say, not looking at him, but he doesn't move. I tilt my head back to stare up at him, frowning. "I told Laurel I'd make a salad."

"We have to play nice this week," he says, tone warning. His voice is only loud enough for me to hear, but I look around him to the foyer to check and see if anyone else might have heard. Davi joined Laurel and Gabe, and they're laughing about something.

"This week isn't about us," I say.

"Exactly," Everett replies. "So we can't make it about us by bickering all the time."

"I don't think we're *bickering*," I say.

One of Everett's brows tugs upward, doubtful. "How'd you do with those pizza boxes?"

"Great, thank you."

I can see one corner of his mouth twitch bitterly, and I'm surprised at the thrill that runs through me, like I've won. I don't like it.

"We'll play nice," I say. I wave a hand around him, shooing. "Now may I please get to the fridge?"

"Of course," Everett says in far too cheery a voice, pivoting on one foot to let me past. "Do you need help?"

Yes. No. Not from you. I smile tightly. "Sure."

Laurel plops onto one of the island stools as Everett washes his hands before I hand him an apple and a knife. Gabe claps a hand on his shoulder as he walks into the kitchen, and Everett momentarily sets down what I've given to him to hug him hello, exchange greetings with Davi.

"Seems like everyone's getting along?" Laurel says, catching my eye as I yank a bunch of kale out of its bag with a little too much force.

"Mmm-hmm," I say, ripping the leaves from their stems. "Everything's great."

"Can we get to talking now?" Davi asks as Everett returns to the cutting board, picking up the knife.

"Have you been sitting here in silence?" he asks.

"That's exactly what I said," Davi exclaims, throwing Laurel a wide-eyed stare.

"We were waiting for you to arrive," I say, and it's not the words exactly, but the tone in which they slide out of my mouth that turns it into a barbed comment. Which, depressingly, makes it all the easier to keep going. "No earlier flights?"

"You know, I tried to convince Delta to make Dubrovnik to Los Angeles their headline flight, but it wasn't really the boon they were hoping for," Everett says. Again, a sarcastic comment that might have gotten a laugh from me before, but now is delivered with enough vitriol laced into it that I rip into the next piece of kale like I'm trying to tear a flag down.

"You were in Croatia?" I ask when I see Laurel eyeing me.

"Filming the next movie," Gabe says. He's rounded the counter and is pulling wine bottles out of the box, stashing whites in the fridge and uncorking a red.

"Have things been as rough as they were a month ago?" Davi asks Everett, and I am suddenly on the outside. It's clear the four of them have their own group separate from the five of us, just like I do with Gabe, Laurel, and Davi. Just like I never wanted to happen.

"You didn't have to come straight here," Laurel says, skipping over Davi's question. "You've got to be so jet-lagged."

"Are you kidding?" Everett says, slicing into the apple. "Wouldn't miss this. And things wrapped up fine," he says to Davi. "But I'm glad to be off a film set for a while."

Gabe pours everyone wine while I finish the salad, Everett grabbing the goat cheese from the fridge while I make the dressing in a move that feels competitively helpful.

Everett sets a salad bowl in front of me. I yank it a little too harshly and have to catch it before it careens to the floor and we have to explain broken porcelain to Ralph. When I straighten, Laurel is watching me, assessing. I clear my throat and set the bowl on the island, forcing a smile onto my face. Everett is right. We have to play nice this week, even if that's all it is. Pretend.

five

First Summer

I couldn't find a moment to talk to Everett alone that first night, and that quote from *Gatsby* kept ringing in my head, about large parties and how there isn't any privacy at small ones. I'd never been more irritated with the size of our friend group than when I'd meet him in the kitchen and he'd look at me with a grin like we were in on the same thing, and suddenly Davi would be there, grabbing another beer from the fridge. Or when he was standing out back and I hurried to stand next to him only to discover Laurel there too, consoling Gabe. The fact of our small party never bothered me until I needed to talk to someone alone without drawing attention to it.

But if I thought Everett wouldn't keep our secret, I underestimated him. He coolly navigated the whole evening like we'd never met before, shaking my hand and asking what my major was at dinner, while I in turn responded like Laurel did to the Bronco as if I'd never seen it before, demanding we all drive along the coast in it at some point on this trip, and pretended I was surprised to learn he wanted to be a director. To be fair, that was new. I'd learned he was in film school at the party where we met, but he hadn't told me exactly what he wanted to do. I was quickly made aware that whatever casual intimacy I'd felt with him during our one night together was more a result of Everett's general vibes—easy, sunny, charming—than it was about what we'd learned about each other. Which was to say, very little.

He and Gabe had been friends as kids, I learned, until Gabe moved to Colorado their sophomore year of high school and they lost touch.

"I didn't even know he went to Devon until the first day of that Writers of the Beat Generation class I took last semester," Gabe said as we sat around the living room on our first night there. "Isn't that crazy?"

"Crazy," Laurel repeated before she turned to Everett. "Are you a big fan of the Beats?"

Everett shrugged. "I don't hate them."

"On a scale of one to ten, though, *how much* do you want to be like Jack Kerouac?"

Everett scratched at the back of his head. "I've never really considered it."

"That's a good answer," Laurel said, picking up her wineglass again. We'd made our way through most of a box and were all on the far side of tipsy, save for Everett, who staunchly followed his water-between-drinks rule and was only half as slaphappy as the rest of us. At Laurel's comment, he glanced at me where I sat across from him, like I might clarify.

"Laurel has certain red flags," I said, and ticked some of them off on my fingers. "If they're too into any male-dominated artistic movements, if they think they could be president, if they're too into the ocean."

"*Too* into the ocean," Everett repeated.

"Like, do you want to explore areas you probably don't need to, not do you want to save it."

"Do you want to save the oceans, Everett?" Laurel asked, pivoting a wobbly finger his way.

"Of course."

"Good."

He smiled at me then, and I smiled back, then glanced quickly around, afraid it was too familiar, but no one was paying attention.

It wasn't until later that Gabe started to freak out. "Zoey and I were going to get married," he said. He had a bottle of some expensive rye whiskey his father had given him as a graduation present next to him and kept tipping more into his glass. He was the drunkest of anyone, but none of us were stopping him that night. He looked up at us: Davi in the armchair behind me while I sat on the floor like Gabe. Everett was on the couch over Gabe's shoulder, Laurel on the other end. "We talked about it. I was going to propose to her after we'd lived in Denver for a year. After we were more settled. Fuck." He put his head in his palms, raking his fingers through his hair. "We were moving to Denver so we could be closer to my family when we had *kids*."

"Oh, sweetie," Laurel said, sinking down onto the floor and wrapping her arms around Gabe's wide shoulders. "You'll have kids with someone else. Someone who won't cheat on you with a guy from her biology seminar."

Gabe looked up. "But you and Sutton would have been in the wedding," he said. "Davi too. I don't know—" He waved a hand in the air toward Everett. "If you and I had started hanging out again, maybe you would have been too."

"I'm honored," Everett replied.

"It's okay," Davi said. "We'll still be in your wedding, no matter who you marry. We'll all be in each other's weddings. Well, except mine."

"The point is, you were also supposed to be in *Zoey's* wedding, and now she isn't even here." Gabe glanced morosely around at all of us. "I fucked up the whole group."

"You did *not*," I protested.

"I did."

"Zoey did," I said. "When she cheated on you."

"But just on me," Gabe said. "Not all of you."

"She broke our trust, though," I argued. "That's the point. We don't do that. We choose each other. Zoey could have broken up with you and *then* slept with someone else. She could have talked to you, or any of us, if she was having doubts about your relationship."

"But wouldn't that have been just as bad?" Gabe asked. "It still would have changed things between all of us."

We looked around at each other then. Davi, behind me, shrugged, while Laurel sat back against the couch, thinking.

"Okay," she finally said, grabbing the bottle from in front of Gabe and pouring some into each of our glasses before she raised hers. "From here on out, to maintain the sanctity of our friendship and preserve the family we've chosen for ourselves, we will promise not to date or otherwise fornicate with each other."

"You didn't need to use the word *fornicate*," Davi said. "You never need to use the word *fornicate*."

"Oh my god, you get it, though," Laurel said. "Gabe is right. Dating each other opens the door for things to get messy, no matter how sure a thing you think something is. And we're all too important to each other to risk it."

"Wouldn't we have slept together by now if we wanted to?" Davi asked.

"I think you protest too much," Laurel countered.

"I'm just saying," Davi said. "Are you suddenly going to start dating Gabe?"

"No," Laurel said. "That's the whole point. This—" she waved a finger around at all of us "—is too important to me to risk even considering sleeping with Gabe."

"*Have* you ever considered sleeping with Gabe?" Davi asked.

"Why does that matter?"

"I think we should get any past dalliances out in the open."

"I was faithful to Zoey the whole time," Gabe said, holding up his hands.

"We know, sweetie," Laurel said. "And no, I haven't. Fine, Davi. Anything anyone wants to get out in the open?"

My eye caught Everett's for half a second. We were all looking at each other, like we expected someone to confess, so the moment between us went unnoticed as we communicated something across the circle. We weren't going to tell anyone.

Davi was the one to break the silence. "I had a dream about Sutton once."

I turned to him, nose wrinkling.

"What?" he said. "I've seen you every day for the past three years. I think it's natural. It doesn't mean I'm in *love* with you."

I shoved off the hand he rubbed on top of my head, rolling my eyes.

"Aside from Davi's sex dream about Sutton, have any of us ever, even once, done something that could compromise the friendship?" Laurel asked. "Speak now, or forever hold your peace."

Another glance at Everett. I wasn't sure why, if it was the wine and whiskey or some other reason I couldn't identify, but it seemed like the same thought passed between us, the same decision being made. That whatever had happened between us didn't matter. That the us anyone would know about started now, this weekend, and it could be as simple as that.

"Fine, then," Laurel said, lifting her glass toward the middle of the table so we could all cheers. She slung an arm around Gabe's shoulders. "Then on this night, we make a pact that we are all off-limits. Friendship only." She started to push her glass forward to clink it against everyone's when she realized we were one short and glanced over her shoulder at Everett. He was sitting with his glass balanced on one knee, fingers settled lightly against its sides.

"You too, Bridges," she said. "You're a part of this now."

"I don't—" he said, almost hesitantly. "I'm just here for Gabe."

"No," Laurel said. "Sorry. You're one of us. You've now promised your first week of June to us from here until forever, and you can't sleep with a one of us."

"Okay," Everett said. He leaned forward and pressed his glass into our little cheers.

"To friendship!" Laurel said, squeezing her arm tighter around Gabe's shoulders. "Fuck the rest."

"Fuck the rest," we all echoed, and sipped our whiskey. But Everett's eyes met mine over the rim of his glass, and I felt it: We would be in on this secret together, forever.

After we made the pact, the only real goal of the week beyond cheering up Gabe was to enjoy this week like it was our last together.

We stayed up late and woke up late, drinking the coffee whoever got up first made on the back porch while we stretched off hangovers. Everett excepted, of course, who, beyond that first night, had a hard three-drink limit that he rarely reached. We declared everything a tradition to be re-created the next summer, and every summer thereafter, because time was endless then. There were no responsibilities we could fathom that could possibly keep us from this.

On our fifth and second-to-last night there, we all piled into Everett's car and drove through Topanga Canyon to the nearest In-N-Out, Davi's vacation playlist pumping through the speakers. He sat huddled on one side of Gabe in the back, Laurel on the other, and I had to pretend I'd never been in this passenger seat before.

Everett glanced at me as the three in the back sang along to "Sweet Disposition," alarmingly off-key. "Are you having a good week?" he asked.

I looked over at him, offering up a smile. I'd been a little standoffish with him since the first day, when talking to him alone had been all I'd wanted. Whatever silent agreement we'd made stood: No one would know what had happened between us two months ago. Still, I was having a hard time pretending having him here was normal.

I was the only one, though. I could tell Gabe was thrilled to have his old friend back. It was obvious the two of them had been close when they were kids, sharing that kind of mutual language you only know when you've been young with someone. Davi, usually stingy with his affection but never one to be left out, quickly got over any lingering doubts he had about this new person. That, and he was obsessed with Everett's car. Everett handed him the keys on our second morning there and Davi had a friend for life.

Laurel was, of course, Laurel about it. Her doubts were erased as soon as she saw Everett. Not that Laurel was altogether vain, not that Laurel *wanted* Everett, but a beautiful face could sway her. And Everett, I was discovering, was beautiful. I'd known it that first night, that morning I woke up in his room. But it was something else altogether to see him laughing as he hopped into his car with Gabe to go surfing, or as he paused on a hike high above the ocean to take a long drink from a water bottle, the ocean stretching blue behind him, or as he lay on the sand next to me, chest bare, eyes closed. Or as he glanced over at me again with one hand casually on the steering wheel, the other arm resting on his window, hair rustling in the breeze as the twilight cast everything in blue.

"I'm having a good week," I told him. I motioned at the world around us. "Are you having a good time?"

"You didn't tell me you had such great friends," he said, voice low.

The top was on the Bronco, but the windows were down, and Laurel, Davi, and Gabe were singing loudly enough that they wouldn't have heard Everett even if he'd shouted. Still, it had me seizing up, shifting in my seat.

"They're the most important thing in the world to me," I said. I met Everett's eyes when he glanced at me, almost in a challenge.

"It seems like you all take care of each other."

"We do," I said. "We're family."

He navigated us around a sharp curve before he spoke again. "Do you want to tell me about Zoey?" he asked.

The sting the question sent through me surprised me. "She betrayed Gabe," I said. "She's not one of us anymore."

Everett glanced sideways at me, back at the road. "She's got to be missing this," he said.

"She caused the breakup," I said, defensiveness edging my voice. "She broke Gabe's heart."

"I'm not saying she's in the right," Everett said. "Just that it would be hard to lose this."

"Then don't screw people over," I said.

Everett did that huff of a laugh again: just an exhale, really, through his nose, accompanied by a barely there smile, like he knew something I didn't. I would have found it annoying if it didn't have me leaning in, curious, every goddamn time.

"You're not big on chances, are you?" he asked.

I crossed my arms over my chest as we continued to climb

out of the canyon. "I don't think what Zoey did really deserves a second chance."

"I agree with you," Everett said, in that easy way of his. I prickled at it, his levelheadedness. His ability to just carry on a conversation even when I was irritated. "I just wouldn't ever want to do something you deemed unforgivable."

"You don't even know me," I said then. "How do you know what I find unforgivable?"

"I don't," he said. "But it strikes me that you set a pretty high standard."

"What, and you just let people get away with anything?"

"Oh, no," he said, surprising me. We came up on a stop sign at the top of the road, and he glanced over at me, a crooked grin on his face. "I think I might be as unforgiving as you are."

I laughed a little, out of shock or relief, I couldn't tell, but as he looked back at the road again, I realized that I didn't believe him. Not at all.

We got our food and Everett drove us to an overlook he knew about, where we could see all the way to the water. We grabbed a blanket from his trunk and spread it directly on the gravel in the parking lot and passed around French fries and milkshakes, and it was another one of those nights that had made me fall in love with my friends in the first place: In the middle of all the mad rush of the world, we were always a safe place where I could be still.

six

This Summer

After Everett and I finish up the salad, we all grab pizza and take it out to the table on the back deck. The sun has mostly set, but Laurel plugs in the globe lights strung on the pergola the table sits under, flicks on the heat lamps sitting in the corners.

"The cottage didn't even have a real table *inside*," Davi says as he sits down next to me, a black fleece tugged on over his shirt.

"Bet you'll be happy to cook in a real kitchen this week," Gabe says to me from his spot next to Everett across the table. Laurel is at the head presiding over all of us, her hands folded under her chin like she's surveying her children. Her eyes catch on me, twinkling.

"Ask Sutton about her cookbook," she says.

Gabe jerks upright so aggressively he almost drops the slice of pizza he just picked up from his plate. "Seriously?"

"Seriously," I say. I got the news just a few weeks ago. Laurel had been the one to first set up the account where I shared recipes after I started appearing as a guest in the videos of a few former coworkers who had found success as internet chefs. I was resistant to it then—still am—but it led to this.

"What does that mean?" Gabe says, glancing at Davi, who already knew because we talked on the phone last week and who reserves his enthusiasm for things like final products. "What do you need to do? When do we get it?"

"We've barely started recipe development," I tell him. "It's still very early."

"Will you put the pistachio mint cookies in there?" Davi asks, interest apparently piqued.

"You have that recipe," I answer, picking up my wineglass and taking a sip.

"Yes, but I'd like it in cookbook form, please."

"I'll think about it."

"If you're taking requests, that white bean thing you used to make for us in college should absolutely be in there," Gabe says.

"There'll be a riff on something like that," I say. I shake my head, rushing forward before things get too out of hand. "It's seriously still so early, but yeah, the cookbook is happening."

"We knew her when," Gabe says, forming a marquee with his hands.

"Please, we knew *them* when," Davi says. "Everett had award season by the balls last year."

"Gross," Laurel says. Davi shrugs.

I realize I haven't looked at Everett since Laurel mentioned the cookbook. I could feel his eyes on the side of my face as I talked, and I knew, or suspected, why. It was a reminder, the first of many I was afraid of coming up this week. Of what used to be. He was one of the first people I told I actually wanted to write a cookbook. Telling him, telling anyone, made it real. But that doesn't matter now. I look across the table at him, jaw set.

"I don't think I ever congratulated you," I say. "On the win." I am pointedly leaving out the seven nominations and two other wins that *Cooney*, the ode to the coming-of-age, science fiction greats of the eighties, garnered last year. Suddenly Everett's name was everywhere, because winner of best director is one thing, but a young, hot, and eligible best director is another entirely.

"Thank you," Everett says, eyes locked on to mine across the table. "Congratulations on the cookbook."

The moment lasts just a breath too long, spreading unease through me. I set my wineglass down, clap my hands together. "Enough about that," I say. "What about everyone else?" It feels strange to have to ask, a poke at a sore spot in me, but I school my expression into something neutral.

"The twins are starting preschool in the fall," Gabe says, looking almost teary. "I can't believe it."

"I am up for a promotion," Davi says.

"No work this week," Laurel says, leveling him with an accusatory stare.

"Remind me what you were doing in your room this afternoon?" Davi asks. Laurel tosses what's left of her crust in his direction, but he dodges it, laughing. "I'm also officially the legal counsel to a musician who cannot be named but whose name you absolutely all know and give so many shits about."

"Tell us," Gabe says. "I promise we won't tell anyone."

"You'll tell Mia," I say, pointing an accusatory fork at him.

"You always tell your spouse," Gabe counters before looking back at Davi. "Mia won't tell anybody."

"I'm not at liberty to say," Davi says, holding up his glass. "But this artist may or may not be on your workout playlist, Gabe."

"That narrows it down to roughly two thousand people," Gabe, who has famously never made a new workout playlist and instead just keeps adding and adding and adding to the existing one, mutters.

"I'm doing a campaign with Alaska Airlines starting this summer," Laurel says from her spot at the head of the table.

She tips her wineglass toward Everett. "Maybe *they'll* add more flights between Dubrovnik and Los Angeles."

We go around the table like this, the talking that Laurel wanted us to postpone until now, a circle of updates that we never used to need but that are now essential for all of us to truly be caught up on one another's lives. It's obvious when it comes to something either I or Everett don't know, and it quickly emerges that it's not just the three groups that exist among us, but four. Laurel, Davi, and Gabe are their own. I try not to let it bother me. We each have our own, unique relationships with each other. But I want us to feel cohesive again. Right now, it seems more like we're just round-robin-ing our life updates.

"Mia and I are thinking about a different house," Gabe says. "The four of us are starting to outgrow the space where we are now. But we love that house."

"It's a great house," Everett says. I add it to my mental list of Things to Keep Track Of. He's been there. I haven't.

"See, this is another reason I don't want kids," Davi says. "Who can afford to level up their real estate every time they pop out another gremlin?"

"Maybe an entertainment lawyer representing someone we all *give so many shits about*?" I tease.

"And they aren't gremlins," Gabe says. "Except around the holidays, maybe. They get really insane in December."

"Our eternal bachelor," I say, wrapping an arm around Davi's shoulders and stretching up to tuck my chin on top of his head.

"What about you?" he asks, shifting so he sits up. "Relationship status?"

I shrug. "Same as always. Who's to say."

"That means she just dropped the last guy she was seeing for . . . two weeks?" Laurel says.

"I'll have you know I went on *eleven* dates with him," I say proudly. "But he really wanted to define things. Was ready for a real relationship."

"Perish the thought," Everett mutters from across the table, which has me turning to him.

"Let me guess," I say. "You started *something* with an actress you met at some event or other a few months back and you just don't know why it didn't work out."

Everett, worthy opponent that he is, has the audacity to not look rattled. Instead, he relaxes back in his chair, takes a drink of his wine. Says, in his perpetually winning tone, "She was a screenwriter. And it was last year."

Gabe snorts at this, then straightens his mouth, eyes quickly flashing my way.

"Well," Laurel says after another beat of silence, during which Everett and I stare, hard-eyed, at each other. "Since we're on the topic of relationships, I'd like to say thank you to everyone for making this week work."

It's like the fight is punched out of me. I can see it in Everett's expression too, as four faces pivot toward her. Here it is. The moment she lets us know what happened. But instead, Laurel just picks up her glass.

"To divorce!" she cries, holding it aloft.

Davi is the only one who joins in. At the rest of our silence, Laurel takes a swig and rolls her eyes.

"It's okay, guys," she says. "I thought this would be it, and it's not." She swipes her hands together, like she's dusting flour off of them rather than a whole relationship that not just she, but all of us, thought would last.

It's Everett who says something first, and I hate him for it. Not just because I want to beat him to the punch, prove to

Laurel that I am the best friend, but also because I agree with what he says.

"Do you want to talk about it?" he asks.

I don't know what does it. Maybe it's the fact that I think it's what we all want to ask. But I find my hackles rising, and before I know it I'm piping up too, saying something I don't totally agree with, but not quite at Laurel or the group at large. At him directly. "If Laurel says she's okay, then she's okay," I say, grip tight on my wineglass. I thrust it toward the sky, my brown eyes locked on to Everett's cool ones. "Here's to moving on."

There's a brief beat before the others echo me. I stare back at Everett as he raises his glass, last of anyone. His eyes don't leave mine as he echoes the cheer and takes a healthy sip of his wine. He doesn't look away until he's setting it down on the table.

Everett sits back and Gabe jumps in with a story about his flight here, clearly trying to change the subject. I wait as long as I physically can to glance at Everett, not wanting to give him a single iota of proof that I care what he thinks. That he's here. That he exists at all.

But I'm not so lucky. When I look over at him, he's already watching me, lying in wait. I don't look away. I stare back at him as he lifts his glass almost imperceptibly in a private toast of our own, cementing something I hadn't known we'd agreed on. *If this is what this week is going to be like, so be it*, his glass and the expression on his face say.

Let the games begin.

seven

First Summer

On the morning of our last full day at the cottage, Saturday, I proposed my own tradition. We'd make one final, special dinner together that night, and so we traipsed to the farmers market where we wandered between stalls, Laurel sampling everything while I picked out ingredients and put them into the bag I carried and another Everett had dutifully extended my way at each stall. I smirked at him as I placed a quart of tomatoes into it, hand-pulled pasta at another, as I deposited a carton of peaches into his waiting arms.

At the house, Laurel turned on Patsy Cline and poured everyone wine, her one contribution. Gabe sliced the baguettes I put in front of him and Davi grabbed the slivered almonds out of the oven before they went from toasted to burned. It had always been this way with my friends. None of them liked to cook. I'd tried to get them into it on some level during our three years living together, in the hopes I might have at least one sous-chef on occasions like this, but the three of them were much more the drink-and-keep-the-chef-company variety than the cooking variety.

Everett, I discovered, was no better. But he did at least try.

"Have you *used* a knife before?" I asked as he tried to dice an onion next to me. He'd said he could when I handed it to him, like it was simple, like everyone knew how to properly do it. Which I thought everyone should, really, but I wasn't about to tell my friends that.

"Yes," he said as he sliced another painfully slow sliver off the halved onion. He'd gotten that far. "Obviously."

"Okay, here," I said, reaching over and taking the knife from him. I held the onion with my nails against it, sliced it horizontally before cutting a series of vertical slices in it. "And then you just chop, okay?" I said, mimicking the motion with my hand. When I looked up his eyes were already on me, and I felt that same flush rise up my neck that I did at that stupid party. I clapped a hand on his shoulder. "You've got it."

But Everett didn't have it. Eventually, I put him on pasta duty, which was to watch the pot with his hands clasped behind his back and to stir when I prompted him to. I already had a timer set.

"What do you usually eat?" I asked as he watched the pot.

"You know," he said. "Things that don't require a lot of preparation."

"Like what?"

"Coffee," he said. "Apples."

"You eat coffee and apples?"

"Toast," he said. "I'm great with toast."

"Oh my god," I laughed as I whisked the salad dressing. "You are *not* surviving on coffee and apples and bread."

"Okay, I eat other things, but you're making me nervous," he said, smiling sheepishly at me. "You're really good at this."

"I *studied* this," I said. "I'm sure if I came to a film set I'd be equally wowed."

"But your thing is part of basic survival," he said. "No one needs movies to survive."

"Hmm," I said as I set the whisk down. "I might argue otherwise."

Everett grinned. “Can I tell you something?”

“You can tell me anything,” I said, almost unbidden. It was something I’d say to Laurel or Davi or Gabe, and I found myself surprised to be saying it to Everett. Still, I waited, curious.

“I watched a lot of Food Network growing up,” he said, glancing over at me. “And I still can’t cook.”

I slapped the back of a hand against his chest. “You say that like it’s some big secret.”

“Shouldn’t I be able to properly dice an onion if I was raised on Ina Garten?”

“Hey,” I said. “Ina has faith in your abilities yet.”

“Does she,” Everett said flatly, as the timer I’d set for the pasta went off.

I bumped him out of the way, pot holders in hand, but he didn’t go far. Instead, I ended up with one half of my back pressed to his chest, glancing over my shoulder at him. Laurel was right: He was beautiful, and I felt my breath hitch in my throat as I looked up at him, as I remembered his hands skimming down my sides, hoisting me up against him. I tried to smile, brush past the thump in my chest. “She does.”

Everett, Gabe, and I cleaned up after dinner while Laurel and Davi worked on getting a fire started down on the beach. When we joined them, Davi was standing guard over it, arms spread wide in presentation.

“Look at my creation!” he said, clearly pleased with himself.

“It only took us seven tries,” Laurel said. “Proud of us?”

“So proud,” I said, dropping onto the sand next to her. Everett sat across the fire from me.

We all watched the flames whip their embers toward the sky in silence for a while. We could feel it hanging heavy over us, the next step this week had been gently leading us toward.

"I can't believe this is it," Gabe said then. He looked around at all of us. "I kind of thought college would just last forever."

"Me too," Laurel said, leaning her head against my shoulder. I scooped an arm around her, squished my cheek against her hair. "I'm really afraid of being lonely in Seoul."

Laurel had landed an internship at a fashion house in Seoul after deciding she wanted to work abroad for a year following graduation. She had family there and would be living with one of her cousins, but she'd still told me she was afraid of living without us. I felt the same worry, heading back to San Francisco, where my closest friends were my Uncle Hank and the staff at his restaurant.

Gabe took a long swig of his beer. "I'm afraid everyone's going to pity me now that Zoey and I have broken up."

"No," Laurel said, at the same time I said, "If it seems like anyone is even *considering* pitying you, you call me and I'll hunt them down." Gabe tilted his head back, laughing.

"Okay, I'm afraid I'm going to be *too* good at law school and I didn't aim high enough," Davi said. Laurel kicked some sand his way.

"Come on," she said.

"What?" Davi said. "I'm incredible. You all know it." When we all smirked at him, he rolled his eyes. "Fine," he said. "I'm terrified of not having this. I'm scared every friend I make from here on out is going to be surface level and I'll never be a part of something like this again."

"But you *are* a part of something like this," I said. "We're forever."

It was only me and Everett left then, and we looked at each other across the fire, a silent game of chicken. Finally, he sat up a little, cleared his throat. "I'm afraid I made all the wrong choices in college and it's too late to take them back now," he said.

"New guy," Laurel said. "Coming in hot with the cryptic confessions."

"Not the new guy anymore, remember?" Gabe said, clapping a hand on Everett's shoulder. "One of us now."

Laurel and Davi raised their glasses in agreement, but Everett looked at me expectantly. "What about you?" he asked.

"Um," I mumbled, digging around for an answer that wasn't the same as what Davi had said. It's not that I wasn't afraid of the future, but I had some sense that there wasn't much I could do to change it. I was certain our little party was forever, that we would return to this place each year and re-create this magic. I had a plan for the next five years, knew how to handle contingencies. Everything was well-kept around me. So long as things held steady, everything would be okay. But everyone was looking at me, waiting, and I had to say something. "I'm afraid of how much I'll miss all of you." It was a cop-out, I knew, but I couldn't tell exactly why. Still, it had Laurel burrowing her head against my shoulder, and I meant it, so I let it lie.

"Okay," Everett said after a quiet, sad moment. "What about what we're looking forward to?"

"I like that," Laurel said, perking up. "One thing you're afraid of and one thing you're excited for. It can be a tradition."

"Laurel also loves traditions," I said to Everett across the fire, and he smiled when Laurel wrapped her arms around me.

"You love my traditions," she said. "It's what makes us so great."

"Sutton, you first," Gabe said. "You were last to go."

"Fine," I said. This one came easier. "I'm excited to work with Hank and the crew again."

"I knew you'd say that," Davi said, grinning over his beer.

It had been the plan since I'd moved for college. I'd study culinary arts, move back to San Francisco, and work at my uncle's restaurant. I would run the restaurant someday, once Hank retired, so I wanted to spend as much time as I could working under him to learn the ropes.

"Everett," I said, nodding at him. "Your turn."

"I'm really excited to be back in that LA traffic," he said, and when we all laughed, he insisted, "No, seriously. Good music, time to think. Being able to get somewhere in fifteen minutes has been hell these last four years."

"Okay, we need more," Davi said. "If I had to be serious so do you."

"Alright," Everett said, picking at the label on his bottle with his thumbnail. "I'm headed up to Vancouver in October to work on a shoot for a TV pilot and I'm pretty excited about it."

"Gabe," Laurel said. "If you have any other future famous friends hiding in the woodwork, feel free to bring them next summer."

"Ha, ha," Everett said as Gabe rolled his eyes at Laurel.

Davi was excited about going to law school in Illinois because it was one step closer to him living in New York, which he felt much better aligned with his personality; Gabe was excited to have true seasons again; and Laurel was excited to share her travels on social.

After a while, we all huddled together on the same side of the fire. It was a moment when none of it mattered: not the absence of Zoey, not the fear of what life would look like without each other, not even the fact that, mentally, I'd been breaking the promise we'd all made to each other all week, in life and in my dreams. Nothing, not even that, could get in the way of that snapshot: five new adults, caught somewhere between training wheels and growing up. It was the perfect ending to something I don't think any of us could quite name yet.

eight

This Summer

I spend the first night in the house unnervingly aware of Everett in the room down the hall from mine. His presence is a mosquito buzzing in my ear, disappearing for a few minutes at a time only to circle back around when whatever I've tried to distract myself with wears off.

I left today free for settling into the house when Laurel and I planned the week—the re-creation of our usual itinerary starts tomorrow—so in the morning, after a shower long enough to wash off the fact that I can't seem to shut Everett completely out of my mind no matter how hard I try, I tromp down the stairs and announce I'm going into town.

"Why?" Laurel asks, poking her head over the low back of the mid-century couch she's lounging on, one of the many self-help books she lugged with her on this vacation in her hands. Davi is sitting on a stool at the kitchen island, a mug of coffee and his open laptop in front of him.

"I think we need more than chips and wine in the house," I say. I put a hand to my stomach to drive home my point. "We can't eat pizza for breakfast all week."

"That used to be your breakfast of choice in college," Laurel says.

"Yeah, well," I say. "We grow."

"We become professional chefs," Davi says.

"Hey, I'm a ramen girl most nights," I point out. While I love cooking for people, testing recipes to share online, and spending time in the kitchen making dinner for my friends, I usually find that cooking for just myself yields much less joy. If I could have my own private chef after having to chef professionally all day, I'd be so happy.

"Well, I'm in," Laurel says, tossing her book to the side and sitting up, stretching her arms over her head. "Let's round everyone up."

"Oh, actually—" I say, trying to come up with some excuse. I'd been hoping this would be a chance to escape the pall hanging over the house, get away from Everett for a couple hours. But one look at Laurel's face—patient, none the wiser—stops me. This week is about being here for her, after all. And who am I to deny anyone a grocery run? "Never mind."

Laurel runs upstairs to change while Davi clicks away at his keyboard. I slump onto the stool next to him, squint at the screen.

"You're working?" I ask. When he ignores me, I continue, "You know what Laurel said about work this week."

Davi tilts his screen down, not fully closing his laptop. "Didn't Laurel just tell you to go find Gabe and . . . who is it?" He puts an index finger and thumb to his chin. "Your ex-lover?"

"Ha, ha," I deadpan. I tug a bowl of cherries—the only fiber currently in the house and case in point that we need to go grocery shopping, so we don't totally regress to our twenty-two-year-old habits while we're here—and grab out a handful. "You want to do the job for me?"

"No," Davi says. "But I'll watch."

I shove my shoulder against his. "Come on. You can't egg us on. Everett and I are supposed to be *getting along* this week."

"I'm not the one who needs to be reminded of that." Davi grabs a cherry out of my palm and pops it in his mouth, tugs the stem off. "You going to be on your best behavior at the store?"

"Yes, Dad."

"Pity," Davi says around the cherry. "Watching you two bicker is so entertaining."

I'm about to respond when the front door opens and Everett walks in. He's clearly just back from surfing, wearing only a pair of swim trunks with a towel slung over one tanned shoulder, his hair damp. He tosses his keys onto the table in the entryway before he catches sight of us and nods, tugging the towel off of his shoulder to scrub at his hair as he walks over.

He looks up at me as he approaches, and I'm struck, yet again, by the exact shade of his eyes. I remember all the ways I used to think about them: icy in a first-snow way, a cold blue sky alight with a fire's glow. Weather hanging over a hot day, relief when the rain finally breaks. But all of that is gone. Now, the blue-gray of his eyes is more akin to slush in the gutter, getting sprayed on you on your way to the bus stop when a car speeds by.

"Morning," he says to us, shaking me out of my irritated daydreaming.

"Good waves?" Davi asks.

"Not bad," Everett says, grabbing a few cherries from the bowl. "Gabe wanted to go."

"Did you forget him?" I ask, looking exaggeratedly at the empty foyer behind him.

Everett looks a half second away from an eye roll, but he abstains. "He's FaceTiming Mia and the kids on the front porch."

"Ah," I say, eyeing Everett's bare torso. "Had to wait until you were out of frame, huh?"

He narrows his eyes at me, juggling the handful of cherries between his fingers like he's weighing his comeback options. "Why would that be, Sutton?"

"I'm just saying, you couldn't be bothered to put on a shirt between the beach and here?"

"Yes, Sutton. My chest is why Gabe decided to take the call outside."

I hold up my hands. "Listen, I think it's a little weird too."

Everett turns his flat stare to Davi, who's smiling tight-lipped at his computer screen. "What's everyone up to?"

"Oh." At this, Davi slams his laptop closed, looking far too pleased. "We're all going into town. Sutton's idea."

Everett frowns as I stomp on Davi's foot. "Was it."

"Better get showered, salty boy," Davi says. "We're getting groceries."

Everett looks like he'd like to ask more questions, but Laurel comes prancing down the stairs at that moment in a loose white linen dress, hair piled on top of her head.

"Everett!" she sings, like we're gearing up to go drinking instead of stocking up on food. "Get ready! It's time for groceries!"

"Better hurry up," I say when he glances back at me. A deep breath precedes a forced smile before he heads for the stairs.

I'm smiling triumphantly after him. If it were any other point in my life, I would probably be embarrassed by the pride I feel at winning whatever this exchange just was. But this isn't any other point in my life. It's now, and I'm annoyed by him. By the way he seems to always be watching me, waiting for some reaction. By the fact that he's someone who knows, or used to know me, so his comebacks manage to feel pointed every time, even when they aren't. By stupid things, like how the way the gray of his eyes makes every glare that much more intense, something I can't imitate, or how he's still as at ease in his body as he was back then, some cool-guy thing that makes something as mundane as walking toward the stairs an activity to watch.

Which I am, I realize, when Davi snorts so loudly it startles me. I glare at him, angry to have been caught.

"*So* entertaining," he says on a laugh.

We drive by a farmers market we haven't been to before on the way to the grocery store. I'm crammed into the back of the Bronco between Davi and Gabe, so I have to lean between Laurel and Everett and shout over the wind for him to pull over. He almost misses it but turns in at the last second, and I tell myself it was on purpose, grumbling when I slide out of the car after Gabe.

Everett is waiting there, one hand on the door and the other stretched toward me.

"What was that?" he asks as I completely ignore it in favor of jumping out. It's an awkward angle after sitting with my legs scrunched up in the back, and I stumble a little on the landing.

Everett, unfortunately, is there to catch me, one hand grabbing the one I'm already throwing his direction as his other settles on my back to steady me. "Easy there," he says, voice in my ear. I hadn't realized how close he was, warm chest pressed against my arm as my heart batters against my ribs. He smells so familiar, vivid memories pricking with each inhale.

I push away and start down the street after the others, catching up to them just outside the entrance to the market. White tents top the stalls, the scents of freshly baked bread and early summer tomatoes floating onto the sidewalk.

I pull the list I made in my room this morning out of my pocket, neat bullet points on the pale blue resort stationery. "We have Friday set," I say. Friday, Laurel is hosting the mysterious divorce party, what she's calling her Breakup Blowout, at a bar in town. We all received invitations a few weeks ago, as if we wouldn't already be together. As if it isn't the capstone of this entire trip.

"I figured we'd probably get takeout one night," I continue. "And then Saturday we'll do our usual shop and final dinner. But, Laurel, any requests?"

"I'm sure whatever you have planned is great," she says, already distracted by a vendor selling wind chimes. "I'm just going to stop here, but you tell me what you need me to grab!"

"I'll do a coffee run," Gabe says. "Orders?"

"I know them," Davi says, ushering him down the sidewalk toward Fresh Ground, our favorite café.

I feel him behind me. The only one who has ever actually helped me at a market like this, not gotten distracted by something else. In truth, even back then I would have easily and happily done it all by myself, but I used to enjoy his company, sending him off to find things and perusing produce together when he returned to me.

"What's on your list?" Everett asks, coming around to my side.

"It's okay," I say. "Go with Gabe and Davi."

"Sutton." He levels me with a gaze I find irritatingly mature, like he's calling me on our collective bullshit. "Come on. Let me help."

I sigh but relent, not wanting to be the person who loses this argument by being petulantly stubborn. I examine the list for a minute before tearing it in half and extending it toward him. He's about to take it, fingers already gripping one corner, when I snatch it back.

"Wait," I say, running a finger down it. "You know that if you can't find escarole we can do something like kale, but only if the kale is good." Everett's posture stiffens. "And if they don't have garlic scapes we can't just substitute it with green garlic. And—" I stop my finger at another item on the list, teeth sinking into my lower lip. "You know, I really should just do this myself."

The paper is snatched out of my hands before I can blink. I follow after it, a protest on my lips, but Everett holds it out of my reach.

"I know how to pick a good Sungold tomato, Sutton," he says.

I cross my arms over my chest. "Yeah?" I ask. "How do you know?"

Everett is considering the list and doesn't look up at me when he says, "I was trained by the best."

"Who?" I ask, bristling for some unknown reason.

At this, Everett glances up from under his brow, eyes flashing. "You."

It startles me, the sudden flush I feel race into my cheeks, down my neck, across my chest; an animal waking up in my stomach. *No*, I tell myself. *Like an allergic reaction.*

"Okay, well," I say. I shove one of the tote bags I brought against his chest, and, for a split second, his hand covers mine. It bounces the heat that's spread to my fingers right back up my arm to my face again and I wriggle my hand out, wave him off. "Chop, chop."

Everett's smirk seems almost amiable.

I head in the opposite direction after he's disappeared into the crowd. This market is smaller than the one we usually go to, but it has some of the same vendors, people I recognize from over the years. There's something calming about the clamor of it all: parents pushing strollers and dogs leaning against legs, a college-aged couple inspecting summer zucchini next to someone picking up local honey next to someone mulling over a pair of handmade earrings.

Hank used to bring me to markets like this growing up. On Saturdays, we'd go to the pier so he could place his seafood order for the week, early enough that I sometimes wondered if I was still dreaming. Then we'd grab breakfast—always at a different spot, always somewhere Hank somehow knew everyone. We'd eat greasy diner breakfasts at counters before the place opened, grab pastries at the back doors of bakeries, wander long enough for the farmers markets to start.

And it was always the best part of the weekend. The whole ritual of it. When I was little, and still just visiting in the summers, Hank holding me up high so I could see the bright spreads of produce. When I was older, Hank teaching me how to pick out the best cuts of meat, how to spot a good sourdough from a mile away. By the time I was old enough to help out in his kitchen I was splitting lists with him, right down the middle, a tradition I've only ever shared with one other person.

The thought startles me as I'm picking up a carton of crimson strawberries, my grip almost slipping as it makes contact. "Sutton!" A hand wraps around my arm, startling me enough to firmly dislodge Everett's face from my mind.

Laurel is turning me away from the table, something pointed in her tone. "You'll never guess who I ran into," she says, grinning at me toothily as she flicks her eyes toward the man next to her.

My eyes land on his shoes first, mostly because I'm trying to keep my balance after Laurel spun me around so suddenly, but it means that I do one long sweep up him, like I am full-on, audaciously ogling him. In fairness, it's not a bad sweep. At the top of brown chinos and a cream well-tailored button-down is a set of broad shoulders, a well-kempt mustache, thick dark hair just graying at the temples. He's holding a bag of lemons in one hand, the other casually in his pocket. And he smiles at me.

"Cooper, this is Sutton," Laurel says, piloting me into a handshake with the guy holding the lemons. "Sutton, this is Cooper. A *chef*."

"I'm guessing you're a chef too, if she's saying it like that," Cooper says, pulling one large hand out of his pocket and holding it out for me to shake. I take it, feeling like something of a damsel in distress about to be tossed over this burly man's shoulder, in a good way.

"Something like that," I say. The words taste sour in my mouth as soon as I say them. It's one of Everett's catchphrases, and I realize now I don't know when it made its way into my vernacular.

"She's writing a cookbook," Laurel says. She plucks a strawberry from the tasting tray and bites into it. "She's brilliant. Cooper here—" she discards the strawberry stem "—lives just down the beach from us."

"Oh?" I say. "How do you two know each other?"

"I've done some private events for Laurel before," Cooper says. "She's one of my favorite clients."

"Please, Cooper, we both know we're excellent friends," Laurel says. "We're in the same support group now. Cooper is recently divorced."

"I'm sorry to hear that," I say, as Laurel mouths *single dad* over his shoulder and shoots me an enormous thumbs-up, a grin splitting her face in two.

"Thanks," Cooper says as Laurel dances to the next row of samples behind him, leaving us relatively alone. "It's okay. You know, I'd love to pick your brain about what it's like writing a cookbook sometime, if you're free."

I fight the cringe I feel at the words *pick your brain*, a deep-seated pet peeve I have that Gabe used to tease me about (*Can I pick your brain about the history lecture I missed this morning, Sutton? Any time for me to pick your brain about what to get Zoey for Valentine's Day?*) and smile at Cooper. "Of course," I say. "I'd love to chat."

"Great," Cooper says. He pulls out his phone. "There's a great lunch spot a few miles down the coast that does the best fish taco around. You can't miss it while you're here."

"Sounds amazing," I say.

"Well, let me grab your number," he says, and passes his phone to me just as I feel an invisible presence behind me.

"Your tomatoes," Everett says flatly. Almost involuntarily I let out an excited little "Oh" and pause in putting my number into Cooper's phone to turn and inspect the two heavy boxes of Sungolds Everett is carrying before I remember exactly *who* is holding them.

"Cooper, this is Everett," I say, turning quickly away from the tomatoes and jabbing a thumb over my shoulder.

"Have we met before?" Cooper asks Everett. "You look familiar."

"Maybe through Laurel?" Everett suggests, which sets my stomach to simmering. *She texted you first*, I remind myself as envy settles in. I was the first person to know something was wrong. Even with the distance that's grown between us over the last five years. Even if she and Everett see each other more than I see her, Laurel and I are still best friends.

"I don't think so," Cooper says. When I look up at him, it's clear he's digging for the answer, rubbing a thumb over his chin before it inevitably comes to him, face lighting up. "I know," he says. "You directed that movie that everyone was so into a couple years back—what was it?"

"*Cooney*," I say flatly, before Everett can answer.

"That's it," Cooper says, grinning at me before looking back at Everett over my head. "My daughter wouldn't stop talking about it. She's twelve, but already knows she wants to go to film school. Where did you study?"

"Devon College," Everett answers, sparking a hundred memories from one single night in my head, and I am suddenly so incredibly done with standing in the middle of this conversation.

"Here you go," I say. I hand Cooper his phone back, tossing my ponytail in an arc that I hope is high enough to whack Everett in the face. "Let me know when you'd like to get together, okay?" I tilt my head and smile up at him, turning just enough for Everett to see.

"I will," Cooper says, attention back on me. "Hey, crazy idea." He glances at Laurel, to make sure she's listening. "What if you all came down to my house for dinner while you're here?"

Everett shifts behind me. I can feel the edge of the top tomato box dig into my back and I lean against it, pushing it back toward him.

Laurel lets out a thrilled laugh, clapping her hands together at the idea. "Wait, but what if you two did it?" she asks, looking between me and Cooper.

Everett coughs behind me, and I press my heel into his toes.

"Did what, Laurel?" I ask in as saccharine a tone as I can muster with Everett's infuriating scent floating into my nose.

"Cooked!" she exclaims again. "Two chefs are better than one, am I right?"

Cooper is looking at me, a knowing smile on his face, like he's familiar with Laurel's antics. "That's what they say," he says.

"Free this Wednesday?" I ask.

"Wednesday's great," Cooper says. His phone buzzes and he glances down at it. "I've got to take this, but I'll call you, okay? We'll set up lunch and I'll clear Wednesday's menu with you."

"It's a party," Laurel says.

"Looking forward to it," I say.

The tomato box jabs into my spine.

nine

First Summer

We said tearful goodbyes outside of the cottage on our last morning there. Laurel's eyes were puffy and red by the time she climbed into the back of Davi's car, Gabe in the passenger seat.

"You'll be okay?" she asked, leaned out her window as I crouched down to squeeze her hand one last time.

"I'm fine," I said. I'd woken up to an email that morning that my flight had been canceled and the next one I could get a seat on was Tuesday morning. I could take the change or cancel and get a hefty travel credit, and now that my best friends were going to be living so far away, I'd decided to get a rental car and make the drive back up to San Francisco rather than fly. But I also wanted to milk one more afternoon of lying on the beach before starting the drive.

"Maybe someday we'll all live here," Laurel said through a fresh round of tears.

I squeezed her hand, smiling. "Maybe we will."

I walked back to the steps, where Everett was also standing, to watch as they drove away. Davi had to reach behind him to grab Laurel by a belt loop as she leaned out her window, waving one arm so thoroughly she almost toppled out onto the road.

"You okay?" Everett asked when their car rounded the corner.

I looked up at him, hands wrapped around my elbows. I knew the tip of my nose and the tops of my cheeks would be red, the one tell I couldn't master. I nodded, swallowed. "Great," I said.

"Hey," Everett said. "It'll be alright."

I looked at him and nodded again, though I wasn't sure I believed him in that moment. I'd started to settle into just being friends with Everett—or friends adjacent, because calling Everett my *friend* didn't really seem to sum up our strange relationship—so much so that I'd agreed to his offer to drive me up to Los Angeles later this afternoon. I'd find a rental car there and crash in a hotel for the night.

We had to be out of the cottage by noon. Everett wanted to surf one last time, and I had my sights set on downloading enough podcasts to get me through the drive while lounging on the warm sand, so our plan was to head to his favorite beach and leave from there.

But by eleven, an hour after everyone else had left, it was clear we wouldn't be spending any time in the ocean today. Rain started pelting down hard and fast, the driveway in front of the cottage quickly turning into a river.

"Do we just wait it out?" I asked Everett as we stood by the front window, watching.

"Maybe," he said.

After another hour, though, the rain had hardly let up, and the weather service was recommending emergency travel only because of a landslide warning.

I squinted out the window as Everett called the front desk, asking after a later checkout. Apparently, it was a no-go, and so we ran with our things to his car where we sat, soaked through.

"Are they seriously going to send someone down to clean in this right now?" I asked. "We couldn't hang out for fifteen minutes?"

"I don't know how much fifteen minutes would help," Everett said. He glanced over at me. "I think we should probably find somewhere to stay tonight."

The thought of staying in a room with Everett—only Everett—landed in my stomach, fluttering around, but I tried to quickly shake it off. The pact, I reminded myself. Anything else with Everett was off-limits.

He drove us up to the main building and parked out front. I tried to distract myself from the way his wet T-shirt was sticking to him as we walked in, but there was only so much looking at the ceiling I could do. Luckily for me, though unluckily for our prospects of a new room, Ralph was standing behind the desk, grimacing at us as we approached. The sheer hatred emanating from him was distraction enough.

"Hi," Everett said. Ralph eyed the still-damp elbow he leaned on the counter.

"Hello," he said in a pinched tone.

"We just checked out of Poppy Cottage," Everett said. I let my eyes roam around the lobby as he explained our situation. I'd only been here at check-in and hadn't paused to do much inspecting of the building, but it was beautiful, from the original tiled floors to the intricate gold sconces on the dark wood walls. The place was historic, I knew, started by some starlet from the golden age of Hollywood and her third husband, a fact Laurel had cited when she managed to book a cottage at all.

I was dragged out of my daze by Ralph's nasally voice telling Everett that the only available accommodation for tonight was the six-bedroom Palomino Villa, a half mile down one of the roads that zigzagged its way around the property, and ran for two thousand dollars a night.

Everett hesitated for only a minute before he nodded and said, “Okay.”

“Okay?” I echoed, voice rebounding off the walls. Ralph narrowed his eyes at me. There was literally no one else around to hear me.

“Don’t worry,” Everett told me in a low voice. “It can be on my dad.”

I raised an eyebrow. “Your father won’t mind you charging a two-thousand-dollar villa to what I’m assuming is an emergency credit card, the lease on which is probably about to run out given the fact that we just graduated college and are now supposed to be real adults?”

Concierge Ralph looked like he’d like very much to sigh.

“He won’t care,” Everett said. “It’s not an emergency credit card. It’s more of a ‘buy whatever you want because I’m such an absent dick of a father’ card.”

This stopped me. If I knew about anything, it was absent parents, and in particular not wanting to rely on them or owe them for anything.

“Let’s just find another place,” I said. Ralph looked up hopefully, but Everett shook his head.

“My dad won’t ever see this bill,” he said. “And this can be its last hurrah anyway. Ralph, could you send a bottle of your best champagne to the room, please?”

Ralph looked at us skeptically. Before I could say, *Hey buddy, this man is throwing down a cool two thousand dollars for one night in a rainstorm*, Everett’s arm was coming around my shoulders, warm and heavy in the best way, squeezing around me. I’m not sure what possessed me, but I leaned into his side like I fit there.

"Did I forget to mention?" he asked. "We're celebrating our engagement."

Ralph looked between us. "Are you."

"Yes," I said, stepping in front of Everett so his arms looped around me, pressing back against his chest. "We were celebrating with our friends, but his dad—" I reached up, patted a hand to Everett's cheek "—just insisted we stay another night to celebrate on our own."

Bullshit! Ralph no doubt wanted to cry, but he just grimaced at us and swiped the card. "Typically," he started. "We offer our guests golf umbrellas in inclement weather like this, but I'm afraid all I have left is . . ." He trailed off as he offered up a maroon umbrella that looked like it might have come from the back corner of the antique mall we'd all walked by in town earlier this week, and smirked.

"Excellent, sir," Everett said. "Thank you so much for your help. We promise to be on our best behavior in that villa of yours."

Without another word, Everett took the umbrella from Ralph in one hand and mine in the other, pulling me outside behind him. We paused for a minute in the door as Everett fiddled with the umbrella, and I watched him, thinking.

"What exactly does your dad do that he won't ever see or care about this bill?" I asked.

Everett cleared his throat. "He works in the film industry."

"Ah," I said, the pieces clicking into place as he fiddled with the umbrella. Everett, so cool and collected, hair perfectly right, had been navigating Hollywood crowds his whole life. "So you're in the family business."

The umbrella unfurled with a creak. Everett's mouth ticked upward as he glanced askance at me. "Unfortunately."

We ran for his car, where he opened my door first, keeping the umbrella over me until I was firmly inside. I watched through the windshield as he jogged around the front, lowering the umbrella as he went, so by the time he did get in next to me, breathless, he was soaked all over again, T-shirt sticking to him and water dripping from his hair into his eyes. I stared at him for a minute, heart ramming in a frustrated way against my ribs, until he looked up and grinned, like he *knew.* Like we hadn't spent this whole week avoiding moments exactly like this.

We didn't talk on the drive up to the villa, and when we got there Everett shooed me inside, insistent he'd bring our bags in. I obliged, both because I was freezing and because I didn't think I could be in a car with Everett and the contours of his chest through his wet T-shirt for a minute longer.

When he did come inside, bags in tow, I was dripping rainwater onto the terra-cotta tile floor of the entryway, head tilted back to look up at the blown-glass chandelier hanging high above us.

"No wonder concierge Ralph hates us," I said as Everett paused next to me, setting our bags down and following my gaze. I looked over at him, eyes tracking the line of his neck for a minute, the angle of his jaw, the short beard there. "You're probably used to places like this, though, aren't you?" I asked, now that I knew he was the son of some industry person.

It took him a second to look at me, but when he did, there was a flash of something there that wasn't just humor. "Something like that," he finally said.

"Something like what?" I asked, pressing. He'd leaned down to grab our bags, and he paused, gaze flicking my way.

"We should probably figure out some food, right?" he said. "Are you hungry?"

"Everett," I said, following after him as he started toward the living room. "Something like what?"

"Something like what you said," he answered. "I've been in houses like this growing up, yes."

"Did you grow up in a house like this, though?"

He set our bags down next to a lush white couch, big enough to fit our entire friend group and then some. There was a huge kitchen to one side, a dining space set two steps above the living room, a staircase off the foyer we just left leading to the six bedrooms this place advertised, a pool out back. A massive stone fireplace sat under the mantel across from the couch. Everett headed toward this and busied himself with an amber-colored jar of long matches.

"Everett," I said.

"Not exactly," he said in my general direction, not quite over his shoulder, as he leaned toward the fireplace to set a match against the kindling already set on top of the wood there.

"*Not exactly* is the same evasive answer as *something like that*," I said. I wanted to sit down on the couch but I was still in my raincoat, water running down my shorts and onto my legs. "*Not exactly* tells me nothing."

Everett straightened and turned to me, running a hand through his wet hair. He paused before he answered, a struggle playing out on his face. To tell me or not, I assumed. To let me in or keep me always a few inches away. It was what I'd been feeling about him all week, this push and pull. A desire to get to know him better but a nervousness over what that meant, where it took us.

"My father is Ben Astor," he finally said, voice devoid of emotion. A simple delivery of information that he had to know would shock me. Would shock anyone he told.

"Ben Astor, the actor?" I asked after a quiet, stunned moment. Everett nodded. "The *really famous* actor?"

"Yes, he's the guy who was in all the heist movies and World War II movies and rom-coms in the nineties," Everett said, in the most disinterested tone I'd ever heard from him, before walking over to the kitchen.

"I didn't even know he had a kid," I said.

Everett huffed out a laugh as he opened the fridge. "He has kids."

"Plural?"

"Plural," he said. The fridge was stocked with exactly two bottles of water and he pulled them both out, setting one on the counter in front of me.

"Thanks," I said. I considered Everett as he took a drink, trying to reframe him in this new context. He'd had some energy about him, almost like he'd been tailor-made for his exact life, and I wondered how much this revelation informed that now, if at all. But something else poked at me too, nagging. "Why didn't you tell anyone else this week?" I asked.

Everett had leaned his elbows on the island, hunched over his water bottle as he twirled it back and forth on the marbled surface, and he looked up from under his brow at this. "My dad and I aren't close," he said. "I don't tend to bring him up. And I'm not . . ." He shook his head. "I've never really been part of a friend group as close as this one. You guys seem to know everything about each other."

I nodded. "We do," I said. "One time, Davi asked me to look at a zit on his back."

"Did you?" Everett asked.

"Of course. I'm a good friend. And he was going on a third date with a girl he was obsessed with that night. Davi is very self-conscious of any weird bumps on his body." Everett laughed. "So it wasn't just because you wanted to tell only me?" I asked jokingly, trying to keep the mood light.

"Oh, you're the only person I want to share anything with," he said.

My heart skipped a beat, and I had to glance away for a minute before I could look at him again. "See, you're always saying things like that," I answered. "Making me think we're more important than we are."

"Are we not important?" he asked then, looking fully at me.

It knocked me silent for a minute, the sudden shift in tone. "We're not I-only-want-to-share-things-with-you important," I said.

"Hmm," Everett mumbled. He didn't add anything else.

"So your dad is an absent dick of a father," I said, quoting his words from earlier. It was clear Everett didn't want to talk more about it right now, and I wasn't going to force him to, curious as I was. Everett's gaze flicked up to mine again, confirmation enough for me. I nodded toward the living room. "Want to raid the minibar and rack up a tab on your dad's card?"

"Yes," Everett said, wincing a little. "But I'm fairly certain the minibar is included in a place like this."

I scoffed as I stood up. "Something only a son of the rich and famous would know," I said.

Everett laughed as he followed me.

ten

First Summer

The rain finally cleared after an afternoon of watching Food Network reruns on the couch, so we left the house in search of dinner.

We pulled up to a quiet pier, the sky a brilliant pink in the post-rain glow, lights diffused in the mist that still hung in the air. We grabbed food at a burger stand and stood at their counter, dipping fries into milkshakes and wondering if anyone on the Food Network had ever acknowledged what we both thought was the general superiority of the combination.

After a while, we started walking toward the end of the pier, where there was a wide view of the last streaks of light across the sky.

"So, what about you?" Everett asked as we walked.

I cast him a sideways glance. "What *about* me?"

"You've heard my whole sad story," he said. "What about you?"

"You haven't told me your whole sad story," I pointed out. "You've told me one tiny part of your whole sad story. And what makes you think I have one?"

"Don't we all?"

I smirked. "Spoken like someone who wants to make movies."

Everett laughed and clapped a hand to his chest, like I'd wounded him. "Come on," he said. "You've got to have *something*."

"What if I don't?" I said. "What if I was raised in a household full of marvelously well-adjusted people and never encountered a setback in my entire life? What then?"

"Did you?" Everett asked me. "Grow up in a household full of well-adjusted people and never encounter a setback in your entire life?"

I looked at him, sucking at my lower lip to try to hide the smile that always seemed to pop up around him. Even then, when he was asking a question like that, I couldn't seem to help it. He stared at me, waiting me out. Finally, I shook my head. "No."

He nodded as if in confirmation. "See," he said. "Even if your answer had been yes, I still think there would have been something."

"How's that?"

"Everyone has some kind of setback," he said. "Or thing or issue or whatever it is. I think even that thinking you don't have a thing would probably constitute having a thing."

"And your thing is your famous father," I clarified.

Everett gave me a look like he might wink at me, like he was just taking all of this so lightly. "He's part of it."

We were walking toward the end of the pier, where the water stretched out underneath the sunset, residual stormy waves cresting gray under the final fades of the brilliantly colored sky.

I could always not tell him, I knew. Leave our relationship as it was: somewhere between something and nothing, a sort of safe place to be whatever version of myself I wanted to be. But I was finding it hard to be anything but myself with Everett in a way that startled me. Outside of Laurel, I'd never been so immediately comfortable with someone. She told me once it felt like Gabe and Davi, Zoey too, had had to earn knowing me, that there was some wall almost visible to her when we were all together at first. That it wasn't until six months in that she noticed it missing. *You can talk to anyone*, she'd said. *But it's like there's some point system. Only once they've proved themselves do you actually relax.* It hadn't bothered me. I knew what she meant, and it seemed bizarre to me that all relationships weren't formed this way. *Show me you'll stay, and I might let you.* But she'd proved me wrong. As soon as I met her, waiting outside our freshman math class wearing a shirt that read *Kirsten and Sandy Cohen Adopted Me*, I knew we'd be friends. There was no probationary period with her.

I looked over at Everett, a breeze rifling through the soft wave of his hair. Maybe it was something about that night, being without my friends, that made this happen. Maybe it was the secret we shared. Maybe it was the fact that there was something in his sadness that matched mine, even if I didn't know all of it. Maybe it was that we just had that tiny slip of time together.

"I was mostly raised by my uncle," I said.

"Hank," Everett said, and I nodded confirmation. "I've heard that name a few times this week."

"He knows everybody," I said. "He feeds everyone when he's in town."

"Ah," Everett said. "So the apple doesn't fall far from the tree."

"If we're calling Hank my tree."

"I think we are," Everett said. I grinned sideways at him. "How is that your thing?"

I'd said it before; to Laurel, to Gabe and Davi, to Zoey. It always came up somehow. People tended to be curious why I grew up with my uncle instead of my parents. I'd added the *mostly* a while ago—I was *mostly* raised by my uncle, because there were the years I still lived with my parents while school was in session and with Hank only in the summers, but even then, the summers seemed like the time most of the raising was actually being done.

"My parents love their jobs more than much else," I said finally, Everett's eyes finding mine in the quickly fading light. "My mom is in finance, my dad is in tech, they're always busy. I think having at least one kid was kind of something to check off a list?" I tried to tell the simplest version of it, none of the ins and outs, none of the stretches of silence or darker moments. Just facts.

"Anyway, every summer, they would send me to stay with Hank in San Francisco. And there was this one summer, right before seventh grade, when my mom called me the night before I was supposed to get on a plane to fly back to New York, and she told me I was going to stay with Hank awhile longer. That I might even start the school year there."

"Did you?" Everett asked when I went quiet for a minute, the conversation replaying itself in my head. *We're coming out at Thanksgiving anyway,* my mom had said, like all my things weren't back home, like I didn't know what was happening. *We'll revisit things again. Revisit* was a word I'd heard her use a lot growing up, on the phone with clients during things like dinnertime or our walk to school in the morning. *Revisit, circle back. Pick your brain.* I hadn't thought those things applied to her kid, until they suddenly had.

"I did," I told Everett. "And I never moved back home."

Everett shook his head at this, the motion barely there. I knew I'd skipped over about a hundred steps in the process—the first school year I spent in San Francisco without seeing my parents at all, when the trips for Thanksgiving and spring break and my birthday were all canceled, when another year went by and my mom tried to pick me up and I had to tell her I wanted to stay. I'd been ready for a fight, but it didn't come. She'd almost seemed relieved.

"What about now?" Everett asked. I raised an eyebrow at him. "What's your relationship with them like?"

"We talk on the phone once a month," I said, without adding *if they can make it work*. "They helped pay for college."

"Did they come to graduation?" Everett asked.

I shook my head. "Hank was there," I said. At Everett's expression, I insisted, "They're not bad people," the same strange defensiveness I felt for them cropping up whenever I told this story. Most of me really believed it, maybe because I'd loved living with Hank so much, had been instantly happier than I ever was with them. And it was so routine to not talk with them much that I didn't question it. Didn't want to. "They just . . . they love their work. And honestly, sending me to live with Hank is the best thing they could have done. They didn't have the time for a kid. So—" I tilted my head toward him, said around my straw as I brought it to my mouth "—*that's* my thing."

Everett's brow pulled together momentarily, relaxed again. It was a look I'd seen before, a rote response. It wasn't pity, exactly. Somewhere more in the realm of concern, of disbelief. On Everett, it looked almost like recognition.

Everett huffed. "Hell of a thing." Something in my expression must have shifted, because he asked me, "What?"

I opened my mouth, closed it. This was the hard part, the part I hadn't ever really been able to put into words. Hadn't tried to, even with my friends, because I didn't want to seem insensitive or insincere. "It is," I started. "I know that. But I almost think it might seem worse to other people?"

We'd reached the end of the pier by then, and Everett settled against the railing next to me, our elbows just brushing.

"Like, if I spent my whole life sitting around thinking about how my parents just decided they didn't really want to parent anymore, I'd go crazy," I continued. "If you spent all your time contemplating all the ways your dad fucked you up, you wouldn't get anything done. So just—you're right. We all have our thing, but it's *our* thing, and I think it always sounds worse to someone who hasn't been through it." I laughed. "I'm Laurel's worst nightmare," I said. "She still thinks I'm not dealing with my trauma."

"Are you?" Everett asked.

"I think I already did," I said. "Hank had me talk to someone when I was younger. They helped a little."

"So you don't think there's anything in your life now or in the future that could be a result of what happened," Everett said. "You've worked through it? You're done?"

"I just don't see the point in revisiting it," I said. "Rehashing what's already been—" I waved a hand, searching for the right word "—hashed."

Everett smiled, and I knew he got it. All of his sunny-eyed smiles, casual jokes, easy confidence. He didn't want to revisit his shit either. I was sure of it.

"Whatever you say, Sutton Hale," he said. "Let's not rehash the already hashed."

"Hear! Hear!" I said, extending my cup his way so he could tap his against mine. "To leaving the past where it should stay."

And so we didn't rehash it. We started back toward the car once the sun had set, walking past the restaurants and shops, and didn't bring up my parents or his dad. Some measure of space between us was gone, taken up by what we now knew. But it didn't have to matter. It didn't have to change things.

"Interesting to know this is what we've been missing out on," Everett remarked after a while.

"What do you mean?" I asked him.

"I'm just saying, this is nice," Everett said. "We could have been hanging out like this for a couple months now."

"Yeah, because you called me up so many times since then." I knocked my elbow against his playfully.

"I didn't have your number," Everett pointed out.

"Couldn't be bothered to ask for it?"

"Hey, if I recall correctly, you were the one who was trying to sneak out the next morning."

"Fine, point goes to you," I said. He laughed around his straw.

We walked in silence for a few minutes before he said, "Maybe we wouldn't have to keep this secret if I'd asked for your number."

I glanced over at him. We were passing by a bar and the purple glow of a neon sign in the window splashed over his face, made his hair darker, like it was when he came out of the ocean, when he'd just showered. Only a week, and I knew those things about him.

"No," I said, once we'd passed the window and were back to the orange glow of streetlights spotlighting the honey of his hair. "If everyone knew we'd hooked up, it would be this thing."

"Thing?" he repeated.

"Laurel would have read into everything," I said. "Like if you and I went to a movie alone, she'd be convinced it was code. Davi would have asked all the time if you were sleeping over because he has a very strict bathroom schedule—"

"Oh, *that* I discovered this week," Everett said, grinning.

"—and Gabe, well." I waved a hand in front of us. "Before

things fell apart, Gabe would have wanted nothing more than another couple in the group. He would have pushed us into situations that he'd hoped would make us fall in love with each other."

Everett mulled this over. He tossed his cup into a trash can as we passed, and I followed suit. "What you're saying is, this worked out the best it possibly could have for us."

"Exactly," I said. We stopped at the entrance to the pier, looked back at it one final time. It stretched out into nothing, only the few boat lights bobbing off in the distance a reminder of what it looked like during the day. We stared out at it for a minute before we both turned to each other. "Now we can actually be friends."

Everett reached up and brushed my hair behind my ear. The move startled me, but I didn't flinch, didn't move away. "Friends," he repeated. I swallowed. "So, because I didn't ask for your number, because we have this secret now, we can manage to uphold this pact that Laurel has proposed?"

My breath caught at his question. At his wording—*this pact that Laurel proposed*, not *this pact we made*.

I nodded quickly, hoped he didn't notice. "Look at it this way, even if we had hung out with each other the last two months, we would have been upholding it anyway," I said. I'm not sure why, exactly, it sounded like I was trying to convince us both of something. "We just wouldn't have known the pact existed yet. So technically we'd end up in the same place."

Everett squinted, a small smile playing at his lips. "I don't know," he said then, edging closer to me. "I don't think I would have done a very good job just hanging out with you if I had asked for your number."

His answer was a trickle of warmth moving from my neck down. "I thought you weren't looking for anything," I said, voice a little scratchy.

"I wasn't," Everett said. He left it at that.

The drive home was laced with whatever started on the end of that pier, something crackling in the air between us. That, or we were both silently acknowledging it now. That whatever had so quickly drawn us together at that party was still alive and well.

Back at the house, Everett leaned against the jamb of the door into the house, still wide-open, like he was dropping me off for the night instead of coming inside with me, ready to retreat to our opposite rooms. I stood in front of him, closer than I should have, not as close as I wanted to, pulled closer still.

We leaned together and kissed on an inhale, bodies fitting together as easily as they did before. I fit into all the places he wasn't, and he molded to me where any gaps remained. It was a hell of a kiss, as kisses go, tongues skimming against lips until our mouths opened against each other and Everett's hand came up to cup my face, something I remembered him doing two months ago and something that still made my knees go weak. It was his toothpaste, I realized, that the cinnamon came from.

His free hand slid against my lower back, pressing me closer to him, my pulse picking up as our hips rolled together. My hands were about to skim under his shirt when I remembered. When every reason *not* to do this came back to me.

"No," I said as I pushed away from him. Everett's hands left me immediately, his brow drawing down.

"Of course," he said. "I'm sorry."

"No," I said again. "Not—not *no*." I pressed a hand to his chest, let the warmth of it seep into me for a minute before I realized it was starting to pull me under again and I let go. "I want to—trust me, I *want* to. But we're not supposed to be doing this."

His concern morphed into confusion, like we hadn't *just* covered this on the pier. "Because . . . ?"

"Because of Laurel's rule," I said again. It wasn't lost on me that I'd done the exact same thing he had earlier. Calling it hers, not ours, making it something we existed outside of. "Because of the pact."

Everett's mouth quirked. "We already broke the pact."

"No one knows that."

He leaned a little closer to me. "*We* know that."

Pine, salt, cinnamon, eyes that feel like the ocean rushing in on you. I paused to clear my throat. "Semantics."

If I'd been honest with myself, I wished he would have closed that gap between us again. I would have let him do whatever he wanted in that open doorway, and I wouldn't have told a single soul about it.

But instead, he nodded and stepped away. Held a hand out to me, like we were closing a business deal. He did it all with that trademark charm, a casual grin on his face. I took his hand, shook it, tried not to show what the rub of his palm against mine did to me.

"Friends?" he said.

I almost laughed. "Or something like that."

It was the first lie I ever told him. I couldn't have been just friends with Everett Bridges if I tried.

eleven

This Summer

After the farmers market, we wander the shops in town for a while, our usual traditions popping up unintentionally. Laurel buys everything that even slightly piques her interest: a pale pink cashmere scarf at one shop and Frye boots at the place next door, an All-Clad pan I tell her is my favorite at the fancy kitchenware shop that she will most assuredly never use, a vintage wedding ring at another place that she says signifies her *marriage to herself.*

Between that and our stop at the grocery store, we arrive back to the villa bogged down with packages, more things on order to be shipped to Laurel's place in LA.

"Hey," she says to me as she straightens her laden arms and lets bags carelessly slip off of them into a heap on the floor of the foyer. "We re-created our first day without even trying."

"We did," I say.

Davi comes in behind her, a paper grocery bag in his arms. "We never used to spend money on—" he pulls a bottle out of the bag, squints at it "—hyperoxygenated water? Laurel," he says. "How much was this?"

"It flushes out toxins," she says. "I need to flush toxins out of my life right now."

"Okay," Davi says, ever-skeptical eyes already rolling, "but—"

I stop him, snatching the bottle out of his hand as Laurel flits into the kitchen. "Let her have her water," I whisper. Davi completes his eye roll but drops the issue.

Gabe and Everett bring the rest of the things in while I start unpacking in the kitchen. Laurel says she's going upstairs to change into her swimsuit.

"Anyone is welcome to join me on the beach!" she calls, picking over the bags at the foot of the stairs before she finds the one she's looking for and leaves.

Gabe watches her as she goes, waiting until she's out of earshot to say, "Do you think she's secretly still dating Stephen?"

"What?" I ask, at the same time Davi says, adamantly, "*No.*"

"Why would you think that?" I say, closing the fridge door. Everett opens it again as soon as it closes, eggs and butter in hand. Our gazes lock for half a second, annoyed, before we both look away.

Gabe shrugs. "She just seems . . . off."

"And the only explanation is that she's secretly dating her cheating ex-husband?" Davi asks.

"Who said anything about cheating?" I say to him, trying to moderate my tone but failing. It comes out shrill, bouncing off all the marble countertops in this kitchen.

"Come on," Davi says. "He *had* to be cheating, right? To break those two up? They were like—" he waves a hand "—Goose and Amy, or whoever."

We all look at him in silence, and even Everett closes the fridge door to squint at him.

"You know," Davi says. "*If I can fly, you can fly*, or whatever the hell it is."

"*The Notebook*," Gabe translates. "Ryan Gosling." Everett and I nod.

"That's what I said," Davi says. "They're meant to be. You don't just break up when you're meant to be."

"People break up for all sorts of reasons," I say as I dig into another bag, pulling out a box of cereal and a wedge of Parmesan. "Meant to be or not."

Everett makes a sound behind me. It could have been a cough, a clearing of the throat, something entirely unrelated to what I said. In all likelihood, it was, but in my mind, there is no world in which it wasn't a scoff. I pivot on my heel to look at him where he's placing apples in a fruit bowl on the counter.

"Why do *you* think people break up, Everett?" I say.

"Hmm?" he says, casually, like he didn't hear me.

"We're trying to figure out what exactly happened between Laurel and Stephen," I say, gesturing to where Davi and Gabe are standing on the opposite side of the island, watching us. "So what's your take on why people split up?"

Everett turns fully toward me, hips sinking back against the counter behind him, hands sliding casually into the pockets of his jeans. He shrugs his shoulders, the movement hitching his sleeves a quarter-inch higher on his arms, revealing more of his tanned biceps. My eyes snap back to his face.

"I think that sometimes it just doesn't work anymore," he says. "Maybe they just got tired of it."

"Tired of it," I repeat. "So you think that if you get bored you should just leave?"

"I think if you're bored in the first place, it's probably not the right relationship for you," Everett says.

"Tired of what, then?" I ask. "Of being with someone? Of being married?"

Everett draws in a deep breath, eyes glancing across the surface of the island behind me. I think he might not answer, so

I turn to the counter again, tugging another bag toward me a little too forcefully.

"Tired of the work of it," he says, finally. I bristle, an aggravated pinch running down my spine.

"Shocker," I mutter, yanking a jug of orange juice out of the bag.

"Excuse me?" Everett says. I can hear it in his tone: irritation, something I so rarely used to hear from him before. Even then, it was always about something else outside of us. Something at work, bad weather. His dad, usually. Except, of course, the last time. When anger seemed like the only thing left between us.

"Nothing," I say. "Just that four months seems to be about your cutoff in a relationship, so I don't know how valuable your take is."

"You *asked* me what my take is," he points out. "And besides, what's your cutoff? Two weeks?"

"At least I don't call them relationships," I say, looking back at him.

"Which means you probably aren't qualified to comment on one either."

"Okay, whoa," Davi says, from behind us. I turn to see him waving a hand, Gabe watching silently next to him. "White flag, or whatever."

"Only one of *us* can wave the white flag," I say.

"Then, I don't know," Davi says. He motions at Gabe. "Whatever you and Mia say to the heathens when they won't shut up."

"We usually tell our *children*, Riley and Chloe, to use their words better," Gabe says with an annoyed glance at Davi. "And we don't use the words *shut up* in any context."

"Whatever," Davi says. He sighs and looks at us. "Can we use our words, Everett and Sutton?"

"What, we're children now?" I snap.

Gabe winces slightly. "A response like that would usually mean reflection time in their rooms."

Davi's face goes flat. "What the fuck is reflection time."

"It's like a time-out, but that language is too harsh now," Gabe says, voice low as if Riley and Chloe are in the room with us, learning all of his secrets. Davi holds up his hands.

"I'm never getting married, I'm never parenting," he says. He points between us. "You two. Reflect. I'm going to the beach with Laurel."

"But look!" Gabe insists as he stands up and follows Davi. "You're a natural already!"

I narrow my eyes at Everett as soon as they're out of the room.

"Glad to know we've moved past things," he says, voice dripping with sarcasm.

I think about the last time I saw him, at Laurel and Stephen's anniversary celebration just last year. I'd volunteered to do a grazing board for them, and was out back at their house when Everett arrived, a tray of radishes and French butter in one hand and three baguettes tucked under my arm. I thought I'd moved on since seeing him at Gabe and Mia's baby shower, when we'd ended up partnered together for games, and a diaper that was supposed to end up on a stuffed animal wound up torn in half. Since we'd gotten in an argument at the bar where we gathered to celebrate Davi's thirtieth birthday party.

I couldn't even remember what had sent things south each time, why we couldn't even manage to be civil for a few hours for our friends, but I had a sneaking suspicion it was whatever started simmering under my skin when he walked onto the back patio of Laurel and Stephen's Larchmont house. Some angry thing that still lived in me, some part that hated that I couldn't get rid of him, erase him from my life completely. Whatever it was, Everett seemed to mirror it. Even our hellos were terse, as if we wanted to fight. The spark that had once existed between us didn't give way to something good anymore. Instead, it was the hot, angry edge of a pan just pulled off the stove, a burned fingertip that sent rage flooding through both of us.

Wherever it came from, it ended with a hand accidentally smashed into the butter and a baguette flung toward the pool where it floated, waterlogged, as we both wilted guiltily under Laurel's cold stare from where she stood framed in the back door.

So this week has to be better. *We* have to be better.

Everett sighs and runs a hand through his hair, a little roughly, draws in a deep breath, like he's been living in this particular memory too. Like he's also remembered that this trip isn't about us. "We're being a little immature, don't you think?" he asks.

It's at this moment that I remember my arms are crossed. I drop them, try to appear far more adult than I feel right now.

"You're right," I say.

The words feel like barbed wire coming out.

We make it through the rest of the day unscathed, largely because we simply don't talk to each other. Our only slipup is when I'm sitting in the living room, talking to Hank while Laurel and Gabe nap and Davi answers some emails in his room, apparently banished there by Laurel, who got tired of him staring at his phone on the beach. It hadn't occurred to me to care where Everett was or what he was doing.

"How's work, kid?" Hank has just asked me when the back door opens. I twist to see Everett coming in, a book and a notebook tucked under his arm, a pen in its spiral spine. Our eyes latch for just a minute, that same frustrating tingle running along my neck before I turn around again.

"Um," I say. I usually spend the summer working various private chef gigs, away from the restaurant. But this summer is different. This summer is about the cookbook, and so I haven't taken on clients. "Work's great. Mostly the same."

The lie stings a little coming out, but I still haven't been able to bring myself to have this conversation with him. The one that would make him hate me.

I don't *want* to be lying to Hank about what I'm doing with my time. But we built the whole original plan together, over the dinner table and when I learned to cook in his kitchen and when I started applying to schools. Hank would need someone to take over the restaurant someday, and when I was younger, it seemed like an absolute dream come true. I loved Half Moon House, loved the diner aesthetic that lent itself to its weekend brunches and could transform into something cozy and cool for the pre–dinner rush happy hour. I loved everyone who worked there. I learned from them and Hank how to perfectly poach an egg, how to sear a scallop, how to match ambiance to a meal. It was where I fell in love with the idea of running a restaurant. As a seventeen-year-old, carrying on his legacy was all I wanted.

But things have shifted since then. Slowly, at first. When developing recipes was my favorite part of my culinary classes in school, I knew I'd be able to do that at the restaurant too. Try new things out when there was time. Maybe after the first few years, once I really had my feet under me. And when I started to share those recipes online—with Laurel's help, of course—I assumed it would stay just a hobby. It never occurred to me it could lead somewhere. More than that, it never occurred to me to follow it. I was already doing something I loved; I wasn't looking for anything different.

Until I was. Until I'd suddenly signed a publishing contract, and cut back on my hours at the restaurant, and I still, for whatever reason, hadn't told Hank.

"Well, we're all looking forward to having you back in the kitchen," Hank says. My teeth sink into my lip almost painfully as I nod, like he can hear me.

"Mmm-hmm," I say noncommittally. "Me too."

I toss my phone onto the coffee table after we hang up, the conversation crawling under my skin, and wander into the kitchen in search of a distraction. Everett is there, lifting the electric kettle off its base. He raises it when he spots me on the other side of the island.

"Tea?" he asks. It's his version of the white flag Davi tried in vain to wave between us earlier, I think.

I shrug, my mind still too fixed on my call with Hank to bother being irritated by his general presence right now. "Sure," I say, slipping onto one of the stools. He grabs another mug from the cupboard, sets it next to his on the island.

I pick up the book sitting on top of Everett's notebook.

"*Hypothetical Physics*," I read from the subtitle. I glance up at him. "Considering a career change?"

Everett stares unwaveringly at the mugs in front of him as he fills them with hot water. "It's just research."

"Hmm," I murmur, briefly flipping to one of the pages he has marked before setting it down again. "For the next movie?"

"Maybe," he says. He still isn't looking at me.

"Okay," I say. "Hollywood is confidential, I get it."

He does glance up at that, away from the relentless bobbing

of the tea bags in the mugs, having been alternating between one and the other methodically as a way, I'm assuming, to avoid my gaze. But now he meets it, and when he sees my expression schooled into what I hope is an open, if slightly apathetic, one, he relaxes a little, eyes taking on just a hint of the glow I know so well. Our exchange from earlier, however brief, echoes in my head. *We're being a little immature, don't you think?*

"It's a whole space movie," he says. "I'm still trying to figure out if it's even feasible."

"*Star Wars* or *A Space Odyssey*?" I ask.

Everett thinks for a second. "*Arrival*," he says. "*Interstellar*, maybe."

I nod. There's a lot I could say, but being a little more mature doesn't necessarily mean going back to who we were before. To me, it just means not arguing in front of everyone else.

Everett, however, picks up the thread. "Was that Hank?" he asks, tilting his head toward where I'd been sitting in the living room.

I push my hair behind my ear and sigh, settling my forearms on the countertop. "Yep."

"How's he doing?"

"He's great," I say. "Hank is always great." He is, and the steadiest force in my life. It had bothered me when I'd first moved in with him. I thought his perpetually sunny attitude was the result of having a preteen thrust upon him, that he felt like he always had to make everything great for me to compensate for what my parents did. But I'd quickly learned it was just how Hank operated. He is an eternal optimist. It makes lying to him now all the worse.

"He must be excited about the cookbook," Everett says.

I tense as he slides one of the mugs toward me. There's no way Everett could know exactly which nerve to hit, but it's like he's found it, raw and exposed, and pressed a finger to it. I wrap my fingers around the mug and grip it tight.

"He doesn't know," I say, voice low.

Everett pauses with his mug halfway to his mouth, eyes narrowing.

"Yeah, I know," I say. "How could I not tell Hank."

The corners of Everett's eyes soften at the same time his mouth tightens, openness and tension braided together.

"I wasn't going to say that," he says quietly, and takes a drink of his tea.

I wait, silent, to see if he's going to offer up what he actually *was* going to say. When he doesn't, I shift forward, drum my fingers against the sides of the mug. "He will be excited, you're right," I say.

Everett glances up from under his brow. "When you do tell him," he says.

"Of course."

We stare at each other, the silence stretching taut. I'm wondering why I came over here at all, when I know nothing good lies on the other side of this. The us of the past is a ghost I have no interest in getting to know again. Letting Everett make me tea and asking him questions about his book and trying to explain the Hank of it all are best left to the girl I used to be.

"Look," Everett says on a sigh, rubbing a palm over his collarbone. My gaze settles on the movement for all of a half second before it shoots back up to him. His eyes are cool, but there's something behind them that's familiar, some look I used to see when it was just the two of us. Something almost hopeful. "Can we—"

Footsteps sound from the direction of Gabe's room, his door creaking open. Everett straightens, eyes darting that direction, but it takes me a second to mirror him. I'm stuck on whatever it was in the way he looked at me that had me falling back into some memory of him. If it was even real at all.

"Well, look who's talking," Gabe says as he moseys into the kitchen, rubbing one eye with the back of his fist. He glances between us when we don't say anything. I offer him a grim smile.

"Tea?" Everett says, nodding toward the kettle. "Water's hot."

Gabe glances at the clock on the microwave, considering. "Think I'll grab a beer and head down to the beach," he says, opening the fridge. He fishes a beer out, finds a bar key in a drawer, flips it open before turning back to us. His eyes flick between us again as we watch him, silent. He tries for a grin and raises the bottle. "It's five o'clock somewhere."

Everett beats me to an answer, and I add it to the mental tally I have of who's winning favor more easily. Of course it would always be Everett, no matter how much history I have with everyone in the house. He's always been that way, had an air of ease around him that draws people in, makes them want to be his friend.

Everett holds up his mug. "Cheers to that," he says as he follows Gabe to the back door. He doesn't look back at me as he goes.

twelve

Second Summer

Ralph wasn't any happier to see us that second summer than he was the first, but Laurel and I happily collected our keys from him anyway. She blew a kiss over her shoulder as we walked out of the lobby to our waiting rental car.

"I'm so happy we're together!" Laurel crowed out the window as we wound our way down to the cottages, her hair streaming out the window. After her year in Seoul, the heavily documented exploits of which had gained her a hefty social media following, she'd decided to move back to California. Her arrival had coincided with the trip, so after my flight from San Francisco yesterday, we'd spent the night at her new, empty apartment in Silver Lake before we wound our way to the coast.

Davi was already there when we lugged our things inside. He remained lounging on the back deck in swim trunks and sunglasses, beer in hand, until it was clear he wouldn't have to help unpack.

"There's our world traveler," he said as Laurel launched herself at him, wrapping her toned arms around his neck. He hooked an arm around my shoulders once she let him go and I patted him on the back.

"That's it?" Laurel asked, looking between us. "We're reunited for the first time in a year and you two look like you're congratulating each other on your favorite sports team winning."

"Sutton hates the Pirates," Davi said. "And we saw each other two months ago."

"Yeah," I said. "We grabbed a quick lunch last time he was in town." It was a joke. In reality, Davi had crashed on my couch for his spring break—he was in law school in Illinois, which Laurel knew, but she still rolled her eyes.

"You two are so unsentimental," she said.

We joined Davi on the back porch where he filled us in on what the life of a law student looked like after Laurel refused to share any details of her trip abroad until everyone had arrived. (*You can tell them again*, Davi had said. *I know, but then it won't be as* fresh, Laurel replied.)

The sun was starting to dip toward the horizon when we heard a car pulling up out front. Laurel bolted out of her seat, Davi and I following behind as she raced through the house and out onto the front porch. Davi paused to grab another beer from the fridge and pull on a T-shirt.

Laurel and Gabe were hugging in the driveway when I walked out onto the front porch. It was one of those that goes on for a while, a lot of cooing on her part and rocking back and forth on his.

"I can't believe it's yoooou," she practically sang as he swayed her. Gabe's hair had grown out from its usual short crop into something wilder than I think any of us ever expected from him in the last year. It stuck up in tufts now, had to be routinely pushed back with a hand or, currently, his sunglasses.

"I can't believe it's you!" he said, easily matching Laurel's enthusiasm. They were hugging in front of the Bronco. The sight of it sent something unexpected through me, like a soft brush of wings just roused from slumber in my stomach.

I didn't have time to think about it. Gabe was rushing over to me before I could, thick arms coming around me and lifting me off the porch in a bear hug that squeezed all the air out of me. I heard the car door slam as he spun me around before setting me back on my feet.

"Hi," I said as Gabe held me away from him. I beamed up at him, only part of my brain fixating on the sounds of a Laurel greeting ensuing behind us.

"Can you believe we're here?" Gabe asked, eyes sparkling, so far from the heartbroken person he was a year ago.

"Believe it?" came a voice from behind us, and his attention was drawn toward Davi, who had emerged from the house. "We've only been planning it since we left last year. You and Laurel act like it's some big surprise."

Gabe scrubbed a hand over the top of my head before he started toward Davi and I could turn toward the car again, following whatever it was that knotted in my stomach and tugged me in that direction.

Everett was looking down at Laurel, hands on her shoulders and smile wide as she said something to him. I caught snippets of it—*hang out all the time* and *show me the best spots*, because they'd be living in the same city now, which Laurel had reminded me of last night as we ate takeout Chinese on the floor of what would become her living room.

"You could move in with me, you know," she'd said. "I've heard people in LA need chefs or whatever."

"Seriously?" I said, widening my eyes and prompting a laugh out of her. I speared a water chestnut, pulled my knees up to my chest. "Much as I'd love to be roomies again, things are good in San Francisco." They were, and Laurel knew this. I'd been on full time at the restaurant all year, and was taking July and August off to cook for private clients in the area. I already had a whole week lined up with a family in Half Moon Bay.

"That's okay," Laurel sighed. "I'll just have to hang out with all my other amazing friends." I kicked her foot, scowling jokingly. She nabbed a spring roll from the box between us, biting into it before saying, "Oh, and Everett, obviously."

The rice I'd swallowed suddenly wasn't going down so easily, turning into a dry mass in my throat. I took an enormous swig of water to wash it down. "What about Everett?"

"He lives here, duh," she said. "He'll have to hang out with me."

"Right," I said. "Duh."

I knew Everett lived in Los Angeles. He had a place in West Hollywood and, after a stint in production on a show that wasn't ultimately picked up, landed a gig as second assistant director on an indie movie one of his friends from film school was working on. He still surfed. He'd had a birthday and he'd let his beard get a little longer and he'd trimmed it again and he took care of his friend's dog for a couple months while said friend was making a movie in Spain or somewhere and his eyes were just as bright through a computer or phone screen, which was why, for the most part, I knew all of this. Our group chat wasn't enough for Laurel and so she'd scheduled monthly catchups for all of us.

Like today, I knew he'd picked Gabe up at the airport and that they drove down together. I knew they'd be arriving in the Bronco, and that they'd be getting here around this time, and I knew that my eyes seemed to drift, almost of their own volition, to his little square every time we were on one of those calls, my mind casually wandering back to that kiss in the doorway. Which was probably why, when his eyes lifted toward mine over Laurel's head, I was right back at that party, drawn toward him by what I told myself was some primal reflex, whatever was in me urging me toward whatever was in him because we'd make great babies, or something scientific like that.

Laurel said something else before rushing back to the porch, joining Gabe and Davi, and leaving me to wander over to Everett alone.

"Sutton," he said.

"Everett." There was a half second when I swore he smirked at me before he pulled me into a hug.

"Good to see you, Hale," he said. I leaned away from him, returned his smug expression. He tugged at the ends of my hair lightly, rubbed them between his fingers. "Gotten longer," he said.

I moved out of his reach, pushed his hand away. "Crazy how hair does that when you don't see someone for a year."

Everett frowned. "Not if you cut it."

"Yes, Everett, I did notice your haircut," I said, which turned his mock pout into a grin. "What a roundabout way to tell me you want me to say you look good."

He did look good, in a way that couldn't be wholly communicated over FaceTime. He looked a year postgrad in all the best ways: jawline a little sharper, facial hair a little better kempt, arms a little more toned under the sleeves of his T-shirt, muscles shifting as he reached into the open back window of the Bronco to grab his bag.

"Hey," he said as we started toward the house. The others had pushed inside, and I could hear them rustling around in the kitchen, the hiss of beer caps being twisted off and the crinkle of a bag of chips being opened. I looked back at Everett, expectant. "The cottage is still available after we check out."

I smirked. "Working for Expedia now?"

"Ralph's been keeping me in the loop," he said sarcastically. "He wants to make sure his favorite patrons keep returning."

"That, or you throwing down your dad's credit card last summer has something to do with it."

He smiled at that, and I felt like I'd just won at some arcade game on the pier, tickets shooting out.

"Interested?" he asked.

I almost stumbled, heart leaping into my throat.

I *was* interested, and that, we'd established last summer, was the problem. I seemed to have a real issue keeping my proverbial clothes on when it came to Everett. "You sure know how to proposition a girl, Bridges," I finally replied, kicking the can of decision further down the road and taking another step toward the house.

"No proposition," he replied, and when I looked at him, I could see he meant it, and was then startled to feel a small jolt of disappointment. "Just cooking shows, pier food, two more days at the beach."

"I'll think about it," I said.

"Good. Can't watch Ina all alone." I shoved him away as he laughed and it trickled down my esophagus and straight to my stomach like I swallowed the sound.

"This one," Laurel said, holding a silky tank top up in front of her. "This will be the top that tells everyone *Laurel's got a new life.*"

"What's the focus now?" I asked, checking the price tag on a pair of shorts. "Laurel does LA?"

"No, no more travel content or city checklists," Laurel said.

She examined the top for a minute before shaking her head and hanging it back on the rack in the tiny boutique we were perusing. Apparently *not* the choice for her newest path. "You know the meditation retreat I went on?" I nodded, trailing her to another rack. "It *opened my mind*, Sutton," she gushed, the same thing she told me just after the retreat itself. "So I'm thinking like, lifestyle and wellness? In a totally normal way, of course."

"Of course," I echoed.

Laurel was pawing through a rack of bandanas. "You know, you could advertise yourself on socials," she said.

"Could I."

She turned to me, eyebrow raised at my tone. "It's not as evil as you make it out to be, Sutton. And you should get in now. There will be so much more noise in a few years to contend with."

"I don't think it's *evil*," I said. "I just don't want to share my life online."

"That's the best part of it, though," Laurel said. "You only share what you want to."

"Maybe," I told her. "I think I'm good with how things are going for now."

"If you insist," Laurel said. "But remember, I could run it for you." She grins at the idea. "We'd have so much fun. And your face wouldn't even have to be in it. Though—" she reached over, holding a red, floral bandana up next to my face "—it's such a great face, we could totally market that."

I knocked her hand away playfully. "We're not marketing anything, thank you very much."

"If you insist," Laurel sighed. She held up her arms, laden with clothes. "I'm going to try this stuff on. You coming?"

"I think I'll check on the guys next door," I said. "Meet us when you're done?"

Laurel waved me off and headed in the direction of the dressing rooms, but paused halfway there to call over her shoulder. "No shenanigans!" Her voice echoed around the light wood space as she winked. "Remember the pact."

I laughed, a little guiltily, before wandering over to the bar where Gabe, Davi, and Everett had ended up after we'd meandered between shops for a couple hours. The front windows were all thrown open, letting the early summer heat in. Gabe and Davi were playing shuffleboard against a far wall, Everett seated at a table near them.

"Not a shuffleboard man?" I asked as I dropped my lone bag on the table.

Everett grinned at me as I sat next to him, where we could both watch what looked like an increasingly competitive game.

"I lost to Gabe," he said.

"He *is* the athlete among us," I said.

Everett picked up his water glass. "Can I get you something?" he asked.

I shook my head. "I'm good. I just came over to see what debauchery you were getting up to while Laurel cleans out the boutique next door."

"A little different than last summer's window shopping, huh?" Everett asked.

"For Laurel, at least," I said. He was right—where last summer none of us had had any real money, this summer we had roughly 1 percent more, save for Laurel, who, after a year of not paying rent and scoring three brand deals while she was abroad, was currently the richest among us.

"So," Everett said, elbows leaned on the table in front of

him as he turned his head to look at me. "How's your year been, Hale?"

"You know how my year's been," I said. "We've caught up with everyone."

"Yeah, but I'd like to hear it from you," Everett said, bumping his elbow against mine. A tingle zipped up my arm from the spot. Laurel's voice echoed in my head. *Remember the pact.*

I hadn't expected to feel this way around Everett. I'd spent my drive north to San Francisco last summer replaying our kiss, the three months I'd lived in my childhood bedroom at Hank's before I could find my own place dutifully redefining our relationship in my head, and by Halloween, I was sure I was cured. I no longer wanted Everett Bridges in some insatiable way. But my body had other ideas. His elbow touched mine, and I was weak at the knees.

It didn't matter, though, I reminded myself. I could want him like that and not act on it.

"Let's see," I said. "I'm in a tiny place with a great kitchen—my bedroom is mostly bed, but I have a gas stove, so." I shrugged and Everett smiled, and the flash of his teeth had me pressing my knees together. "I love being back in the kitchen at Hank's. I'm taking on some private clients. Everything is going according to plan."

The smile on Everett's face turned into something smaller, softer. "I'm happy for you and your plans," he said.

"What about you?" I asked.

"I'm not sure I'm as well organized as you," Everett said. "My *plan* is more of a loose sketch."

"I can help you," I said. "I love coming up with a five-year plan."

At this, Everett turned further toward me, knee pressing against mine under the table. "Stay with me on Sunday," he said, and my stomach flipped over itself. His mouth twitched, eyes sparkling. "You can rip my plan apart."

I felt my mouth open, could taste some sarcastic reply on the tip of my tongue, but nothing would come out. I was stuck like that when Laurel's voice echoed through the bar, her footsteps rapidly approaching.

Everett and I were still caught, staring at each other.

"I'll think about it," I said quickly, the same rote reply I'd given earlier. I grabbed his glass of water and took a long drink.

thirteen

This Summer

Come Tuesday morning, I'm desperate to even the score between me and Everett. At dinner the previous night, he had everyone else hooked with his wild stories from set, everything from outlandish demands (his lead actor wouldn't shoot a single thing before everyone participated in an hour-long group meditation at sunrise every morning) to weather restrictions (they spent four long days trying to film a desert scene in ten-minute bursts between monsoon-level rainstorms). I sat swirling my wine in my glass, my brief triumph of re-creating Laurel's favorite dish from a restaurant in LA quickly diminishing under the weight of learning just how bizarre the world of filmmaking really is.

I'm in the kitchen at five the next morning so that by the time Laurel comes down the stairs I'm pulling a perfectly timed tray of biscotti out of the oven and handing her a mug of coffee.

"I don't know how I feed myself without you," she says as she accepts it from me, sinking onto a stool at the island.

"Lemon ricotta French toast will be ready in half an hour," I tell her. She sighs dreamily.

Everyone else is quick to follow once they start to smell breakfast and coffee. By the time they're all around the island, loading their plates with French toast and bacon and strawberries from the farmers market, Everett is leaned against the wall opposite me, hair still messy from sleep, the sleeves of his sweatshirt pushed up.

He lifts his mug in my direction, a barely there, devilish grin on his face that tells me he's not so clueless about how all of this is going, after all. I return his gesture.

When I turn back to Laurel, she's watching us.

We all load into the Bronco a while later (point: Everett, always Everett, with his stupid vintage car) and head to the marina to catch a sailboat with Captain Isaiah, the same man who ran a discounted special that first summer here, when we were twenty-two and the worst thing Everett and I had ever done was lie about when we met. *How* we met.

The salt spray sent back by the hull of the boat calms my bruised ego, but only a little. Everett is talking with Gabe, apparently impervious to my presence, so I settle in between Davi and Laurel on the cushioned seat at the back of the boat. Davi passes me a glass of the same sparkling wine we've been drinking on this boat since we first started coming here, made by the captain's cousin. Now he seems to be running an aboveboard wine business, rather than passing out experimental basement hooch.

"Thanks," I say as I take the glass a little too forcefully from him.

"Looks like you could use it," he mutters. I ignore his comment and toss back half the wine. "And looks like we'll need more," Davi says before standing up and wandering off to find some.

I turn to Laurel, but she's stiff, clearly uncomfortable. I settle back next to her and raise my glass to the sky.

"Isn't this beautiful?" I ask.

"Beautiful," she says shortly.

"Remember when this wine used to give you the worst

hangover?" I ask, probing lightly. If we're not allowed to ask Laurel how she's doing, and we're not supposed to ask what happened, and if I can't change the facts of *why* things are so tense right now, then the only option remaining seems like distraction. "Hopefully he's gotten that sugar content under control."

"Right," Laurel says. She hasn't looked at me.

I stay quiet for a minute, chewing on my lip. Across the deck, Everett laughs at something Gabe said, the sound seeming to drift directly from his mouth to my ears, pulling my gaze toward him. I stare at his profile, seething. The wind ripples through his hair, the sun catching on the golden hues in it, the tendons in his neck flexing when he turns his head to look at something on the water that Gabe points out. I hate that I once buried my face against that neck and found comfort there, or that I used to marvel at the color of his hair while we all played volleyball on the beach. I hate the way that—

"What are you doing," Laurel says, brusquely drawing me out of my furious reminiscing.

"What?" I ask, turning quickly to look back at her. Even if she sounds angry, I'm thrilled she's finally looking at me. "Nothing."

"You grind your teeth when you look at him, did you know that?" she asks. "You only do that when you're mad. You sound like you're going to break a molar."

I brush this comment away with a wave of my hand. "Just stressing about the cookbook."

"No." Laurel crosses her arms over her chest. "I know you, and I know you're not stressed about the cookbook. You and Everett have been fighting since we got here."

"We're not *fighting*," I say, though I can't totally deny the accusation. "*Bickering* is probably more accurate."

"No," Laurel says again, the word sending a wash of shame

through me, like a child scolded. "You two used to bicker, but that was sweet, like you were an old married couple or something. That was when you two still liked each other. When you used to flirt with each other and think that none of the rest of us noticed."

My chest goes hot. I don't know what to say to her. There's so much unsaid in her short speech, so many things I thought we just wouldn't acknowledge this week. But there's also a kernel of truth to it, I know, and my gaze is drawn briefly back to Everett. For a minute, I try to picture what it would be like to just be friendly with him again. I swear I do.

I look back at Laurel. "You're right," I say.

Her expression, which has been cloudy up to this point, darkens further. "Are you two seriously still mad at each other?" she asks. "It was, like, a thousand years ago."

The words slice a little deeper than I want them to, but I'm not sure I can explain the reason for that to myself, let alone Laurel. If I could own up to the reason why, after five years, I can't seem to fully move on, maybe this trip would feel different. Instead, I force a smile. "We'll stop arguing," I say. "I promise."

Laurel looks unconvinced. She shrugs, dropping her sunglasses from the top of her head over her eyes, and sits back against the cushions.

Davi flops down on Laurel's other side, back with more wine. He pulls his phone out of his pocket and lifts it high above his head, searching for a signal as mine chimes in my own pocket. I pull it out to a text from Hank—

Happy Tuesday! Sailboat this afternoon? My heart sinks, guilt twisting through me at the same time Davi's attention jerks toward me. "You have a signal?" he asks.

"I think it's already gone," I say even as he leans over Laurel toward me, phone extended.

"Oh my god," she says, shoving his arm away. "Can you stop responding to emails for two seconds."

"I'm waiting to hear—"

"About the promotion, I know," Laurel grumbles. "They won't be able to tell you it's yours if your phone is at the bottom of the ocean."

"And why is my phone at the bottom of the ocean, Laur?" Davi says, pocketing his phone and slinging an arm around her shoulders. I see her suppress a slip of a smile as he squeezes her arm, jostling her jokingly. "Is someone grumpy enough to put it there?"

She shoves him off as I stand, wandering in what I hope is an unassuming manner over to the railing, biding my time. When they seem fittingly immersed in conversation, Laurel's mood vastly brightened when it's just Davi, and not me, sitting next to her, I turn and march over to where Everett and Gabe are still talking.

"I need to talk to you," I say. I grab Everett's hand and yank him, stumbling along behind me without looking at either of them.

"What the—" Everett says as he finds his footing. "Sutton, Gabe was just on picture forty-five of Riley and Chloe's first ballet class."

"You can look at pictures another time," I say, pulling him to one side of the deck where the rigging blocks us from view.

"Do you *know* what a Gabe slideshow is like?" he asks.

"Yes, I've been through more of them than you have," I point out. Technically, though, I realize, there's a chance this isn't true. I know Gabe was already a big fan of the photo montage in college, sitting us all down and running through the literal hundreds of pictures he took over summer or winter vacation, on weekend trips he and Zoey would take, at least 40 percent of them always blurry or duplicates. But while I had assumed the habit originated back then, there's a chance he's always been like that. That even in middle school, he was showing his friends—read, Everett—slideshows of his science projects or his three cats. I wouldn't put it past him.

Everett, I can tell, is thinking the same thing, but to his credit, he doesn't say anything.

"We have a problem," I say.

Everett raises an eyebrow. "Do we."

"Laurel caught on to our—" I wave a hand between us, because while she would define what we're doing differently than I would, I don't want Everett to know that "—bickering."

"Sutton," Everett says. "The captain picked up on our bickering. Everyone at the marina picked up on it. Hell, the other *boats* on the water right now can probably—"

"I get the point," I cut in, holding up a hand to silence him. "It's a problem."

"I didn't come here to argue with you," Everett says.

"Neither did *I*," I say. But I didn't go to Gabe's baby shower to argue with him either, or Davi's birthday party, or Laurel and Stephen's anniversary. And yet. I realize that my back molars are, in fact, gritting painfully together. I try to unclench my jaw. "But we are, and it's what's putting Laurel in a weird mood this week."

Everett's mouth ticks, like he might find what I just said funny. "You don't think she might be a little more focused on, I don't know, her divorce? Herself? I don't think our issues are front of mind for her this week, Sutton."

"Are you joking?" I scoff, disbelieving. "Everett, *we* are the whole reason this trip hasn't happened for the last four years."

A dubious expression flits across Everett's eyebrows before he's shaking his head. "I think you think we matter too much."

"I don't think *we* matter," I say, gesturing between the two of us. "I think the fact that we broke a very important pact with absolutely no consideration for our friends and what it would do to them matters."

"Oh my god," Everett says, almost groans, tugging a hand roughly through his hair. "When are you going to let go of the stupid pact? It sounds so childish."

I balk. "Excuse me, it is not *childish*. It's the thing that made this work for so many years."

Everett runs a hand down his face. "It was a joke," he says. "The pact was a joke to begin with."

"What does that mean?" I ask. Everett opens his mouth to respond, shuts it again, and it's enough to drop a new hot thread of anger through me. "Right," I say, throwing up a defeated hand. "You can't believe any of this. You're just so above it all."

Everett's brow creases. "That's not—" He breaks off, eyes drifting over my shoulder and mouth pressing into a thin line. I glance behind me, heart jumping into my throat and excuses flooding my mouth at Laurel standing there, cheeks flushed.

"Are you kidding?" she says, and the look on her face could shrink me down ten sizes.

"Laurel," I say. "We were just talking—"

"Clearly," she says. Then, shoulders hunching up to her ears, "No, you know what? I don't want to hear it. I'm sick of this."

"Laurel, we really were trying to talk things through," Everett says, and it feels odd, uncomfortable even, to suddenly be on the same side.

"Great," Laurel says. She pushes us in the direction of where the captain is sitting by the wheel, looking bored. "Then you won't mind continuing your *conversation*." Her words drip with sarcasm, disdain, and I don't blame her.

"What—" I say, feet slipping against the boards as she marches us along. "Laurel—"

"In you go," she says, stopping us in front of the door to the little cabin.

Everett and I exchange a glance. "We'll behave," he says to her. "Seriously."

"I don't want you to behave," Laurel says through her own gritted teeth. "I want you to move past this shit between you."

The sound that escapes me is half scoff, half snort. I regret it as soon as it's out, Laurel turning to me with fire in her eyes.

"You want to know why I've been acting so off?" she asks. "It's not because of my divorce, or the media circus around it, or the fact that half of *my money* is going to someone I'm not going to share my life with anymore." I fight the urge to argue with her on all these points, because the way she delivers them certainly makes it sound like she's upset about them.

"I'm upset because this trip was supposed to be *fun*," she says. "It was supposed to be a distraction from all the garbage going on. It wasn't supposed to be about the two of you hating each other. So I'm pissed that the two of you can't get over yourselves long enough to just act civil for one stupid week!" Her voice gets louder as she says it, the last words ending in a high-pitched crescendo that sends Everett hurrying down the narrow set of stairs into the cabin and me following quickly behind him.

"Figure it out," Laurel says, Davi's and Gabe's faces appearing on either side of her, looking curiously down at us. "You have thirty minutes until we let you out."

Everett and I exchange the same panicked glance we did earlier before looking back up at her. "Let us out?" I say.

But Laurel is already slamming the door, the lock sliding into place.

fourteen

Second Summer

If I'd thought it was hard to ignore Everett that first summer, the second was torture. I told myself it had to be something about not being able to have him every time I caught myself staring at him a minute too long, or letting my arm brush against his whenever we were close enough.

He did nothing to help. Aside from not looking away first when our gazes would catch and possessing arms in the first place, he asked me twice more about staying, always dropped casually, almost jokingly into conversation, my answer always the same. *I'll think about it.* Because as much as I told myself I would say no the next time he asked, almost *hoping* he would, the word seemed to completely flee my vocabulary when it came up.

On Friday morning, a full forty-eight hours since the last time he'd asked me—something that was nagging at the edges of my brain and I was actively trying to ignore—Everett sat on the coffee table across from me, putting a finger on the edge of my book and tilting it down.

"Excuse me," I said, acting annoyed. In reality, I'd been aware of his proximity as soon as he walked into the room, read the same line over and over until he sat in front of me.

Laurel and Davi were lying out on the beach while Gabe was still sleeping. "I was reading that."

Everett grinned. "I'm teaching you how to surf."

I shook my head, nerves tinged with the possibility of very real fear racing up my throat. "I'm not a huge ocean person."

"Shocked you're Laurel's friend, then," he said. I smirked. "Shocked you're on this trip at all."

"Plenty of people don't want to dive into shark-infested waters."

He leaned in then, eyes narrowing playfully. "I'm going to let you in on a little secret," he said. "The sharks around here?" He shook his head. "Not actually all that interested in you."

I closed my book and set it next to me. "You say that now. But what happens if I crack my head open falling off the surfboard? They'll come swarming."

"Sutton," he said, still leaned in close to me. I had my legs curled under me, but if I didn't, his would have been bumping against mine, and something about the sheer possibility had me sweating. "I promise you that I would never let you crack your head open. And—" his eyes flicked down to my knees, like he'd suddenly had the same thought as me "—I happen to know you're at least half lying about the whole ocean thing. You swim every day here."

"I *am* afraid of sharks, though," I reiterated as his gaze latched on to mine again.

"Probably healthy to be at least a little afraid of them." He held a hand toward me. "Now, are you in or out?"

"I'm not sure surfing is really on my bucket list," I said, even as I grabbed his hand and stood up.

I hated to admit how much I liked riding in his car, one hand gliding through the air out the window and the music up loud. He drove us a few miles down the coast and parked in the lot of a bar that had two-for-one deals we'd taken advantage of earlier this week and last summer.

But it turned out that, where surfing was concerned, I was *not* an ocean person.

Everett ran me through jumping up on the board on the beach. By the time I'd paddled over my tenth wave, though—tiny, hardly a speed bump in the ocean—without trying to stand up, Everett knew it too.

"You've got it," he said, returning to my side. "I believe in you." He sat up so he straddled his board. Water droplets sprayed off his hair as he shook his head back, trailed down his chest.

"That's the thing," I said. "I'm not sure *I* believe in me."

He leveled me with a serious look. "Sutton."

"What?" I said. My pulse was thumping in my throat in a way I was convinced he could see, some muscle twitching as rapidly as water boiling on the stove.

"You believe in yourself," he said. "You're not afraid of anything."

"You know that's not actually a compliment." My eyes furiously scanned the water in front of me like I might find a spot of dry land on it. We weren't actually that far out, seeing as this was supposed to be a *beginner's lesson*, but for some reason, I was feeling the same kind of bottomless sensation in my stomach you get when you're about to drop on a roller coaster or, I'd imagine, before you do something like jump out of a plane, off a bridge. "I think someone not being afraid of anything would indicate a certain brand of narcissism. And, hey—" I glanced over at him, suddenly irritated "—you're the one who said it was probably healthy to be a little wary of sharks earlier, and— What?"

Everett was grinning, which only irked me more. "Still feeling nervous?"

"I—" I started, confusion rising and waning in the space of one breath. "Oh my god, I hate tricks like that. Just replacing one emotion with another isn't—"

"You've got to paddle now," Everett interrupted.

"What?"

"No matter how you feel about my teaching methods, you've got to start paddling now if you want to make this wave," he said, but in my moment of hesitation, it was too late, and this time the drop in my stomach wasn't just from nerves but from the sudden lurch of the board beneath me, the wave bigger than either of us had anticipated.

"Everett!" I yelped as the board rocked, falling forward to grip it with my hands. He steadied it immediately, leaning over to wrap an arm across the front.

"I'm sorry," he said as he held me there. I watched as the wave bobbed toward the shore in front of us now, and considered, for a moment, how ridiculous I must look from that vantage point, a dot of a person screaming as the water rose like a tiny wrinkle in a blanket beneath them. I looked over at Everett, breathing hard. "Come on." He waved me in the direction of shore. "I shouldn't have pushed it. Let's go."

"No," I said as he started to lean forward, ready to paddle back to the beach. "I still need to stand up."

"You did great," he said. "We can try again another day."

"We don't have another day," I said. "We leave after tomorrow."

"Then we can try again next summer," he said. I'd expected him to ask me to stay again, was almost disappointed that he didn't.

I glanced over my shoulder. Another small wave was rolling in toward us, far enough for me to prepare. "This is the one," I said to him. "I'm standing up."

Everett's eyebrow tugged upward. "You sure?"

I nodded, even though it was shaky. "Yep. This is it."

The corners of Everett's mouth turned down as he considered, but he nodded and dropped forward to paddle a little away from me, giving me space.

"You can do it!" he called to me as I fell forward, feet on my board behind me. *Like a push-up*, Everett had told me while we practiced on the beach. *Or a burpee.* He'd laughed when I'd glared at him about it.

The same nerves Everett told me he didn't think I had started to bubble up, but the wave was under me before they could take root, and Everett was telling me to "Paddlepaddle-paddle!" And I was pushing up, getting my feet under me, and Everett was cheering, and for one tiny second I wasn't afraid at all. It felt a little like flying.

I fell immediately.

But Everett was there when I popped up, in the water too, his board bobbing gently toward shore, and I was wrapping myself around him, laughter jostling out of me.

"You did it!" he said, pulling his head back to smile at me. We were pressed together as much as we could be as we both pedaled to stay afloat, salt water sluicing off his shoulders under my palms.

"And here you thought it was time to go," I said. Everett threw his head back, a laugh barking out of him. I wanted him to kiss me, I realized, when he looked back at me and I could see the water clinging to his eyelashes, wanted to taste the salt on his lips. He seemed to realize it then too, hands tightening on me for a split second before he was loosening his grip.

"Is that enough for today?" he asked.

No. "Mmm-hmm," I mumbled, nodding as we let go of each other and kicked off in the direction of our boards.

We didn't waste any time lingering on the beach. We walked

in silence back to the rental shop and rinsed off our boards there before returning mine and heading back to the car. Everett leaned his surfboard against the trunk and reached inside to retrieve two towels. He slung one around his neck and returned to me where I stood with my back against the driver's side door. It was warm out, hot even, but there were goose bumps on my arms.

Everett wrapped the towel around me, rubbing his hands up and down my arms. We were staring at each other, too serious. He pulled the top of the towel up over my head and scrubbed a hand on top of it, dragging a laugh out of me. I squirmed my head out from under his hand but didn't move away from him, even though I knew I should have. Instead I grabbed onto the ends of the towel he still had hanging around his neck, his bare stomach brushing against mine.

"Better?" he asked, hands still on my arms. I could feel the heat of his palms through the terry cloth, the rise and fall of his breath against my abdomen.

"Loads," I said. We had been this close in the ocean, his arms wrapped around me as he pedaled his legs below, heart thrumming against mine; and yet, it hadn't felt like this. Maybe because I was just a *little* afraid of drowning out there. Maybe because I was warmer and back on dry land. Maybe because I'd been trying all week not to think about Everett like that, look at him like that, dream about him like that. But at his car, bodies pressed together, it was all I could think about. My eyes traced along the sharp angle of his jaw, up to the achingly soft curve of his lips, the straight bridge of his nose. By the time they landed on his eyes, my hands had climbed to his shoulders, the pads of my fingers brushing over his skin and the remaining hints of salt water there.

Everett stared at me as I traced the tips of my fingers to his collarbone, over his sternum, down until he was lifting an arm to lean it above my head, forehead dropping to the car just next to mine, breath against my ear. He pressed a kiss to the spot just below it and I gasped, curling closer toward him, adding to the pressure between us.

Everett looped his other arm around my waist and drew me against him, moving his mouth up to mine in slow, hungry movements. I arched against him, bringing my hand back up to thread into his hair, the other grasping for the side mirror like I was losing my balance. It was as good as our last kiss was—better even, sharper, a want behind it that felt somehow time sensitive. Which it was, I remembered as Everett's hand dropped to the small of my back, pressing me against him, and I moaned into his mouth, an incriminating sound.

"Stay with me this weekend," he said, the words a rasp against my lips as his thumb pressed into my hips, fingers urging me somehow closer to him. It was the question I wanted him to ask in the ocean, the one he'd been asking all week even when he wasn't actually saying it, in lingering glances and the way we spoke to each other, in elbows bumped together in the kitchen and invitations to teach me how to surf. It was pointless to deny wanting it, and as his other hand raked up my side, drew circles over the damp fabric of my bikini top, I wondered if we even needed to. If it could just be instinctive. He kissed me again, tongue dipping into my mouth. That sound came out of me again and he drew back, leaning his forehead against mine. "Sutton."

"Okay," I said, nodding. I didn't even think to say no. Of course I was always going to say yes. "I'll stay."

fifteen

This Summer

Everett stretches up to try the knob, but it is, in fact, locked.

"Can you seriously still lock people in?" I ask. "Is that legal?"

"Yes, it's legal, Sutton," Everett says flatly.

I narrow my eyes at him as he sits on the edge of one of the narrow bunks. There are two facing each other, a row of cupboards the same dark wood as the floors at the end, a small porthole on either side. The rocking of the boat is more noticeable down here, vaguely like I'm being tossed around in the waves, and I'm suddenly very aware of how little separates us from the miles of deep, dark water below us.

Everett looks up at me as I cross my arms across my chest and pace to the end of the cabin. "Are you okay?" he asks.

"Fine," I say. I glance out the porthole, which is a mistake because there's water halfway up it, which means that we are, literally, partially submerged in the ocean. Which, clearly. I know how boats work. But that doesn't mean I like it. I feel much more comfortable aboveboard, with my whole body bathed in air and sunlight.

"So," Everett says as I pace back to him.

"So, what?" I ask.

"So, we talk," he says. I eye him skeptically. "Right?"

"We have talked," I say.

"Are you referring to what happened up there?" he says, which sends a roil through my stomach. Words like *up there* are not helping my nerves right now. "I think you could loosely categorize that as an *attempt* at talking. *Biting each other's heads off* might be more accurate."

"Look," I say, stopping in my pacing to face him from the end of the bunks. "We sit down here for thirty minutes and tell Laurel everything is great when she opens the door. Okay?"

Everett looks like he doesn't want to agree with me, and I sigh, slumping my hip against the mattress and pressing a hand to my face. "I'm sure you have some witty comeback ready to go right now, but can you please just save it for later?"

"What's wrong?" Everett asks. "Are you feeling seasick?"

"No." I shake my head, face still hidden in my palm, so I only hear Everett move. I think maybe he's going to check the door again, so I jump a little when I feel a hand against mine, lowering it from my face as the other rubs over my shoulder.

"Your head?" he asks, and I'm so startled by the gentleness in his voice, the soft way he's touching me, his proximity, that I almost forget I'm mad at him for a minute. A memory flashes through me: a migraine the kind of which I hadn't experienced in years, a cold morning with Everett, feeling cared for.

I swallow, shake my head, try not to breathe in too deeply, lest I be lured further in by Everett's historically intoxicating scent. "No."

"Is Cousin Hugh's wine still iffy?" he asks, which prompts a small laugh out of me. I watch as one corner of his mouth lifts.

"I'm sure it is," I say, forcing my gaze up to his. "But that's not it."

Everett nods. For one quiet, breathless moment, his eyes skim down my face, and I'm questioning if it really is just the waves and the small space that has my stomach doing somersaults.

Everett's expression goes cloudy, whatever was there suddenly blotted out. He clears his throat and drops his hands from me. I miss the warming pressure of his palm against my shoulder. But that realization sends a shock wave through me, and I step back—or try to, but there's only bed behind me, so it seems more like I'm rearing away from him.

Everett appears to take the hint, because he nods toward the bunk. "Why don't you sit down," he says, voice returned to its previous flat tone.

I sit and watch as he wanders into the space at the end of the cabin, bends to look out the porthole, hands in his pockets; he straightens again and tips his head back, squinting at the ceiling. It feels like five minutes must pass, but in reality, it can't be more than a painfully quiet sixty seconds.

"I keep thinking about the water," I finally say. Everett's attention snaps back to me.

"The water?" he asks.

I nod. "How deep it is," I say. "If there's some shipwreck or giant shark or dead body beneath us."

Understanding clears his cloudy expression. "Ah," he says. "The water." I swear I can hear what he would have said if this were five, ten years prior, can picture his wry expression in my head. *The odds are there might be*, maybe. *But I'll get you out of here long before we find out.*

"I like the ocean," I insist, shaking the image of past Everett from my head and forcing myself to focus on the present. "I like this whole boat tradition."

Everett nods. "I know you do."

"Good," I say. "Just wanted to . . . clear that up. My phobia isn't that pervasive."

"Well," Everett says. He walks down the narrow aisle between the bunks and drops onto the same spot he was in before, directly across from me. "I've seen you master this phobia before."

I don't say anything, just widen my eyes in confirmation at the memory, mouth set in a straight line.

I haven't done a lot of dredging up the good memories Everett and I share. That effectively means I haven't really dredged up *any* memories we share in the last four years. There's just one, really, that I've examined more than I ought to. The one that defines us for me now.

But the memory he's talking about is one of those good ones, even if it's laced in nerves. There's also an excitement there, the same kind I used to associate only with Everett, and a feeling of triumph, and a deep want that colors the whole thing in swirling reds and dark purples. That whole second summer with him is like that for me, somehow shimmering ephemeral and heavy at the same time. The most I've ever wanted someone and that desire's quick answer, two days of giving in to what we hadn't that first summer.

"I'll get Laurel to let us out," Everett says and stands, starting toward the door.

"Wait," I say. He turns back to me. "I can do it," I say. "I'm fine."

"You sure?" he asks, which only sends another current of stubbornness through me, a need to prove that I can sit in a boat's cabin for thirty minutes without freaking out.

"Yes," I bite out.

Everett sits down across from me again, elbows on his thighs and his folded hands hanging between his knees. He looks a little like a coach about to give a player a pep talk. I steel myself, the waves in my stomach matching the rhythm of the waves around us.

"So," he says. "The cookbook."

I raise an eyebrow at him. "What, are we talking now?"

He shrugs one shoulder. "We can sit here in silence for half an hour, or—" he holds one hand out to read the watch on his wrist "—twenty-four minutes and about forty-five seconds, if you'd rather."

I don't say anything in response, which I guess Everett must take as confirmation that I *would* rather, because after a moment he kicks his feet up onto the bed and lies down, hands tucked behind his head.

"Are you going to nap?" I ask after another minute.

"Not a lot of options down here, Sutton," Everett says. His eyes are still open, staring straight ahead.

I look around at the room, at the dark blue of the quilts on the bunks, the wobbly light coming in from the portholes, the clasps on the cabinets. Think about how the mattresses stay put. Wonder what the light looks like when the boat is docked. Consider the effectiveness of the clasps in rough water, until I can't take it anymore.

"I'm nervous about it," I blurt. "The cookbook." Everett turns his head to look at me, something like disbelief on his face. "What?" I ask.

"Nothing," he says. "I've just never known you to be nervous about something in your professional life. Sharks, sure. But not cooking."

I shake my head. "This feels different. It feels . . . important."

Everett sits up at this, like it's caught his attention. He swings his feet to the floor and fixes me with the full force of his gaze. A spark shoots down my spine at it, as I remember what it's like to be the subject of his undivided attention, how it feels to have Everett Bridges interested in only you.

"Was cooking in Hank's kitchen not important?" he asks.

I sigh, shaking my head. "It was," I say. "Of course it was. But I don't know if I've ever wanted anything this much. I *thought* the thing I wanted most in the world was to take over the restaurant once he finally decided to retire."

Everett nods. "Last I remember, you were still pretty hell-bent on that," he says.

I let myself think about the last time we were really together, weeks before everything went south, for exactly two seconds. San Francisco. A chilly pier. Things I thought were true finally spoken out loud.

"Why haven't you told Hank?" Everett asks softly after I've gone quiet for too long. I glance up at him, still wary of this conversation. Not just with him, but with anyone.

At some point in the last few years, I stopped wanting to own a restaurant. Or maybe I never really wanted that. Maybe it was the impression of it all: If I was ambitious enough, if I achieved enough, I would somehow matter. To the world, to people paying attention, to the people who already loved me. To my parents. But the truth was, the people who loved me didn't mind. I could be the person sticking hot dogs on the rotating rack at a 7-Eleven and I still mattered to them just as much as if I were crafting Michelin-starred meals comprised of things like tallow foam and lavender essence—served under a glass dome on a pillow, of course.

But I didn't want to run a business. I wanted to feed people. I wanted something akin to the feeling I got when we all sat down to our last meal at the summer house every year—here is how food brings us together. Here is one of the most human, basic things, and we've gathered around to make something beautiful.

It seemed harmless not to tell Hank at first. To keep my good news to myself. While I knew Laurel texted her mom and grandmother every minute detail of her life, Hank and I had always been a little more need-to-know. *Things are good, I'm safe, yes I want to go to the game next weekend, no we don't need to talk about that guy I was seeing for a while.* That sort of thing.

And I told myself it didn't mean much anyway—I'd let him know eventually, and I could couch it as more press for the restaurant. A whole new client base to bring in, now and when I started running the place. Which I was partially convinced I would still do. Even if I didn't want it, I hadn't fully let it go. A pattern, it would seem, in my life. Selective fixation.

Everett is still waiting for my response, ever patient, ever focused. "I just . . ." I start, kicking a toe against the floor. "Hank has done everything for me." I swallow, afraid to say the next part out loud. "How do you disappoint someone who's done everything for you?"

Everett's brow draws down. Half of me can't believe I've said it, and to him of all people. The other half is relieved to have it out there and, if I'm honest, not all that surprised that it's Everett I've said it to. Laurel and I aren't exactly having many deep talks lately, and while I know Gabe and Davi would be sympathetic, they think differently about this sort of thing than I do. To Davi, it wouldn't be a big deal. Gabe would ask why I couldn't do both.

"I know what you're going to say," I cut in, needing to beat Everett to the punch. "Hank loves me, he just wants me to be happy, I'm not a disappointment. It doesn't change anything."

At first, Everett doesn't respond. He just looks at me, and I know I'm right. But then, just as I'm about to start talking again, he responds.

"I wasn't going to say that."

I frown. Everett leans a little closer to me.

"All of that is true," he says. "Hank loves you, he does just want you to be happy, and you aren't a disappointment." He pauses. "But maybe this does disappoint him," he continues. "And that's okay."

I suck in a breath like I might respond, like a retort is already brimming behind my teeth, but nothing comes. My shoulders tense, eyes narrowing in Everett's direction.

"It's your life, Sutton," he says quietly. "You've got to do what you want with it."

For a minute, I let those good memories rise up to the surface. How it always was between us before the one moment I now let define Everett for me. Easy, I used to think. Simple. But further down, if I linger long enough in the past, something deeper. Not as surface level as I've convinced myself it was. A connection no one could make up. I think about who we used to be, and it makes these past forty-eight hours seem so foolish.

"I didn't come here this week wanting to fight with you," I say.

I see one corner of Everett's mouth twitch, and I almost want to say it for him, for the past version of him that seems to have followed us into this cabin. *Could have fooled me.*

"Neither did I," Everett says instead, and I'm almost disappointed. "Seems like we both failed."

I almost want to ask why, where he thinks all the fight in us came from if neither of us intended it, but there's a shadow lurking on the other side of that question, too big for me to consider right now.

"How would you feel about a truce?" he asks.

I'm surprised at the small chime of disappointment that rings through me. A truce seems almost temporary, acknowledges that there isn't anything beyond this week. But I know that already. Everett hasn't been in my future for years now, so it's unreasonable to feel a little duped by a *truce* for the rest of the week. It's what Laurel asked of us, after all.

I nod and hold a hand out to him to shake. His palm is warm against mine as he takes it. "I can't promise I'll be your best friend," I say.

Everett grins as he squeezes my hand. "Wouldn't expect any less from you, Hale," he says, the old nickname sending a zip down my spine. We let go and I tuck my hands quickly under my legs as Everett glances at the watch on his wrist.

"Well, thirty minutes is about up," he says. "You proved yourself."

"Proved myself?"

Everett nods. "You mastered your phobia," he says. "You're never one to back down from a challenge."

"Hey," I say as it dawns on me what he did. "Offering to get Laurel to open the door isn't exactly a *challenge*."

"It was enough of one for you," he says. "Congratulations, Sutton. You're two for two."

"That was sneaky," I say.

Everett shrugs. "Worked last time."

For a minute, the tension in my body relaxes. I let myself just sit here with Everett as if nothing is wrong. As if we didn't hurt each other, and all the anger between us has just floated off into the ether. As if we've actually, finally moved on. "Yeah," I say. "I guess it did."

sixteen

Second Summer

I hated that I felt the smallest bit happy to see the taillights of Laurel's car fading on Sunday morning. Hated even more the lie I told her to keep me here two more days, that I was interviewing with a potential client tomorrow. It was based in some reality. There was a woman with a house down here who was a friend of a friend of a family I'd cooked for this spring who had reached out, wondering if I did any live-in work. But I'd told her I wouldn't be available this summer weeks ago.

"At least you'll have Everett to keep you company," Laurel had said when I told her. He'd said he was staying behind to catch another weekend of surfing before leaving for his next project that was filming in Georgia. She'd leveled a pointer finger at me, added playfully, "Remember the pact." It only made me feel guiltier.

But it didn't have me getting in the car with her. It didn't have me changing my mind. I don't think anything could have after that day by Everett's car, after the surfing lesson. It awakened something in me I'd been keeping locked down since our kiss last summer. I wanted Everett Bridges, plain and simple. In a move surprisingly out of character for me, I wasn't concerned with how flimsy my willpower was when it came to him. There was something exciting about giving in to it. In some decision that was just ours.

He was washing breakfast dishes when I walked back in and I pushed myself up onto the counter opposite him, watched his shoulders move as his hands did.

"I don't think anyone has ever watched me wash a mug so closely," he said after a while, without looking at me.

"You're being very thorough," I commended him. He laughed and set the mug in the drying rack and grabbed another. I kept watching.

"Everyone's gone," I finally said.

At this Everett turned off the tap, grabbing a dish towel and drying his hands as he turned to face me. "Sutton Hale," he said as I swung my legs, hands tucked under my thighs. "Did you run in here to tell me we're alone?"

"Me?" I said, loosing a hand to press it to my chest in mock surprise. "Of course not. I came in here to supervise your dishwashing."

"And?" Everett said, tossing the towel over his shoulder and walking over to me, my knees parting for him to step between like some cause-and-effect question on a test. *If Everett Bridges approaches you, what is the most natural response?* His hands raked up the outside of my thighs, my skin tingling in their wake.

"Like I said, *very* thorough."

We both smiled just before he kissed me. Any remaining guilt fled from my body as one of his hands came up so he could settle his fingers in my hair, hold my jaw with his thumb.

It was always like that with Everett. He kissed me, and the rest of the world turned off for a minute. It was part of the reason I gave in to our secret so easily, this sort of ease around him. We were simple, and there was a kind of joy in that, in two perfect, hazy days that I could look forward to each year without any long-term consequences.

I was reaching for the hem of Everett's shirt, his hands already exploring under mine when he pulled away from me. I let out a disappointed sound.

"Come on," he said, waving me off the counter.

"What?" I asked.

"Come on," he said again. "We've got to go do something."

I hopped down, hand quickly sliding into his waiting one. "What do we have to do?"

"I don't know," Everett said. "Something."

"I thought the whole point of these two days was to do something *here*," I said. Everett laughed as he pulled me through the living room toward the front door.

"Isn't it about hanging out with each other too?" he asked. I felt my cheeks go pink as Everett grabbed his keys from the hook by the door and pocketed them. He turned to me, took my face in his hands, and kissed me once, long and slow, again. "Let me at least buy you dinner or a coffee or those weird marzipan things you like so much from the candy store first."

I felt one corner of my mouth tug down as I tried not to smile. "Sorry I was only thinking about getting you into bed."

Everett grinned at this, throwing an arm around my shoulder and walking us outside. "Don't ever apologize for that," he said.

The rest of that first day was exactly what Everett talked about: coffee, and the candy store, where we filled a bag with two of each of their overpriced bulk options. We wandered around the same streets we had with everyone else just a few days ago, sucking on extra-sour pineapple twists and trying to land chocolate-covered peanuts in each other's mouths. We stopped at the bougie market on the corner and bought two mini bottles of some fancy premixed cocktail and snuck them and the rest of our candy into a matinee of *Stand by Me* at the tiny theater down the street. The cocktails tasted a lot like the watered-down cosmos they used to serve at a dive bar I frequented with Laurel and Zoey in college. Everett knew which one I was talking about, and it was another tiny reminder that we'd been orbiting, never getting close enough to touch, for a while now.

"You know what would be a perfect double feature with that?" I asked when we swung out of the theater. "*Now and Then*."

"Great movie," Everett said. "Agreed."

Everett did buy me dinner, at a pizza place down the street. We sat out back, at a little table on a mosaic-tiled patio, under globe lights strung between trees. Around us, people in bikini tops and shorts sat next to women in boxy linen dresses, tennis bracelets winking in the fading light, dads in board shorts picking up orders for the families waiting back at their rentals, groups of friends not so different from ours.

"Dating or friends?" I asked, nodding surreptitiously at a couple sitting a few tables away from us. Everett glanced askance at them, eyes roving casually over the other tables until they returned to me so the couple wouldn't notice him looking.

He shrugged. "Maybe they made a pact with their friends not to date each other, so they have to spend two secret days here together after everyone else has gone."

"I hear it's a pretty common practice," I said. Everett grinned, and for a minute it was quiet between us, just the sound of muted conversations and the cool indie music the place was playing drifting in. "I'm glad Gabe chose you," I finally said.

"For kickball in the third grade?" Everett asked.

"Well, that, obviously," I said. "And then to replace Zoey last summer."

Something flickered over Everett's face, quick, before the same calm, lazily happy expression he usually wore slid into place again. "I am too," he said.

It felt so much like that first night we'd met as we drove back to the cottage, the briny evening air whipping in through the windows. There were pieces of Everett that still felt new, exciting, that were distinct from who he was with everyone else.

The bedroom I'd shared with Laurel that week became ours for the next two days, and maybe I should have cared about that, but I didn't. The only thing I cared about was the golden glow of the sunset against the white sheets, Everett's skin against mine, for once just giving in to something. Not thinking about any *next* moment. Everett's hand pressed into my hip, his head dipped between my legs, and nothing else mattered.

I wore his T-shirt while we made breakfast the next morning and turned on the Food Network in the background, yet another microtradition we'd established. We ended up tangled together on the couch, breathless and fast compared to last night's drawn-out exploration of each other. Afterward, we changed and ran across the warm sand to the water, splashing in and ducking under, replacing the sweat dried on our skin with salt water. We warmed up on the beach and swam again, over and over, until our stomachs and the dipping sun dragged us back to the house.

On our last morning together, I turned onto my side to look at him. He was already awake, hair rumpled from sleep and where I'd dragged my fingers through it. "Can we do this again next summer?" I asked.

Everett smiled slowly, eyes still a little tired. "Of course," he said.

Neither of us acknowledged the pact or other people. Not

just our friends, but other partners, potential relationships that couldn't be further from our minds in that moment.

I wasn't sad saying goodbye to him when he dropped me off at the airport that afternoon. We'd spent the drive from Malibu talking about what was next for us, no mention of when we'd talk again or what this meant. We both seemed to tacitly agree that, as soon as the door to the cottage closed behind us, we were back to our usual selves. Friends, or something like it. Just two parts of a larger group.

"See you in the group chat," I said as Everett hauled my suitcase out of the back seat, setting it on the sidewalk next to me. He had his sunglasses pushed to the top of his head, and for a minute I thought about him driving home from here, pictured him in his life. Traffic and film sets and flights to new places. It was a good image, but one that was quickly replaced by Everett shaking ocean water out of his hair, laughing across a bonfire, moving around a tiny kitchen with me. Summer Everett. The only piece of him I'd ever really known. Funnily enough, summer was just beginning, still around the corner on the calendar. We were each other's shoulder season.

We hugged each other goodbye, friendly, familiar. "Pencil me in to your calendar," he said as we pulled away. "Two days next summer."

"Already have you down in pen," I said. Everett smiled at me, that brilliant flash that I'm sure had hearts skipping all over LA. It had caught my eye at a party two years ago, after all. He nodded toward the airport. "Get out of here, Hale."

I grinned. "Bye, Bridges." I waited for the guilt to show up then, rear its head now that we were back to real life. But it didn't come.

seventeen

This Summer

Everett and I manage to make it through most of Wednesday without openly—or privately, for that matter—bickering. Whatever truce we struck in the cabin of the sailboat seems to have stuck.

We spend the morning at Laurel's favorite hiking spot, a few miles down the coast. It's a trail that takes us far up and away from the road at first, before eventually flattening out and winding its way along a brush-dense path, high above the ocean.

Our second summer here, Everett and I lagged behind, arms brushing as we tried to walk side by side on the narrow trail. We pointed out the dots of people on the beach, tried to make up stories for them. A family here for a reunion, half of them happy with the location and the rest wishing they'd picked a ski trip in the winter. A young couple in an argument over who was supposed to pack the sunscreen and forgot. A lonely wanderer, maybe here from a different time, collecting information to take back to wherever he was coming from.

This summer, we end up at the back together out of sheer coincidence. Or, I'm pretty sure it's coincidence. Laurel links arms with Davi and calls to Gabe over her shoulder as we reach the top of the incline, in a move that leaves Everett and me to bring up the rear and that I'm not sure I trust is entirely unintentional. She's testing us, seeing if we actually worked through things yesterday.

But Everett and I walk in silence. He's behind me for a while, until I stop under the pretense of taking a long drink of water and he draws ahead. Then he needs to stop to tie his shoe and I prance past him, before I have to peel off my T-shirt to hike in my sports bra, the sun beating down heavier than anticipated, and he overtakes me.

Eventually our game of leapfrog gets boring, and I keep pace with him from behind, attention caught by the way the sun in his hair makes it look almost dark blond. When he turns around, ostensibly to check I'm still there, I just smile at him, ignoring the faint press I feel against my sternum.

That evening, I get ready in Laurel's room for dinner at Cooper's. We're both in front of the mirror above the dresser.

"I'm sorry," I tell her for what I think has to be the fourteenth time. She's still been distant today, pointedly avoiding being alone with Everett or me. Laurel pauses, an eyeshadow brush in hand, and meets my eyes in the mirror.

"You don't have to keep apologizing," she says. "Just keep not fighting with each other and I'll forgive you."

"I know," I say. "I'm just sorry that we distracted from the week at all."

Laurel looks away from me and leans into the mirror. "Let's just focus on making the rest of it good."

"Of course," I say. I almost say *I'm sorry* again, this time for things long past, but I don't.

Laurel and I didn't talk about what had happened right away. At first, she wouldn't answer my calls. Then, for a while, I think we were pretending it hadn't happened at all, until the guilt of *not* saying anything finally got to me and it just burst out one day when I was visiting her for a long weekend in LA. The thing, even then, was that she hadn't seemed all that interested in my apology. *Thanks*, she'd said quickly, and when I asked if she wanted to talk about it, she just shook her head, and that was that.

I knew it was because she had to be angry, had to feel so betrayed by what Everett and I had done, that the only way forward was to pretend it hadn't happened. But the longer we didn't talk about it, the more I felt like I had to atone for it, until that was a new, permanent facet of our relationship. I would forever need to prove to Laurel how sorry I was. It was why this week had seemed so perfect. Here, maybe, was an opportunity to finally settle things. If we went back to how we all once were—FaceTiming every month, texting every day, going on this trip every year—the small, proverbial step she'd taken back from me would disappear.

I'd let my anger at Everett get in the way of the most important goal this week. I wouldn't let it happen again.

"Cooper's cute," I muse idly as Laurel blends her eyeshadow, hoping to draw her back in, out of her anger at me.

It seems to work. Her eye catches mine again in the mirror and she smiles—a real smile, not the distracted one she's been wearing so often this week.

"I knew you'd like him," she says. "I bet you two will be making out in his kitchen by the end of the night."

"Okay, let's not get ahead of ourselves," I say. "I don't even know if he can properly poach an egg yet."

"Can't marry a man who makes a bad egg," Laurel parrots, half rolling her eyes in a jovial way. I laugh, and lean into the mirror next to her.

This, I think as we keep getting ready, laughing like we used to when we were in college. Our rooms were across from each other, and we'd huddle in front of the shitty, ten-dollar full-length mirror that sat at the end of the hall. Zoey was usually with us, refilling cups with cheap liquor and juice, whatever we had on hand. Laurel would ask to do my makeup until I'd give in and let her while I played music on my phone. If Davi or Gabe came upstairs we'd shoo them away. The second floor was girls only on those nights, some small oasis just for the three of us.

So *this*, this tiny moment with Laurel, is exactly the type of thing I won't give up for anything—or anyone.

Cooper's house is a rambling ranch-style home six miles away, tucked down a road lined with orange trees and perched high enough that he has a spectacular view of the ocean. A huge deck wraps its way around three sides of it, floor-to-ceiling windows reflecting the sky.

Gabe lets out a low whistle as we all climb out of the car. "You could fit three of my house in this yard alone," he says.

"What kind of chef did you say he was, exactly?" I mutter in Laurel's ear as we walk up to the house. I'm carrying a bottle of wine, Laurel balancing a bouquet of flowers in the crook of her arm. The sweet scent of citrus mingles with salty air as we start up the front steps.

"He got this house in the divorce," she hisses back as Davi rings the doorbell. "But a very successful one. The last restaurant he worked in got a Michelin star while he was there. You should see the house his ex-wife got."

My mouth curves down, eyebrows raising in an impressed frown. "Suddenly my cookbook feels pretty stupid."

Laurel makes a tsking sound, elbowing me.

"Your cookbook isn't stupid." I jump a little, twisting to see Everett standing behind us. I hadn't even realized he was there.

"Thanks," I say after a second of staring at him, his eyes gone a little shadowed. He nods as the door swings open.

"Welcome!" Cooper says, throwing an arm wide in greeting. "Come in, come in." He's wearing beige pants and a navy-blue cashmere polo, the sleeves tight against his biceps. "Good to see you," he says as I walk by, leaning in a little closer than he did to anyone else.

"Good to see you too," I say, pausing in the doorway to look up at him. His eyes crinkle as he smiles, a dimple appearing in his cheek. He'd called me yesterday to confirm tonight's menu, and I hadn't hated hearing his voice over the phone. What I said to Laurel earlier was true. Cooper is cute. I can get on board with this, especially if it means distracting from Everett.

But like he heard my thoughts, Everett clears his throat behind me.

"Come in!" Cooper booms again, turning his attention to Everett as I hustle forward after Laurel.

Cooper takes our things and hangs them in a coat closet by the door, thanks us for the wine and flowers, which he grabs a cool ceramic vase for from a bookshelf in the entryway before gesturing for us to follow him.

"This is the place," he says, sweeping a hand out as we pass by a huge sunken living room, dark beams on the ceiling catching the light filtering in through the windows. He leads us over to a wet bar in one corner, where he sets the flowers and the vase. "Dining room is through there," he says, nodding toward the room adjacent. "And kitchen," he says, seemingly directly to me, "is that way. But what are we drinking, first?"

He examines the wine bottles we handed him, a red and the sparkling white the captain's cousin makes. "Seems like we should save these for dinner."

"Actually, Hugh's Hooch is great at any time of the day," Davi says, leaning forward to point at the label on the sparkling wine that had, our first summer here, read *Hugh's Hooch* in Sharpie but is now professionally designed and named.

"Oh, I know Hugh's work when I see it," Cooper says, setting the wine on the counter. "Sure you want to dive in now?"

"He's kidding," Laurel says, which I'm not entirely sure Davi was. "If I remember correctly, you make the best Manhattan on the West Coast."

"My specialty," Cooper says. Gabe and I exchange a glance, and I'm relieved to know I'm not the only one who's feeling like things are suddenly a little different than they were before we got here. This is a side of Laurel I don't think anyone—save Everett, maybe—is very familiar with. Some subtle shift in her mannerisms, away from the girl who ate Funyuns for breakfast and more toward someone who loves a Manhattan made by a Michelin-star chef at his wet bar in his multi-million-dollar Malibu home.

Cooper makes everyone drinks before leading Laurel, Gabe, Davi, and Everett toward the pool patio, leaving them at a table there and walking me toward the kitchen.

"Oh my god," I say, rushing over to the six-burner Wolf range as soon as we walk in. "My kingdom for this stove."

"Wouldn't cook on anything else," Cooper says. I eye the rest of the kitchen, clocking what we have in common. Design-wise it's a little industrial for my liking, but he has good taste in appliances, though I think he must have taken out an insurance policy on this kitchen alone.

"Are we still doing chicken Marbella?" I ask as I spot the ingredients Cooper has laid out methodically on the counter, everything set at perfect angles.

"It's been marinating since the morning," he says. "Just need to get it finished and in the oven. I've got some good arugula in the fridge. You want to work on the salad?"

"I want to work on this chicken," I say, rolling my wrists around so they crack before pulling my hair back into a ponytail, which has Cooper laughing. "What?"

"Nothing," he says. "It's always an apron and an ice-cold deli container of water for me before I get started cooking. You need anything else?"

"I'm great," I say, grabbing the roasting pan Cooper has set out just as the door to the kitchen swings open and Everett walks in.

"The director!" Cooper says. I can see Everett flinch, just a tiny bit. "What can I help you with?"

"There might be an issue with the firepit," Everett says. "In that Laurel might be breaking it."

"That thing is tricky," Cooper says. He's just picked up a knife, a loaf of crusty bread on the cutting board in front of him, and eyes Everett.

"Think you could handle this?" he asks. I watch as what I'm sure Everett would like his response to be plays out on his face and have to look down, bite my lip to keep from smiling.

"I think I'm up to the challenge," Everett finally says, smiling in a way that doesn't reach his eyes.

Cooper grabs the wine for the chicken as he passes me. "I'll open this for you," he says, before pushing out the door.

Everett and I work in silence for a minute, but I can feel him glancing up at me every now and then, and I do the same, never able to fully catch his eye.

"Are you having a good time?" he finally asks after a while. I look up from where I'm sprinkling brown sugar over the chicken, but his eyes are on the work in front of him. He seems to be slicing the bread at a much slower clip than is strictly necessary. "Cooking with Cooper," he clarifies. He says it a little like he's announcing a show, a segment on *Good Morning America*.

"Oh," I say. "Yeah. It's always fun to see how another chef works."

"Hmm," Everett says, like this is something he needs to mull over. I watch him for a second, waiting, but it's not until I look down again that he says anything. "Surprised Laurel thinks he's your type."

I set the sugar down, plant my fists on my hips and stare at him. "And why would that be, Everett?" I ask. I'm exasperated, but I'm trying hard not to show it. To follow the rules we established for ourselves on the boat.

Everett sets the point of his knife against the cutting board in front of him and looks up at me, shrugging.

"I just didn't know you wanted to date another chef," he says.

"I've never said I wouldn't date another chef," I say. "Besides, *why* wouldn't I date another chef?"

"Hard to coordinate your schedules," Everett points out.

"Great reason," I say. "Is that all you've got?"

"Isn't he a little . . . ?" he asks, trailing off.

"What, Everett."

"Outside the age group in which you'd normally date?"

I snort. "He's, like, ten years older than us. I'm not exactly grave robbing."

"Never met a forty-two-year-old named Cooper," Everett mutters at a decibel that makes it clear he wasn't trying to hide what he was saying on any level.

"I find that highly unlikely," I say.

Everett shrugs. "Seems like a young name."

"Coopers grow up."

"Still."

"What's your point?" I ask.

Everett shrugs. "He's just in a different phase of life. I mean, he has a kid."

"So does Gabe."

"He has a *twelve-year-old*."

"He looks like Pedro Pascal," I say in a breathy voice as I pick up Cooper's salt cellar.

"I don't see what that has to do with anything." I ignore his point, which apparently only adds fuel to his fire. "You want kids," he points out.

I furrow my brow, focusing for a minute on sprinkling the salt onto the chicken. "I don't see what *that* has to do with anything." I'm surprised by the small spark it ignites in me, that Everett is bringing up this point. That he *knows* this about me, an intimate detail I don't readily share with, say, Sandy at SoulCycle or my hairdresser.

"Do you think he's open to having more kids?" he asks. "Do you think that after raising a daughter he wants to have a newborn around the house again?"

"Okay, whoa," I say. "It's not like we're getting married."

"Yet."

"Why do you care?" I ask as the door to the kitchen swings open and Cooper reappears.

"I don't," Everett says. Cooper walks over and retrieves a wine opener from a drawer.

"Can't seem to get the damn corkscrew to do anything," he says, shaking out his hand. Everett's eyes widen behind me, like Cooper is somehow proving an invisible point. I wait until he's left through the swinging door with the wine opener in hand to look at Everett again.

"People get sued for how you're acting right now," I say.

"For what?" he asks.

"*Ageism*," I hiss at him, glancing at the door like Cooper might reappear.

"Okay, I didn't say he was *old*," Everett says. "Just that maybe he's a little older than someone you'd usually date."

"And now you wheel it back," I say as Everett returns to angrily slicing the bread next to me. I let the silence stretch between us for a minute before I ask the obvious thing, the thing that started rattling around inside my brain as soon as he first brought this up. "Why do you care who I'm interested or not interested in dating anyway?"

Everett's slicing slows, almost instinctually, his shoulders hitching the smallest bit. No one else would notice, but I do. I've realized this week that I know Everett's tells better than I thought I ever did, and something about it is disconcerting to me, like there was a key detail about our relationship I missed. Like the arrangement we had revealed more about ourselves to each other than I knew.

He looks over at me, finally, and I think he might say *I don't.* That I'll roll my eyes and we'll be on our way, back to disliking each other in private and pretending to generally get along in front of Laurel. But instead, his expression softens. "I just want you to be happy," he says.

It's simple. Standard, even. Something you say to a friend, or an ex, or the sort-of-ex Everett and I are to each other. But something about it smacks me in the chest, has my breath not coming as easily for a second, and try as I might to scramble for a reason, a logical explanation for how I'm feeling, I can't come up with one. Everett tells me he wants me to be happy, and all rational thought flees my brain.

The door to the kitchen swings open behind us and I look quickly away from Everett.

"Got it!" Cooper exclaims before plonking the wine down on the counter. "This looks great," he says, coming over to us and putting a hand on both of our shoulders, peeking between us. "I can take over here, man," he says to Everett, reaching a hand toward the cutting board.

Everett sets his knife down, stepping quickly away. "Sounds great," he says, in a voice a little rougher than usual. He walks out the door without another look back.

I sit up front on the drive back to the house after dinner, Laurel insisting she hasn't had any back seat time this whole trip. She and Gabe and Davi start up their usual karaoke as soon as the radio turns on. Everett and I are silent the whole time, but I can feel every minute shift in the air as he turns the wheel, as he lifts his eyes to glance in the rearview. As soon as we're back at the villa, I hop out and march toward the steps, determined to get up to my room before anyone can stop me.

But Laurel has other plans.

"I saw Taboo in the cupboard!" she says excitedly, back to her normal self. "Everyone in their pajamas and we'll meet out back in five."

Everett is standing in the foyer, door still closing behind him as the others scamper off toward their rooms like excited, overgrown teenagers. I'm standing at the base of the stairs, one hand on the banister, knocked a little to the side by Davi and Laurel in their enthusiasm.

"Going up?" Everett asks, nodding at me. I follow his gaze

to where I can see the second-floor landing, look back at him, a little dazed. By what, I'm not sure, but something settled in back at Cooper's. *I just want you to be happy.* I shouldn't read into it, I know. Shouldn't think about the way he said it, or how he looked at me as he did. But it was there all through dinner, something that kept dragging my gaze to him, even if he hardly glanced my way, my mind on the almost ragged edge to his voice as he said it. And, further down, on some moment years ago, just the two of us, promises made that neither of us were ever going to be able to keep. Some kind of hope lodged between us that we couldn't hang on to.

"Yep," I finally say, but I don't move.

Everett walks over to me, pausing on the other side of the banister. He puts his hand just above where mine is sitting, his index finger settling against my pinky. Innocuous enough, and yet it sends a spark zapping down my spine, straightening my posture, chest tilting toward his.

"Did you mean what you said?" I ask in the quiet, my own voice low. Everett's brow furrows. "In the kitchen. You want me to be happy."

He steps closer to me, mere inches between us now. "Of course I want that," he says. His next inhale is a little shaky, deeper than the last. "I've always wanted that."

"I want that too," I say. "For you."

I wish I could somehow record every unspoken thing zipping between us right now. All the conversations we should have had and never did, all the things we actually mean. Of course we want each other to be happy, in the same way we want Laurel and Davi and Gabe and most people, generally, to be happy. But it feels so much bigger when Everett says it. I want to ask where he wants that happiness to come from. I want him, I realize in that moment, as his fingers slide just over mine. This. Worst of all, it feels so familiar I worry that it's been with me this whole time. That I never fully stopped wanting it.

It's enough of a shock that I startle back, sucking in a breath. Everett's hand slides off of mine as I do, his gaze dropping for a second before he looks up at me again.

"After you," he says, gesturing to the stairs.

"Thanks," I say, nodding.

It takes me a moment longer than it should to turn away.

eighteen

Third Summer

Davi couldn't come our third summer. He'd tried and failed to get work off, or at least, that's what he'd told us. He'd gotten an entry-level job at his dream firm in New York, and we all knew Davi's main goal in life was to be partner by thirty. This vacation didn't quite seem to fit into that plan.

I didn't blame him, understood things came up, but something about it unsettled me when he confirmed he wouldn't be joining us. The countdown on my calendar was suddenly a reminder not only of the trip, but that we wouldn't be whole this year. Still, there would be Laurel and Gabe and Everett, and those two promised days after the week ended. There were things to look forward to.

Our first morning there, while Laurel and Gabe played gin rummy in the living room, it was just Everett and me in the kitchen. Everett helping me cook had become enough of a routine at that point that it didn't seem odd, but I was still more aware of the proximity of his forearms than ever.

"Excuse me," I said, glancing down at Everett's cutting board. "Where did you learn those knife skills?"

His smile was faint but full, like he was waiting for me to notice. "Someone had to be your actual sous-chef here," he said. I waited until he looked at me, popped a few perfectly brunoised chunks of red pepper into his mouth, grinned with his full force. "I took a cooking class over the winter."

It was kindling added to the always burning ember in my stomach, the one with Everett's name on it. I fought to keep the smile off my face, but it was fruitless. For a moment, it didn't matter that anyone else was around. I would have kissed him then and there, without thinking.

"I hope this means you're subsisting on more than just toast and coffee now," I said.

He nodded, a smile playing at his mouth. "Knowing you has improved my life immeasurably, Sutton."

"Well," I said, eyes still locked on to his. I had to shake my head a little to clear it. "Show me what you learned, then." I nodded toward his cutting board, and we continued on. My burst of affection for him fled without causing any permanent damage.

After sliding the frittata into the oven, I grabbed my phone to see if Davi had time to talk. Something sharp and painful jumped in my chest when I saw the missed call on my screen.

"Everything okay?" Everett asked from where he was washing dishes.

"Hmm?" I glanced in his direction, but didn't quite find his eyes, my gaze quickly drifting back to my phone. "Oh, yeah. I just have to make a call."

I stepped out onto the deck and slid the door closed behind me, heart hammering in my throat.

My mom never called me outside of her scheduled times, and sometimes not even then. Only once before had I gotten something unprompted from her, and it was to tell me in a clipped, five-minute call that my father's father had passed away. I hadn't been close with him, but I was still shocked when she said *anyway, we'll be in touch*, before she hung up with me, like I was one of her clients she was trying to schedule a meeting with, not her daughter trying to wrap her head around the death of a family member.

I called her back, crossing an arm around my middle as the phone rang. She answered at the last minute, her voice the same tight pitch I was so used to.

"This is Heather," she said. It was Monday, already ten o'clock in the morning on the West Coast, so I knew I was catching her during her workday.

"Mom?" I said. "Is everything okay?"

"Sutton?" I swore I could hear her take her phone away from her face, as if to check it was actually me. "Why are you calling me?"

With Hank, it was always *kid* or *bug*, occasionally *sweetheart*. My parents didn't even use pet names with each other.

"You called me," I said. "It's not the fifteenth."

"Oh, you know what?" she said. "I meant to call another Sutton."

"Another Sutton," I repeated. "How many Suttons do you know?"

My mom let out a snort. "You'd be surprised."

Okay. "Well, I'm the daughter one," I said, an uncharacteristically snarky response for me when it came to my mom. I usually kept things light. Didn't, as I told Everett, rehash the already hashed. "Is Dad alright?"

"Of course," she said. "He's on a business trip in Santa Monica."

"I—" I started, breaking off as the door slid quietly open behind me, shut again. I didn't know what to say. My mom didn't know anything about the annual trip to Malibu. And Santa Monica wasn't San Francisco. But it was a hell of a lot closer than New York, and I felt it, a small twist at my core, my younger self flinching at the fact that my father hadn't bothered to tell me he was going to be in my time zone.

"Well, maybe—" I said, not sure what I was going to suggest. That I'd call him. That she and I could talk sooner. I wasn't going to do either of those things, didn't even want to. But still, I wanted something. What I had told Everett was true: This didn't bother me most of the time. I didn't let it. But it was there now, a small hurt in the center of me.

"Listen, Sutton, I have to go," my mom said. "Slammed with meetings today. I'll call you on the fifteenth, okay? And I'll be sure to add in those last names to my phone so we don't have this mix-up again."

"Okay," I said, instead of the obvious, that I hoped she didn't need to add my last name, which was hers, to her phone. "I love—"

The line went dead before I could finish.

I stared at my phone screen for a minute, trying hard to push down the anger, sadness, hurt swirling through me. I jumped when I heard the shift of feet behind me. I'd completely forgotten about the door opening.

I turned around to see Everett standing there, watching me. He didn't ask if I was okay then, didn't ask who it was, like maybe he already knew. I opened my mouth, fighting back a burning in my eyes that I hadn't felt in relation to my mom in years.

I shrugged after a minute, still in some suspended state of disbelief. *Another Sutton.* "I hate parents," I finally said, because I couldn't think of anything else. It felt like something my fourteen-year-old self would say, unable to sum up her emotions. Which, maybe, I was still incapable of.

Everett stepped tentatively toward me but I was already closing the space between us, folding myself against his chest as his arms came around me. I closed my eyes, breathed him in, felt my brain quiet as he held me. I didn't care that we were in full view of the living room. He was all I wanted in that moment, this person who knew, without my having to expound upon the problem, what I was feeling.

After a minute, I looked up at him. He ran a hand over my hair, smiled softly. "Come on," he said. "Breakfast, then farmers market?"

I nodded and would have taken his hand as we walked back inside if we were alone. Instead, I tucked the sound of his heartbeat under my ear away, somewhere deep inside me.

"That's a good lime?" Everett asked, extending the citrus toward me.

"That's a good lime," I affirmed. Laurel and Gabe had left us almost immediately in favor of the coffee shop when we got into town. I was feeling better, the conversation with my mom banished to the furthest recesses of my brain, but I still didn't mind time alone with Everett.

I ran a finger over the lime's rind. "See how it's shiny and smooth, kind of heavy? That means it's juicy."

"Juicy is good," Everett said, smiling at me like we were in on some joke. I laughed even though I wasn't totally clear on what it was.

"Juicy is good."

"Advice for cooking and for life," Everett said as he leaned back over the stand, inspecting the other limes.

"We'll need fifteen-ish," I said, moving down the table toward a pile of oranges.

"Fifteen limes?" Everett asked, incredulous.

"We're making margs, friend," I said. "Margs take a lot of limes. And I need more for guac too."

"You know, for someone who abbreviates so much, you sure call your friends by their full first names."

I wrinkled my brow at him as he added limes to the bag in his hand. "What does that have to do with anything?"

"I'm just saying—*margs, guac, parm, toms, mozz*—you seem to shorten most foods."

"Trick of the trade," I said. "You've got to save time in a kitchen."

"I see," Everett said, joining me by the oranges as I plopped a few into a bag. "But no abbreviations for your friends. Just Laurel, Gabe, Davi."

"Everett," I said.

"Yes?"

"You forgot—" I stopped at the look on his face, cool and amused, and bumped his shoulder with mine. "Okay, smart-ass."

"Good to know, though," he said as we handed the vendor our spoils. He pulled out his wallet and handed the guy cash before I could stop him. "Here I was thinking we weren't friends."

"I mean, we're at least friends-adjacent," I said. For some reason, I found myself blushing. "I don't know. What do you think we are?"

Everett's smile turned playful as we started toward the next stall. "I think you're someone I look forward to seeing every year," he said, mouth dipping close to my ear. "Especially when we have two days to ourselves."

"You know, you almost had me at that first part," I said as I directed him toward another stall. "For a minute, it sounded like we really are just friends."

"I'm sure we can come up with a term for what we are," Everett said.

"Fuck buddies?"

He clapped a hand to his chest with a wounded expression, and I laughed. "Surely we're more than that."

"I mean, a friend you look forward to spending two less-than-innocent days with . . ." I said, shrugging as I grabbed two bags of locally made tortillas. "What else would you call it?"

"That first year was incredibly innocent."

I fixed him with a flat stare that I hoped would remind him of our kiss in the doorway on our last night together, which was, at least to my memory, decidedly *not* innocent and more realistically what set this whole thing in motion.

"Fine," Everett said. He pulled out his wallet to pay but I stopped him again. "But I don't think we're just fuck buddies either."

"Friends with benefits?" I suggested as we headed back toward the entrance to the market.

"I think that's the same thing," Everett said.

"Well, then, sir, I believe we are at an impasse," I said. We'd made it to the sidewalk, the coffee shop in view.

"We'll keep thinking about it," Everett said. "Come up with something uniquely our own. Maybe one of your abbreviations."

"Friends with bennies," I said, prompting a groan out of him. "F buds."

"Okay, let's decide on something that sounds less like a dispensary," Everett said. He grabbed the tote bag I was carrying and added it to the one already over his shoulder as we started down the sidewalk.

"You know, for a fuck buddy, you're certainly a gentleman," I said. If it were just the two of us on this trip, I think he might have slung an arm around my shoulders on his laugh. But because we tended to keep that level of familiarity firmly within our planned forty-eight hours together, save for our hug that morning, his smile wasn't paired with any physical mark of affection, instead just a warming to his gaze as he looked down at me that had me feeling a little like I'd been plunked into a bath, muscles relaxing.

"Summer people," I said suddenly.

"What?"

"Maybe that's what we are," I said. "We're each other's summer people." It made sense. It was something beyond just friends with benefits, which didn't really seem to sum up this weird relationship. I looked forward to spending time with just Everett as much as I did sleeping with him every summer. There was something to our containment that made me feel freer than ever, that made the two days we spent together precious. Our time together was equivalent to a perfect summer day. Clear, sunny, fleeting.

Everett nodded, smiling, and for some reason, I was relieved. "Summer people," he said. "I like that."

nineteen

This Summer

Cooper calls me Thursday morning to ask if I want to grab lunch that afternoon and talk about the cookbook. We're all gathered around the table out back drinking coffee, and Laurel waggles her eyebrows at me, urging me forward as soon as I say "Hi, Cooper!" in an overly cheery falsetto.

"I'd love to get together today," I tell Cooper. Laurel claps her hands together across from me, and despite a conscious effort not to, I glance at Everett sitting next to her. His eyes slip away from mine as soon as I look at him and he takes a long drink of his coffee, expression inscrutable.

Still, I can't shake the half second our gazes locked for the rest of the morning as I sit on the beach with Gabe and look at the pictures he showed Everett on the boat, as I rinse the sand off my feet, as I slip on a green dress that makes me technically a little overdressed for this lunch place and swipe on mascara before heading downstairs to leave for lunch with a man who is very much not Everett. Which is a good thing, I remind myself as I say goodbye to Davi where he's on his computer at the island and grab Laurel's keys from the table in the entryway. Because Everett and I are not something, and we haven't been for a long time.

But it's him I see as soon as I walk out of the villa, shutting the door to his car, surfboard sticking out the back. His hair is still damp, a towel in one hand.

"Good waves?" I ask as I approach him.

"Pretty decent," he says.

"At least you remembered to put a shirt on for the drive back this time," I say. I don't know what it is, this need to say things like that to Everett, small comments delivered in a barbed tone. We agreed to a truce, but after last night, standing so close to him on the stairs, it somehow feels easier to talk to him this way than to be altogether friendly. That would be too close to inviting him back in.

He's in my path when I reach him. When he doesn't move I tilt my head back, squinting up at him. "Where are you going?" he asks, not unkindly, but with enough intention behind it I know he's trying to delay me.

"I'm going to lunch with my future husband, if you don't mind," I say, stepping around him. He turns sideways as I do, letting me go.

"Send my best to Mr. Pascal," he says.

"Oh, I'll let him know *the director* sends his regards," I say over my shoulder.

I expect Everett to respond. Want him to, so I can prove to myself that we're both feeling the same way. We toed some line last night that we need to steer clear of. But he doesn't say anything. When I get into Laurel's car, he's still standing there, watching me as I drive away.

It would make things so much easier if Cooper could be the great love of my life. And maybe that would be possible, if my mind weren't so stuck on the way Everett—who Cooper does want to spend a fair portion of our lunch discussing—

watched me drive away from the house. I can feel the spreading cracks in the dam I've put up when it comes to Everett, pressure mounting behind it the longer the sun bakes down on my shoulders, the more Cooper and I discuss recipe testing and award-winning movies and his daughter.

I'm a terrible date, I'm sure of it. I'm distracted and a little annoyed and by the time we're hugging goodbye in the parking lot, I'm positive any interest Cooper might have had in me has to have waned. But he surprises me, asking if he'll see me at Laurel's divorce party tomorrow, says that he's looking forward to it.

I drive back to the villa in silence, windows down, stewing over a problem that still feels nebulous to me, a storm cloud I can't seem to penetrate.

I drop Laurel's keys on the table in the entryway and kick off my sandals. The house is quiet as I walk into the kitchen and grab a glass from the counter, fill it at the sink.

"How was lunch?"

The rim of the glass clinks against my teeth as I jump nearly out of my skin. I slam the cup down on the counter and turn to where Everett is sitting in one of the armchairs in a corner of the living room, his finger holding his place in the book balanced on his knee.

"What—have you been lying in wait or something?" I ask, heart hammering in my chest.

Everett lets out a sound somewhere between a scoff and a grumble, like his larynx can't make up its mind, and doesn't answer my question.

"Lunch was fine," I say as he stands up from his chair, tosses his book back onto it, and walks over to stand on the opposite side of the island, arms crossed in front of him.

"This man is supposed to be your future husband," he says. "And lunch was *fine*?"

I start walking around the island, not looking at him. "I just said that because I was mad at you."

"That seems to be our main motivator this week," Everett says. The space between the kitchen and the living room is narrower than I realized, and when I meet Everett in the middle of it, he doesn't immediately step aside, just like he didn't at his car earlier. I cross my own arms and lock eyes with him, ready to win whatever face-off he's decided to drop us into.

"Where is everyone?" I ask.

"They went into town," he says.

"Why?" I ask.

"*Lunch*," he says, and I've never heard such a mundane word quite so charged. Everett makes lunch sound like a slap in the face and an innuendo all at once.

"You didn't want to go?"

"I had some reading to catch up on."

I glance at the chair. "Right. Movie research couldn't wait."

"Why was lunch just 'fine'?" Everett asks.

It catches me off guard. I want to have some perfect comeback, but the one that shoots to the forefront of my mind, like a lightning bolt launched out of that storm cloud and aimed directly at my psyche, is inconveniently *I wasn't with you*. That, more than his question, stymies me. It's so far from what I've been thinking about Everett this week that I almost wonder if my mental health has taken a sudden hard left and I'll just have to live with intrusive thoughts forever now.

But it's not out of nowhere, I know, deep down. The place Cooper took us to was a restaurant that had moved into a spot where Everett and I grabbed dinner once, during our third summer here, and the entire time all I could think about was him across from me on that deck, looking like he was made for this environment with his sun-golden hair and well-loved

T-shirt, the endless stretch of the ocean behind him. When Cooper excused himself to run to the restroom, I tried fruitlessly to tamp down what had happened after that dinner, but it kept coming back to me with every wave that crashed on the sand. Hands clasped as we walked back to his car and later on the way into the house, sheets pulled over us and drying sweat and some twinge in my chest that I hadn't felt before.

I shrug one shoulder. "Cooper's great," I say. "But he might just not be the guy for me. No big deal."

I try to step around Everett, but he catches my hand and pulls me back to face him. I look down at where he's touching me, our first real contact this week, save for the way he tried to comfort me on the boat. "Then why was it such a big deal for us?" he asks. When I don't answer, too frozen to think of what to say, he continues. "Why can't we move on from what happened?"

I'm still silent, all the things I want to say to him trapped at the back of my throat. There must still be some lingering irritation on my face because Everett drops his hand from mine and tugs it through his hair.

"Come on, Sutton," he says. "Why are you *so* mad at me?"

"You're mad at me too," I point out, deflecting.

"I wasn't," Everett says with a shake of his head. "Until I showed up and you were clearly still just as angry with me as you were five years ago."

"It was a big deal to me," I say, unintentionally reinforcing his earlier point, that whatever this is—or was—between us matters.

"It was a big deal to me too," Everett says. "But I thought we'd at least be able to talk about it by now. I thought we could at least be civil this week."

"We *are* being civil."

"We're *pretending* to be civil."

"Same difference."

"Sutton," Everett says, looking almost desperate to fix this. "I'm sorry for my part in things, but we've had five years to try to move on. So why, again, are you *this* mad at me?"

"Because it ruined everything!" I burst out. Everett's brow draws together. "Because our lie broke apart the most important group of people in my life."

When he answers me, his voice is soft. "We all grew up. We got busy."

"But we were the nail in the coffin," I say. "We never came back here after that argument."

"No one *could* come back here," he says. He takes a cautious step closer to me. "Come on, you know that. We floated the idea for two summers after what happened. Everyone had something else going on. Is that really the only thing you're mad about?"

I think that maybe he's right, even if I'm not totally convinced. We did try to make the trip work again, but it had been nearly impossible to get everyone here that last summer. People had been falling off for years, and I hadn't wanted to admit that it meant anything. That we couldn't hang on to what we'd once had. Our lives were expanding in ways I looked forward to in college, but couldn't have predicted the consequences of. Jobs and marriage and homes and successes beyond our wildest dreams also led to settling down, getting used to places, moving to new locations that were better for work, establishing ourselves in them. And it shouldn't have been an insane ask, one week with the people I'd once thought of as my family, but maybe it was. Maybe all our effort was never going to be enough, in the end.

I look up at Everett, something hard lodged in my throat that makes it a little difficult to talk. "I trusted you," I say. "And we let each other down."

I can see how it hits him, and a not-small part of me wants to take it back.

"I'm sorry," he says, and I can tell he's going to say more, but I jump in before he can.

"I don't want you to be sorry," I say, which is the truth at the center of all of this, the thing I won't admit. That it has far less to do with everyone else than I'll ever let myself acknowledge. "I want it not to have happened."

Everett stills at this. I didn't realize how much the distance between us has shrunk. We're standing closer than I think we've intentionally been this whole trip, and I can feel it in all of me. The heat radiating from his skin, the way the air starts to spark and pop between us. It crawls from the soles of my feet and trickles down from the top of my head, meeting in the middle, drawing me even closer to him.

Everett's hand finding my waist hitches my breath, makes my head go a little woozy. I try to steady myself, to not get lost in this. In him. It's always been so easy to.

"All of it?" he asks. "You wish none of it had happened?"

I shake my head, pulse jumping as he bends closer to me, two magnets pulled ceaselessly together. "Not all of it," I say. I know what's about to happen. Could—*should*—stop it right here. But I don't want to. "Just the last part."

Everett's lips against mine are a revelation, every good thing my anger let me forget about in the last four years. I remember the taste of him so well that some sleeper agent part of my brain whirs to life like it's a trigger phrase. He hooks his arm around my waist and pulls me into him, his other hand wrapping into my hair, and I remember all of it so well, how it's always felt a little like we were made for this. How I don't respond to anyone the way I do to Everett.

He turns us so we're against the counter, lifts me deftly onto it and steps between my parted legs. My fingers are clawing into his shirt, his hair, some cocktail of every emotion I've ever felt toward Everett spilling out of me. I want him aggressively, have been starved of this and haven't even let myself entertain the thought of having it again. I tilt my hips closer to the edge of the counter and feel his length press against me, bask in the rough, breathless sound that comes out of him.

"Lunch was only fine because it wasn't with you," I say, crazily, when he moves his lips to my neck, my collarbone, my hands in his hair. "I want someone like you." Having Everett this close to me again has me confessing things.

"There's no one like you, Sutton," he says. Which is a much better confession than my clunky one, and at it I'm pulling him back up, kissing him again, chasing that same taste, feel, the friction between our bodies.

Everett urges me toward him with a hand on the small of my back, my dress hiking up around my thighs, and I think I'd let him lie me down right here if it weren't for the beep at the front door, the lock whirring.

There isn't any time to do more than jerk away from each other. Everett walks over to the fridge and opens it, pretending to inspect the contents as I slide off the counter and race back to my water glass, filling it at the sink again and trying to keep the rise and fall of my breath out of my shoulders.

"Hey," Laurel says, dropping her bag onto the island loudly enough that we both turn to her. Everett looks a little dazed, just how I feel. "Better get ready. We're going out tonight."

"We are?" I ask, rifling mentally through the plan for the

week as my pulse pounds in my throat. "I thought we were laying low tonight."

"We were," Laurel says, something mischievous sparking in her eyes. "But I found an outdoor movie night. Sounds more fun than hanging here."

"Great," I say. I'm convinced she knows, that my voice comes out two pitches higher than usual. "What movie?"

Laurel's focus narrows on Everett, a rabbit in a wolf's path as she grins. "*Cooney.*"

twenty

Third Summer

Friday night, we headed to a new bar in town that Laurel had heard about from some of her social media friends. It was a detour from our traditions, but it was good, she said, not to get too stuck in a rut. The place struck a bewildering balance between an early aughts all-ages music venue and a maritime-themed bar: all-black floors and furniture, the hint of a possible blacklight in the corners, anchors and fishing nets adorning the bar, a carved wooden captain statue at the door.

An hour in, it was clear something was going on with Gabe.

We were sitting in a booth, Laurel and I on one side. She'd been responding to comments on her phone for the better part of the hour, while Gabe nursed what, on the menu, was called a "Siren's Call," a bright red drink that came in a beer stein and was served with a skewer of tropical fruit.

"Hey," I said after he morosely sucked on another pineapple wedge. "What's up?"

Gabe finished the pineapple before dropping his face into his palms. His already broad shoulders expanded on a sigh. I glanced at Everett, who looked as confused as I did.

"Hey," Everett said, patting a hand on Gabe's back. "It looks like there's a nautical pinball machine in the back. You want to give it a go?"

"No," Gabe said. Then, out of nowhere, "I miss Zoey." His voice was muffled from where he still had his head in his hands. We all exchanged a glance as he lifted it. "Did I just say that out loud?"

"You did, pal," Everett said.

Gabe groaned, rubbing his palms down his face. "I don't mean that," he said.

"It's okay if you do," Laurel said.

"I don't," Gabe insisted. "I don't miss *her,* I just miss . . . I miss heading toward something. I wanted to get married. I wanted to have kids. I wanted a house and vacations and music lessons and soccer games and the whole stupid thing."

"You'll have that," I said, reaching across the table to pat his hand. He gave me a grim, disbelieving smile.

"Okay, I have an idea," Everett said. We all looked at him. "Gabe, we're going to help you meet someone."

"Meet someone?" Gabe said, like it was a foreign concept. "Where?"

"Here," Everett said, gesturing to the bar at large.

"I don't live here."

"That doesn't matter," Everett said. "You don't have to meet your wife tonight, but you do need to get back on that horse if you're ever going to find her."

"I've been on the horse," Gabe said glumly. Everett raised an eyebrow at him. "I haven't been on the horse."

"I think it's a great idea," Laurel said, already scanning the crowd like she was searching out potential prospects.

"Me too," I said. "We'll all help."

"But I don't know how to just talk to someone," Gabe said. "I'm all or nothing. I'm a relationship guy."

"Well, then, good thing you have these two here to help you," Laurel said, gesturing at me and Everett. "Last I checked, they're both experts at no strings."

Everett and I exchanged a quick, panicked glance, but Gabe's puppy-eyed expression told me we weren't caught.

"Gabe," I said, ignoring the small sting Laurel's comment left behind. "Everett and I will guide you through finding someone for *tonight* rather than forever. Okay?"

"Okay," Gabe said, sitting up, an eager student.

"I'm going to scout out the bachelorette party over there," Laurel said, picking up her drink and nodding toward the far side of the bar.

Everett moved from his side of the booth to mine so we were both facing Gabe, who still looked glum. His arm brushed against mine, and I had to fight the urge to lean against him, let his warmth seep into me. I stayed still.

"Okay," I said. "Gabe. What would you say to a girl you just met?"

"This is stupid," Gabe said. Then, quickly, "Come here often?"

"You wouldn't say that," Everett said.

"Why not?"

"Because you're not looking for a *pickup* line," I said. "More of an opening line."

"What's the difference?" Gabe asked, leaning forward. He kind of looked as if he'd like to take notes.

"One runs the risk of you looking like a sleaze," I said. "The other one is just human. You're just talking to another person."

"Hmm," Gabe mused, before looking at Everett. "What would your opening line be?"

Everett squinted a little, rubbing at the back of his neck. "Contrary to Laurel's belief, I'm not actually picking up women all that often."

"Sutton just said it's not a pickup," Gabe pointed out.

"Okay, I'm not meeting women in bars all that often."

"But you're the one who said I should do this," Gabe said. "This was all your idea!"

"You're right," Everett said. "I'm sorry."

"Where *are* you meeting women, then?" Gabe asked.

Everett shifted a little. I could feel him glance down at me, so I looked up at him, face curious as Gabe's. If we were going to give him advice, we couldn't worry about hurting each other's feelings by talking about the other people we saw during the year. Besides, in our arrangement, that didn't matter. We were nowhere near exclusive.

"Through friends," Everett said, turning back to Gabe. "At work, events and stuff."

"Parties," I added, smirking when Everett's elbow dug into my side.

"But that's not the point," Everett said. "Where do you meet anyone? We're at a bar right now, which I've heard is a great place to meet people."

Gabe glanced around morosely. "I met Zoey in a history seminar."

I nudged Everett. "Didn't Gabe ask what your opening line would be?" I asked. Everett narrowed his eyes my direction.

"You could just say hi," Everett said.

"Hi," Gabe repeated.

"I've heard it works," I said.

"I need hypotheticals," Gabe said. "Give me a scenario."

"Maybe you say you're a fan of the beer she's drinking," I said, nodding toward a woman at the bar who had been nursing the same craft, tastes-like-a-pine-tree IPA since we arrived.

"Okay," Gabe said, nodding.

"You love her jukebox choice," Everett said, as Talking Heads came over the speakers and a chorus of cheers erupted in one corner.

"I could do that," Gabe said. "And then what?"

"Then you . . . talk," I said. "Hopefully she'll respond."

"Don't bring up wanting kids or a house," Everett said quickly. "You're just practicing talking to someone."

"Right," Gabe said, nodding. "Just talking." He looked at Everett. "About what?"

I sat back in the booth as Everett coached Gabe through talking points and the natural flow of conversation, like Gabe didn't already talk to people all day, every day. But his nervousness was endearing, a trait of Gabe's I'd always loved.

Laurel came sailing back through the crowd, her drink held high above her head until she reached the table. "There are at least *seven* single women over there who would be thrilled to meet someone like you tonight, Gabe," she said once she reached us. She looked at me and Everett. "Did you prep him?"

"He's ready for surgery," I said, nodding at him.

"I think I might throw up," Gabe said.

"All part of it, pal," Everett said, grinning at him.

"I'm going to post myself at the bar," Laurel said. "So if anything goes awry you can tug your ear and I'll intervene." She held her hand out to Gabe. "Up, up, up."

Gabe gave us one last nervous glance before he took her hand and let her lead him through the crowd.

We watched as Laurel pushed him toward a blond woman. Even from our spot, we could easily make out Gabe's crimson cheeks.

"He'll do fine," Everett said. He had one arm thrown across the back of the booth, eliminating any barrier between us.

"You don't *really* feel like you're going to throw up when you talk to a girl, do you?" I asked him. He looked away from where Gabe was anxiously smiling his way through the interaction to me. His mouth curved, eyes warming.

"You make me pretty nervous sometimes, Hale," he said. The words rooted into my stomach with all the others, fluttering around. Pleasant. But that wasn't the right word. Things were more than pleasant with Everett. I couldn't think of anything better then, though. It was like floating in the water on a warm day, something bobbing gently in me.

"I'm not supposed to make you nervous," I said. "I'm your pit stop before the real thing, remember?"

Everett's gaze roved over my face, his expression going serious. For a minute, I worried the joke had gone too far, that I'd poked the same thing in him that Laurel's comment had scraped against in me earlier, this idea that neither of us were interested in a real relationship, something I didn't think was true.

"I wouldn't call you a pit stop," he said, voice low. "Didn't we decide we're summer people?"

"Right," I said. "Summer people."

For a brief, breathless moment, Everett's gray-blue eyes flashing as he looked at me, I wished the week were over. I wished it was the two days we'd promised each other, however foolishly. I wished that everyone else didn't care so much about the stupid fucking pact, and that I could kiss the half-smug smile that showed up on his face the longer we watched each other, the longer the silence stretched. That maybe it wasn't just two days ahead of us.

But, rule aside, he was right. We were summer people, Everett and me. If the rest of us were year-round, constant, then the two of us only came around once a year. And there was something exciting in that, in a way. In the anticipation of it. In knowing there was nothing permanent here that could go away. We couldn't disappoint each other if the only expectation was showing up. Romantic as a life outside of this time with Everett might seem, it was impossible; or so I kept reminding myself.

My phone buzzed on the table, and I looked down to see Laurel calling me. We both whipped our heads to where she was sitting. She was pointing toward the group, smile huge, directing our attention to where Gabe was fully making out with the blond girl.

"That was fast," Everett said.

"He never needed our help," I said. "Let's just hope he doesn't fall in love with her."

Everett laughed, but Gabe would bring the girl back over to our table a little while later and introduce her to us. She was a pediatrician, visiting from Denver for her friend's bachelorette party. Her name was Mia.

twenty-one

This Summer

It's a marvel we get Everett in the car at all.

"No," he said at first, adamantly, after Laurel announced her plan. He headed immediately in the direction of the stairs, like he might lock himself in his room.

"Oh, come on," Laurel had said, dancing after him. "Don't be one of those *artistes* who can't bear to look at their own work."

"Laurel," Everett said, turning to face her. "I don't watch anything I've made after the final cut is done. I leave my own premieres."

"I know," Laurel said. "They reported on it in *People*."

Everett rolled his eyes sky-high, turning to go again, but I was the one who called out to him, making him stop and turn once more.

"We've never been able to see one of your movies all together," I said, hip against the island he'd just had me on top of. His eyes met mine, chilly steel gray, but almost interested. Not in watching his own movie, I knew, but maybe in why I'd said anything. I wasn't quite sure myself, other than the fact that I still had the taste of him on my lips and didn't want to watch him walk away.

He'd looked back down at Laurel, sighing through his nose. "Fine," he said. "I'll come. But that doesn't mean I'm paying attention."

Laurel squealed, clapping her hands together. "Perfect!" she said, spinning around. "We're going to need to pack wine, and blankets . . ." She threw tasks to each of us as Everett's eyes locked on to mine once more across the room, the air still sparking between us.

At the park, we set up camp on the wide lawn that slopes down toward the giant screen, spreading blankets around and Davi flopping into the low-sitting chair he brought, stretching his legs out in front of him and pouring his first glass of wine as we settle in to wait for sunset. It's more of an event than Laurel let on, apparently. There was a banner we walked in under that read *Malibu Movie Series: Cooney!*, and two massive posters on either side of the ticket table that made Everett's cheeks flame red as he ducked behind me.

Food trucks are set up around the perimeter, what looks like a small kids' carnival set up to one side, likely an homage to the massive carnival sequence in the movie, when the teenage heroes take on the mysterious threat that's invaded their town. This is more of a ring toss, a carousel, and a lone cotton candy cart, but the effect is charming.

I'm next to Everett at one end of our blanket setup, but if I'd thought there would be any covert glances tonight, hands brushing in the dark after what happened in the kitchen, apparently, I was very wrong.

Everett is sitting with his forearms resting on his knees, the hood of a dark blue sweatshirt pulled up over his head. I examine him as his eyes dart around the crowd, teeth working at his lower lip.

"I don't think anyone's going to *recognize* you," I say, more out of any remaining glimmers of irritation I'm feeling toward him than any truth in that statement. *Cooney* is something of a phenomenon, and an event like this would undoubtedly draw some superfans.

Nevertheless, Everett's eyes flick toward mine, a frown curving his mouth as he yanks off his hood. "I'm not that vain," he grumbles, low enough so only I can hear. At that moment a group of women walk by, one of them pausing to do a double take at Everett. Though I think it has less to do with her recognizing him and more to do with his rumpled hair, the sharp jaw underneath his short beard. Every other thing that's drawn me into Everett Bridges over the years. I watch her as she passes.

"People love *Cooney*," I say, turning my attention back to him once they've gone. "It won awards." I don't know what I'm trying to do, exactly. Maybe coax Everett into relaxing a little. I reach into the bag of potato chips in my lap, staring down into it as I say quietly, "It's a great movie."

I can feel Everett's attention land on me, but I don't look at him, focusing on picking out the largest chip I can.

"You saw it?" he finally asks.

I feign exasperation, crunching down on the chip as I nod, but I meant what I said. *Cooney* is a great movie, and it infuriated me when I snuck into a matinee of it like I was trying not to be seen, my own hood up and a box of Sour Patch Kids in my pocket.

It had been out for a few months at that point, but I'd avoided it as best I could. It was bad enough to have to see the poster for it on my commute to work, or hear about it from everyone I knew. *Have you seen that new sci-fi movie yet? Not even sci-fi, it's, like, a love letter to all those eighties movies we used to love*, Hayes, front of house at my uncle's restaurant, had said when it first came out, his words lifted directly from all the pull-quotes they'd used for publicity. *The next* E.T., *filling the* Stranger Things *void, a tapestry of nostalgia, growing up, and the sci-fi we used to love.* I heard it everywhere. On social media, the radio, in snippets on the street. Try as I might, *Cooney*, and reminders of Everett with it, was unavoidable.

The irritation in me flickered and then started to fade as I watched it, though, steadily marching through my candy until my hand hit the bottom of the bag only halfway in. I'd been that absorbed, and the sugary cellophane against my fingertips was enough to yank me out of it for a second, to remember to watch the movie with Everett in mind.

And I did. For the second half, I watched it searching for reasons to be angry, like he might have left a piece of us somewhere in there. He had writing credits on the movie too, had been working on the concept with a buddy of his for years, I knew, even if he'd been secretive about it then. We hadn't talked much about his work, I realized as I sat in that theater, as I watched the two leads fall in love while they unraveled the mystery of what was plaguing their small town.

But I could see him all over it, in ways I didn't expect. *We* were in it somehow, all of us, in the friend group that formed. They were all on the brink of the next phase of their lives, this one last hurdle to cross before they could grow up. And logically I knew that was the point, that the message here wasn't specifically for me, but for everyone who'd ever felt something like that. Even so, by the time the credits rolled, my cheeks were wet, and I sat through to the bitter end and then a minute longer, until a kid the age of the characters in the movie came in to sweep up.

It was the only time I'd let myself cry about Everett Bridges since things had fallen apart between us. And it had been his shining, brilliant, award-winning movie that had done it. I hated him for it.

So it's a little hard for me to admit it's a great movie to him now. Not because I don't mean it, but because of what it meant to me. Something outside of what it meant to the millions of other people who saw and loved it.

Everett is still watching me when a kid in what looks like a homemade Cooney High School sweatshirt comes bounding up to us, cheeks ruddy. His mom is with him, beaming down at us. Laurel, Gabe, and Davi crane their heads to watch as the kid holds the hem of his sweatshirt out toward Everett, wordless.

"We love your movie," the mom says, not even bothering to ask if he is, in fact, Everett Bridges and not some doppelganger here to enjoy some popcorn and a little sci-fi horror. "Would you sign Kit's sweatshirt?" She produces a Sharpie, extending it toward Everett.

It shouldn't surprise me that Everett just smiles and takes the marker from her, signing a quick signature on the light blue fabric. He's the picture of cool as the kid watches with shining eyes. He'll tell everyone about this, I think.

"Nice to meet you, Kit," Everett says as he caps the marker and hands it back to the mom. "Enjoy the movie."

As soon as they're gone, and Laurel, Gabe, and Davi erupt into *oohs* on my other side, Everett retreats back into himself. If he still had his hood up, I swear he'd be drawing his head into it like a turtle.

"Shut up," he says to our friends. Laurel pelts him with a peach ring, Davi cooing his name loudly enough for nearby moviegoers to hear while Gabe claps. I reach for the open bottle of wine, pouring heavily into one of the mishmash of cups we tucked into bags and handing it to Everett.

Because I get it, I think. It's not that he isn't proud of his work, or that he hates signing middle schoolers' sweatshirts. He isn't vain enough to think everyone here is going to recognize him, or care if anyone does. But there's something so personal in it that it's like we've all sat down to watch a naked Everett on an operating table for the next two hours, ogling something he's powerless to hide. Everett can be the charming guy, self-deprecating enough that he's not an asshole. But he's never totally had to be that with us. This trip, this place was once a sanctuary. And even if coming to see his movie isn't the reason it's not, even if some of the magic faded from this place a long time ago, tonight makes him feel like he isn't safe. Like we're examining him somehow, the same as everyone who has watched *Cooney* and made some assumption about the people who created it.

"Thanks," he says with a grateful grimace as I hand him the wine, filled to the top. I nod, pour my own glass, and settle in as the screen flickers to life in front of us, ads and announcements starting to roll as the sun dips beneath the horizon.

I startle a little when Everett's arm brushes against mine, looking over in time to see him glance away from me and back at the screen, where an ad for a local credit union is scrolling past.

I look down at where our arms touch, the blue of his sweatshirt against my denim jacket. And I shift, the same way he did, just close enough to mean something, pressing back.

An hour in, Everett is miserable.

I glance away from where the two leads are breaking into the abandoned medical facility and look over at Everett, who's watching the screen like it's a car crash happening in front of him, vehicles piling up, maybe an explosion or two.

"I'm going to check out the food trucks," I say, loudly enough for the others to hear. Everett jerks his gaze to me. "Anyone want anything?"

"Fries," Laurel says without looking at me.

"More fries," Davi echoes. Gabe holds up a hand on the other side of him to add a third order.

"Great." I slap my hands on the ground behind me, look at Everett. "Can you help me?"

He's already standing up.

We wind through the crowd toward the arc of food trucks arranged around the lawn, Everett's shoulders visibly relaxing the farther we get from the screen. Though, when there's a particularly loud crash as the love interest knocks into a rack of rusty medical instruments, they shoot back up to his ears.

"You really hate this, don't you?" I ask as we get in the short line for a burger truck, its side boasting an illustration of smiling French fries in a red plastic basket.

Everett glances down at me, appearing to weigh his words before he finally gives in and shrugs. "Yeah," he says. "I hate it."

"I should keep it in mind for the cookbook," I say. "That I'll hate it someday."

"I don't hate *Cooney*," Everett clarifies as we move forward a spot. "I love the version of it in my head."

"Ah," I say, tugging my jacket a little tighter around me. It's not cold out, but something about being with Everett like this, talking normally, has a shiver running through me. That, or the memory of earlier, his hands scraping up my thighs, like some dream I had. "So it didn't turn out how you wanted it to."

"It's not even that," he says, shaking his head a little as he thinks. "I don't know how to explain it. It's like I thought things would go one way and they didn't. And the way they did go is fine, great even, in a lot of ways, but . . . I keep wondering about the other possibilities. I can't seem to let go of them . . . If that makes sense."

I stare up at him, quiet for a minute. Because it does make perfect sense to me, but not in the context of his movie. And as Everett looks at me a beat too long, I wonder if he feels like we're not just talking about *Cooney* anymore either.

"Next!" We both yank our gazes away from each other to the woman hanging out of the window of the food truck, looking a little exasperated, like it's not the first time she's tried to get our attention.

"Sorry," I say, quickly stepping forward and trying to leave the buzzy feeling in me behind.

The woman tells us they're running a few minutes behind after we place our order, so we wander over to the small carnival area while we wait. All the better to distract Everett.

It's quiet over here, most everyone watching the movie or getting food while watching the screen over their shoulder now. A group of teenagers are on the rickety, carted-in carousel at one end, laughing and shouting to each other while a set of grandparents and their grandkids stand at the Whac-A-Mole game, losing spectacularly.

Everett and I wander in silence for a while, but there's not much to explore. After two laps I nod toward the ring toss. The bored-looking attendant takes our money and quickly returns to his phone.

"Green or red?" I ask Everett, holding up the stack of rings that look like they've seen better days. Everett takes the green from me and I nod toward the milk bottles we're meant to land the rings on. He misses his first shot.

"Better luck next time," I say, as I throw and miss too.

Everett grins at me as he throws the next one, narrowly making it around the neck of one of the bottles.

"I swear I used to be better at things like this," I say as my next one bounces off and lands in the grass.

"Yeah? When?" Everett asks. "Was ring toss big on the San Francisco sports circuit when you were growing up?"

"You have no idea," I say. I toss one and it lands on top of Everett's green ring.

"Hustler," Everett mutters sarcastically, shaking his head. "Here to take me for all I'm worth."

"Didn't realize we were betting on this game," I say as he picks up his next ring, misses again. "What's on the table?"

Everett thinks for a minute as I throw and land a red ring. When I turn to look up at him, smiling, something in his expression has heat rising up my neck, into my cheeks.

"Lunch with me," he says, chin tilting forward as if in invitation. "Not Cooper."

I'm grateful that the carnival lights are already casting everything in shades of reds and oranges, or Everett would see how flushed my face is at this, as if he just offered up strip poker as a bargaining chip instead of a meal together.

"I already told you," I say, fingers curling around my final ring. "I'm not having lunch with Cooper again."

Everett's eyes are locked on to mine, holding me there. "You never told me that," he says softly.

I swallow, try to keep my shoulders steady as my breathing hitches. It takes everything in me to tear my gaze away from his, toss the ring in a lackluster movement toward the bottles. I don't really want to win this bet.

But the ring flies in a perfect arc right toward the milk bottle in the middle and lands cleanly, no spin at all.

"Winner," the attendant says flatly. He rummages around

in a plastic storage bin behind him, eyes on his phone screen as he finally produces a rolled-up T-shirt and extends it in my direction. I have to lean over the booth to grab it from him.

We fall into step next to each other as we head away from the game, the T-shirt tucked under my arm. When I risk a glance up at Everett, he's already looking at me.

"What?" I say, a breathy, nervous sort of laugh shaking out of me. When he doesn't say anything, just opens his mouth and closes it like he's reconsidered, I face forward again and try to appear nonchalant. "We could still grab lunch sometime," I say.

"Right," Everett says. "Meet somewhere between LA and San Francisco?"

I shrug a shoulder that feels about as casual as a marriage license. "Stranger things have happened."

"Stranger than us happening again?"

I look sharply over at him, breath catching in my throat. But he's staring straight ahead, at the spinning colors of the carousel. I follow his gaze toward the winking lights. Something about it feels like a memory, sharp edges sanded down by time.

I worry sometimes that there isn't enough proof of us to call the time we spent together real. We were only ever seen by people when we were falling apart. Everything else comes in shimmering flashes and washed-out hazes, lens flares in corners blocking things out or letting memories mix together. I can't call up Laurel or Hank and say *remember when*, because we're the only two who do, truly, remember. We are a carousel of moments that fell apart as soon as we tried to show anyone else.

I look up at Everett, something steeling in my chest. "I didn't know we were even a possibility anymore," I say, instead of the thousand other smarter things I could say right now. Things like, *We should talk about what happened*, or *Up until two days ago we were locked in a who-hates-the-other-more competition.* The answer to this question seems more important.

"I don't know if I'm the one who needs to decide that," he says. I glance down at my feet, the grass beneath them, because I don't know what to say. There are too many things to sort through here, and half of me thinks it might be less complicated to just let it lie. But then I think about Everett's lips on mine in the kitchen, his expression at the bottom of the stairs after dinner at Cooper's, the way he touched my face in the cabin on the sailboat. How my heart reacted every time: a jump before it settled into some sure, steady rhythm, like I was exactly where I needed to be.

"Cooper and I went to that place on the beach that we found our third summer here," I say finally, unsure why it's the response I go with. "Do you remember?" *Please remember,* I think.

Everett looks fully at me, eyes the color of stormy gray waves, rough and intense. "I remember everything, Sutton," he says. "I think all of my best days have been with you."

It catches my breath, has me moving closer to him, startling as my chest brushes his and his hand grips my waist. I want to be able to say things like that to him. Want to be the one who opens the door to the possibility of this, but there's still some part of my brain that snags on our history. On Laurel and Davi and Gabe, and how fragile our whole group is, how the two of us going anywhere near this again would inevitably destroy that.

But I still find my head tipping back, face tilting up toward Everett's. My eyes are still closing when we press together, a breath apart. My phone buzzes in the pocket of my jacket, loud and jarring. I take a step back, blinking as I pull it out. "Food's ready," I say, holding my screen up like proof.

Everett doesn't press or try to keep us here any longer. Instead, he nods us back in the direction of the trucks, and something about it reminds me of the way he was with the kid who asked for his autograph earlier, or who he was at a college party a decade ago. That was always one of the confusing parts about us. We could go from what felt like huge moments to casual in seconds. It was also what made it exciting.

But that was then. Now, it doesn't feel quite as fun. It feels like we were just standing on the precipice of something and were yanked violently back from the edge, sprawling on the ground. I can't fully get my bearings.

"Hey," Everett says as we near the food trucks. "What's your prize?"

It's only now that I remember the T-shirt under my arm. I unroll it, a small smile eking onto my face before I turn it toward Everett, who groans.

"You can't keep that," he says, running a hand down his face.

"Oh, this is going to be a collector's item someday," I say. I'm glad for the distraction, feel the quick relief of our back-and-forth settling over me as I twist the shirt to look at it again. The original artwork for *Cooney* is on the front, large and undeniable. "I'm going to sleep in this every night. Can you sign it for me, Director?"

"Nope," Everett says. He swings an arm around my shoulders and plucks the shirt out of my hands, tucking it under his opposite arm. Easy. Casual. No *I think all of my best days have been with you* in sight. We could be two friends or a couple in love to any outsider as I lean around him, try to grab at the shirt he stole. "We'll get you something better to sleep in."

I lean into his side as we near the food trucks, letting myself, for just this moment, feel like I used to with him. Enjoy it. Whatever that means.

twenty-two

Fourth Summer

We slid into our fourth summer after a marathon of planning: tweaking dates so we could overlap as much as possible, moving things around again when new plans came up, cutting things short and extending them again and trying out every possible variety because we'd all just gotten so busy over the last year. And still, after everything, Gabe wouldn't be there.

I have to take two weeks off for the wedding in August, he'd said the last time I'd talked to him about it. *I'm using up enough vacation time as it is. I just can't swing it this year.*

I understand, I'd told him. Because logically, I did. Not everyone had the luxury of setting their own schedules, and we'd all see each other for a few days surrounding the wedding anyway. But the other part of me, the part that railed against any kind of change, the wholly unreasonable part, wanted to tell him to quit his job and make the trek to California so we could all be together. *We promised each other this one week*, I wanted to say. *How big of an ask is one week a year?*

On top of us being down one person again, this summer wouldn't be the same for another reason. There wouldn't be two extra days at the end of the week, because Everett, surprise of all surprises, had a girlfriend.

"What's it like dating the most beautiful woman in the UK?" Laurel asked after we'd all arrived and settled into the living room of the cottage. Davi was grabbing water in the kitchen, and Everett and I sat at either end of the couch, like holding space between us was important.

Laurel leaned across the coffee table, holding up her phone to Everett as if he needed a reminder of who his girlfriend was. On her screen was a picture of him with Maud Turner at the red-carpet premiere of her last film, looking as much like a Hollywood couple as they did at Cannes for the showing of his most recent project the month prior. Everett in an expensive black suit, Maud in something bespoke and fashion forward.

They'd even been papped a couple times, coming out of Osteria Mozza or sitting outside Stir Crazy. It was those that bothered me the most, for some reason. Not that any of them should bother me. But I would zoom in on Everett's face whenever Laurel sent me the photos, eyes hidden behind a pair of sunglasses, like I could find clues there about whether or not he was happy. On the red carpet he was a presence, charming, laughing, and chatting. Everett at a party. But in these pictures some of that fell away, and so I studied them for signs they were real. If he loved her, if they did things like cooking together or surfing or if he turned on Ina Garten on Saturday mornings while they sipped coffee and woke up slowly. Probably. Probably those things weren't just ours. And it was silly of me to think so.

"You're just returning to us from France, aren't you?" Laurel asked, when Everett just waved off her first question. "Fancy man." And he did look fancy, tanned in a way that suggested yacht decks rather than mornings on his surfboard, his shirt so soft against my skin when I hugged him that I had to double-check it was, in fact, just a T-shirt.

The movie Everett had worked on two summers ago—*Just an indie*, he'd called it, *nothing special*—had been making its rounds at film festivals to much aplomb, garnering award buzz and landing him his next jobs and, maybe most importantly, budgets. While he was no household name, he was becoming increasingly well-known in the film community. And his relationship with a certain gorgeous, up-and-coming actress didn't hurt his growing reputation either.

"You're just getting back from a month in Bali, aren't you?" Everett asked Laurel, deflecting her question.

"I am," she said. "The wellness retreat was a success."

"Remind me," Davi said, as he flopped onto the couch next to me and it made a disagreeable sound. "If we have a wildly successful influencer and the next Spielberg in the room with us, why are we still staying in this shithole?"

"Take that back," Laurel scolded him. "This place is not a shithole."

Davi looked around skeptically at the tiny room, but didn't say anything else.

It had come up, briefly, when we booked the cottage this year. A discussion of whether we should upgrade to something a little more comfortable, but Laurel had dismissed it, saying the whole point of the trip was staying here, specifically.

"Is Winona still coming down for a couple days?" Everett asked Laurel.

Her face clouded at the mention of her girlfriend of a year. Everett and I exchanged a quick glance, the first we'd shared since he arrived. "I don't think so," Laurel said, voice going a little far-off. Her expression matched, gaze drifting out the door. She would have made a great close-up in one of Everett's movies.

"Everything okay?" I asked her, but she just gave me a wan smile.

"Fine," she said. It was a small sting, unintentional, but there nonetheless. Laurel wasn't telling me something, and as far as I knew, we told each other everything. But, I reminded myself, she would tell me when she was ready.

I stood up, brushing my hands on my shorts. "Should we head to the beach?" I asked.

Laurel brightened at this. "I'll grab the wine!"

Davi followed Laurel into the kitchen while I scooped beach towels out of the basket by the back door. When I straightened, I smacked into half of a solid chest and an arm, stumbling back a step and almost landing back in the basket before Everett caught me around the waist and hauled me upright again.

"Thanks," I said, taking pains not to breathe him in, let the familiar smell of him light up any neural pathways that only led to bad decisions. A bad decision couldn't be made this week anyway, so there was no point in even letting my brain go there.

And yet, as I looked up at him, eyes latching on to his, those usual nerve endings flared to life regardless, sparking everywhere we touched.

Everett let go of me and waved me toward the door at the same time I nodded him in the same direction. We repeated the dance until we both stepped forward, bashing together again.

"After you, really," he said, moving back to give me a wide berth and not meeting my gaze.

I hurried through the door, ignoring the way his mere presence made every tiny hair on my neck stand on end.

I didn't care that Everett had a girlfriend. I hadn't imagined that our arrangement would continue forever, that we'd be octogenarians meeting up for two days of shenanigans in a beach shack and still not telling our friends. We'd grow up, we'd change, we'd move on.

But I couldn't deny the fact that I sensed him as he walked

out the door behind me, as we started down the steps and he helped me lay out towels, even as he lounged at the opposite end of our row, almost pointedly. For some reason, not being able to have Everett made me more aware of him than ever.

It was, inconveniently, going to be a long week.

Laurel broke up with Winona on a phone call two days later, hours before she was supposed to arrive. We were about to head out to catch Isaiah's sailboat, when Laurel walked back inside from the deck, where she made the call. She sniffed, plonked her floppy sunhat onto her head, and grabbed her bag from the counter.

"Ready?" she said to the three sets of eyes staring at her. "Come on." She waved us toward the door. "Captain Isaiah will be pissed as hell if we're late."

Isaiah had never once scolded us for being late, but even so, we scrambled after her, throwing bags over our shoulders and shoving our feet into sandals, grabbing jackets off hooks. Everett was walking behind me and caught my elbow when I tripped on the lip of the door on my way out, in the same way he'd saved me from tumbling into the basket on our first day here. Something about avoiding him made me clumsy, taking pains to steer clear of his path and only throwing myself into less convenient ones. I turned back to him, every iota of my attention homing in on the scrape of his warm palm against my skin. I looked down at it, trailed my gaze slowly back up to his. When our eyes caught his were wide, almost startled, that icy gray in his irises flashing even brighter as his pupils dilated.

"Careful," I said, nodding back down at his hand. "What would Maud say if she were here?"

He frowned and dropped his hand.

On the boat, Laurel finally relaxed. She curled up at the bow next to me and dipped her head onto my shoulder, sighing.

"I'm relieved," she said, before I could even ask her. "But I'm a little sad too."

"Of course you are. You loved her."

"I don't know," Laurel said. She straightened, squinting out at the water. "I think I really wanted to."

"You'll find someone you're sure about," I said. At this, she leveled me with a skeptical glance, like I'd said something ridiculous. "What?"

"Come on," she said. "You don't believe in things like that."

"I—" I started, eyes flicking of their own accord toward where Everett stood with Davi a few feet away, shielding his eyes from the sun as he looked out toward where Davi pointed at something. A dolphin or a wave or some speck in the distance. For a half second, I pictured him like this with Maud, surrounded by wealthy, artsy people on a boat somewhere halfway across the world, and he suddenly felt like a stranger to me.

I cleared my throat, looking back to Laurel. Luckily, she was staring down at the water, and hadn't caught my slipup. My not saying anything had been as good as a confirmation for her, that I didn't believe in things like real love.

"I do think you'll find your person, Laurel," I insisted, drawing her attention back up to me.

"Sure," she said. "It's just kind of hard to think you mean it when you don't want that for yourself."

My throat went dry at her words. "I want that," I said, voice not much more than a rasp. I took a sip of the wine that Isaiah had handed us as we'd boarded; better this year than others. When Laurel gave me the same look as she had before, I felt my eyes widen, my shoulders hitch. "Why do you think I don't want that?"

"Sutton," she said. "You have *situations*. Maybe you go on a few dates with someone, but it never lasts. You don't do relationships."

"And that means I don't want one?" I asked, surprising even myself at the irritation in my voice. I never snapped at Laurel.

She shrugged. "You're like Davi," she said.

"Davi has a theory that no relationship should last longer than six months," I said. "In college, he used to lecture us on monogamy not being natural. Just because I'm not currently in a relationship I'm like Davi?"

The look Laurel gave me was almost pitying, mouth turning down at the corners. "You've never been in a relationship, Sutton," she said.

I flipped through my mental Rolodex of our shared experiences, trying to find something to prove her wrong. The guy I spent a semester hanging out with sophomore year of college, or Jake, the line cook at Hank's restaurant who I slept with for three months straight. But none of those things would equal a relationship to Laurel. Or, if I was honest, to me.

I'd thought Laurel knew me better, though. That she understood that just because I wasn't like her—someone who loved being with someone else, who chased it like staying single was a death sentence—didn't mean I didn't eventually want to find someone. But that it was easier said than done. Finding someone who wouldn't let you down. Who would stay.

One memory did pop up, though, as I kept digging for evidence. *Everyone will disappoint you*, I'd said to her through her first breakup we'd experienced together, her head in my lap as she cried over the TA with a pierced eyebrow who'd left his dirty socks in our kitchen sink. *Don't let them.*

I looked up at Laurel. I didn't know how to explain to her that it wasn't that I didn't believe in love as a concept. It was that I knew the person who would be worth it had to be exceptional. Extraordinary. Someone you would never have to doubt and who would never let you down. And when I thought about it that way, maybe she was right. Maybe I wouldn't find someone, because the person I was looking for didn't exist.

I knew she could tell I was upset as she reached out to squeeze my shoulder. "I believe you," she said. "If you say you want that, then I believe you."

I forced a smile, nodding, marveling at how I'd gone from having a good time with my friends to spiraling into self-doubt in a matter of minutes.

Laurel stood up to grab more wine. I let my attention be pulled back to Everett after a while. The breeze washed out the crisp lines of his pale blue shirt. If I unfocused my eyes, he almost blended in with the scene behind him, shirt just another part of the water, golden hair the sun sparkling above.

Something occurred to me as I continued to stare at him, a sharp twist in my stomach. I blinked away the blurriness, tried to shake away the thought, but it stuck.

No one could let you down, ruin anything, if all you ever gave them was two days.

twenty-three

This Summer

When we get back from the movie that night, Laurel grabs another bottle of wine out of the fridge, holding it aloft.

"Let's get drunk on the beach!" she says. Davi cheers, and Gabe, who is already tipsy on one glass of wine, grabs glasses from the cupboard.

"You coming?" Gabe asks, glancing at where Everett is standing near the stairs, and at me, hovering near the island.

"I'm pretty beat," Everett, who has never in his life gotten drunk on a beach, says.

"Aw," Laurel says, pouting out her lower lip. "Did we go too far with the *Cooney* commentary on the way home?"

Everett laughs, shaking his head, but I saw the way his grip on the wheel flexed the more Laurel leaned between the seats, pretending to be a reporter and asking about his inspiration, his process, his idea for his next project. After a while I'd leaned forward and turned up the radio to just below blasting right as a U2 song came on. If I didn't know that Laurel had already had her fair share of wine that night, I'd have believed the song was her all-time favorite, given the verve with which she started singing along as Everett cast me a grateful glance.

"I'll catch up," I say when the three of them glance my way, holding up my phone. "Promised Hank I'd give him a call."

They leave, whooping and hollering, through the back door, the bob of the flashlight Gabe grabbed their only giveaway as they make their way down the beach.

I turn at the creak of the bottom stair, Everett heading up.

"Are you—" I blurt, heart jumping into my throat when he glances back down at me. We stare at each other for a minute, Everett's eyebrows raising, before I finally shake my head. "Never mind. Sleep well."

Everett looks like he may say something else, lips falling apart, and I want him to. I want him to tell me to come upstairs with him, or to close the gap between us and take my face in his hands, continue what we started earlier. But I can't find it in myself to do either of those things, so I don't blame him when he nods, tells me to say hi to Hank, and continues upstairs.

I wait a beat before I follow him. When I get into my room, I toss my jacket onto the chair in the corner and sit cross-legged in the middle of my bed, staring down at my phone in front of me like I might actually call Hank. I didn't promise Hank that I'd call him tonight. But Everett going to sleep felt, for a minute, like some kind of code we were both in on.

It takes three steps to cross to my door, Everett's face burned into my brain as I throw it open. Halfway down the hall, though, I lose my courage and pause. I hover, half turned toward my door, listing every reason I shouldn't knock on his door in my head.

You haven't talked about anything that happened.

What happened did *happen.*

Laurel would kill you.

You're not twenty-two anymore.

Laurel would kill you, Laurel would kill you, Laurel would kill you.

I whirl on my heel at the last echo of it in my head, something like indignation rising up in me as I march toward his door.

But just as I'm almost there, my hand starting to lift so I'm ready to knock before I can lose my nerve, it opens.

Everett, in the short-sleeve button-down he had on under his sweatshirt, freezes at the same moment I do, a skip on a DVD. Until some muscle near his mouth twitches, like he's trying not to smile.

"Hi," he says as my own lips start to curve. I press them together to no avail.

"Hi," I say. Suddenly *you're not twenty-two anymore* feels like such a lie. Every version of me that has ever hooked up with Everett is in this hallway right now, all shoving me directly toward where he stands, one arm braced on the doorframe.

"Going somewhere?" he asks. The grin on his face is familiar, one I know well. It says we're in on the same secret, that there's something going on here only the two of us could understand. Something about it emboldens me.

"I don't know," I say, squarely in front of his door. "Are you?"

He pretends to frown, thinking. "Thought I heard something in the area of your room."

"Funny," I say. "I swear it came from your room."

He drops his arm, steps close enough to me that I have to tilt my head just a little to look fully at him. Still, he doesn't touch me. "Heard there's a party on the beach," he says.

"Mmm-hmm," I say, nodding. "Heard there's something better going on in here."

This is the piece we're good at, I know. The flirting, the banter, the lead-up, and what comes after. And my rational brain knows it's a bad idea, but my animal brain gets one whiff of Everett and all logic switches off. Moves my hand so my fingers graze against his, flicks my eyes over his shoulder, lets him pull me into his room and lean me against the door, smiling up at him until he kisses me again.

There's still some small voice listing all the reasons this is a bad idea in my head, but it's muffled, drowned out by our bodies pressing together, Everett's hands gathering mine and pinning them above my head, skimming back down until they land on my hips.

"I hated thinking about you at lunch with him today," Everett says when he dips his mouth to my neck, breath warm against my skin. "I didn't go into town with everyone else, because I was losing my mind every second you were gone."

"I hated being there," I admit, the words rushing out of me before I can think about it. I arch against Everett as his hand falls to my ass, pressing me closer to him. "I wanted to be with you."

"Then be with me," Everett says, voice vibrating against my skin. "I'll come to San Francisco."

His grip on me tightens. Even if what he's saying is impossible, it has me swimming in memory, things I've been denying for years now, like how we seem to notch perfectly together, or how every single one of my sighs is swallowed up by him like something rare to be collected. Our kiss in the kitchen was a frantic rush to fit something in before we were caught. But this is slow and heady, hands taking their time exploring and any gaps between us slowly filling in, a sort of melding together.

Instead of answering him, I kiss him again, roll my hips against his and revel in the rough sound he makes.

"You used to be such a T-shirt man," I say, looking down at the button I'm fumbling with until I get it. "You never used to wear shirts like this."

"You never wore a dress like this," Everett says, palms skimming up over my arms to my shoulders as I finish unbuttoning his shirt.

"Sure I did," I say, though I'm not sure it's true, am too distracted to really think about it as I slide my hands over his stomach, his muscles jumping under my touch. "Maybe you just weren't paying attention."

"I paid attention to everything, Sutton," he says before lowering his face to mine again, kissing me slowly. His fingers slide over my exposed sternum before dipping underneath the fabric of my dress, palm curving over my breast, drawing a soft sound out of me as I curl into his hand. I deepen the kiss, fingers lacing into his hair as Everett pushes the straps of my dress off my shoulders.

We should slow down, I know. I should pause to consider what Everett's *then be with me* really means. I should think about the others, should think about what happened, should think about the fact that I've spent the last five years angry with him. But I'm so tired of *shoulds.* I'm tired of worrying about what everyone else wants. I'm tired of trying so hard to pretend I don't want this.

I nudge Everett toward the bed, straddling his hips when he sits down underneath me. "Sutton," he says, palms skimming up my back. "Are you sure we should do this?"

"Not at all," I say on a sigh, hands diving into his hair. "But I want to. Just once, at least."

I lean down, move his shirt out of the way so I can kiss his shoulder. He stiffens underneath me, and for a minute I think he's going to stop this. But in the next breath, he's hooking his arm across my lower back, the other steady on my waist as he flips us, holding me to him to shift me farther onto the bed before he lowers himself over me.

"Okay," he says in an uneven voice as his lips skim down my neck, skate across my chest.

I draw Everett back up to me and push his shirt off his shoulders, hands dragging down his back, every muscle in him tense. He unzips the side of my dress and I arch up so he can pull it off of me. I'm not wearing a bra, and Everett immediately dips his head to my chest, his other hand hooking into the waist of my underwear, pressing into my hip.

My fingers coil into his hair as he returns to me, kisses me again. We shed the rest of our clothes quickly, impatiently, kicking things to the side of the bed and grinning into each other's mouths until he slides against me. Any laughter is replaced by harsh breaths, sounds stifled against shoulders because part of keeping this between us tonight is staying quiet in case the others return from the beach, which seems impossible the more we move together, chasing friction, connection.

"Condom?" I ask him.

He reaches over to his nightstand, fumbles with his wallet for a minute before he sets it there again, the ubiquitous foil packet balanced on top. He's starting to move down my body but I stop him, reach over and grab the condom from where he set it. He gives me a quizzical look.

"It's been five years since we've done this," I say to him as I rip the packet open. "The rest can wait." I don't pause to think about the fact that I'm implying there will be a next time.

"Sutton," he starts, but anything else he was going to say is lost as I work the condom onto him, as I pull him back down to me and cant my hips up toward him.

"*Please*," I whisper in his ear. The hand he has on my hip flexes.

Everett's head drops into the curve of my shoulder, teeth just sinking into my skin there as he pushes into me, a deliciously aching stretch that I've been missing for years. *This*, I think as our chests meet, as we breathe together before we start moving again. *This is what you were always avoiding. What you were missing.* Some connection with Everett that sat on the other side of fear, of worry that the two of us would ruin each other. Sex with each other was always amazing, but in a fun, no-holds-barred way. We explored and learned each other in a way only our agreement could produce. There was nothing to be embarrassed about, so it was almost like a lesson each time—*here, this is what you like*, *and let's try this*, and *we should definitely do more of that next time.* Vulnerability in a way that only came from how we both managed to keep our deeper, darker emotions always just out of reach. The only goal was to feel good.

But now, after this week, after five years of denying him, there's a pleasant ache in my chest too, some sort of awe at being this close to a person. To him.

Everett kisses me as we rock together, his mouth soft against mine. I moan into his mouth when he shifts his hips just so, hitting a spot deep inside me, letting him capture and keep the sound. Eventually, our pace starts to quicken, Everett hiking my thigh up against his hip. I bite his shoulder, the same place he did mine, to muffle the sound when I cry out. His head fits into the curve of my neck again, but he turns it this time, kisses my neck so gently it makes that place in my chest balloon, swell until I'm afraid I might burst. The combination of sweat on skin and fingers digging in with a kiss so soft it's barely there is enough to send me over the edge, but I wait until I can tell he's there too, until I can pull him over with me.

I say his name, as barely there as his kiss on my neck, but his lips find mine and I know he heard it.

twenty-four

Fourth Summer

Laurel's words echoed in my head all day. Through the drive back to the house, while I sat in the passenger seat of Everett's car and stared out the window, grateful that the wind whipping in was too loud to hear much of anything. Through stirring orzo on the stove and turning on the ancient grill out back, waving off any help from him. Was I really someone who didn't want to find their person? Was I so afraid of disappointment that I wasn't even trying?

The rest of the week felt different, like we were all out of step, moods sour and some of the fun sucked out of everything. Laurel blamed it on Gabe not being there.

I scrambled to try to make it better. I suggested we go into town, get drinks at the cool new place Laurel had wanted to try when we'd driven by it earlier in the week, but there was a line out the door, and when we ended up at our usual dive bar she sat and twirled the base of her beer glass around in its circle of condensation, looking bored. I suggested pizza and movies back at the cottage, but when we got there, the only movie we could find on TV was the second half of *Ghost Rider* and they'd given us the wrong pizza.

Laurel went back to the room we were still sharing and flopped onto the bed with her phone.

I caught Everett watching me eye the gap in the door. He sat in an armchair across from my spot on the couch, and I straightened, trying to look bored.

"She's okay," he said softly. Even if he'd shouted it, I'm not sure Laurel would have heard. "She's probably just sad about the breakup."

I nodded, glancing quickly in the direction of the room again.

The truth was, it wasn't just this week. Laurel and I had been talking less all year. I'd written it off at first; we were both so busy, it's not like I was responding to every one of her texts either, and a few unanswered voicemails didn't mean that much. But after a few months I could feel it, some empty space in my life that she used to occupy. When we did talk it was brief, about surface level things, and I told myself that was just life. Highs and lows. But I missed her. It was why this week felt so important. It had gone from something to look forward to, to the only surefire way to maintain our connection. Which struck me as odd, because I'd never felt that way about this trip and Everett.

"Come on," he said, dragging me out of my head and back to him. I turned to face him, some sense of comfort washing over me that I quickly tamped down, angry at myself for even going there. He had a girlfriend. I couldn't feel things like that with him this week. Yet another reason things were different.

Everett nodded toward the back door, the dark beach beyond. It had been a gray, muggy day, but the sun had finally broken through in the evening, leaving the moon and stars bright. "Let's sit outside for a while."

The night air was warm, the edge of hotter days to come hanging in it. We sat in the sand just a few feet outside the glowing sphere of the light coming from the back of the cottage, close enough for us to see inside but too far for Laurel and Davi to see. And suddenly it was just us, somehow, like we were sitting under one of those rainbow parachutes from gym in elementary school. The air would rush out eventually, but here was some vestige of our two days together, no need to pretend anymore. I felt my shoulders relax, my racing thoughts about what was going on with Laurel momentarily quieting.

"Hey," I said to Everett's profile.

He smiled, turning to face me. "Hey."

"Long time, no see," I said, nudging my elbow against his. He laughed, eyes crinkling, and I felt it in my chest. "How you been?"

"I've been good," Everett said, glancing away as he said it. A muscle flickered in his jaw.

"I'm convinced," I said, still watching him, still holding on to this bubble. The warm breeze played at his hair, and I couldn't be sure why I wanted to lean in a little closer to him. If it was because this felt like it was a solution to the gaps in my life left by all of us drifting further and further apart. If it was because I'd missed him too.

Everett didn't respond for a minute, eyes scanning the black horizon. He'd had a good year, as far as I could tell. Professional and romantic success. At that thought, a tiny bit of air seeped out from under the sides of our parachute.

I looked away from him, swallowed. "Seems like you have a pretty cool girlfriend."

"Maud is great," Everett said, for roughly the twelfth time that week. It was like a mantra, a response when Laurel asked about her, when she came up in idle conversation, as if he was trying to prove something. If he said his girlfriend was great enough times, maybe we would all really believe it. The trouble was, none of us had any reason to believe otherwise. But then, he continued. Changed things. "My dad loves her."

I glanced over at him, lips parted in surprise. "You introduced her to your dad?"

"Not exactly," Everett said, something souring in his expression. "They met at an event a couple months back. Apparently, he approached her and said, *I believe you're dating my son*."

"Worse opening lines to have, I guess," I said.

"Yeah," Everett said. He looked down at the sand between his legs. "Complicates things a little when his follow-up was *Guess that means I have to wait my turn*."

"Okay, fuck your dad," I said, without thinking. "Sorry." But I glanced over at Everett to see him laughing softly.

"No, my thoughts exactly," he said.

"What did Maud do?" I asked.

"Oh, she told me about it like it was funny. She actually said it was charming. Told me I shouldn't be so worked up about it."

He'd dropped his gaze again, reached down and trailed his fingers through the sand before shaking them off and resting his forearm on his bent knee again. I wanted to say something helpful, meaningful, but all I could think was *your dad is an asshole*. And while I was sure Everett agreed, I didn't think it was the best comment at the moment.

We were quiet for a while until he said anything again, but when he did, his eyebrows tilted together, throat bobbing before he asked his question. "What was your impression of Ben Astor? Before you knew me."

"He seems . . ." I trailed off, not sure exactly what descriptor I was looking for. Nothing quite seemed to sum up how Ben Astor appeared on the surface. He was the kind of celebrity who was always just kind of there, ubiquitous in a way only a long and prolific career and early status as a heartthrob could create. I might have said something else before I met Everett. I finally settled on what I hoped was the most judicious, "He seems charismatic."

Everett smirked at me. "He does know how to work a red carpet, doesn't he?" he asked. I shrugged and Everett looked toward the horizon, something like bitterness on his face.

I leaned in a little closer to him, hoping he might look up at me. When he didn't, I still pressed forward, said what I thought was important in the moment. "If he said something like that to me, I think I'd knee him in the groin."

Everett chuckled. I wanted to ask him everything—what his relationship had been like with his dad growing up, why he didn't want to talk about him—but I knew I had to wait him out. Let him say it first.

"He was drunk, when he said it," Everett said, mouth twisting as he shook his head resignedly. "Or I'm 90 percent sure he had to be. Not—" he said severely, holding a hand up "—not that it excuses it at all. He's a dick when he's sober too. But Maud didn't really seem to care."

"I'm sure she cared," I said softly, uncertain if he'd even hear me.

"My dad is an alcoholic," Everett told me. I watched the bob of his throat as he swallowed. "Though he'd never call himself that. He's an addict in every sense of the word, though. Drugs, sex, fucking . . . *attention*." He shook his head, and I found myself wanting to slide my fingers between his or anchor them against the back of his neck or use them to rub circles on his shoulder. "But he keeps it so well hidden, he's so high functioning, no one would ever know. I don't think he even knows.

"He met my mom when she was sixteen," he continued, and

I found my hand snaking closer to his in the sand, not touching, just there, like if I did make contact he'd stop. I didn't want him to stop. I wanted to know everything. "He was twenty-four. She was an extra on some movie he was in. She was pregnant with me by the time she was eighteen. I wasn't his first kid, but I was the first he stuck around for. For a few years, at least. Anyway, he left when I was four, and I already had another half sister by then. Do you know he has eight kids, that he knows of? Only two of them with the same woman. His PR team should win a fucking award." He said it like he was sharing something he read in a tabloid, gossip about some beloved celebrity, but I could see it there, the question in his eyes. *That's fucked up, right? Tell me you think so too.* But before I could say anything, he was looking away again.

"Anyway," he said, like he was shaking it off. "We're all terrified of becoming our parents, right?"

Something twisted in my chest. Because I knew exactly how he felt, but also because of how he was lumping his experience in with everything else, like it made it matter less, sweeping an arm across a table laden with all his experiences to clear it.

"I don't think so, Everett," I said. "I don't think everyone feels that way." When he didn't answer me, I tried for another route. "What about your mom?"

His face changed at this, a smile just lifting one corner of his mouth. "She's a makeup artist," he said. "And she's happy. She got remarried when I was seventeen, and they have two kids together." He gave me a wry look. "I have a lot of siblings."

"Are you close with all of them?"

"No," he said. "My mom's kids, I guess? I want to be, but they're eight and six. I feel like more of an uncle to them. And the sister my dad had when I was four—Amy—we're really close. She lives up in Santa Barbara. I've tried to reach out to the others, though. One of them, my brother, keeps in pretty close touch. And some of them were friendly enough, but some of them weren't interested or never answered my messages. I think having a shared disdain for your father isn't necessarily enough to make you want to strike up some close sibling relationship."

"That's got to be hard," I said. I considered my next words carefully, teeth sinking into my lower lip. "But I think the siblings you are close with are pretty lucky." I looked out at the water, swallowed over the tightness in my throat. "All I wanted was a sibling when I was growing up. Someone who got it. Even if it was just Amy, at least she has someone who gets it. What it's like to have not just a *parent like that* but *that* parent."

Everett was quiet for a minute. I could feel his eyes on my face before I looked at him, and when our gazes did lock, there was some understanding there. "That's why they're all so important to you, isn't it," he said, voice soft.

I shrugged, trying to brush it off. "Everyone's friends are important to them."

Everett shook his head. "I don't care about *everyone*," he said. "That's why they're so important to you, isn't it?" His tone was firm the second time, like I couldn't avoid it.

I looked at him dead on, trying to shove the Laurel of it all out of my head when I said, "I think anyone who stays is important."

A shadow passed over his face, clouding it for half a breath, before he was nodding, mouth twisting into a small knowing smile. "We make quite a pair," he said.

Something occurred to me as he said it. "Is that why you don't like drinking that much? Your dad?"

"Yeah," Everett said slowly, rubbing a hand at the back of his neck. "Something like that. Some shitty childhood memory lodging itself into my psyche and informing this habit." I could tell there was more to it, whatever memory he momentarily retreated into as he stared at the sand in front of him, but I could also tell it wasn't something he wanted to relive just then. Something he would share with me only if he wanted to. He looked back up at me suddenly, a blaze in his eyes I hadn't seen there before. "Maybe it's not true for everyone," he said. "But I'm fucking terrified of being anything like my father. I hate that the only thing I want to do with my life is so closely tied to who he is. I hate that I want anything close to something he's done."

I did reach for him at this, cupping his face in my hand and rubbing a thumb across his cheekbone. I was still surprised at the way the closeness to him made me feel, a fluttering in my stomach and a heat in my cheeks, a pull at my center. "That might be the one good thing you got from him," I told him, hoping he knew how much I meant it. "That passion for something. But you won't be him, Everett. You're too good."

I wished so much there wasn't a Maud, in that moment. I watched as his eyes dipped to my mouth, briefly, and I realized with a deep rush of dislike for myself that I would have let him kiss me then, that I would have let him do more than that.

That was always the problem with Everett. Our time together was like some break from reality, the one time I let go of control in any real way. He wasn't part of any plan, couldn't possibly fit into any real plan, and that was part of the allure of it. I was a different version of myself with him, someone who let the world rest lightly on her shoulders, who was open to whatever our brief time together would bring. There were no repercussions to be felt, no aftershocks save for sometimes seeing him in my dreams. We were free of consequences.

But other people were a consequence. Other people were

real, could be hurt, and Everett knew this, drawing away from me and hopping to his feet, holding out a hand to help me up. I could see it in his eyes—he knew. Even if we hadn't done anything, a line had been crossed. Not only in the way I touched him, but in what he'd shared too. Everett didn't talk to people like that, didn't share things readily, and I had a sneaking suspicion Maud didn't know any of it. But I did. And I was far from just a friend.

"Hey," I said, waving a hand at the beach around us. I wanted Everett to know he hadn't done anything wrong. That he was the one to pull away, and it counted. "It's just this place."

He looked at me, something sad flickering across his face. The wind played at his hair as I waited. Finally, he shook his head. "It's not just this place," he said.

The words slammed into me, sunk into my bones. I'd keep them there for the next year, returning to them every once in a while, long after I'd returned to my normal with no Everett around to make me go a little crazy.

We walked back to the house, a marked distance between us. Laurel and Davi were waiting, and Everett still had a girlfriend, and we were still supposed to be nothing more than just friends, no matter what he'd said. No matter what molecular thing between us had shifted.

twenty-five

This Summer

I stay in Everett's room that night. I spend the night, like I told him I never do, like I always have with him. We fall asleep wrapped together and wake up in the same position.

Everett plays with my hair as I hug an arm around his chest. I'm happily still ignoring everything we haven't discussed, the impossibility of all of this, when there's a knock at his door.

"Everett? You up?" Gabe says from the other side of the door.

Everett's hand freezes in my hair. I widen my eyes at him. Gabe knocks again.

Pretend you're asleep, I mouth at him. Everett's eyes flick to the doorknob, like Gabe might just come in. Which, I realize with a sinking in my stomach, is true. Gabe used to barge into my room in college whenever he felt like it.

"Um," Everett calls as I scramble out of bed, grabbing my dress from the floor and launching into the bathroom. "Just a second!"

I hear Everett root around as I partially shut the door behind me, probably trying to locate a pair of pants. Gabe knocks a third time.

"Sorry," Everett says as he opens the door. "What's up?" I

press myself closer to the counter in here, shutting my eyes, as if that would make me invisible to Gabe if he came in.

"Do you have any Tylenol? Ibuprofen?" Gabe asks. "Usually I'd ask Sutton, but I can't find her."

"Yeah," Everett says, and something in his voice has me casting around the bathroom, heart pounding when my eyes land on the bottle of ibuprofen sitting near the sink. I hear Gabe move into the room as Everett starts toward the bathroom.

"Man," Gabe says. "Might have to fight you for this room next time. You know, if there is a next time."

"It's yours," Everett says as he leans around the door. I already have the ibuprofen stretched out toward him, his fingers brushing mine as he takes it. "Here you go."

"Thanks," Gabe says, in his tone that unmistakably means *settling in.* I hear him sit on the edge of the bed, the sheets of which my underwear are undoubtedly tangled in.

"You good?" Everett asks. I'm still holding my dress in front of me, and I settle in against the counter, repressing a sigh. I love Gabe, but now is not the time for one of his talks.

"I don't know," Gabe says. "Has this week felt off to you?"

"Hmm," Everett murmurs, and I try to picture him, standing with his arms crossed and a frown on his face. "Maybe a little awkward."

"Forced is what I was going to say," Gabe answers. My head straightens at this. I'm surprised to hear this coming from Gabe, of all people. Affable, comforting, never one to really complain.

"I think it's just been a while," Everett says.

"Maybe." I listen, trying to parse the silence. "I'm just worried about how disappointed Sutton will be if this is our last time here."

I wish so much, in this moment, that I wasn't standing naked in Everett's bathroom. It's a unique embarrassment to have to listen to other people talk about you, even if it is just Gabe worrying. Am I truly the only one who thought this week could mean something? That we might start this tradition again?

"The trip was Laurel's idea," Everett points out.

"I know," Gabe says. "But I think this trip might have always meant more to Sutton than the rest of us, you know? I don't want her thinking this week means we'll start coming back here again."

I bite my lip, look down at my feet. I don't want to hear this, don't want to know that my friends feel *sorry* for me. But then Everett is answering. "This trip meant a lot to me too," he says, something like defensiveness edging his voice.

I don't get to hear Gabe's response, because there's another knock at the bedroom door, followed by Laurel's voice. "Did you—" she starts, then, "Oh, thank god you have ibuprofen." I listen as she flops onto the bed next to Gabe, my pulse racing anew. "Have you seen Sutton? Her room's empty."

"Yeah, no, I haven't seen her," Everett says, and I can imagine him dragging a hand through his hair, anxious to get them out of there. "I was about to take a shower."

"Okay," Laurel says. There's no other sound of movement.

"I—" Everett says, then, "Okay."

I press myself into the counter as he trudges into the bathroom. He shuts the door behind him and flicks on the fan, eyes locked on to mine as we try to communicate something silently, all *What the fuck was that* and *What else was I supposed to do* and *Kick them out!*

After probably a minute of this, Laurel and Gabe murmuring on the other side of the door about lord knows what, Everett turns on the shower before leaning against the wall across from me.

We stare at each other like that for a while, wary at first, until one side of his mouth twitches. I can't help smiling, clamping my lips together to keep it from growing but failing miserably. After a minute, I have to press my hand to my mouth to keep from laughing, Everett's shoulders shaking silently as he drops his head back against the wall behind him.

I close the space between us, checking to make sure the door is locked as I do. His chest is warm under my palm. My dress falls to the floor between us as I press against him. His gaze goes heavy, no laughter left there anymore.

"Everett, we're going to go on a coffee run!" Laurel calls as Everett's hands skate up my back. "Want anything?"

"I'm good!" he answers, my lips running along his collarbone.

"Tell Sutton where we are if you find her!" Gabe shouts before they're gone.

Everett tilts my head up, kissing me as soon as his bedroom door closes behind them. I don't think we've ever been quite this reckless before, and I can't bring myself to care.

"Did you mean what you said?" I ask after a while, breathless. "That this trip meant a lot to you?"

"Of course it did," Everett says. "Though maybe not in the way it did to you."

I pull away from him a little, just enough to see his face. Something about his words has my spirits falling, the same way they did when Gabe said what he did about me. "What do you mean?"

Everett's fingers skim across my shoulder blades, down my spine. "I loved the trip," he says. "I love everyone here." His eyes scan my face as his throat bobs, before he continues. "But those two days with you always meant more to me, Sutton. They were always the most important part."

My breath catches in my chest. Suddenly, last night becomes

infinitely more complicated. My *just once* feels insane. I don't know if I can tell him I feel entirely the same, because it was like the week and the two days existed separately for me. The week was something sacred, this time left with the people I called family, and the two days were just ours, special. I hadn't wanted to admit how much they meant to me then, have been actively ignoring how much I've felt the absence of them, of him, since it all ended.

But for Everett, I realize, all of this had been new. All of us, and even his renewed friendship with Gabe. We might have absorbed him easily, but he didn't have the same history of those four years together. What he did have, though, was the two of us. And what we had was sacred in its own way too.

"They were important to me too," I say, eyes locked on to his as I do. I want him to know that, even if this doesn't continue outside of this room. If I walk out of here and last night and right now are nothing but a memory, a cap on whatever complex, beautiful, maddening thing our relationship has been.

The idea leaves me feeling a little empty.

twenty-six

Fifth Summer
San Francisco

It was May, and the first notes of summer were just starting to simmer in my bones. If I told anyone else this, they would think I was crazy, but I swore I could feel it, smell it when I walked out the door, taste it in the tomatoes we used at the restaurant and the lemon I squeezed into my water in the mornings. Summer was already weaving its way into my life.

Part of this feeling was just my usual connection to this time of year. But this summer, it was partly due to the fact that, after a Herculean effort, everyone would be coming to the beach house. And the other part (maybe the biggest part, though I was still a little hesitant to admit it to myself) was the fact that Everett was coming to visit me that second weekend of May.

Well, not *visit me* per se. He had a few meetings here, and he'd called last month to tell me, to see if I wanted to hang out while he was in town. I'd been surprised to see his name pop up on my phone. We didn't really call each other, though we had been texting more, just the two of us, since he'd broken up with Maud last fall. Nothing of particular note, but it felt significant, somehow, like our summer selves had leaked into our real lives.

But by the time he knocked on my door at noon the Friday he was set to arrive, I had only the foggiest memory that someone was coming over, because of the sharp, senses-obliterating migraine pulsing behind my right eye.

I squinted against the light streaming in through my living room windows as I shuffled toward the door, tugging the blanket around my shoulders up over my head in a makeshift hood to block it out further. Something about the cold metal of the doorknob under my hand made my stomach turn, and I had to swallow against the bile that suddenly rose in my throat.

"Fuck," I said when I opened the door. Everett's winning smile faltered, understandably, but his expression quickly morphed into concern as he took me in: gray sweatpants, one leg bunched above my calf, a faded Devon College T-shirt, hair that needed to be washed falling out of a braid I'd thrown it into yesterday afternoon when the first hints of a migraine started to creep in and I went through my usual routine: ibuprofen, a Diet Coke, and a bacon, egg, and cheese sandwich. I hadn't had consistent migraines in over five years and so had stopped filling the prescriptions I used to take to prevent and mitigate them, and started cursing myself for that decision as soon as none of my home remedies helped and I started to see spots.

Everett was at my door because Everett was *supposed* to be at my door. But somewhere between the black dots that had started flashing across my vision last night and trying not to puke this morning, I'd forgotten about our plans.

"Are you okay?" he asked as I closed my eyes.

"I remembered you were coming," I said, leaning against the doorframe. "I promise."

I startled a little when a palm settled against my forehead. "You don't have a fever," Everett said. "How are you feeling?"

"I have a migraine," I explained. Something about the gentle pressure of his hand against my head seemed to infinitesimally ease the pain there. If I were feeling better, I would have paid attention to all my better judgments, but they didn't even exist at the moment, and so I leaned into it. "I'm sorry."

"Why are you apologizing?" Everett asked. His other arm slipped around my shoulders, familiar, taking my weight as I rested against him.

"I didn't tell you," I said. "We were supposed to—"

"Hey," he said. "No apologizing, okay?" He rubbed at my shoulders and I let out a contented sound that quickly morphed into a groan when the vibrations sent a new wave of pain through my entire brain. "Come on."

I remember Everett directing me back into bed, pulling the blankets up over me. I remember him refilling my water glass and handing me more ibuprofen when I asked for it and checking to make sure I had everything I needed, and I remember him pushing me back down when I sat up, insistent we *do something*, that I wouldn't let this weekend pass us by, that I knew, historically, the migraine would run its course in a few more hours. *I'll be right here*, he said, or something like it, as I shut my eyes again, maybe *I'm not going anywhere.*

It would have horrified me to be like this in front of any other man I'd dated, or slept with, or whatever it was Everett and I did. If I hadn't set twelve extra alarms to get up and do everything to look as human as possible, to avoid canceling plans, I wouldn't have let them in the apartment. I would have pretended I wasn't home and then that I forgot about the date and I would never tell them I felt bad. I wouldn't let them tuck me into bed with my morning breath and my laundry basket out in the open and then just wander, unchecked, into my apartment.

But as soon as my bedroom door clicked softly closed behind Everett, I started to drift off. I didn't worry about disappointing him, about being perfect. I felt better with him here. More than that, I realized, I wanted it to be him. Not Laurel or Gabe or Davi. Everett.

I didn't have time to mull it over. I was asleep before I could consider the why.

When I woke up, my apartment was quiet. The long lines of late afternoon sun slanted in through my blinds. I groaned when I checked my phone; I'd been asleep almost four hours. But it had helped. The headache behind my eye had reduced to a dull pulse, and the nausea that usually accompanied my migraines was gone.

I stood and stretched, wondering if I'd dreamed up Everett altogether. But when I wandered into the living room, there he was, flesh and blood, on my couch. Asleep.

Hovering in my bedroom doorway, I watched him for a minute, the faint rise and fall of his chest, the arm he had crooked above his head, before a light in the kitchen caught my eye. I wandered over, following my nose to a pot on my stove that I lifted the lid on.

"You're up."

I jumped at the sound of Everett's voice, turning to where he was sitting up, eyes sleepy.

"You made me soup?" I asked, lid still in hand.

Everett nodded, rubbing the heels of his hands over his eyes. His hair stuck up a little in the back. "You told me once that Hank used to make you soup when you had a migraine."

"I did?" I asked. I looked at the pot, at the soup that he'd clearly gone out and gotten ingredients for, made in my kitchen without my help, and back at him. "I don't remember that."

Everett's hands had fallen, and he looked between me and the stove, chewing on his lower lip before he finally said, "I do."

Something in my chest shifted. I put a hand to the spot, like it was physical, like I might find a new bruise or scar where I felt it, but there was nothing. No permanent reminder of the change, only a certainty in my body that the way I was looking at Everett then was different than how I looked at him before, and I started to worry there wasn't anything I could do about it.

I swallowed, settled a hand against the counter in an attempt to appear casual. "Can we have some soup?" I asked.

Everett sprang up, came over to me. I watched as he opened cupboards and drawers like he knew where things were, which he must have because he made the soup to begin with.

Having him there, in my small kitchen, felt off-limits, somehow, like I was breaking a rule. Inviting him into my life outside of the trip, something I did with the others but we'd never done with each other. The days at the beach always felt more innocent, like they were some continuation of a version of ourselves we never got to be. But this, having him in my apartment, having him take care of me, the sudden ache in my chest at the sight of him, was new.

He nudged me after I'd been standing there in silence for a minute, eyes stuck on his movements as he navigated my kitchen. "Go sit down," he told me, and I complied, let myself be taken care of. Everett brought me soup and a blue Gatorade, another thing he remembered, and we ate and turned on the cooking channel and watched Molly Yeh make a hot dish and I was so happy that I almost started crying.

Later, when my headache was almost gone and Everett was washing our dishes, I ducked into the bathroom to take a shower, rinse off the feeling of having lain in bed all day. When I came back out, wrapped in my robe, Everett was sitting at my table, coat on.

"Hey," he said, glancing up at me. "Feel better?"

"Loads," I said. I hovered near the end of the table. "Thank you for taking care of me."

He stood up, reached out, and tucked a damp strand of hair behind my ear. "I liked doing it."

My lips parted as his hand fell, and I worried that if I didn't say something then, I never would. I turned to follow his gaze to my front door, and noticed, for the first time, his suitcase sitting there.

"It's getting late," Everett said as I looked back at him. "I should probably get going."

I swallowed and nodded, the courage I'd felt before still burning in my chest but flickering now.

Everett brought a hand up to the back of my head, brow furrowing almost like he was concentrating. He let out a breath, a small *hmm* at the back of it, a sound of consideration, before he kissed my forehead. When he drew away, I forced my eyes wide-open. "Text me when you're up in the morning, okay?" he said. "We can still do something."

"Okay," I said.

I turned as he started down the hall, picturing, for a minute, if he did stay. What would happen if Everett was in my apartment in his sweaters and socks every Saturday morning, if we weren't just summer people, not just group-text people, not two people who kept a secret, but two people who did this all the time. What would happen then?

"Or—" I said. Everett was at the door, one boot in hand, but he looked back at me. My pulse felt like the drum of an overeager middle school marching band kid, almost painful. I wanted him, enough that I found myself forcing the words up and out of my throat so they lay bare between us. "Or you could stay."

Everett hesitated for just a minute. My heart hammered in my throat the entire time. "Are you sure?" he finally asked.

I nodded. "If you don't mind."

His face softened into his usual, amused-at-the-world smile then. "I've never minded spending the night with you, Hale," he said. Then, expression going serious, "I mean, not that we're *spending the night together,* just—"

"It's okay," I cut in quickly, something about his own embarrassment easing my nerves. We were both a little new to this whole part of things. "I know what you meant. We'll sleep."

And so we did. Everett left his boots by the door and grabbed his toothbrush out of his bag. There was a brief exchange about the couch that I quickly ended because I hadn't meant he could stay so he could crash in my living room. He slid into bed next to me and we both rolled onto our sides and after a loaded, silent moment, he kissed me. A kiss good-night that wasn't going anywhere, but maybe, if I thought about it, was leading everywhere.

In the morning, my migraine gone, I took Everett on the tour of Saturday morning San Francisco that I'd gone on with Hank so many times and now regularly embarked on myself—minus the early-morning fish market.

We wandered the farmers market, arms around each other to ward against the bite of the morning chill. Everett held the bag I'd brought while I filled it with things and we planned out a menu for that night: short ribs that I'd braise, Parmesan polenta, and minty greens.

We picked up coffee and too many pastries from a shop a few blocks down and sat on a bench outside, trading bites of orange rolls and a blueberry muffin. Everett liked his coffee hot and strong, I liked mine milky and iced, even in the relative cold of the morning, and Everett brought my hands around his own cup when he saw me shiver, held them there.

We walked down the pier at Fisherman's Wharf. At the end Everett stood behind me, arms around me as we looked out at the gray and stormy water.

I leaned back against his chest, turning my head so my cheek brushed the soft cashmere of his sweater.

"Can I tell you something?" I asked, glancing up at him.

"Anything," he said.

"I like this," I said. "I've been here a hundred times alone," I continued. "And I'm good at being on my own. Most things I like doing alone."

Everett looked skeptical, not about what I said, but that it was really what I wanted to tell him, so I hurried to add the important part.

"But I like it better this way. I like being here with you."

He smiled at that, chest rising under my cheek on what seemed like it might be a relieved sigh. I looked back out at the water. "I think I like doing most things better with you," he said, voice low.

I smiled, staring out at the water as his words worked through me. It felt impossible, saying the things I was thinking out loud, and yet I couldn't seem to stop them, as if all my willpower had been ground down to dust.

"Are you happy, doing what you do?" I asked him, eyes tracking a seagull diving toward the waves.

"Yeah," Everett said after a while. "I am. I mean, it doesn't come without its hard days, but I can't imagine doing much else."

"Are the hard days because of your dad?" I asked. "Because of how close your work puts you to him?"

Everett sighed, and I reveled in the movement of it, in being this close to him. "You might be the only person who knows how much I hate that part," he said. "But I meant more about the general stress of the job. I think I'd rather deal with the hard parts of making a movie than the hard parts of a different job any day."

"Hmm," I mused, burrowing in a little closer to him.

"What about you?" he asked. "Do you feel that way about taking over the restaurant?"

The skip in my chest was familiar at that point, like a heartbeat missed because of a loud clap of thunder or a door slamming suddenly. It echoed through me, touching on all parts of my history: Hank and everything he'd done for me, how he'd raised me. The kitchen where I'd learned to cook and fallen in love with the breakneck pace of it all. The promise that someday too that would be mine.

"I want to," I said. "But there are some other things I'd like to do too."

"Like what?"

"I'd like to write a cookbook someday," I said, quickly, like it was a foolish dream. "I'd probably have to let Laurel start managing my online life if I really want to accomplish that."

"Hey," Everett said, turning me gently toward him. When I looked at him, he shook his head, brow furrowed like he'd caught on to the tone of my answer. "No. That's a great thing to want, Sutton. You can do that if you want to."

I nodded toward him. "I'd need your input," I said.

Everett laughed softly. "How's that?"

"You'd have to let me know if the recipes read well, from the perspective of a home cook."

"You overestimate my abilities," Everett said.

"That soup last night says different."

Everett's eyes sparkled at this, his hands locking around my back so our chests touched. I kept my head tilted back, looking at him, ran my hands over his shoulders. "I mostly learned to cook to impress you," he said.

"You learned how to properly dice an onion so I'd agree to spend two extra days with you at a beach house?" I asked. Even as I joked about it, the idea planted something in me, spreading roots from my chest.

Everett's expression shifted. I understood enough about him then to know that serious conversations sometimes felt dangerous, like he had to keep some sort of smile on his face or laugh in his voice in case things went sideways. But he looked at me like he wanted this part of things to be committed to memory, like even if it went poorly, we'd both remember the good. "I think it was always about more than two days with you, Sutton," he said. "There were just too many other things standing in our way."

I nodded, but I couldn't quite look at him when I replied. "We promised everyone we wouldn't do anything like this."

"Maybe," Everett said. His tone drew my gaze back up to his. "I think we've also gotten in our own way well enough."

"What about now?" I asked, breath catching in my throat as I waited for him to answer. It felt so frightening that I wished I could laugh my way through it, turn it into a joke if his answer didn't live up to what I wanted him to say.

"I'd like to help you with that cookbook," he said, eyes hopeful. It wasn't the full *let's stop getting in the way of ourselves now* I'd imagined. But it felt somehow better, bigger, a stepping into each other's full lives that we hadn't worked our way to yet.

My fingers drifted into his hair, and I bit down on a smile as I said, "I'd like to come see how you make one of your movies."

A small exhale shook out of him, almost a laugh but not quite. "Yeah?" he asked, his grip on me tightening.

"Yeah," I said. It was as big a promise as we'd ever made to each other.

When we got back to my apartment that afternoon, he immediately fell into place in my kitchen, like he belonged there.

It wasn't until after we'd eaten that it came up. The big, unspoken thing sitting in the middle of this day.

"Only three weeks until the trip," Everett said. We were on my couch, dishes drying in the rack in my kitchen. I was holding my glass of wine against my knee, twirling it between my fingers. This stopped me. "Everyone will be there this year."

"No small feat," I said.

"We haven't talked about staying," he said.

"No," I said. I took a sip of my wine, set it on the table, dragged a hand through my hair.

"Maybe it's time that tradition died," Everett said, almost cautiously.

I faked a pouty frown. "You don't want to spend two days alone with me anymore?"

He laughed and hooked his hands behind my knees, tugging me over to him so my legs were slung across his lap. I smiled as his hands skimmed up to my face, one thumb brushing over my lips before he said his next words. "Maybe we should tell everyone," he said. "About this."

I captured his wrist in my hand, placed my fingers over where I could feel his pulse. Fast. Like mine. "What is this?" I asked.

Everett's mouth went soft. "I don't know," he said. "But I don't feel like we're just summer people anymore. I want to find out what this is." He brushed my hair behind my ear, let his hand linger there. "And I know I don't want to keep hiding it from everyone."

I turned my head to the side so I could kiss his palm, looked at him again. "I don't want to hide it anymore either. But they might be angry with us."

"I think they'll forgive us."

"And if they don't?"

Everett's jaw jumped, his eyes flicking between mine. I was nervous for his answer. "You're more important to me," he said quietly, roughly, my heart glowing with it. "But," he continued, grip on me loosening just a little. "They're your best friends," he said.

"They're—"

"Mine too, I know," he said. "But they're everything to you, Sutton. If you'd rather we don't tell anyone because it could risk upsetting the order of things, I understand that. We can—we can forget this."

He looked so hopeful then. It needled at something tender in my chest, that he thought I wouldn't agree with him. That this—us—might not be more important to me. But he was right, in a way. If being with him came at the cost of the dissolution of the most important group of people in my life, I wasn't sure we should tell them. And yet, here he was, real to me in a way that made me feel whole. There were so many moments with Everett that I wouldn't trade for anything.

"We tell them," I said. "On the trip. In three weeks." I nodded. "I want to."

Everett kissed me, relief washing over his face, and I felt it too. As his hands roamed over my skin and we moved together, pulses syncing up perfectly, as sweat dried on our skin and I lay with my cheek against Everett's chest. Some sense that this was right. That they would all understand. That everything would be okay.

twenty-seven

This Summer

I sneak out of Everett's room while the others are still gone, text Laurel to say I was on a walk and will she grab me an iced latte. The worst part, maybe, is that I don't feel guilty in the way I think I should. Some part of me loves it, having this secret again, like I've reclaimed something that's mine.

But even so, by the time evening rolls around and Laurel leaves us all to head to her party, none of us allowed to join her until it starts, I start to worry. That what Gabe said in Everett's room is correct—this trip won't continue. That I'm the only one who will be bothered by that. And that Everett and I, by so easily giving in to something I swore we never would again, have played some cosmic role in the final dissolution of this friend group, rendering all my hopes for this week pointless.

The invitation we received listed a black-and-gold dress code. Laurel left with a garment bag over her arm, so I have no idea what she'll be wearing, but I slip on the swirly, pleated gold dress I found just a week before the trip. When I walk out of my room, Everett is shutting his door behind him dressed in a pair of black chinos and a soft black T-shirt, a cool black jacket slung over his shoulder.

"Look at you," he says as I walk over to him, spinning once so my dress fans out around me.

"Did I do it justice?" I ask, pausing just shy of him. Davi's door is still cracked open.

"Do what justice?" he asks.

I look down at myself, lift up my hands. "An Oscar."

Everett laughs, eyes drifting over my shoulders. "I so prefer you to an Oscar," he says quietly.

We meet Gabe, also in all black, in the kitchen, and wait for Davi to descend. When he does, he's in a gold shirt more sparkly than my dress, typing furiously away on his phone.

"Now *that's* an Oscar," Everett says, nodding in his direction. I stifle a laugh as Davi looks up at us.

"What?" he says. "I wore this shirt for New Year's last year. I'm not wasting it."

"You look amazing," I tell him as I start to herd him toward the door. "And we're late."

Everett drives us all to the party, placing bets on what we think it will be like. I laugh when he says he thinks Laurel will be carried out in a coffin, throwing herself a literal funeral for her past life.

When we arrive, though, I don't think it's what any of us expected. "Okay," Gabe says as we all stand in the doorway to the bar Laurel has rented out for her party tonight. "This is . . . something."

Davi lets out a low whistle on Gabe's other side, eyes scanning over the black decorations dripping on every surface, hints of gold poking through.

"*Is it* a funeral?" I ask, reaching out to cup a hand under a flower so purple it almost looks black.

"I don't think so," Gabe says. "It feels more . . . roaring twenties."

I tilt my head back to look at the gold star lanterns strung above us, light bouncing off the gilded ceiling. "Pretty," I say. "Not Laurel's usual style."

"Maybe that's the point," Everett says from next to me. I drop my gaze to find him doing the same, eyes meeting mine. He shrugs a shoulder. "She does keep talking about her new life."

A blur of sparkling white comes racing toward us, bright against the dark backdrop of the bar. Laurel holds her arms out wide as if to engulf all of us, a smile I haven't seen all week splitting her face open.

"My babies!" she cries, squeezing us tight to her.

I meet Gabe's eyes over her head. *Babies?* I mouth at him. Laurel has never called us anything remotely close to that before. He shrugs as she releases us.

"You look great, Laurel," I say to her. She's in a drapey white dress that sparkles like it's made of something pearlescent, glitter in her hair and tiny jewels dotted in a line above her eyebrows, highlighter on her cheekbones bright enough to strobe.

"It's my new life outfit," she says, holding her arms up and spinning. I catch Everett's eye. He was right.

Another party enters behind us, and Laurel points us in the direction of the bar before greeting them with the same level of enthusiasm she did us, which stings, somehow. Glancing around the room, I realize I don't recognize anyone here. No one who was at Laurel and Stephen's wedding, except us. None of her LA friends I've met when I've visited her. Everyone looks either as enthusiastic as Laurel or casually bored, like being here is checking an item off a list.

"Did Laurel ever tell you why she didn't want us to plan this party?" I ask Davi as we reach the bar.

He shrugs, the shoulder of his shirt catching the light drifting down. "Who cares," he says. "Are you mad you didn't have to plan a party in addition to organizing this whole week?"

"I didn't—" I start, but Davi raises an eyebrow at me. "We all helped organize this week." I think back to our texts, conversations, the feeling of seeing Everett's name pop up on my phone so frequently after years of avoiding it as much as I could. Confirmations we were a go, that we'd pay Laurel back for everything. But it's true that I was the one who picked the house we'd stay in. Who called to book the sailing tour. Who reminded everyone of our itinerary the week before we were set to arrive so we could be on a schedule if Laurel wanted us to be. So we could be organized without looking too organized. So we could avoid any painful, awkward silences, but mostly so we could be reminded of what this week used to mean to us.

"Maybe," Davi says as the bartender approaches. "But Laurel didn't call the rest of us when she wanted it to happen. She called you. You're the one who's always making sure everything is perfect."

He turns to the bartender and orders for both of us, leaving me with his words bouncing around my head as they try to land, burrow in.

I'd thought Laurel called me for the same reason she always did: because there was something between us that went just one level deeper than it did with everyone else. It was a secret I thought she and I had both harbored; that we would always be each other's first call.

But maybe I've been wrong. Maybe I'm not always her first call. Maybe I'm the best at *organizing* things, at *making sure everything is perfect*. It starts to settle, to take root, this idea that I am a function to Laurel instead of her undisputed person.

I try to dislodge the thought. Tell myself that maybe it's just a mark of our friendship, instead of something damning.

"Sutton?" Davi's voice brings me back to the present. He's handing me a martini. "Got you three olives."

"Thanks," I say. At the other end of the bar, Gabe and Everett are laughing about something, and as Davi wanders off to talk to a woman in a backless black dress, I start to feel completely alone. It's not fair, I know. I told Everett we should act normal, and this week, at least after the boat, normal for us is a sort of cool friendliness. I could join him and Gabe, or follow Davi, or track down Laurel, or find someone else to talk to. I could stand here alone and drink gin martinis all night.

But something about Davi's words are still ringing in my head, the implication behind them, and being the only one without someone to talk to, and really, the very fact of this party has something sinking in me. Like whatever supports I've put in place to hold this week aloft have eroded away, and all my expectations are finally crashing down. The magic sheen I've been trying to force onto everything is fading, replaced instead by the glossy facade of this room, where I know exactly four people.

Except, there might be five. A head of salt-and-pepper hair catches my eye as it approaches the bar, several pairs of eyes watching the same way I am as he passes, as his gaze meets mine and he smiles.

"Fancy meeting you here," Cooper says when he reaches me. He leans one arm on the bar, effectively blotting out my view of Gabe and Everett. He's in a black button-down, the sleeves accentuating his biceps. Arms that take work, I think. A body like that requires a lot of effort.

"Cooper," I say, lifting my glass in his direction. "I forgot you'd be here."

Cooper claps a hand to his chest, like I've wounded him. "Am I that forgettable?" he asks. "Wasn't it just yesterday I saw you?"

It startles me, the fact that it was only a day ago that I had lunch with Cooper. That I came home and Everett lifted me onto the kitchen counter, and everything changed from there. I'm shocked by how much can shift in such a short time.

"Not forgettable," I tell Cooper, forcing a smile onto my face. I can't figure out how to fix things right at this moment, but I can fake my way through a good night. "A pleasant surprise."

Cooper grins and nods at my drink. "You good?" he asks. I nod, and he orders before asking if I want to find a place to sit down.

I glance over my shoulder as I follow Cooper toward a wall of low-sitting tables. I *want* Everett to be looking at me, I realize, and for a minute I can't sort out why. I wonder what part of me hopes he'll be watching. If it's the ugly, angry part I came into this week with, hoping in some way to make him jealous. If it's the part that drove me to his room last night, that hiked my pulse every time we were caught alone today, searching for some confirmation that there's more to this than revisiting the past. That this isn't just another party, and I'm not just another person, and we matter.

But when I do find him in the crowd, he's frowning at his phone, no cool gaze for mine to latch on to at all.

I look away, focusing on Cooper's broad shoulders as I follow him, surprised when I can't tamp down the sinking feeling in me like I used to.

I wish I could sort out why I can't seem to make myself actually want Cooper, especially as yet another person passes by, eyeing him until they realize his attention is undividedly on me and they move on, disappointed. I wish I could pinpoint what it is, exactly, about this handsome, successful, incredibly decent man that isn't doing it for me, that seems to be doing it for absolutely everyone else.

The only thing that comes to mind, again and again, is a breathy admission on a kitchen counter, every lie I've told myself unraveling as I told Everett *he's not you*. Last night, and this morning, and how it felt every minute before we walked into the party.

As if Cooper can read my mind, he glances around the room, searching for someone. "You know, I'd love to track down that director friend of yours," he says. "Talk to him about film school. My daughter was furious she missed meeting him."

"Everett?" I say, stupidly, like the mere mention of him doesn't have warmth shooting through me. "He's around here somewhere."

Cooper glances at me, a crinkle by his eyes as he gives me a soft smile that has me feeling utterly exposed. I throw back the dregs of my martini and stand up, hopeful that if I face the topic of Everett head-on, Cooper won't suspect me of anything. I can't have *Cooper*, a veritable stranger, thinking he knows something about me, understands it even before I do.

"Let's find him," I say. The martini Davi ordered me was strong, and his comment about why Laurel called me is still buzzing incessantly around my head, some undercurrent to it that I can't seem to fully ignore, something about this whole night rubbing me the wrong way.

Cooper follows me into the crowd. Laurel has been a white blur all evening, but I haven't talked to her since we arrived. Right now, she's laughing loudly with a circle of people underneath a sign that reads *Laurel's New Life!* in looping golden script, a motto that's starting to dull. I want to be clued in on what, exactly, Laurel's new life is going to look like. Our collective place in it.

I track Gabe and Davi down, making friends with people I

don't recognize. Neither of them have seen Everett in a while, they tell me, and so I resume my dogged march through the crowd with Cooper trailing behind me.

"Hey, it's not a big deal," he says at one point, leaning down so his breath is against my ear. I'm not exactly tipsy, just less than, nursed the martini long enough that it feels less fun and more like a headache now, making me unnecessarily cranky.

"No, he'll want to talk to you," I say to Cooper. I can feel doubt radiating off him, think he'd probably be wise to veer sideways into the crowd and away from me right now, find someone who isn't acting like I am. But I can't seem to stop searching the room, feel almost desperate to find Everett, like my nerves won't settle until we do.

"Sutton," Cooper says, with a gentle brush of a hand against mine.

"There he is!" I exclaim, pointing with the same hand Cooper's fingers just found across the room, to the doors that lead out to the deck attached to the side of this place, where partygoers flow outside. Everett is leaned against the wall, a drink in hand, and something about the sight of him has whatever has me so angry dissipating, quieting for now.

But when we reach him, I know instantly that something is wrong.

"Hey," I say to him as he glances up.

"Sutton," he says flatly. Then, eyes flicking to the person next to me, "Cooper."

Cooper, to his credit, knows when to make an exit. "Can I get anyone drinks?" he says, eyeing both of us.

"No thanks," I say. "But didn't you want to—"

"I'm going to grab another," he says, giving my elbow a squeeze that feels a lot like a goodbye before he nods at Everett. "Enjoy the rest of your evening."

I feel a little guilty as I watch him go. When I turn back to Everett, he's taking a sip from his glass, something in it that looks stronger than anything he usually drinks.

"He wanted to ask you about film school," I say. "His daughter wants to go to Devon."

"I don't want to talk to Cooper about film school," Everett says, voice low.

I shake my head. "He's a nice guy."

"So? I don't know him," Everett insists, and I can tell that he's angry, something simmering just below the surface. "Did you want to spend an afternoon telling him how to land a book deal?"

Not really, I think, but that's not the point right now. The point is whatever has caused Everett's sudden shift in attitude.

"Are you mad that I was talking to Cooper tonight?" I ask. Everett shakes his head, looking exasperated, which has the same frustration I felt with him at the beginning of the week flaring to life in my chest. "We're not exactly together," I say, before I can think about it.

Everett's eyes flash for a split second before something fizzles out there, fight and defeat all at once. "Oh," he finally says. "That I know."

It feels like the world has been flipped upside down, like we drove into some other dimension on the way here. Everything was fine, and now it's not, and I can't tell if I just didn't notice that things really *weren't* okay, or if something has actually gone wrong.

"Everett," I say, reaching out to lay a hand on his arm. "What's going on?" He glances down at where I'm touching him, something seeming to still in his body. "Listen, we'll talk. Just—once this is all over, okay? Once we're past this week. Now just isn't the time."

Everett's eyes flick to mine. "Right," he says, but it doesn't sound convincing. "Of course we will."

"Everett," I say, as he steps out of reach, apparently heading somewhere. "I promise you."

"I know you do," he says, and he gives me a quick smile that doesn't quite reach his eyes. "I'm going to get some air, okay?"

"Do you want me to come with you?" I ask.

He shakes his head, and I can't tell what it is, exactly. I don't know if he seems angry anymore. Not at me, at least. But there's something there that I still can't grasp. "No," he says. "You stay. It's a party. Here." He digs his keys out of his pocket, hands them to me. The cool weight of them surprises me, like I've been handed his most prized possession, but I don't think to protest. "In case anyone wants to head home early."

"Everett, what's wrong?" I ask, but again, he shakes his head.

"Nothing," he says. "I promise you."

I can't tell if he meant to echo me. If the words should land and sting, or if it was unintentional. But whatever he meant, he goes. Backs away toward the door until he turns and makes it the rest of the way out, one hand in his pocket.

And I let him.

twenty-eight

Fifth Summer

I had three weeks to prepare for a trip my brain had previously been careening toward in anticipation, and yet, by the time Davi parked the car in front of the cottage, I still didn't feel prepared.

Everett and I had agreed to wait until the end of the trip to tell everyone about us, but that felt like its own kind of torture. We'd spent every night on the phone since he'd been in San Francisco, and I swore even my nail beds missed him. Something had broken open in me when he'd left my apartment the weekend he came to visit me, and out had spilled years of repressed longing, tangling with the goopy mess that came with finally giving in to this. Suddenly I was someone I never thought I would be, dragging Everett by the hand back to my doorway every time he started to leave, face splitting in two every time it was his name I saw on my phone screen, almost falling asleep at the prep station at work because neither of us wanted to hang up the night before.

Laurel and Everett both had work to wrap up that day, so they were heading down in their separate cars that evening. Davi, Gabe, and I stopped at the grocery store on the way into town, and after unloading our things and stocking the fridge, Davi and I headed to the beach and left Gabe inside to call Mia.

"Think you'll ever want to talk to someone like that?" Davi asked me as we spread our towels on the sand.

"Hmm?" I said, twisting the cap off my water bottle and taking a long drink, pretending like I hadn't heard him. *Yes*, I wanted to say. *Yes, there's someone I want to talk to every day, all of a sudden, and I don't know what to do with myself now that it's happened. I'm the person you and I used to make fun of.*

Davi dropped onto his towel and stretched his legs out in front of him. The sun glinted off the water in front of us. It had been a hot May, and it seemed like the earth had trapped some of that, holding on to it for our visit here. He glanced back at the house. "I'm just happy Gabe's happy. Remember our first summer here?"

Every comment felt like some jab designed to get the truth out of me. I knew it wasn't *about* me, but the secret had clawed its way to the surface and almost scratched its way out, some monstrous thing I was now desperate to get off my chest.

"Yeah," I said, sitting on my towel next to Davi. I pivoted my mind away from what I wasn't saying, reminded myself that no one knew anything. "I'm still so mad at Zoey."

Davi shot me a look then, one I couldn't quite read.

"What?" I asked.

"Nothing," he said, then, when I wouldn't stop staring at him, "just that Gabe is really happy now. He wouldn't have even met Mia if things hadn't fallen apart with Zoey, you know?"

"I know," I said. "But what she did is still messed up."

"Sure." Davi shrugged. "I'm not saying you have to be best friends with the girl again. But we all mess up. If Gabe has moved on from it, isn't it time we do too?"

His words rolled through me, knocking against years' worth of grudges I'd staunchly set up in my lifetime. The girl sophomore year of high school who had made up a rumor that I'd been internet stalking my homecoming date for months, because she wanted to go with him. The guy Laurel briefly dated junior year of college who forgot her birthday. The professor who told Davi he wasn't cut out for law school. The big one, of course; my parents. But Zoey too. Her betrayal loomed larger to me than so many others, for some reason, and I'd assumed it did for all of us. The idea of the others moving on from it rattled against my foundations, unsteadied me.

But then, Gabe's laugh trickled down to us as he stepped out onto the back deck. I twisted to look at him, at the way he smiled as he talked to Mia, and felt something gentle brush against my ribs. Gabe wasn't worrying about Zoey anymore. He was happy. He was in love.

Unbidden, Everett's face flashed into my head, jerking my gaze back toward the water. Something glimmered at the edges of my mind, an idea brought on by Davi's words. Maybe, if everyone had moved on from Zoey, what Everett and I had done wasn't such a betrayal. Maybe things would be okay.

It was a big maybe, though. I thought about what I would do if I learned one of them had been lying for so long, what kind of wall I'd erect between myself and all the hurt it caused. You didn't treat people you loved like that. You didn't put others before them. It was what I'd done since I'd met Everett. I'd kept some piece of him to myself, and I'd enjoyed it.

Davi picked up his book and opened it before setting it on his face, tucking his hands behind his head. "Wake me if a tidal wave comes," he said, voice muffled.

"Sure," I said, distracted.

By the time evening rolled around, I'd planted myself in the kitchen, the only place I could think to go where I wouldn't confess everything to Davi and Gabe or combust from waiting to see Everett. *Three weeks*, I reminded myself as I stabbed skewers through zucchini and mushrooms and peppers, perhaps a little too forcefully. *It's only been three weeks*. I wasn't some kid with a crush. My brain couldn't possibly be rewired like this in such a short time. And yet, here I was, almost taking out my thumb when tires sounded in the driveway and I missed the slice of red pepper I was holding.

I set the kebab down on the tray of completed ones, wiping my palms on the tea towel hanging from the oven handle before trying to casually follow Gabe and Davi out the front door where Laurel was pulling in behind Everett, the two of them having driven down in tandem.

She was the first out of her car, the key barely out of the ignition before she hurled herself across the driveway at us, shoving herself into the middle of the circle so we could all hug her at once. "Everett!" she shouted over her shoulder when he hadn't joined us in the split millisecond it had taken her to climb out of her car. "You're missing something!"

I watched over her head as Everett swung out of the Bronco, the orange light of sunset slanting across his face as his eyes cut straight to mine, my breath immediately hitching when he smiled.

"Hurry *up*," Laurel whined. Everett wrapped his arms around Davi's and Gabe's shoulders, never breaking my gaze. Not even the chant Laurel started, something like *beach week, beach week*, could force my eyes away from his as we all huddled together in the driveway. His fingers found the back of my hand, my wrist, sending sparks shooting their way up my arm and straight to my brain.

Three weeks, I heard in my head, but only vaguely, as Everett's eyes sparkled in my direction. Maybe it was just three weeks. But a lot could happen in less time than that.

It was a perfect four days. Sun-warmed sand, sleeping with the windows thrown wide, drinks on the beach, dinners on the back deck, salty hair, and talking like we all used to, and laughing until we couldn't breathe. It all lasted four wonderful days until the clouds went gray and the kind of weather that never fully breaks into a storm, just hangs heavy above you, descended.

"Okay," Laurel said, dropping down next to me on the couch where I had my laptop open in front of me, a spreadsheet on the screen. The others were in town, on a mission to find the things we needed for the seafood feast we were making that night. "It's time to talk wedding."

Laurel met Stephen roughly two weeks after breaking up with Winona. It wasn't surprising—that was her usual timeline—but what did surprise us was their engagement approximately ten months later. Laurel, it seemed, had finally found the person she had been so ardently searching for since we'd met. I was her maid of honor, like we'd always planned, and she was eager to nail down the specifics.

"The place in Mendocino is free next June," I said, scrolling to the venues column on the spreadsheet.

"My number one?"

"Your number one," I said. "I called last week and they have you and Stephen penciled in. You'll need to put down a deposit by the end of the month if you want to lock it down."

"I love you!" Laurel crowed, flinging her arms around my neck. "What else have you planned for me?"

I ran her through the list. Potential vendors and her top two bands and weekends we could set aside for me to come to LA, help with whatever she needed. By the time we got to the florist she'd been eyeing since before she met Stephen, she sat up, squeezing my hand and leaning over to lower my laptop screen.

When I looked over at her, her eyes were watery. "What's wrong?" I asked, worry flickering through me. "Do you not like the catering options for the rehearsal dinner? Because I'll call the sashimi guy again—"

"No, it's not the sashimi," Laurel said, almost laughing. "It's just that I love you a lot."

"I love you too," I said. I pushed my laptop aside, turned fully to face her. "That's why we're going to make this the best wedding ever."

"I know it will be," she said. "But I don't just mean the wedding. I mean—" She sniffed, glancing quicky away before looking at me again. "I mean everything, Sutton. I don't think anyone has ever made me feel more cared for than you do. I mean, you're basically working a second job as my wedding planner. You always do so much to make this week happen." She gestured around the cottage. "You love all of us so well."

It should have been amazing to hear. It should have finally contradicted something I'd secretly worried about for years, that it was all too much, that nobody really wanted to be on this trip as badly as I did, that I was overbearing. But instead, all that came to my mind was Everett. The lie we were keeping, to be sure, and the guilt of keeping it, but the fact that he made me feel that way. *Cared for.* Not that Laurel didn't, of course she did. But there was this other person, someone I felt so much for, that understood me. That helped me to put down the things I was carrying every time we were together. And he was the one person it would hurt Laurel to learn I wanted to be with. It could never be simple between us.

"Promise me," Laurel said, dragging my attention back to

her. She took my hand in both of hers, staring seriously at me. "Promise me that we'll never let anything come between us."

Every hope I'd had for our last day here, every confidence I'd felt that it would be okay once Everett and I came clean, that our friends would be happy for us, wilted.

"What would come between us?" I asked, voice a little hoarse.

She shrugged. I was a horrible person. I knew exactly what would come between us, and I was just letting her carry on. "I don't know. Sometimes I just think about Zoey, and how she was our friend too. I feel a little guilty about what happened there." I didn't say anything, could tell there was more she needed to get off her chest. "But then I think about you, and how loyal you are, and how you would never do something like she did. You would talk to all of us first if something was going on that could mess up what we all have. I think that you'd put us before anything else. And we're all just so lucky to have that."

I didn't think I'd felt such an acute sense of guilt before, if it had ever sliced so deeply, turned me inside out and shoved all the terrible things I'd done into my face. Laurel was right—I prided myself on putting our group above all else, but that wasn't what I'd been doing at all, not for years now. I'd chosen someone else, someone new, over them time and time again. I'd thought it was innocent. But I was awful, a liar, disloyal to the people I considered my family.

"Do you promise?" she asked, giving my hands a little jostle.

"What?"

"Promise that nothing will ever come between us." Laurel let out a small laugh, almost rolling her eyes. "Not that you ever would."

All I could see was Everett. I could feel the perimeters of

my heart curling inward, protective, blotting out some truth I'd only just started to feel comfortable admitting to myself. How I felt about him. The things I wanted with him. Some future that now felt like dandelion seeds on the wind. I was never meant to keep it.

"Of course," I finally said, just as the front door opened and the others came in, Davi chattering on about some work thing or other. Laurel squeezed my hand one final time, the period on our promise.

"Did they have the good scallops?" she asked, pushing herself up from the couch and walking over to peek into the bags they'd brought in, as if something hadn't just ended, as if life was just supposed to carry on.

The conversation dulled around me as they carried things into the kitchen, as I turned my head and caught Everett's eye when he came in last, shutting the door behind him. He held up a carton of the peaches I'd told him to find if he could, and I tried to smile at him, but it was strained. Earlier this morning, he'd grabbed my hand and pulled me back into the house when the others raced out onto the beach to catch a quick five minutes of sunlight breaking through the cloud cover. We'd tucked ourselves against the wall, kissing and roaming our hands over each other's bodies until I almost shouted to the others that we had something to tell them, that there was a secret I couldn't keep a minute longer.

But keeping what had happened between us secret mattered more than ever now. What was most important had suddenly crystalized. There was only this group, and the new promise I'd just made to Laurel, and the fact that I wouldn't allow my heart to break; not over someone who was never really mine.

twenty-nine

Fifth Summer

That first summer I'd searched for a private moment with Everett and failed, but on that last day, after I forced myself to be fine during dinner and almost no sleep afterward, it was almost too easy. Gabe walked up to the main hotel while he called Mia, the sun finally out again that morning. Laurel and Davi went on a mission to get wood for our bonfire that night, the tradition we always ended the trip with. I'd anticipated some excuse to get him out of the house so we could talk, so I could end this before it went any further, but I found myself alone with Everett far too soon.

He was standing near the couch, frowning at his phone when I came out of the room I shared with Laurel, and he looked up immediately, face clearing.

"Is it work?" I asked, gesturing to where he tucked his phone into his pocket. "You should finish it."

"It can wait," he said, and I wished he hadn't. I wished he would delay this longer. Give us more time, but it was the same as my conversation with Laurel yesterday: I knew something that he didn't, so it was unfair of me to want more.

"What's up?" he asked, and for a brief second I wondered if I was wrong. If he could sense something was off. He hadn't closed the space between us, hadn't pulled me into his arms like he usually would.

I considered him before I said anything. We wouldn't be the same after this, I realized. There wouldn't be stolen days or the hope of them. The secret we'd shared would be in the past, buried, and with it, whatever thread tied us together. But the only way to fix this was to end it here, before anyone else knew, before it could hurt anyone beyond the two of us.

"I don't think we should tell everyone," I said, finally. "About us."

Everett was quiet. "Now?" he asked after a long minute. "Or ever?"

I swallowed, my chest aching. "Ever."

His lips just parted, and it wasn't until that moment that I realized there was no better outcome here. The idea of hurting Everett hit me as hard as hurting everyone else, but for some reason, I could convince myself we mattered less. There would be other people, had been other people. What I felt for Everett wasn't unique. It couldn't be.

But I saw something in his eyes, just a brief flash, that had a deeply specific, personal corner of my heart fracturing because I knew it so well. It was the thing Laurel always told me I wasn't addressing: how what my parents had done had shaped me. And it was what Everett's father had done to him. It was being left behind, having someone choose something else over you time and time again, feeling safe and having the rug ripped out from under you. I was doing it to him now.

I knew Everett too, though, and just as predicted, the hurt was only legible on his face for a second. He brushed it away with a practiced, level expression. "Okay," he said, but then, "Can I ask why?"

It surprised me—we were so much the same that I'd assumed

he'd want to get it over with quickly, not spend too much time picking over the wreckage. "Because of everyone else," I said, shaking my head. "Because we would hurt so many people. It's better if it just dies here."

"Right." Everett's eyes glanced across the ground at my feet before he looked at me again, assessing. Something in the way he watched me raked against my skin, like he was seeing too much. "It's not just that, though, is it?"

"What?" I asked, irritation starting to spark in me. *Just let it go*, I wanted to say to him. *Don't make this harder.*

"I don't think this is because of hurting everyone else," Everett said, not unkindly. "I think it's because it could hurt you."

My defenses sprang fully to life then, a familiar shuttering of anything else I might be feeling. It was how I always dealt with things: keeping them in strict order, compartmentalizing. But I'd let Everett spill over into so many areas of my life in the last few years, without even realizing it. Something about it made me angry, that I couldn't shut him out so easily. "Excuse me?" I asked.

"Come on, Sutton," he said. "You hate the idea of not being in control. A relationship comes with some measure of that. There's a chance we both get hurt here, and you might not have a say in that."

"We aren't even a couple, Everett," I snapped, because what he said dug too deep, hit a dead center bull's-eye in my chest.

"Of course," he said. "Neither of us do relationships."

It was too close to what Laurel had said on the boat last summer. It seemed almost like some sort of challenge—one I didn't want to back down from.

"There's nothing here to hurt us," I said. "But there's a lot to hurt everyone else. The way we've been lying."

"Nothing," Everett repeated then. "There's *nothing* here that could hurt you?" When I didn't say anything, he continued. "The last five years meant nothing to you."

For a brief, bright moment, my anger faltered, and I could almost feel his hand on my waist as he said it, like he'd closed the space between us and this was all just some stupid joke, some scene we were rehearsing in case anyone else got word of us. We'd kiss, and it would all be fine.

But he hadn't closed the distance between us. We were still two islands. "Not nothing," I said. Everett was right about one thing, no matter how little I wanted to admit it, I wished I could control this, but he was a variable I'd never expected. I shrugged a shoulder, said as casually as I could muster, "They were fun."

"Fun," Everett said. "Five years of lying to everyone, of sleeping together, of breaking this pact you care so much about—that was fun for you?"

I'd been too focused on Everett to hear the lock of the door turn behind me, but the sound of the door banging open had me jumping, turning to see three of the most important faces in the world to me ranging from shock (Gabe), to something like humor (Davi), and finally, to anger, pure and unfiltered, on Laurel's perfectly sun-kissed face.

"You're joking," she said. I choked, no sound coming out of me. "You two are sleeping together?"

"Were," Everett clarified behind me, too fast, and I whirled, expecting to find some smug expression on his face but he just shrugged, like *What else am I supposed to say?*

I wanted to ask when they got there, know how much they heard, but I knew none of that mattered. What mattered was that Everett and I had broken the only real promise we'd ever made, the one we'd all sworn on in this very room, and lied about it.

"I'm so sorry," I said quickly, turning back to face them.

"You're unbelievable," Laurel said, stomping past us into the kitchen, where she set down the bag she was carrying with a loud clink.

"Laurel," Davi said. "Come on. We've talked about how much they flirt with each other."

"Don't *come on* me," Laurel spat at him, which had Davi stepping back, holding up his hands, and the reality that they'd discussed this descended on me. She looked at Everett and me, still standing a good few feet apart. I'd lost my one ally. "You've been sleeping together for five years?"

That, at least, cleared up how much she'd heard.

"When did you even find the time that first summer?" she asked. I winced before I could stop myself.

"We met at a party," Everett said, stepping in at least for this.

Laurel's gaze pivoted to him. "A *party*?"

"It was before graduation," I said. "We—" I broke off, unsure of how to say it.

"We hooked up," Everett said. "It was nothing."

His voice was flat, emotionless as he said it, and that was it. Whatever had started in San Francisco was gone. Truthfully, whatever had started five years ago was gone. It confirmed what I'd always been nervous about. Even through our time together, that one night hadn't been some magical thing. The connection between us was the same as it was between anyone else. Predictable. Something that could be easily ended. No harm done. But I felt something close to that in that moment, hurt pricking up like I'd never felt before.

"Hold on," Laurel said. "You two knew each other?" Our silence seemed to be the tacit confirmation she needed, because she laughed once, a bark of a sound. "Round of applause, really. I mean, you had me fooled."

"Laurel, it was for two seconds," I said. "It didn't matter."

"Two seconds?" Davi said from where he and Gabe still stood in the doorway, mostly to Everett. "That's pretty short, man."

"Davi, not now," I said, shooting him a pleading look that made him go silent again. "It was one night," I said to Laurel. "He was just another guy." I hoped it sunk in for Everett, that I could play this game too. If it meant nothing to him, I would convince myself it was true.

"Except he's not just another guy," Laurel said, crossing an arm over her middle. "He's Everett. He is very much a *very important guy* to everyone in this room. And you didn't think you should tell us, at any point? Maybe, I don't know, when we specifically asked about it when we made the pact?"

I hated the word *pact*. Hated that it made us sound like a bunch of Boy Scouts sitting around a campfire. And yet it loomed so large in my life, held so much weight that it felt almost sacred, this promise we'd made to each other at such a pivotal point in our lives, when we were all heading our separate ways.

It was Gabe who broke the silence, finally, after Everett and I had stood there for a solid minute, both of us apparently unable to offer up any sort of explanation or apology.

"You should have told us," he said, almost surprising me. I'd been so wrong, that they wouldn't care, that because they'd forgiven Zoey they would forgive this. And of course that was the case. What Zoey had done was in the past, faded for everyone but me, the person who couldn't ever seem to let anything go, but this was now. I touted this group as unbreakable, but here I'd been for years, so casually destroying it. "We deserved to know."

"You're right," Everett said, beating me to it. "I'm sorry we didn't tell you."

"I'm sorry too," I said.

"Are you two together now?" Gabe asked, glancing between us.

"No," Everett and I said at the same time, voices laced with the same level of vitriol. Gabe raised an eyebrow.

"There is no world in which Everett Bridges and I would ever be a couple," I said, not bothering to glance at Everett for his reaction.

"But there's a world where you might have been, isn't there?" Laurel said. I looked at her. "You're still lying to us."

"We—" I started, feeling like something was strangling around my throat. I wanted the hard, ugly parts of this to be over. "We discussed it," I finally said. "But it would never work."

Laurel crossed both her arms at this. "Did you think at all about what would happen if you two broke up? What that would mean for all of us?"

"Of course we did," I said. "That's why we're not—" I broke off, her next possible words bouncing to the front of our brain. *Oh, so it's our fault.* An anticipated accusation that I couldn't prove she'd say, but could see the possibility of written on her face.

I watched as Laurel took a deep breath, closed her eyes for a minute. I hated being on the outside of it, being the reason for it. I wanted to be the solution. But I stood still until she looked at all of us again, expression cool.

"Listen," she said. "There's still plenty of daylight left. I don't really want to be here anymore."

"Laurel," I said, but she shot me a look that told me I was the last person she wanted to hear from. Our conversation from yesterday shattered around me, along with all my efforts to get this thing with Everett over with quietly, quickly, so there would be no collateral damage. I'd ended up hurting everyone.

"I don't care what anyone else does, but as far as I'm concerned, this trip is over."

"Laurel," Gabe said as she shoved her way toward our room. "Come on. This doesn't have to be such a huge deal."

"No, I think it's an enormous deal," she said, whirling furiously on Gabe. "I think that two of our best friends thought it was fine to lie to us for *years*, and I'm not going to stick around to find out what else they're hiding. I think we're done here."

She slammed the door to the bedroom, rattling the framed picture that hung on the wall next to it.

Davi and Gabe looked at where Everett and I still stood, both of us frozen. "She'll get over it," Davi said. "She always does. Just give her some time."

I nodded, but I didn't totally believe him. Laurel needed time when she was upset about other things: when Davi ate the last of her cheese from the fridge, when she went through a breakup, when she was stressed out. But she'd never needed time because of something I'd done. Something like this.

"We'll pack, I guess," Gabe said. "Are you good to leave tonight?"

"Mmm-hmm," I mumbled softly, arms crossed protectively in front of me.

They headed upstairs, leaving me alone with Everett in the living room.

"Davi's right," Everett said after a minute. "We can try to talk to her again in a couple of days."

My gaze jerked up to him then, and I didn't care that everyone was in earshot, that we were standing in a tiny house with absolutely no privacy, where I'd thought it would be a good idea to have what needed to be a private conversation with him in the first place.

"There is no *we*," I snapped.

Everett, who had returned to his usual self, the brief fight in him from earlier gone, looked surprised. "Sutton," he said. "Let's not—"

"No," I cut in, a shimmering kind of rage settling in the pit of my stomach. I didn't care that Everett was looking at me like he used to, that there was something like hope behind his eyes that we could move past this. Something had occurred to me as Laurel stormed into her room about Everett's position during our argument, his view of the front door. "Did you know they were coming?"

Everett's eyebrows slanted together. "What?"

"When you said everything out loud earlier. When you summarized our whole pointless relationship, did you know they were at the door?"

"Of course not," Everett said, disbelief flashing across his face. "Sutton, I wouldn't do that."

"I don't believe you," I said. I could hear Gabe's and Davi's movements still above us, our voices carrying up to them. "All I know is that the three most important relationships in my life are ruined, and it's because of you."

I could see my words slam into him, hitting home. Three relationships, and one person at fault. The person I never should have welcomed into my life the way I did. Maybe Laurel was right. Maybe I didn't give anyone a second chance. But in that moment, I was fine with it. I owned every problem she and Everett said I had, decided to wear them like a badge of honor.

Everett was nodding. "Pretty sure we did the ruining together, Sutton," he said.

I didn't answer him. I turned on my heel and marched out the front door, slamming it shut behind me.

We never stayed at Poppy Cottage again.

thirty

This Summer

I don't see Everett again for the rest of the party. I wait for him to come back in through the door, keep a watchful eye on the crowd for him, but he never comes back. The worst part is that no one else seems to notice.

When it's nearly midnight, I ask Gabe if he's heard from him. "He isn't here?" he asks, and when I shake my head, he shrugs. "He's got to be around here somewhere."

Davi hasn't seen him either, so I finally track Laurel down at a table in the corner, holding court with a group of beautiful people I don't know and have never heard her mention.

"Hey," I say, sliding into the spot next to her as she bids the group goodbye. They slink off into the party like they're her personal NPCs. "Have you seen Everett?"

"I'm sure he's somewhere around here," she says, waving a dismissive hand. "Now, did I see you talking to Cooper earlier?"

"Laurel," I say, something like impatience flickering through me. I tamp it down, remind myself this is *her* night, *her* party, *her* week. "I *can't find* Everett."

One of Laurel's eyebrows ticks upward. "Is there a *reason* you're suddenly so concerned about him?"

I bristle at the comment, even though I know I'm keeping a secret from her, yet again. In that moment, though, I'm exhausted. Tired of Laurel being mad at me, of trying to atone for what happened for *years* now. Of making something up to someone who can't seem to decide if she actually forgives me or not.

I watch for a minute as she waves at people milling past, nothing but her public self. I think back to every time I've watched her shift, a social chameleon I used to envy. Now it has me questioning if the version I've always had of her is even real. *Look at me*, I want to shout at her. But instead, the question bubbles up in my throat and bursts out of me, sharp and sudden. "Why did you text me first?"

She moves her face like she might glance at me, but her eyes don't leave the crowd. "When?"

I know Laurel is going through something. I know she might be heartbroken. I know that my only job is to be here for her right now, but suddenly, I can't do it anymore. I can't keep pretending things are fine, that this week is in any way normal. When she'd texted me that she needed me I'd felt some kind of pride wash over me, like it was proof she still needed me, but I don't feel needed, or even wanted, right now.

"When you and Stephen split up," I say. "Why did you text me first?"

At this, she does finally look at me. "I knew you could make this week happen," she says.

"That's it?" I ask. "You wanted to start up this tradition again, and you knew I'd be the one to plan it for you?"

She's taken another sip of her drink and almost laughs as she sets her glass down on the table again. "Sutton," Laurel says. "This trip was never about tradition. We all know what this week really is."

I shake my head. "What is it?"

Laurel's head tilts, almost like she pities me. I still don't know what I'm missing until she says it. Until she's speaking to me like I need to be helped along. "Look at all of this," she says, gesturing to the party at large. "Honey, this week was never about going backward. It was a goodbye."

I'm still not caught up. Or, maybe I am, but I don't want to be. Don't want to hear what she's saying. "To what?" I ask. "To this place? Because we can go somewhere else. We can plan other trips, we—"

"Sutton." The tone in which she says it is grating in its condescension, like I'm a child she's carefully delivering news to. "Be realistic. This week was a way to say goodbye to us."

My throat seizes. "To you and me?" I ask.

If Laurel catches my reaction, she dismisses it. "To everyone," she says. "To the family we used to be. To my old life."

"Used to be," I repeat. Laurel nods, and for some reason, it sparks an angry ember in my chest. "What, do Davi and Gabe feel the same way?" I don't include Everett. I can't bring myself to.

"We haven't been talking about it," Laurel says. "But everyone knows."

"*I* didn't know," I say, almost shrilly. A man in a gold suit startles a little, looking at me, then Laurel, raising an eyebrow as if asking if she needs help. *I'm her best friend!* I want to yell at him, but instead she waves him off, nodding that she's okay. Her expression flattens when she looks at me again.

"Everett and I—" I start, swallowing over the burgeoning lump in my throat. "I know we messed things up when we broke our promise to everyone. I know we shouldn't have lied to you for so long, but, but we're fine now, we—" I break off, unsure of how much to say. Knowing it can't be much without

Everett here with me. Then I remember that there might not even be anything to tell anymore, given how he seemed at the party tonight, his disappearing act.

But Laurel is looking at me like I just said something crazy. She shakes her head, brows drawn together. "Sutton, no one cares about you and Everett hooking up what, five, ten years ago? God," she says, looking almost baffled. "We aren't in college anymore. We made that pact ages ago."

"But it's why we stopped coming on this trip," I insist, sure this has to be the reason. Because it has been the reason—I've *believed* it's the reason—that everything fell apart. I've blamed myself for it since it happened, thought that my poor decisions caused the fracturing of my family. I've put so much energy into fixing things, railing against people who didn't seem to *want* to fix things, that it's impossible that Everett and I breaking the pact isn't what caused this. "It's when everything fell apart."

Laurel shakes her head again, slowly, like I'm once again that child she has to help arrive at the right conclusion. "I was mad about you lying, sure. But things had been changing for a while before that, Sutton," she says. "No one could even come on this trip anymore. We were spread out all over the place." She shrugs a shoulder. "We grew up."

It's that, such a general statement accompanied by such a casual gesture, that does it for me. It settles what she's saying over me somehow, presses down.

"We've been trying these past few years," I say, almost to myself. "We text. You and I still—"

"Talk on the phone every few months?" she says. "Collab on socials?"

I nod. Stupidly, I guess, because Laurel rolls her eyes, like it's nothing. I thought I'd been giving her the space she said she needed after my relentless apologies following that last argument between me and Everett. The one that ruined everything, that left us all shattered.

"The most we've *really* talked has been to plan this week, though," Laurel says, like the rest of our relationship doesn't mean anything. "Doesn't that say something?"

"But this week has been great, hasn't it?" I say. I need my effort to mean something. "I mean, it's been like it was."

"Nothing is like it was," Laurel says softly.

I stare at her for a long, quiet minute. Her tone is so final, so assured. It dawns on me, finally, that she's been thinking about this for a while. That what the rest of us thought was support was actually a last hurrah for her.

"No," I say suddenly, something almost manic pushing at my chest. "What we have is rare, it's important, it's—"

"What?" Laurel says when I stop short, aware that my next words will sound melodramatic to her.

"It's worth saving," I say.

Laurel, to my horror, scoffs.

In that moment, I know it's not my former best friend sitting in front of me. It's someone I can't reach. I've been fighting for a friendship she might not even want anymore.

I stand up, rifling in my purse for Everett's keys.

"Where are you going?" Laurel says behind me.

"I still have to find Everett," I say.

"Why do you care so much?" she asks. She waves a hand toward the party. "What about Cooper? You have this perfectly great guy following you around all night, a *chef* with a kid and a house who wants to be with you, and you're still chasing after someone you've been mad at for years now. It's like you want to be disappointed sometimes, I swear. Why can't you just be happy?"

It's almost as if I don't have room in my brain for anything more, can feel her words circling, but taking a while to settle. She's not wrong. Cooper is great. Maybe I should be trying to find him, should have paid him more attention this week. But if being happy is the point, it seems like the most obvious thing in the world: It isn't Cooper that would make me happy, wonderful as he may be.

"I can be happy," I say to her, a vivid image, or maybe a memory, crystalizing in front of me. A cold pier, and warm hands, and hopes shared out loud. My life, but better. What I already have shared with someone who I can't find right now. "Everett's still missing," I tell Laurel.

"He's a grown man," she says, lounging back in her seat. "He'll come back when he wants to."

"Everett never disappears," I say.

"Who cares," she mutters, sending a new flare of disbelief through me.

"Laurel," I say. "Everett is our friend, whether you want him to be or not."

"Yeah, for now."

I should go, I know, give her space, let her enjoy her party, but I take a step closer. I don't know this person, this Laurel, at all. "What does that mean?"

"What do you think it means?" she asks. "Everyone disappoints you. You used to agree with me about that."

"No, *you* used to agree with *me* about that."

"Same thing," Laurel says.

"No, it isn't," I say. "Because I don't believe that anymore." It seems odd, to have this be the moment that fully clicks into place for me, when Laurel has just told me our friendship means nothing to her, that the funeral or whatever it is she's thrown for herself tonight was also a funeral for our friendship. But I mean it. I'm tired of thinking that way, in such black-and-white terms, tired of not leaving any room for not only everyone else to be human, but also for myself.

There are a million ways I know I've worked myself into the corners I have. I've been stingy with second chances and I've expected the people I love to be superhuman, to never make mistakes, but for some reason, all of that feels foggy now. I don't want Cooper, who hasn't disappointed me once this week, who would probably do so many things perfectly until I got close enough to him to discover the crack in his immaculate veneer. I want Everett, who I've hurt, who has hurt me, whose flawed, human pieces I know, and have only made me love him more.

I wait for Laurel to say something, anything, to be the friend I used to know so well, but I can't find any of it there. "Well, then, you're the one who taught me," Laurel says. "Everyone disappoints you."

I feel it like she reached out and slapped me, heat radiating from the spot. I stare at her until she stands with a fed-up expression, swiping her hands on the skirt of her dress and starting to march past me.

"Well, I'm going," I say before she's out of earshot. She stops in her tracks, turns back to look at me. "And I give a shit about saving us, the people you called when you needed support. Not any of your internet friends, or all the people you hang out with in LA and Paris and Tokyo. Not your actual fucking sister. Us. And no matter how badly any of us have acted this week or in the past five years, we're worth saving."

I brush past her, headed in the direction of the door, Everett's keys jangling in my hand.

"Don't be so naive," Laurel calls after me. I pause, not looking back at her. "We'll never talk to each other again after this week."

I frown to keep my chin from shaking. When I look back

at her she's watching me, artfully disheveled in her white dress, framed on all sides by her party, like even when she's saying things like this, she can somehow still maintain perfection. She's never felt more like a stranger to me than she does right now.

"If I find Everett, we're leaving in the morning," I say.

I walk away without another glance backward.

thirty-one

Sixth Summer
Laurel and Stephen's Wedding

I spent most of the year between our last summer together and Laurel's wedding trying to mend things. By the time the day of her actual wedding rolled around, we were back on steadier footing, but I think it was due largely in part to the fact that she didn't want any drama surrounding the weekend, and less to do with the fact that she'd totally forgiven me. I could see the way the crack that I'd put in our relationship spidered out. Case in point, it was always the plan that I would be Laurel's maid of honor, but at the last minute, she'd decided she wouldn't have bridesmaids at all, revoking her bridal party invitations to all of us. I told myself it wasn't about me, even as she started to ask me to help her again, assigned me tasks that I would have been doing had I still been her maid of honor. It wasn't about what I'd done.

Davi and Gabe were quick to come around. They knew Everett and I were sorry, and so we were fine. But I worried about our foundation, something I had thought was unshakable. Our group chat had gone quieter than ever. There would be no trip to Poppy Cottage this year. Even if we were fine on the surface, there was permanent damage below.

I spent weeks hunting down the best revenge dress I could find for Laurel's rehearsal dinner, and hated that all Everett had to do was put on a suit tailored to him to make a point when he walked in.

My anger at him had slowly settled into a simmer, always there, but something I could move to the back burner. I dumped every thought I had about him into that pot, the good and the bad. The idea of Everett next to me at the farmers market as I wandered the stalls, a head of tousled golden-brown hair on a patron at the restaurant and the sharp ache that followed, the fire that leapt up in me when Laurel posted a photo to her story that included a hand I'd recognize anywhere wrapped around a beer glass—all of it went in, stewed together until I couldn't sort the pieces out from one another.

So by the time I saw Everett arrive at the restaurant in Mendocino where Laurel and Stephen were holding their rehearsal dinner, the impact of him was already muddied. I was angry, I knew, but mostly it felt like something itchy I was forced to wear. I wanted nothing but to shake his presence off, couldn't deal with the fact that the whole argument hadn't just made him and our entire history disappear, that he was here now, a part of this, no matter how I felt about it.

He arrived with Gabe and Mia, and I watched as Laurel hurried over to them, throwing her arms around all of them in a group hug.

"Careful," Davi said from his seat next to me. We'd been here since this afternoon, had helped set up, and hadn't received that kind of greeting from Laurel. He plucked the olive out of his empty martini glass. "Better school your face into something more pleasant."

I stared at where Laurel was beaming up at Everett, felt like a feral creature had just awakened in my stomach. "She certainly forgave him quickly," I muttered so only Davi could hear me.

"Yeah, well, Everett isn't her best friend," Davi said. My gaze snapped to his, lips parting. He shrugged. "We're all best friends, I know. But you two are different. I don't think Laurel even knew you had that kind of lie in you. We all just thought you and Everett liked flirting with each other."

It stung, sharp and shocking, but I knew he was right. He'd confirmed, twice now, that everyone else was at least aware of whatever sparked between Everett and me, a fact that embarrassed me to no end. I pictured myself every summer for the last five years, thinking I was treating him like anyone else, when I must have looked ridiculous, bantering with this guy who I could never have. I understood what Davi meant too. That I was Laurel's best friend, so the hurt went deeper. But still, I couldn't shake the jealousy I felt over the way she'd forgiven Everett and might never forgive me. I worried that if it went on too long, our positions would be flipped, and he would be the best friend, while I was the one who didn't have to rise to any higher expectations, an afterthought.

I vowed to myself, at that table, to not let that happen. I would prove myself to Laurel until she trusted me again, the way she used to.

The evening passed quickly after that. I said a terse hello to Everett and ignored him the rest of the night, not even glancing his way except for the few moments I could feel Laurel eyeing me like she was checking in on my behavior, and I would force myself to look at him when he talked, smile and nod until I knew she'd looked away.

Laurel and Stephen's wedding day dawned perfect and sunny, not a single cloud in the sky. I felt the sharp reminders of what this day was supposed to be everywhere, though. When I spent the morning on a hike with Gabe and Davi instead of with Laurel, or all of us together. When I showed up to Laurel's room just an hour before the wedding and she was already in her dress. When I watched from the fifth row instead of standing beside her, as they were married with the ocean sweeping out behind them.

It was a perfect wedding, though, and even if I didn't participate, I could see the things Laurel had let me help her with everywhere, in the flowers and the music and the lighting and the favors, tiny details we'd pored over on the phone and on my trips to LA. Proof, I thought, that we weren't entirely broken.

It wasn't until the end of the night that he found me. I thought I'd almost made it through unscathed, as the dancing wound down and Laurel threw her bouquet and the bar started to close up. I stood next to a low stone wall on an overlook near the tent where things were wrapping up, just outside the golden glow of the party, and had been looking out at the dark ocean, the sound of the waves crashing in drowning out any approaching footsteps.

"Sutton." His voice sent a familiar flutter through my stomach, one that now had my shoulders rising up toward my ears, one I didn't want to feel. I turned my head to look at him, unsmiling. The sleeves of his white button-down were rolled up, jacket abandoned somewhere, his hands in his pockets. I'd avoided looking at him all night, and still he'd been there. Two seats down from me at the wedding, at our table at dinner, spinning Laurel's gleeful grandmother on the dance floor. Everett was a point of light wherever he went, *the most popular person in the room*, and I couldn't deny it any more than I could pretend it wasn't what had drawn me to him in the first place. Beautiful, golden boy who would only break your heart.

I looked back out at the dark horizon, not saying anything to him.

He waited a minute, quiet next to me until he said, "We don't have to talk. But—"

"Good, then," I cut in, casting him a sideways glance. "I don't want to talk."

Everett's mouth closed, his brow furrowing the smallest bit. "Okay," he finally said. He stood for a moment longer before turning, starting back toward the tent.

Something lodged in my throat. Words or an ache, I couldn't tell, but before he was out of earshot I turned, calling after him. He looked back at me, and the small glimmer of hope on his face plunged straight into my chest, pinning me in place for a moment until I brushed it into that pot that simmered on the back burner of my brain. "There was a better way to do it," I said. "You didn't have to trick me."

He glanced down at the ground, shook his head before he looked back up at me. "I didn't do what you think I did, Sutton," he said. "I wasn't paying attention to anything but you that day." Something about that, the almost angry way he said it, punched at the tender spot near my sternum, but I didn't let myself hang on to it for long.

"I just don't see why I should trust you," I said, not because I wanted to be cruel. Because it was a question I'd been turning over when I did let myself pull him to the forefront of my mind. If I'd made a huge mistake this whole time, misjudged him entirely.

Everett's eyes narrowed at this. "You don't see *any* reason to trust me?" he asked. "After everything?"

I thought about what he was referring to. Our whole history. Secrets shared and secrets kept and something between us that felt frighteningly important. But I could so easily reduce it to just two days every summer. Two days together, without any outside context, and it became simple to say I didn't know him.

"I hurt the most important people in my life because of something that should have never happened," I said. It was different than what I'd said before, that it was his fault. I still blamed him, but my part in all of it had crept up more recently, reminding me that Everett wasn't alone in this. "I can't remove you from that."

"What happened wasn't just about you," Everett said. "You think I cared so little about everyone else that I just wanted to make you look bad? They're my friends too."

"But they heard *you* say it."

"Oh my god," Everett said, rubbing an exasperated hand down his face. "So you wouldn't be so mad at me right now if *you'd* been the one they overheard?"

"I wouldn't have done that on purpose—"

"I didn't do what you think I did," Everett cut in angrily. "Whether or not you want to admit it, Sutton, we created this problem together."

He stared at me, waiting for a response, but I could clearly see us here, going in circles, for the rest of the night. So I crossed my arms over my chest and shrugged.

Everett's expression morphed into one of disbelief for a second before his shoulders fell. I wanted him to say something else. What, I didn't know, because nothing could fix this. That same ugly part of me that would shut down any attempt he made to remedy things was still alive and well.

"All the best to you, then, Sutton," he said after a long minute of silence.

And he left.

That should have been it. I should have let him walk away and figured out how to forgive him, in my own way. And I might have, on some level, for the next four years. Four years without a week in a house with him helped to dull what had happened. But every time I thought I'd moved on, there he was, at some gathering that, if I weren't still so obsessed with Everett Bridges on some level, should have been nothing. Instead, it was arguments that pulled us all further apart, tiny jabs that proved that no matter how much time passed between us, the wound was deep enough that we both still felt it.

And as soon as Laurel's text came in, *I need you*, as soon as the concept of the trip being re-created was even born, it all came rushing back to me again. I'd let things sit without proper attention for so long that the emotional snarl in me that revolved around Everett had grown to behemoth proportions, something that overwhelmed me the closer our arrival date at Wild Horse Villa loomed. And it seemed like it might have been the same for Everett. We had both silently stewed in our hurt for so long, reminded of it just frequently enough to feel it anew, that as soon as we saw each other we were right back in that living room saying ugly things, never having faced what happened at all.

thirty-two

This Summer

I don't know where to look for Everett. I have a sinking feeling he might be on the beach somewhere, impossible to find in the endless dark, and so I decide to try all other options before heading out there. I call the front desk of the resort in case he got a car back. Concierge Ralph hasn't seen him, and actually sounds concerned when I ask. Everett is high-profile enough for him now.

He isn't at the bar across the street or sitting on a bench. He isn't walking on any of the streets I circle, or at the twenty-four-hour market where we sometimes get late-night provisions. I drive toward the surfboard rental shop and scan the buildings in between, moving so slowly someone honks at me and I have to pull over, rest my head against my hands on the steering wheel, and take in a series of deep breaths until the shaky feeling that's been in me since my conversation with Laurel subsides.

I'm making a U-turn from the surf shop when I spot it: a neon yellow arrow pointed toward the door of a bar we went to a handful of times in our first couple years here. And even though I think it would be the last place Everett would go, even though I'm starting to think I might have to head out to the beach, I turn across the road and park in the lot, jog up the ramp toward the door.

It's busy inside, people lined up around the U-shaped bar and others at the two pool tables at one side of the room. Eighties music drifts down from speakers long past their prime, crackling and popping. I crane my neck to look around, and I'm about to go, about to give up what I already knew was an unlikely option, when I spot him.

Not all of him, exactly. The top of his head, fingers raked into his hair as he rests his elbows on the bar on the far side, sitting next to the wall. I push through the crowd to get to him.

"Everett," I say when I reach him, spreading a hand across his shoulders. "Are you okay? I've been looking everywhere for you."

When he lifts his head to look at me, it's like it takes him a minute to recognize me. But when he does, that smile that first charmed me ten years ago spreads across his face.

"Sutton Hale," he says, spreading an arm out toward me. I half hug him, his arm settling heavy over my shoulders. "How are you?" he asks.

"I'm fine," I say, trying to get a good look at his face as he slides his arm off my shoulders again and drops a clumsy hand to the neck of the beer bottle in front of him, toying with it. "And you might be drunk?"

"Am I?" Everett frowns, picks up the bottle and considers it before he looks at me. "Maybe."

The lone empty stool in this place is next to him, and before the college-aged girl standing behind me can slide onto it I grab it and drag it closer, sitting down.

I've never seen Everett drunk, can count on one hand the number of times I've even seen him tipsy, and something about it sets off alarm bells in me. I reach out, spreading a hand over his knee.

"Everett, what happened?" I ask him. He's a little slow, but he looks down at my hand on his leg, beer hovering between his mouth and the bar, still frowning.

"What happened when?" he asks. I tilt my head, give him a second to figure it out. "Oh, at the party?" I nod and he laughs, takes a long drag of his beer.

"Could I have a water?" I ask the bartender. I take the bottle Everett's balancing against the lip of the bar and set it out of his reach, replace it with the cup of water the bartender hands me.

Everett watches it all with a sort of sleepy fascination, a soft smile on his face. He reaches out at one point and untucks the ends of my hair from under the collar of my jacket, spreads a hand across them so they lie flat against my back, then rests a heavy forearm on my shoulder again.

"You were right, Sutton Hale," he says.

"What was I right about?" I ask.

He leans in a little closer. "I'm a nepo baby."

My brow creases in confusion, recalling past conversations, self-deprecating jokes he made that never really felt that funny. *So you're in the family business*, I said that first summer, when I learned who his father was. "You've called yourself a nepo baby before, Everett."

"Yes," he says. "But I didn't know *just how much* of a nepo baby I am."

I shake my head. "What do you mean?"

"I got a call a few hours ago. You know that stupid movie I made a couple years ago?" Everett asks. All the edges of his words are rounded, ineffective. "The one with the kids. The one Laurel made us all see this week."

"*Cooney* isn't stupid, Everett," I say. "You love that movie. Everyone loves that movie."

"Well, it turns out," he says, "that my father—you know my father?"

"Yes, I know your father," I say, with less disdain than I'm currently feeling.

"My *father*, Ben Astor, America's favorite actor, is friends with the head of a certain studio that might have given me funding for a certain stupid movie that launched my whole stupid career."

I pause, let the words settle. I can't think of a worse thing for Everett to find out, and yet, I know he knows the sway his father has. Know he's aware that no matter how far he tries to run from him, there are people that just *know* he's Ben Astor's kid, and even if he hates it, he can't escape it. There was always a chance his father might do something like this. But even so, I can't imagine what it must feel like.

"Everett," I say. "All that means is that *Cooney*, which is a *great movie*, got—"

"That's not even the worst part," he interrupts, leaning in even closer.

"It's not?"

He shakes his head. "My dad wants me to repay the favor," he says. He leans in so his lips are against my ear, hot and heavy. "He's going to be the lead in my next movie."

I lean away from him as he does too, stretching toward where I set his beer. He lifts it in a cheers toward me before draining the rest of it, setting it back down on the bar top.

"Can you say no?" I ask.

He shakes his head. "Casting loves the decision. Think he's perfect for the role. Which—" he lifts a hand toward the bartender again "—he probably is."

"No he's not," I say.

"You don't even know what the movie is about," Everett says, which stings for some reason.

"I know you're reading all those books about physics," I say. "I know people are already thinking it will be a contender during award season because it's *your* next movie." I read it somewhere this spring, that whatever the follow-up to *Cooney* would be, everyone was expecting it to be big.

Everett looks confused, then surprised, then away from me completely when the bartender sets another beer and a shot of whiskey in front of him. He hands her a fifty and tells her to keep the change.

"Everett, slow down," I say as he tosses back the shot. He winces, chases it with his beer before looking back at me.

"Isn't this exactly the kind of thing people drink about?"

"People, maybe," I say. "You don't."

Everett stands up, grabbing his jacket from the back of his chair and slinging it over his shoulder. "I don't know, Sutton," he says. "Remember what you said?"

"When?" I ask, twisting on my stool to look at him.

"You said you can't see any reason to trust me." The words run cold through me, twisting deep into my stomach.

"Everett, I didn't mean that," I say softly.

"No, I think it's probably a good thing. Turns out, I can't even trust myself."

I watch as he slaps far too much cash on the bar, even though he's already paid, and starts through the crowd, a little unsteady on his feet as he goes. I can feel it, that pot boiling over, everything we've avoided talking about this week starting to burn. I was stupid to think we could ever ignore it, could just go back to some time before it happened. The moment we fell apart will continue to define us until we address it.

I jump off my stool, swinging the strap of my purse over my

head just as he disappears out the door. By the time I weave my way through the crowd and outside, he's already halfway down the beach, walking toward the ocean like he might disappear into it. I take my heels off and run to catch up with him.

"Everett!" I call once I'm in earshot, but he doesn't turn around. I finally reach him and put a hand on his shoulder. It tenses beneath my palm. "I didn't mean that, Everett. I said it because—"

"I know why you said it," Everett says, turning back to me. He doesn't look angry. He looks a little lost, hopeless, and it's so much worse than mad. "Don't you think I know? We were so close to having it, Sutton. But of course it would never work."

"What do you mean?"

"It means we're the same. We both love being in control, but it's all an illusion. It's why neither of us can be in a successful relationship. We're summer people, remember?"

"Please stop quoting me," I say, a desperate tinge to my voice. "I don't believe that anymore."

"Why not?"

"Because of this week," I say. "Because of yesterday."

"We've had five years of not talking about this," Everett says, that same sad, defeated expression on his face as he looks down at me. "One week can't change that."

"Maybe it can," I say. "Maybe we were just young and stupid, and maybe now that I know how I feel, we—" I break off. Everett is so close to me, chest almost bumping mine.

"What?" he asks softly.

"Nothing," I say. There are enormous things to admit to between us, things to apologize for, and I can't do it on a cold, dark beach. It has to matter. "I don't want to have this conversation while one of us is drunk."

Of everything that's happened tonight, I don't expect that

to be the thing that gets to him, that makes him drop whatever facade it is he's been clinging onto, but at this, he falters back a step. "Fuck," he says. I watch as he drags a hand down his face, as he looks at the beer he's still clutching. "I am drunk, aren't I." He says it like he never has been, like he's just realizing it now. *This is why my head is spinning.*

"I'm afraid so," I say.

Everett looks stymied for a minute, and then he turns around, lifts his arm, and flings the bottle at the ocean. We watch it glide in a smooth arc, end over end, sending the remainders of its contents raining down over the sand before it disappears into the water.

We stand in silence for a minute. Everett's back is to me, so I can't see his expression, just the rise and fall of his shoulders.

"Feel better?" I ask.

He doesn't answer for a long moment. I take a step closer to him, reaching a hand toward his shoulder. "Everett?"

"Shit," he says.

And bolts for the water.

I call his name but he ignores me, and it's so dark out here that before long I have to take off after him just to keep track of him. I don't know what I expected a drunk Everett to be like, but it certainly wasn't this erratic. "What are you doing?" I shout. "Everett!"

I speed up, watching in horror as he hops on one foot, bringing his other up to wrench his shoe off. He manages to do the same with the other without toppling over or breaking his leg, but it too gets launched in the direction of the water, never to be seen again.

"Stop!" I call out to him just as he reaches the water's edge, pants immediately soaked to his knees as a wave comes crashing in. "Everett, you're drunk! You'll drown!"

"I want to save the oceans!" he calls back to me as he goes in farther, up to his waist.

"What?" I'm at the water too now, and I toss my heels onto the sand.

"Laurel asked if I wanted to save the oceans that first summer, and I do!" he shouts back at me. "I'm not—" I'm up to my calves when a wave comes in and smacks him in the chest, momentarily stopping him. "I'm not a completely shitty person!"

"Everett, you're not even a little bit a shitty person!" I shout after him. I'm up to my hips now, the water colder than I anticipated, and he's far enough out that I'm starting to worry, arms working like he might dive in. "Please stop!" I call. "It's just one bottle! The ocean forgives you! You don't owe it your life!"

He looks over his shoulder at me then, almost like he hears how ridiculous this is, like he's going to laugh at it. I'm almost smiling too when the wave hits him, hard, and he goes under.

"Everett!" My voice feels like a tiny shard in the darkness as I go rushing forward, almost getting my knees taken out by the same wave. I shout his name again, over and over until I'm far enough out that when I put my foot forward it doesn't meet sand and I lurch into the water, taking a face full before I start paddling, panic rising in my chest.

He's a good swimmer, I remind myself, in the roughly thirty seconds I've been looking for him. He's a better swimmer than I am, and it's not that deep here. But as the water crashes to shore in the distance, as I hold my breath and bob with another wave coming in and I don't see him, I worry that I'm wrong. I start to feel frantic, arms wheeling, looking in every dark, endless direction. *Everett*, I think, *this one stupid night can't be it.*

An arm wraps around my middle just as I'm about to call his name again and starts hauling me toward shore as another wave crashes toward us. We get our feet under us just in time and manage to outrun it, Everett's arm dropping from my waist as soon as we hit shore and he falls to all fours, coughing heartily like a sailor tossed overboard, just returned to land. I stumble farther up the beach, arms wrapped around my elbows, suddenly freezing and furious and afraid.

"What the fuck, Everett?" I say as I turn back to him. He's pushing himself up onto his knees, still gasping. "You can't—" I say, sweeping an arm toward the ocean. I stumble back a step as Everett gets to his feet in a show of great effort. He's trying to say something, I can tell, but his breath is coming in sharp, full bursts. "You can't do that," I say as he comes stumbling toward me.

"I know," he breathes when he reaches me, arms coming around me easily, one hand sliding to cradle the back of my head. "I'm so sorry." I wrap my arms around him and we sink to the ground like that, huddled together. "I'm sorry," Everett says, over and over and over again, like he might turn back the wheel of time if he gets to the right number. His lips are against my head, moving gently, so I hardly catch it when he says, "I never hated you."

I pull away just enough to look up at him. "I never hated you either."

"I thought you did," he says. "I was so angry that you didn't believe me, but it was just because it meant I couldn't have you anymore. I knew you'd never forgive me. It would have been so much easier if we hated each other. But I never could."

I want to tell him everything. That believing he'd sabotaged things was what was easy for me, that fighting with him was the best way to not want him anymore. But he's shivering, I realize, and he's still drunk, and we need to take care of one problem at a time.

"We've got to get you back to the house," I say, leaning

away from him and taking his face in my hands. Even under my own cold palms, I can feel that his cheeks are frigid. It's only June, after all, and it's nearly midnight.

"We've got to get *you* back to the house," he says through broken chatters, like he's trying to make a joke.

I ignore him and haul him up from the sand, propping him against me as best I can as we make our way up the beach.

"I'm so sorry, Sutton," he says again.

"No more," I say as we reach the parking lot. I pull his keys out of my pocket, push him into the passenger seat. "I know you are."

In the car, I turn the heat on full blast. Everett leans over his knees, head in his hands, and I reach over, rubbing a hand over his damp back until we get to the villa.

The house is quiet when we arrive, no other cars in the driveway.

Upstairs, in Everett's room, I turn on his shower and make sure it's only lukewarm before shoving him toward the bathroom. I creep downstairs for a glass of water while he showers. When I get back I pace around until he emerges, a towel wrapped around his waist, face a little peaked.

"You're up," he says, nodding toward the bathroom.

"I'm fine," I insist, extending a glass of water toward him.

"Sutton, I'm okay," he says. "You shower."

I sigh, but relent, and I'm grateful once I'm under the hot water. I imagine the worst parts of this week spiraling down the drain along with the salt water running off me, wring out my hair and pretend my fight with Laurel goes with it, dry off and picture scrubbing away the image of that wave knocking Everett down.

When I walk back into his room wrapped in a towel, Everett has clothes waiting for me: a pair of his sweatpants and a

T-shirt, a hoodie with the TIFF logo across the back. I could easily go down the hall to my room, I know. I don't care anymore about the possibility of anyone catching us, but I take them anyway, put them on.

After he turns off the light we curl together in his bed, his arm around my waist, holding me closer to him, our heads bent together.

"Sutton," he breathes after a few minutes.

"Don't apologize again," I say. He quiets and reaches up, rubs a piece of my hair between his fingers.

"Thank you," he says instead.

"Do you still feel the same?" he asks in the still of the dark, just as we're both about to drift off. "About whatever you said you wanted to talk about when I was sober."

I smile, hug him a little tighter to me so I can breathe in the clean scent of him, familiar now, untinged by everything he was doing tonight. "Yes, Everett," I tell him. "Even after all that, I still feel it."

thirty-three

This Summer

In the morning, I wake up early and leave a still-sleeping Everett to creep down to the kitchen to make coffee. The house is quiet, everyone still sleeping off last night. Staying out late, hangovers, getting drunk, and flinging themselves into the ocean. Potentially friendship-ending arguments.

I take my mug and my phone out to the back deck, sink down into a chair. A sudden, brutal twist of something that I could only call homesickness followed me down the stairs this morning. Into the beautiful kitchen that didn't belong to the cottage or my apartment or Hank's restaurant. Onto the deck that looked out onto the same ocean as Poppy Cottage, but felt so far removed from it somehow. It felt like we'd all been climbing some invisible hill to get to a place like this since we planned our first vacation here, and yet, being here hasn't felt like winning. I was so focused on this trip proving we could be who we were before that I didn't notice what was actually happening. Where before this week had been the best part of the year, now it was a vacation from who we actually are. Five people, distinct from one another.

So *homesickness* is the only word I have for whatever it is that sends an ache through my chest. *Nostalgia* is too golden. I'm worried I'll never get back what I've lost.

Everett's face flashes across my mind, soft as he sleeps, and the ache dulls a little. I brushed his hair off his forehead when I woke up this morning, watched him breathe and felt, for a minute, like the world could stop right there, and I'd be okay. I'd have been incredibly lucky. But time hasn't stopped, and I want more of it with him, and there's still Laurel to talk to, and a life to figure out around the very real possibility of her absence, something that renews the ache deep within me so viscerally that I pull my knees up to my chest, curl over them like it's some physical pain I can staunch.

I dial Hank's number without really thinking. He's an early riser, like me, probably already at the restaurant or on his way.

"Hey, bug," he answers, and the sound of his voice almost has me crying. I swallow over the lump in my throat, over everything that's happened in the last twenty-four hours, the last week, the last five, ten years.

"Hey," I say. I balance my coffee on the arm of the chair and wrap my arm around my knees. "Just wanted to check in."

"You okay?" he asks, and I think back on all the times he's asked me that, even before I moved in with him, when he'd call me every Wednesday like clockwork, checking in. When he was looking out for me before I even knew I needed it. I think about all the times I dealt in half answers too—not just with him, but with everyone. *I'm fine, work is great, everything is going according to plan* even when the truth was *I'm lonely, I don't know what I want anymore, I think my heart is broken and I can't tell anyone about the person who made it possible to break in the first place.*

"I'm—" I start, head swaying a little under the weight of it all. I feel like I've been swimming for days, trying to keep not only myself but this trip, this group, my feelings for Everett above water, and I've only now crawled onto shore, my limbs weak. Maybe I've been swimming like that for years.

"I'm really tired," I finally say, so quietly I'm not sure Hank can even hear it.

He doesn't say anything. I can hear the creak of the ancient office chair he won't get rid of, no matter how many times I try to convince him to buy a new, ergonomic one, and I know he's waiting me out.

"Why did you never get married?" I ask him, almost at the same time the question occurs to me.

"Hmm," he murmurs, thinking it over. "I just never met the right person, I guess."

"Did you want to?"

"I think if I found someone I wanted to spend that time with, who made life feel a little lighter, sure," he says, which strikes me as odd. Hank only ever makes life feel lighter for me. But then, I think, maybe that's it. We're so much the same. There would need to be someone who could lighten the load for him, even when it seemed like he didn't need it. Even when he was projecting to the world that everything was wonderful. But it couldn't have been easy, suddenly raising a teenager, starting a family he'd never planned for.

"Bug," Hank says after a while. "I think that if you want that person, you should find them. I don't think you need to keep carrying everything on your own."

It's like he's reached through the phone, squeezed a hand around my shoulder. We might not talk like this all that often, but part of it is because we've never had to. Even if we didn't say it out loud, it didn't mean we didn't understand each other.

"I love your mother, don't get me wrong," Hank says, which surprises me. He's avoided talking about my parents with me for most of my life. "But there's a lot of me that's still mad as hell at her." My breath seizes in my chest at this. "I just never want what they did to make you feel like you don't deserve all the love in the world."

"Hank," I say. "I love you for saying that, but . . . I had the best. No one could have raised me better than you," I tell him. I loved it all—the restaurant, of course, but every trip we took together, every tradition we made, the way he taught me how to build a family for myself. How he always gave me a place that felt like home when the concept had been ripped so quickly and cleanly away.

I think about the girl who told Everett on a rain-soaked pier that she'd dealt with it, that there was no need to rehash anything. The version of me who believed he agreed with me, when really, he wore his own pain even more obviously than I did: in every easy laugh, every *something like that*, every quick, casual response. And I suppose it was true that we'd understood each other from the very beginning, but now I know it wasn't in the way I'd originally thought. It wasn't that the things that had happened to us didn't matter. It was that we both had the same scars in us, and that we both held people at arm's length because of them. Except for maybe each other, for a brief, beautiful moment.

"I'm proud of you," Hank says after a minute, and I feel a familiar pang of guilt slice through me, making me wince.

"Hank," I say. "Hypothetically, how would you feel if I . . . were considering a career change?"

"Well, I think it's a little late for medical school," he says, prompting a small laugh out of me. Hank is silent for a moment, the creak of his chair the only sound before he clears his throat and says, almost guiltily, "But I think you might be asking me about the restaurant. And maybe . . . a cookbook?"

My shoulders drop. "You knew?"

I can hear him shift on his end of the line, sitting up straighter. "You might be good at keeping a secret, but that best friend of yours isn't."

Something cracks in my chest, and I pull my knees tighter in, some protective layer between me and the implication of Hank's words. "Laurel told you?" I ask, throat going dry.

"She's already planning," he says. "Wanted to make sure my schedule was cleared in July. Two years from now. Don't tell her I told you. It's supposed to be a surprise. Long time to keep a surprise secret, in my opinion."

I shake my head, Hank's confession not lining up with the conversation I had with Laurel last night. With how our friendship has been for a long time now, really. I can't blame her for this week, even if all I've wanted is for her to tell me how she's really feeling, to tell me what happened between her and Stephen. She's allowed to be distant, sad, if that's what she needs. But last night, she made it clear she doesn't need any of us anymore.

"I'm honestly kind of shocked she told you," I tell Hank.

"Why?" he asks. "This is exactly the kind of thing Laurel would do."

"The kind of thing she used to do," I say. "The kind of thing I used to do for her."

"I don't know about 'used to,'" Hank says. "Didn't you plan this whole week?"

I hear Davi's voice, Laurel's, in my mind. That she texted me first because I'm the best at planning. And suddenly it seems so stupid that I was ever angry about that. Of course Laurel called me—not because I'm the most reliable, but because I'm the person who could plan it *best* for her. Who would be the one to try her hardest to re-create this week just as it was, even if I'd failed spectacularly along the way. I'd thought I was doing it to repair something we'd lost, to prove to everyone we still need each other, but for Laurel, it was comfort. *You're the one who taught me that*, she said last night. It had felt like a slap to the face, but now I wonder if it was Laurel doing the same thing I always have: trying to control the narrative as a way to protect all the pain in her.

And I'd spent half of the week arguing with Everett and the other half lying to her, being annoyed with her, trying to pull something out of her she wasn't ready to hand over to me yet.

"We got in a horrible fight last night," I say to Hank, squinting out at the water, gray in the early-morning light. I try hard not to let my blurry vision give way to anything, but as soon as I blink it does, my voice coming out hoarse. "I don't know if we'll be doing this kind of thing for each other anymore after this week."

"Laurel is your best friend," Hank says, entirely unconcerned. "She's not going anywhere."

She *is* my best friend. It shouldn't surprise me, but it does, after years of more ebbs than flows. But the fact of Laurel being my best friend remains, peeking through all my doubts, my anger from last night.

She's still my best friend, despite it all. In the way that makes you feel like you don't need to worry. *Does she like someone better than me* or *am I being replaced*. None of that mattered, because it was us for each other, always. Even though a divide had spread between us, even if it spread again, I'd still been the person she called when she most needed someone. There was some small thing in me that matched some small thing in her, or maybe it was a big thing, a we-see-the-world-the-same thing, and whether we were talking every day or every six months, the dust was always easily brushed away. Because at the end of the day we were meant to experience this life with each other, to be drunkenly laughing on dorm room floors and holding each other through heartbreak and staring up at an incomprehensible universe on a sandy beach alongside our other most important people. We didn't have girlhood together, but we had life.

"You need to go," Hank says before I can, like he can hear the gears working in my head through the phone.

"Sorry," I say, wincing. "I don't mean to bring up the cookbook and bolt."

"Bug, that's what I'm here for," he says. "And I brought up the cookbook. Let me know how things shake out."

"I will," I tell him, standing up from my chair. "I love you."

"Love you too," Hank says before hanging up, not even giving me the option of a longer goodbye. Sending me off to work this out on my own, with every lesson he's ever taught me tucked into my back pocket.

thirty-four

This Summer

I march into the house determined to find Laurel, but I'm stopped by a familiar figure in the kitchen, hood pulled up over his sleep-messy hair, two mugs on the island in front of him. He looks up as I come racing in, footsteps louder than I intended.

"Hey," Everett says. He starts to slide a mug toward me, but catches sight of the one in my hand, its ceramic now cold. "Thought I could beat you to it."

"You did," I say, walking behind him and dumping the contents of my mug in the sink. I turn and take the mug he's now holding in midair, expression a little confused. "Thanks."

He clears his throat, watches me as I take a sip. "Could we talk?" he asks.

I glance toward the stairs, like Laurel might appear there at that moment.

"Everyone else is still asleep," Everett says. I look back at him, surprised at the worry that shades his eyes, undeniable. "They won't hear us, if—"

"No, of course," I say, nodding quickly as the reality that he's nervous about the two of us being seen together sinks in. I don't want him to feel that way, ever. Not anymore. Still, I think this is a conversation better had in private. "Your room?"

Everett follows me up the stairs, our steps quieter than my marching ones earlier. I glance at Laurel's door as we pass, but it's closed, as is Davi's across from it. Mine is the only one open in the hall.

When we walk into Everett's room I notice that the bed is made, our clothes from last night carefully folded and set near the door, ready to wash later, like he's been up for a while. I glance up at him as he closes the door behind him, that same expression on his face.

"I was talking to Hank," I tell him.

He nods, something like relief passing over his features, and I wonder for a split second if Everett thought I'd just left. That last night caused me to flee at dawn, leaving him and everyone else behind.

I set my coffee on one of the nightstands and settle on the edge of the bed as Everett sits in the armchair across from me, scooting it in closer.

"How are you feeling?" I ask.

"Um," Everett mumbles, raking a hand through his hair. "Like I know why I never drink that much. Like I'm never drinking again."

"Fair," I say, drawing a small laugh out of him. "If it's any consolation, you're handling it remarkably well."

"Oh, I feel like I'm dying, for sure," he says. "But I don't want to delay this conversation any longer."

I nod, and Everett plants his elbows on his knees, holding his mug between them. He considers it for a minute, glances at the nightstand where mine is, reaches over and sets it down. Runs a hand through his hair again. I watch him, waiting.

"I'm sorry," he finally says. My shoulders slump, head tilting as I start to protest, but he continues quickly. "I know you said no more apologies, but I need to tell you I'm sorry when I'm not half drunk and freezing. I was an asshole last night."

"You were hurting last night," I say.

"That doesn't make how I acted okay. The things I said."

"You were quoting me," I say, shrugging a shoulder. "Can't exactly get mad at you for that."

"Yes, you can," Everett says resignedly, running a hand down his face. I wait for him to continue. When he does finally drop his hand he doesn't look at me, instead gazes absently out the window above the bed, like he can't meet my eyes.

"There's so much I do to prove I'm not like my dad," he says, surprising me. "Even things that are supposedly good, things I want to do. My relationship with my siblings, never changing plans, proving myself. But there's a lot of shit too." He glances at me. "Never getting too close to anyone. Never letting anyone know how I'm feeling, unless it's a good feeling. And last night I was just like him. I got that call and I figured, I don't know. If I can't beat him, join him. I just—" He drops his head, shakes it. "I hate myself for that."

"Everett," I say after a long silent moment that I expected him to fill again. I slide off the bed, kneel in front of him, reach up to cup his cheek in my hand. He looks at me then, and I can see it there, that he doesn't think he deserves this, that he's not worthy of any kind of forgiveness, any kind of second chance. I let him believe that, once. I think back to all the moments he would only share snippets with me, tiny pieces of himself that left me hungry for more of him. Every time he omitted something, every time he shared only the shiniest parts, he was constructing a version of himself he thought we'd all like enough to keep around.

The last night of our first trip here suddenly pops into my head, the game he came up with. One thing we were scared of and one thing we were looking forward to. Even though it was his idea, he hadn't told us what he was really afraid of, what he really wanted. He always kept it light, and the thought breaks my heart. Everett at nine, at fifteen, at twenty, at thirty-two, always trying to do just enough to keep someone interested but never show enough of himself to risk disappointing them.

"You are not your father," I tell him. When he almost smiles, tries to glance away like it's a joking matter, I catch his chin in my hand, gently, so he'll keep looking at me. "You aren't, Everett. You never could be."

He blinks as my hand slides back up to his cheek, something clearing in his eyes. "I'm sorry," he says, but it almost comes out as a whisper, rough.

"I know you are," I tell him, rubbing a thumb along his cheekbone. "But I'm also glad I got to be the person there to help you."

A small smile flickers at one corner of his mouth at this. A real one. "Should probably just tell you what's going on next time," he says. "Before I head for the nearest dive bar."

I laugh. "Probably," I say. "But I'm not too worried about a next time."

Everett's eyes flick between mine as my hand falls to my lap. I watch as his expression fades from something softly happy back to somber. He stands up after a while, pacing toward the door. I follow suit after a moment, stopping him in his tracks with a hand on his shoulder when he turns back to find me standing there.

There's still so much conversation to be had, things we can't keep ignoring if we want this to be something. God, I hope he wants this to be something.

"Everett, when I said those things," I say. "When I ended

things with you . . . it wasn't because I didn't want to be with you. I wanted that so much."

"I did too," Everett says, storm-tossed eyes latching on to mine. "And I'm sorry for everything I said. I—" He breaks off, glances sideways like he's collecting his thoughts before looking back at me. "I've never let anyone in like I did with you, Sutton. I wanted it to work so badly, but even if things hadn't ended like they did . . . I wasn't ready. I couldn't even fight to keep you. It just seemed like it was inevitable, somehow, that I would ruin it. So I said things I didn't mean."

"You didn't ruin it," I say. "You didn't ruin anything. And, honestly, you were right." His brow furrows, confusion spreading across his face. "I do love to be in control. I think we both do, in our different ways." He tilts his head, confirming this. "It wasn't just about everyone else. I was terrified of getting hurt, just like you said." I drop my gaze, shaking my head as I say, softly, "It was so much easier to just blame you than admit that."

Everett slides his hand around mine then, intertwining our fingers. I look back up at him. "Sutton," he says, a pleading look in his eyes. "I promise you I didn't know the others were back. I need you to believe that."

"I know you didn't," I say. The truth is, I think I let go of that further back than I realized. I clung to it so tightly as a reason to hate him, even when my heart knew it wasn't true. "I trust you."

Everett's expression softens. "You do?"

I nod. "Of course I do."

I smile, something like hope blooming in me. Everett reaches up to brush my hair behind my ear, lets his hand fall to my cheek.

Everett's thumb traces over my cheekbone. "I think you

care more than most people," he says. "I think you make all of us better."

My throat squeezes. "I expect too much," I say.

"Sutton," he says. "It would be the greatest honor of my lifetime to try to exceed your expectations, if you'd let me."

I look up at him at this, my breath catching. "I don't want you to feel like you can't be a person," I say.

He shakes his head. "I don't feel like that," he says softly. "I want to be the person you thought you could be with five years ago."

I dip my head into his palm. "I'd rather you be who you are right now. Who you'll be tomorrow."

Something in Everett's eyes sparks; maybe the same kind of hope I'm feeling. A sort of nervous animal, peeking out after a long winter. Maybe what we ruined before can be rebuilt, and the essential pieces of us still remain.

I don't want later with Everett. I want now. We've already had our fits and starts. I don't want to wait another ten years to see if this could work. This thing between us has always been real, but it's been trapped in small stolen moments, and I want to bring it out into the open, let it breathe. Give it life. I want to tell him what I was going to say last night. That I love him, after ten years and one life-altering week. That I know it now.

I'm about to say something like this to him when there's an urgent rap on his door and we both turn, not even bothering to step away from each other when Gabe opens the door.

"What's going on?" Everett asks, his hand still clasped in mine.

I've never seen Gabe look so panicked. He looks between us, brows drawn together. "Laurel's gone."

thirty-five

This Summer

"What do you mean she's gone?" I ask, pulse hiking.

Gabe shakes his head. "She's not in her room, she's not anywhere in the house. I drove us home last night, but—" He winces. "Her car is gone."

"*What?*" I say. Suddenly, I realize I've been strangling Everett's fingers with mine. He just squeezes back, gently, when I loosen my grip.

"Did you see it when you got back?" Gabe asks me.

My shoulders slump, guilt washing over me. "No," I say hoarsely. I'd been so focused on Everett last night that I hadn't even thought to look around.

"Sutton," Everett says quietly, like he can read my mind. I look up at him, surprised to find his face a little blurry. "It's okay. Why would you have even thought to check for her car?"

But that's not it, I realize. It's not just last night. I've been focused on Everett *all* week. To the point that it made Laurel angry. To the point that she and I fought. To the point that I told myself she was fine, even when I knew she wasn't, and that I waited to find her this morning in favor of talking to him.

"Wait," I say, pulling my phone out of my pocket. "I think she's still sharing her location with me."

But Gabe stops me before I can even unlock my screen. "She left her phone in her room," he says. "We tried calling and Davi found it."

"Laurel," I say, half growl, half sigh. I'm both annoyed she would be stupid enough to leave without any way to contact her, and guilty that I didn't see this coming.

"She can't have gone far," Everett says. "If she left her things here, she's planning on coming back, right?"

I'm wracking my brain as Gabe and Everett discuss where she might be, why she might have left. *Where would you go, Laurel?* I think of her favorite places in town, but if she left sometime between Everett and I getting back last night and everyone waking up, none of them would even be open. I picture her scrambling up the rocky incline of her favorite sunrise hike alone, slipping on a loose stone and plummeting down the drop-off. Her speeding down the PCH and overcorrecting and—

I stop myself there. Going to the absolute worst-case scenario isn't going to help us find her any faster.

"Did she leave a note or anything?" I ask Gabe. He shakes his head. "When was the last time you saw her?"

"Just when we got back last night," he says. "Davi saw her before he went to bed, I guess. Said they talked about the party and our last night here for a minute, but . . ." He trails off, shrugging defeatedly, but something about his words rings in my head.

"I think I know where she is," I say. "Maybe."

Poppy Cottage has fallen into even further disrepair since we last stayed here. The succulents are gone from the flower boxes and the paint job they were promising when we first checked in clearly never happened. Flakes hang on perilously from its weather-beaten, peeling siding, and for a minute it seems like quite the metaphor for us. A once-steady foundation, left alone to rot for too long. A shiny new place to stay that matches the surfaces of all our lives. But we'll always have come from here.

The door is unlocked when I try it. It's clear no one is staying in these cottages or has been in a while. When we walk in, there's a breeze blowing sand and salt air through the main room. It's coming from the deck door, thrown wide-open by the person sitting out there alone.

"Oh, thank god," Davi says, drawing a hand down his face. He'd been white as a sheet when we went downstairs, gathering numbers for morgues and hospitals at the kitchen island while Gabe tried to get him to stop.

We all start toward the door, one collective body, but I stop halfway, everyone pausing behind me.

"Can I—" I glance back at everyone. "Is it okay if I just talk to her alone for a minute?"

"Probably a good idea," Davi, who needs approximately three business days to decompress after something high stress happens, says. "If we all go rushing out there she might run off again."

"She's not a deer," Gabe says. Davi shoots him a look. "But good point."

Gabe and Davi start toward the front door. Everett pauses for a minute, hand finding mine.

"You okay?" he asks.

I nod. "I'm good." I squeeze his hand—less violently this time. He lets go and gives me a small reassuring smile.

I wait until the front door has closed behind him to turn back toward the deck, where Laurel is sitting. I realize I don't have a great opening line, or really a place to start. All I have is some jumbled approximation of what to say to her, or some point to get to. But there isn't time to get it perfect now. All I can do is be there for her.

Laurel is sitting on the steps that lead down to the beach, facing the water. I walk quietly over and sit down next to her, looking out at the waves. During past trips, we used to sit like this when the sun was going down. Sometimes the other three would be playing some game on the beach that we were either taking a break from or didn't want to join. Sometimes they'd still be talking on the deck behind us, Davi beating Gabe and Everett at Texas Hold'em, picking at the remnants of whatever meal we'd made that night. Laurel and I would talk or not talk or drink or not drink. But the transition from day to night would always go like this: the two of us, side by side, watching the color of the world change.

We sit in silence for a while until I finally look over at her, ready to say something, but she beats me to it.

"They're tearing these places down," she says. "Did you know that?"

I glance at the A-frame behind us, and I can see it, if I'm honest. A slight sag in the middle. A new hole in the deck. A structure not useful to this place anymore. "I didn't," I say, looking back at her. "I'm sorry, Laurel."

"It doesn't matter," she says. "It's just another thing that's gone."

"It matters," I insist, the same feeling I had last night when we fought taking over me. Some desperate need to prove to her that all of this is still important.

"Why?" she asks. "It's just a house. It's not like it's going to save all of us."

It is, again, so at odds with the Laurel Im I know that I'm startled by it, at first. This pessimism she's never had before. I'd thought it was a product of what's happening, the divorce, but maybe it's something I just didn't notice about her. Or maybe she's not the same person I knew, in a half second, would be my best friend all those years ago. But then again, none of us are who we were back then.

"It's important because we grew up here," I say. "It matters because it mattered to us."

Laurel glances askance at me. Her makeup from last night is smudged under her eyes, some of the jewels missing above her eyebrows. "It's not our family home, Sutton," she says. "It's not even our college house."

"It doesn't have to be," I say. "It's like . . ." I trail off, casting around for some comparison. "It's like when your parents would mark your height growing up, you know?" I can picture the place Hank did it in his house, long before I lived with him full-time. A summer tradition when I first arrived every year, some tangible proof of my changing existence. That it was worth something. "We came here every year, and we saw how much we'd changed."

"Yeah, until we didn't," she says bitterly.

"Laurel," I say, in as gentle a voice as possible. "If you hate this place so much, why did you come here?"

I see it happen slowly: a slight pinch by her eyes at first, a twitch at her mouth next, until she's turning her head away from me, until her shoulders shake.

"Laurel," I say. I reach for her, but think better of it at the last minute. I hate it, but I don't know if we're those people anymore. I used to hug her so easily. She used to lean her head on my shoulder, loop her arm through mine, but we haven't been like that in a long time.

"I don't know what to do," she sniffs.

"About all of us?" I ask. "About Stephen?"

She shakes her head, turning to face forward again, so I

can at least see her profile. "About my life," she says in a rough voice. She scrubs the back of one hand under her nose. "I don't feel like I know who I am anymore."

At this I do grab her free hand, dynamics be damned. Like Hank said, she's still my best friend. She's still Laurel, and no matter how many steps we take away from each other, I have some belief that we'll always find our way back. That maybe it's less about always being as close, as connected as we once were, and more about allowing the ebbs and flows of life to happen, and to trust that we'll be there for each other anyway. It's what I'm hoping for, at least.

"I don't even know if I like what I do," Laurel says, finally looking at me. "I've built my whole life to look a certain way, to make it something other people would want. And now I can't even tell if I ever actually wanted it." I reach over and brush away a tear that's run its course down her cheek and to her jaw.

I'd always thought Laurel was so sure of herself, of what she wanted, who she was. That I was the one who needed everything to be a certain way for me to feel safe, steady. She'd always seemed so free, like the world didn't rest as heavy on her shoulders, but now everything she's been holding on to is written plainly across her face.

"I think that's why I came here," she says. "This place was never for anybody else. It was only ever for us. And that's—that's just gone now. I don't feel like I have anything to anchor myself to."

"You still have us," I tell her. "You'll always have us."

"Everyone is busy," she says. "*I* was busy. Now I just have this void to fill."

"Stephen," I say. She nods. "Laurel. What happened?"

She looks back out at the water for a minute before she answers me. When she does, I swear she's almost laughing, at first. "I know all of you think I've been keeping some big terrible secret this whole time," she says. "Like he was stealing my money, or I cheated on him or something. But really—it just wasn't right. I know it seemed right," she says. "But . . ."

"It wasn't what you wanted," I finish for her, and she nods, face going sad again.

"Stephen is perfect," she says. "He's everything I *should* want."

"I get it," I say. I spent so long wanting the one person I wasn't supposed to. Even this week, on a date with someone who, on paper, should be my perfect match, I couldn't stop thinking about the person I thought I couldn't have.

"Stephen told me he didn't think he recognized me anymore a few months before we split," Laurel says. "That I wasn't the person he fell in love with."

"What did you say?" I ask.

"I told him I didn't recognize me either. But that I was interested in finding out who I am now." She shrugs. "And he wasn't."

She's not crying anymore, but her expression is still melancholy, a little far away.

"Hey," I tell her, squeezing her hand so she'll look at me. When she does, I say, "I'm interested in who you are. Always." I nod toward the house. "And I know of a few other people who are too. I think that's how you know who your people are," I say. "They want to keep getting to know you through everything. Every change. So I'd disagree with you." Laurel raises an eyebrow. "I think you *have* been keeping a pretty big, terrible secret. The person who was supposed to choose you over and over again gave up partway through."

Laurel's face goes cloudy at this, and I worry I've gone too far. But instead she says, shockingly, "I'm so sorry."

I lean back a little, examining her. "For what?"

She draws in a breath. "I've been doing that with you," she says. "I've pulled away from you so much because of what happened, and it wasn't even your fault."

"It was at least a little my fault," I say. "Everett and I lied to all of you for a really long time."

"But none of us were making the effort anymore at that point," she says. "We'd all stopped trying, except for you. And I blamed it all on some idiotic pact we'd made years ago, that didn't even *matter.* I just let myself be mad at you, and you were trying so hard to make up for it. Both of you."

"Both of us?" I ask. "I thought you and Everett were BFFs this whole time."

Laurel rolls her eyes, scoffing. "Yeah, no. I've given him so much shit over the last few years—more shit than you," she says, which surprises me, especially with how she's acted around him, what Davi said at her wedding. "We were just in the same city, and I was flailing, and even if I was mad, I needed someone to hang out with that just knew . . . me. You guys know me."

"Every version of you," I say. "Past, present, and hopefully future."

"Can we even do that?" she asks. "We all drifted so much. We just let it happen." I can see the worry written across her face, and it occurs to me that it might be where so much of what she said last night came from. It was less about *wanting* this to be over and more about thinking that it was inevitable.

"I think it will look different," I tell her. "We're never going to be those kids who showed up here two days after graduation again. But that doesn't mean we matter any less. There's just a lot more life for all of us to share with each other now."

Laurel smiles at this. "I like that," she says. "I want to share my life with you again."

At this, I feel my forehead tighten just the smallest bit.

"What?" Laurel asks.

I chew on my lower lip, palms going clammy. I'm not sure that *this* is the moment to tell her about Everett, not even sure what there is, really, to tell her yet, seeing as our conversation was interrupted earlier. Nothing but the truth, I suppose, as plainly as I can put it.

"I don't want to ruin getting the gang back together immediately," I say.

Laurel's face shifts, like she already knows. "Everett," she says.

"I'm in love with him," I tell her, simply.

She nods as if this is obvious. "So is he."

"In love with himself?" I ask. I grin at the snort it draws out of her, some ghost of Laurel past emerging to join all the new pieces of her.

"Who knows," she says, waving a hand. "But no. With you."

"And you're okay with that?" I ask. "Even after . . ." I let the unspoken hang between us. Even after everything. Even after we lied, and things fell apart, and the last five years and this week happened at all. But I realize I'm not so much asking for her permission this time, as just finding out what she thinks. We're too old for a pact like the one we made. And if the point is to love each other no matter what, then here is this new thing too. The fact of Everett and me.

"You don't need to ask me that," Laurel says.

"Still," I say. "I want to know how you feel about it. I want to do it right this time."

Her mouth twists. "I just want things to work out," she says. "I want you both to be happy."

"I know," I say. "I want that too."

"Pretty scary being totally uncertain about things, isn't it?" Laurel asks. "Letting go?"

"Ceding control," I add, throwing a hand out toward the ocean for emphasis. Laurel laughs. "Yeah," I say. "But it's kind of exciting too. Think about all the great and terrible things there are still left to happen."

"Let's start with some great," Laurel says. "Please." At this, she does rest her head on my shoulder, loops an arm through mine. I press my cheek against her hair.

"Agreed," I say, looking out at the same ocean that's sustained moments like these for so long and will again. Maybe not next summer, maybe not the one after. Things will grow and change and shift, and this is probably the last time we'll sit in this exact spot. But it doesn't mean everything is gone. It doesn't mean things are worse. It just means there's more, always, to look forward to. More ways to learn each other and grow together and support one another, even if it isn't from a bedroom across the hall or a daily FaceTime or a there-every-second kind of friendship. Maybe that's the best part of it, after all, that we are the kind of people who will still be there, even after all of that. Even after five long, hard years, we'll come back together and emerge, stronger than ever, on the other side.

I squeeze Laurel's hand as the front door creaks open inside the cabin, one of the others coming to check on us. We'll invite them in with open arms, pull them into whatever this new version of all of us is. But for now, I repeat Laurel's words like some hope cast into the water, where it might catch on a wave and come back to us again and again. "Let's start with some great."

thirty-six

This Summer

"Think Ralph will have us arrested if he finds us out here?" Davi asks that night as we all huddle around the bonfire we've built out back of Poppy Cottage.

After getting a weepy Laurel off the back deck, we went into town and wandered the market and the grocery store until we had enough food for a feast tonight. It was easy to see that some dam had broken as we wandered the aisles of the overpriced corner store, as Laurel tried every sample available at the market, as we sang along at the top of our lungs to The Police and Billy Joel and Linda Ronstadt in the Bronco on the way back to the villa.

We cooked an elaborate meal and ate it out back as the sun went down, racing to fill the gaps that had been left this week. Things we hadn't done, things we hadn't said. It felt like some part of my heart was mending as we sat around the table, a piece that had been hanging on by a thread sewn back on.

Everett was close by all day, but never obviously so. We still had things to talk about, after all, and this last night was about all of us. But I still let my hand brush against his, stood shoulder to shoulder with him at the kitchen island, let my knee find his under the table.

When the sun went down, we drove back to Poppy Cottage, ducking under the caution tape strung between the rows of A-frames and out to the beach, back to where it all began.

"I don't think he can technically arrest us for being on a public beach," Gabe answers Davi, tipping his beer bottle back.

"Don't underestimate Ralph," Laurel says, raising her own bottle toward him.

Sparks dance off the fire and into the air, disappearing into the night sky. I'm in between Laurel and Everett, and I press closer to her as she lays her head on my shoulder, while my fingers reach for Everett's in the sand.

"Good week," Davi says after a while, eyes fixed on the flames.

We all laugh, Davi grinning, but finally Gabe agrees with him. "Yeah," he says. "Good week, after all."

It's quiet for a minute before Everett speaks up. "So are we going to do this?"

It's a tradition that's gotten a little muddied over the years, since we couldn't all be here every summer. On top of that, we're out of practice. But Laurel smiles at the idea, and Gabe leans forward, ready. Davi is the first to speak up.

"I'm afraid I won't get this promotion at work," he says.

"You'll get it," Laurel says. She sighs. "I'm afraid 'Laurel's New Life' is actually going to be a giant dumpster fire."

"Well, with that attitude," Davi says, and she laughs, kicking sand in his direction.

"It's not going to be a dumpster fire," I tell her, pressing my cheek to the top of her head. "It's just one foot in front of the other."

"I'm worried about the kids starting school," Gabe says. "I'm also worried that Mia wants to start trying for another this year."

"You, Greatest Dad in the World, afraid of that?" Everett asks jokingly.

"I'm worried about loving them as much as Riley and Chloe," Gabe says. "How can that happen three times?"

"It'll happen," I say. "You've got nothing but room in that heart of yours, Gabe." He smiles and nods at me, and I realize that this has turned more into easing each other's fears than just listing them. Maybe that was always the point. I take a swig of my beer, set the base of the bottle in the sand. "I'm pretty afraid of starting off on this new path," I say. "I always knew what would happen at the restaurant."

"It could have blown up," Davi points out. "You could have been inside."

"Jesus, Davi," Laurel says, laughing. She sits up straight and looks at me. "I think this is a really good thing for you. I think you're going to be surprised how good it is."

"Me too," Everett says on my other side, and I have to blink, nudge him to go so I don't get too emotional in front of everyone. He meets my eyes. "I'm afraid of what happens after this week," he says. He glances around at everyone, but I think what he says next might mean more than one thing. "I'm afraid of what happens to us."

We sit with it for a minute, the fire taking everything we've said up and away, a release somehow. Jobs, kids, new lives. All of us. Things that we can only hold on to for so long until we have to let them go, trust that the care we've put into them will carry them forward. Carry us forward.

"Funny," Laurel says after a while. "I was going to say that what happens to all of us is the thing I'm most looking forward to."

I smile over at her, find her hand and squeeze it. "Me too."

"Same," Gabe says.

"I was going to say this wine bar opening down the street from me, but that too," Davi says, Gabe knocking the end of his beer bottle against his knee as we all laugh.

I look over at Everett. "I think there's a lot to look forward to when it comes to us," I say. The fingers we've had resting against each other in the sand press a little closer. "I don't think we need to worry."

He smiles before he lifts his water toward the fire. "To us, then," he says, and we all follow suit, lifting our bottles in a toast and echoing his words.

"To every good thing that hasn't happened yet," I add.

It's as good an ending to this week as I think any of us could have hoped for. Better, even. The five of us, in the same place where we started, still together after everything that's happened. Older, with bigger lives that might take us away from each other, but no less important. The reason we can survive apart, I think, is because we had each other. Because we still do.

We say goodbye to Wild Horse Villa in the morning, not knowing if it will be our last time there. Something tells me we'll come back to this place again someday, even if it's in another ten, twenty years.

"You sure you don't want me to come with you?" I ask Laurel as she slams the trunk of her car, the one I drove us here in.

She crosses her arms over her chest, nodding at where Everett is hugging Gabe goodbye. We floated the idea of Thanksgiving in Denver together, but no plans are set in stone. One foot in front of the other, like I told Laurel. Figuring out what our friendship looks like on the other side of this will take time, but I don't feel as desperate to fix it as I used to, as I did just six days ago. I'm not worried about it ending anymore. We'll continue to shift, together.

"I think you still have some unfinished business here," she says, as I follow her nod to Everett. "Besides, I need a solo drive to kick off my new life."

"I thought the party was the start of that," I say.

She shakes her head. "A party with a bunch of people I hardly know isn't what I want things to look like. I needed last night with my most important people." At the look on my face, she draws me into her, making an *aw* sound. "You can't cry, or I'll cry," she says into my shoulder, already sniffling herself.

"I'm sorry," I say. "It's just been so long since I've heard you say that."

We all gather in a circle in the driveway, arms around each other in a little huddle, and while I've composed myself, it's now Laurel who's crying, so we pull her into our center, wrap around her like a cocoon.

"Why do I feel like we're graduating again?" Davi asks as we squeeze together, looking a little misty-eyed himself.

"That *is* what it feels like," Gabe says. He's right. It feels like something ending, and something beginning, and this is the last moment of the space in between.

"I love you all," I say, as Laurel lifts her head up and we move apart again, still in our circle but not squeezed so tight. Everyone echoes it, and then it's goodbye. Last looks and waves out the window, Gabe honking his horn as he and Davi disappear around the corner, Laurel turning up her music. Over as quickly as it began. On to the next thing.

Everett and I stand side by side even after they're out of sight, like they might come careening back around the corner, demanding more. But the road stays silent.

"Correct me if I'm wrong," he finally says. "But wasn't that your ride that just left?"

I knock my elbow against his, laughing as we head back toward the house. "You going to ditch me, Bridges?"

"Never," he says, smiling down at me.

It's strange how quiet the house feels with everyone else gone. Everett and I pass our bags in the hallway and stop near the kitchen, turning to look at each other.

"Fifteen minutes until Ralph comes knocking," I say, glancing at the clock above the sink. "Think it's enough time?"

Everett doesn't need to ask what for. "I do," he just says.

I rub my hands up and down my arms, suddenly a little nervous even if I'm certain of everything I still need to say, the final pieces between us that have to be arranged. I think we both have a thousand things that still need to be said sitting just behind our lips.

"Did you ever think about it?" I ask, finally. "About us."

Everett's hand floats up to my hip, settles there as he gazes intently at me. "You know I did," he says. "That last summer—"

"No," I cut in. "Not in the last five years. I mean before that." I reach down and find his other hand, draw it up to press it over the center of my chest. Everett looks at the spot, back up at me. "Did you ever think about me like this outside of all our summers here?"

It's not a fair question, but it's the thing I've needed to know. That I've been so worried about. Because I've realized now that I've been busy trying to put Everett out of my mind ever since that first summer, and I didn't even think to consider why. I just felt like I had to if I wanted to keep this thing between us alive.

The hard planes of his face soften, and I don't know if it's because he has a good answer, or he's realized he has to let me down easy.

"I thought about you," he says, his fingers a gentle pressure against my sternum. "But not always in the way you're asking."

I nod, duck my head so he won't see the disappointment on my face, but Everett's fingers come up to catch my chin, guide my gaze back to his. "I didn't understand what was happening," he says, "when you'd suddenly just be on my mind in the middle of the day. I'd be halfway through compiling a list of all the things you'd frowned about on our trip before I'd even realized I'd started making it." When I do frown at this, he smiles. "I'd make lists of everything you'd laugh at too. I was trying to piece together this person I didn't know yet, like how I'd get to know a character in a movie. There were all these gray spots, and I'd try to picture you at your job, with your friends, in your life up in San Francisco to fill them in. And then I'd get these new parts every time I saw you, new ways to piece the whole of you together. Every time we got to stay here."

He brings his hand farther up, brushes his fingers over my lips. "I thought about you in other ways too. Of course I did. But I thought more about who you are," he says. "About what it felt like to be with you. And I don't think I totally realized it, or even let myself acknowledge it, until this week."

"Acknowledge what?" I ask.

Everett's thumb runs along my cheekbone, those stormy ocean eyes skimming mine. "That I was falling in love with you. That I've been falling in love with you since that stupid party."

"The party wasn't stupid," I say, softly.

"You're right," he says. "It's where I met you."

I'm not used to things like this with Everett. Hard truths spoken gently, precious things passed back and forth. It feels a little like a dream still, like I might wake up from it. But when

I look up at him, his eyes almost nervous, I know it's tremendously real.

"I was falling in love with you too," I tell him. Saying it is accompanied by a huge wash of relief, my shoulders suddenly a little looser, my mind clearer. It's the key to a lock I've been struggling with for years now.

But it's also frightening. Not so much that there is suddenly more to lose, because there was always a lot to lose, but that I'm suddenly aware of it. Of what all my anger really meant. Of what was really missing while we weren't talking. Now that I'm letting myself feel it, the possibility of heartbreak becomes all the more real.

"We can't guarantee this will work," I tell Everett.

"I know," he says. I want him to say something like, *Yes we can*, or *There's no way this could fall apart*, but I also understand so deeply all the parts of Everett that won't let him. The little boy who was disappointed time and time again, who had one of his most important people choose everything else over him. I'm the same way, and it scares me to choose someone with a scar so similar to mine.

There's another side to it, though. What I think might break us if we do try this could be the exact reason it will work. We might even be stronger because of it. Both of us want to build something different, have something better than the worst parts of what we came from.

"I can promise you I want this to work," Everett says, his grip on me tightening. "More than anything. I promise I'll choose you, every time."

"I promise that too," I say. It's our own small pact. I press a hand against his chest, smiling. "What's your schedule like these next two days?"

Everett grins. "Wide-open. What do you have in mind?"

"I found a place in Montecito," I tell him. Last night, after we'd all dragged pillows and blankets into the living room, fallen asleep there instead of in our own beds, I'd waited until everyone was asleep to pull out my phone and look at different spots on the coast. Everett was next to me, his soft breathing keeping me company while I researched. "I know it's not Poppy Cottage, but it's a little house right on the beach, good surfing, a Tuesday night farmers market." I poke a finger against his shoulder. "I *hear* they might even have Food Network."

He laughs at this. It's my favorite sound in the world, I think.

"I thought we could start our own tradition," I say, the last vestige of nerves floating up into my throat, a tiny knot until he answers me.

"It sounds perfect," he says. He smooths a hand over my hair, lets his eyes rove over my face. "But anywhere with you is perfect." His arm comes around my waist to pull me closer into him. "I love you, Sutton Hale," Everett Bridges tells me.

"I love you too," I tell him, just before he kisses me, like he was waiting on confirmation.

It feels like the sun peeking out on a cloudy day, warming me down to the bone, lighting me up golden. I think about that first night, all the ways we missed each other before then, how we were tied together long before we ever collided. Back then, I'd thought the warmth that came from Everett was just something people like him possessed, some charm I couldn't quite master. Then, I thought it was nothing but a facade, a way to keep everyone at arm's length. But now I know it's at the core of him, some radiating glow that the people lucky enough to get close get to bask in.

I had thought I wanted permanence, some guarantee that nothing would break me away from the most important people in my life. And maybe there is some small guarantee in the five of us—in trips and pacts and traditions, sure, but also in the stretch of it all. In the coming back together like no time has passed. In knowing that there will always be someone on the other end of the line if we call. But what I've come to find, more than anything, is that what I really want is right now. To let go of the two-handed vise grip I've had on trying to keep the right people in my life, and trust that they'll be there. To remember that a plan is just a plan, and it will probably look different in the end anyway. To remember that no matter how I choose, there will always be good and bad on both paths. There was never a right one. There was always just the one I took. But my favorite one, so far, is the one right in front of me. The one I'm about to take with Everett.

now

We pull up to Wild Horse Villa almost to the second five years after we last arrived. I lean forward, squinting up at the terrace I sat on with Laurel on the first day of that trip.

"It looks . . ." I start, trailing off.

"The same?" Everett, in the driver's seat, finishes for me. I turn to him, smile.

"The same," I repeat. "It looks the same."

It hadn't been Ralph at the front desk, a jarring start to this week here that had me worrying it was some kind of sign until Everett had reached over on our drive down to the house, settling a warm hand on my knee.

"It's going to be a good week," he'd said, and he was right. There was no reason it wouldn't be. But it felt big, somehow, all of us gathering like this again. We'd tried and failed to make the trip work for as many summers as we'd missed it before, and while I knew things were different, while I knew that this place or this trip, even, weren't what we were made of, it was still significant. It felt like returning to some time in our lives none of us had seen in a while.

A blur of gauzy white comes barreling out the front door, Laurel's tanned arms pumping as she hurries across the driveway toward us.

"Where is she?" she asks as Everett and I climb out of the

front seats, completely ignoring us in favor of yanking the back door open and leaning in over the car seat there. "My baby June!" she exclaims as she lifts the wriggling body out, settling June onto her hip. "She's grown so much."

"You saw her last week," I say, laughing as June snuggles her head into Laurel's neck, one of her favorite places in the world.

"I know, but they grow so fast when they're this age," Laurel, who is already planning June's second birthday, still three months off, says.

"It's true," Everett says from behind me, settling his hands onto my shoulders. I lean back against him, watching as Laurel walks over to the house, pointing out the flowers in the pots out front to June as she goes.

"I've got it!" she calls over her shoulder before they disappear inside. "You two can go now!"

Laurel took to being June's aunt like she's taken to most things in her life: quickly and with a zeal that shouldn't have, but did, surprise us. It started even before she was born, when she'd come over to the house I'd moved into with Everett two years prior every day after we shared the news, bringing baby books and supplements she'd read about, special tea once we were close enough to June's due date.

We haul our things inside, Gabe and Mia arriving shortly after us, their now three kids spilling into the house behind them.

"How was the drive?" I ask as I hug Gabe hello.

"It was good," he says, bending to pick up their youngest, who is stretching his arms up toward him.

"It was *long*," Mia adds from behind him. "We're glad that we're here."

"When is Davi arriving?" Gabe asks.

"Don't you mean Davi and—" Laurel starts from where

she's bouncing a laughing June on her lap, and we all whirl on her at the same time.

"Don't be weird!" we say in unison, the mantra Davi has burned into our brains since he announced a month ago that he'd be bringing his girlfriend of a year on this trip.

After he didn't get the promotion he was up for at his firm in New York, Davi started looking for other jobs, burned-out on how relentless the pace of his work had been. After a year of hunting, he found one in Seattle, which put four of us in the same time zone again, and all of us a three-hour flight away from each other. The biggest surprise, maybe more to him than anyone else, was meeting Sydney, who changed his tune about relationships almost overnight. He was happier when we talked, lighter, in a way I hadn't really noticed he wasn't until he suddenly was.

"I'm not being *weird*," Laurel says. "It's just that the man swore he'd never settle down and now here he is, *bringing* someone on this, our sacred trip?"

"I think it's already a pretty different kind of trip this year," Everett says as Gabe and Mia's twins go hurtling by him, already deep into some game.

It takes longer to get settled than usual: There are naps and getting more people unpacked and different dinnertimes and very much *not being weird* when Davi and Sydney do show up. It's not until after ten, when all the kids are finally asleep, that we emerge onto the back deck, one by one, like something called us there.

Everett and I are the first outside, and I curl up against him on one of the wicker couches, rest my head against his shoulder. "What are you thinking about?" he asks, lips against my hair.

I glance out at the ocean, where the dark of the water and the starry sky meet at the horizon. I'd thought there were countless nights in my life when I'd looked out at this view, but in reality, there are only a handful. Flashes of perfect summers I thought needed to be flawlessly re-created for them to mean something. But what's happened in the five years since we were last here is better, marked by moments that feel as important as this one.

"Just this life of ours," I say, tilting my head back to look up at him. Everett smiles, and it's as good as it was the first time I saw it, lighting me up from the inside.

At first, because of the structure of our jobs, we were able to work from our respective cities a lot of the time, and so we set up camp in my apartment and in his house in LA. What used to be two days was now two people, two cities, two homes that we traveled between.

Two homes, but really only one: each other. We talked about our future and what it would look like, jobs and homes and kids and places we wanted to visit and things we wanted to do. When I asked Everett where he wanted to be at seventy, his answer was always the same: *With you*. It was my answer too, and we asked each other all the time, more often than we should, because I think we both liked hearing it. A refrain of the promise we made to each other. That we would want this. That we would love each other for as long as we've got. That there was no controlling today or tomorrow or next week, but there was always this—Everett's hand to hold, his shoulder to rest my face on in the mornings, conversations in the middle of the night. Us. Not the us I started out with, but the one I needed.

It still doesn't mean that everything is wonderful every day. After all, there is the bad. A few weeks into things, Everett finally called his father, talked to him about the movie, had the hard conversation, and the studio cast him anyway. His father didn't turn them down. Hank started to talk about retirement and I had to face the fact that the restaurant would go to someone else, if it stayed a restaurant at all.

But with all of that, there came so much good.

In having to see his father every day, Everett carved out a place for him in his life—small, but there, something healing in it. My own parents remained the same: hard to connect with, distant, but our door stayed open to them, phone calls scheduled more regularly especially once June was born.

Because he started to have a little more free time, Hank met Rebecca, an artist who had a place in a small coastal Oregon town where they started spending more and more of their time.

It meant that I slowly began to let go of San Francisco, that I shifted more and more of my life to Los Angeles, where Everett was, of course, but also where Laurel and I started to spend more time together again. Where we repaired the broken pieces of us.

Everett and I turned our home into the thing we'd always wanted: warm, welcoming, a place we always want to return to.

The back door opens and Davi and Sydney come out, settle into chairs across from us. In a few more minutes Gabe emerges, then Mia, and finally Laurel, completing our little circle as I scoot over to make room for her next to me.

"Is it time?" Gabe asks after a while, all of us sitting in comfortable silence. It doesn't feel like our last first night here, when I was so nervous about seeing Everett again, when everything had to go perfectly. Now it feels like people who have grown up together, who know that no matter how much time passes, we can always come back to this.

"For what?" Davi asks.

"What we're afraid of, what we're excited for," Gabe says. He glances at Mia and Sydney. "It's tradition."

"It's a last-night tradition," Laurel says. "We'll get to that part when we're saying goodbye."

Gabe nods, agreeing with her, before he asks her how Grace is, the girl Laurel started seeing a few months back. Her first time dating anyone seriously since Stephen.

I burrow farther into Everett's side as everyone talks, as laughter floats out into the night and some dormant piece of me is drawn back to the surface. The girl I was when we first came here, poking her head out to see what's changed since then.

We never will get to that final tradition. On our last night here, June will be restless and Everett will go upstairs to sleep with her while Davi and Sydney head into town to meet up with friends who are in the area. I'll sit in the living room with Laurel while Gabe and Mia stay outside a little longer, kid-free for a few hours. It will only occur to me that we missed it when Everett and I are halfway back to Los Angeles the next day.

But it doesn't matter, I'll realize. Not really. Maybe we'll re-create the tradition again, when one or all of us needs to, maybe it's gone forever, but that's kind of the whole point. Things will keep shifting, changing, and we'll step into each part of our lives knowing the most important truth. No matter what we're afraid of or excited for, we all have each other.

In another year, Everett and I will move into a new house when I'm pregnant again, and it will be where we stay, where we watch the life we've made unfurl around us, and I'll think sometimes about how we almost didn't have it. How a million things had to line up for us to be here: Gabe making a friend in middle school, a pact on the beach, breaking it again and again, falling apart only so we could find our way back to each other. How it made us who we are.

How it all started at a party I wasn't even supposed to go to.

acknowledgments

Thank you to Kristy Hunter, still and forever the agent of my dreams. You are so kind, enthusiastic, and supportive, and you're always teaching me so much. I feel so lucky to navigate the bookish world with you as my guide. I wouldn't even get to write acknowledgments for a second time if it weren't for you! I don't think I could ever say thank you enough, but here's another one for now.

Thank you to Sara Rodgers for all your patient and thoughtful work on this book! I've loved getting to work with you and getting to know you so much. I think a second book is a uniquely difficult project, but you made it so much easier with every kind word, answered question, and idea bounced around. Really, thank you for making what I thought would be a totally overwhelming process so enjoyable. I am endlessly grateful for that, and for you.

Thank you to Melanie Fried for helping to conceptualize *Summer People* back when *Friends to Lovers* was still in copyedits. It felt so daunting to step into a new world after living in the last one for years, but you worked with me until the idea was just right—even if that meant phone calls that went on for so long they had to overlap with walking your dog. Thank you for championing *Friends to Lovers* the way you did and for believing in the next story too.

Thank you to Leah Morse for all the ways you helped to guide me through being a debut author. I love asking questions, and I'm so grateful to be surrounded by people like you who are so happy to answer them. Thank you to the whole team at MIRA, including but not limited to Gina Macedo, Stephanie Choo, and Elena Gritzan, for all the hard work that goes on behind the scenes. I'm in awe of this whole industry and all of you who do the work of it. Seriously, it's such a feat to put even one single book out into the world. Thank you to Sandra Chiu and Amy Wetton for the amazing cover art for *Summer People* and to Renata DiBiase for the gorgeous interior design. Obsessed doesn't begin to cover it!

Thank you to Patti Murin, audiobook narrator extraordinaire and generally wonderful person. Your book recommendations are the best, you're always doing the coolest things, and I'm still pinching myself that you brought Ren and Joni to life.

Thank you to so many booksellers, reviewers, and people all over bookish social media, but a few special shout-outs to Kalyani Saxena (Conrad forever), Lauren Korn, and Courtney at Books are Chic. Huge, endless thank-yous to Chelsia Rice, Charlie Crawford, and the whole crew over at Montana Book Company for everything you've taught me, for welcoming me into the literary community here, and for always being a bright spot in the middle of everything. You're just the best.

To so many amazing friends: thank you, thank you, thank you. You've all shown up in ways I never anticipated needing in the last year. I write a lot about friendship, but all of you are better than any kind of fiction. You're foundational. Getting to know and love all of you is such a privilege.

Thank you to my family for everything, always. Thank you for reading what I write and telling me you enjoyed it even when I get all uncomfortable about it. Thank you for teaching me so much about life and change and how to handle it all and for always talking, talking, talking. I have a lot to say during those conversations, I know. Thank you for listening long after the point has already been made. I love you all.

Finally, thank you to Levi. Our life together is all the proof I need that magic exists in this world. Here's to this next wonderful chapter, and every one still to come. Can't wait to float around with you as stardust again.